I0787155

NOVEMBER

Queen

Juliana Andrew

WORKBOOK PRESS LLC
187 E Warm Springs Rd
Suite B285 Las Vegas NV 89119 USA

Website: https://workbookpress.com/
Hotline: 1-888-818-4856
Email: admin@workbookpress.com

Ordering Information:
Quantity sales. Special discounts are available on quantity purchases by corporations, associations, and others. For details, contact the publisher at the address above.

Library of Congress Control Number:

ISBN-13: 978-1-963718-34-8 Paperback Version
        978-1-963718-36-2 Digital Version

REV. DATE: 11/12/2024

Also by Juliana Andrew
Vienna
The Curse of the Infinity Bracelets
Seventh Crossing
The Ladies of Avanloch
The Arcadia project
Home Again/Home Again
Beyond the Yellow Doors {Mayria's Dragons}

Dedicated to my family with much love and appreciation
Troy
Cheryl and Rod
Kayla and Jeff
Vienna and Jaxx
And
My husband Roy in Heaven

CHAPTER 1

Homecoming

I threw the Frisbee towards the shore for Leo. He let out a yelp and took off in the opposite direction towards the road. A woman was standing on the sidewalk talking through an open window to a man behind the wheel of a limousine. Leo completely ignored my calls and made a beeline for her. Surprisingly, he sat at her feet and politely waited for her to notice him. She bent down and proceeded to give him all her attention. Somewhat out of breath I apologized for Leo's behaviour when I got close enough for her to hear me.

She looked up and smiled demurely. "This dog is a perfect gentleman; just as his master is. I wonder though how you were able to ignore Johanna's pleas all those years for a puppy. I guess your new wife has more persuasive powers than your daughter did."

This woman was no stranger; she was my ex-wife, November Queen DuMaurier.

"This is a surprise Emmy. After six years you drop by for a visit?" I glanced around. "Are you here to see me or someone else?"

"I came to see you. Do you think you could buy your daughter's mother a coffee?"

"I think I can manage that. By the way, Leo is not my dog; I'm looking after him for my neighbor, Jock Reynolds."

"Of course; I should have known. If your wife is home I prefer to have coffee somewhere else if you don't mind."

"It just so happens that I am alone at the moment. Go around the back;

the door is open. I'll just be a minute locking Leo up." I gave Charles the limo driver, a quick hello.

He told Em that he would be back in an hour. She said that half an hour would be adequate. For what I wondered.

She was in the kitchen when I returned. "Hope you don't mind, but I snooped. I wanted to see how my husband's second...or is it third wife decorates?"

I did not comment on the wife thing. Johanna had told me that her mother was not delusional or despondent anymore, so I chose to believe it was only her silly little attempt at humor. She had taken her coat off and draped it over the back of a chair. She was as voluptuous and beautiful as ever. She did justice to a sweater like no one else could. I did not see one strand of gray in her dark brown wavy hair. It was shoulder length and bounced when she moved. She did not look much older than she had at eighteen when we had married almost nineteen years ago.

I told her to continue her tour of the house to see if it met with her approval while I made the coffee. She called to me from the living room saying that the warmth from the fireplace was nice. I asked her if she was cold.

"The weather here isn't that much different than it is in London. You'd think I would be used to it by now wouldn't you? Some things one never gets acclimatised to I guess." She said wistfully looking away and focusing on the photographs on the wall and the bureau.

She pointed to a portrait. "I take it that this is your wife...why are there no pictures of you and her? Where is your wedding photo? Johanna says she's nice."

What could I say? Did she want me to say that no one could hold a candle to her. It was true, no one could. She didn't wait for an answer.

"I suppose you want to know why I'm here."

"I gather it's regarding our daughter's upcoming nuptials because surely you didn't come all the way from London just to see me." It was more a question than a statement.

"I want to have another child."

Well, that caught me completely by surprise. "Is there a reason you're telling me this?"

"Yes, because I want all my children to have the same father."

What the hell was she saying? I shook my head. "That is not possible is it Emmy? Are you saying that you want James to legally adopt Johanna because she's a little old for that, and neither she nor I would agree to it."

"I'm divorcing James, so no. It has to be you Johnathan. I already told you that I want all my children to have the same father."

"James is Joey's father; so how in hell does that make sense?"

"Are you sure…have you never wondered?"

What was she insinuating? No, no, it couldn't be. She wouldn't have kept Joey's parentage from me to punish me because she believed that I had cheated on her. No, I was pretty sure that even in her mixed up mind at the time of our divorce she still wouldn't have done that to me.

"If you are asking me if I have ever wondered if Joey is my son, the answer is no because I know he isn't. The timing is not right. We divorced, and you ran off to England, married James, and a year later Joey was born."

"It's your timing that is off. I guess you forgot about the night I came to say goodbye?"

"I've never forgotten that night, but there is no way it ended with you becoming pregnant. On the very off chance that it did, you'd have to really hate me to keep me from knowing my son."

"I never hated you Johnny, not even when my confused mind led you to be unfaithful. My love for you was more powerful than hate, and it still is. It just isn't powerful enough for me to ever trust you again. No, your lust for other women is just too destructive, but there is no one else I want to be the father of my child. I will be forever grateful to you if you will do this for me." She smiled coyly.

I was a little dumbfounded, yet amused. I decided not to address her remark about me being unfaithful. "How would that work Emmy? We couldn't make a baby together even when we tried to for four years, and yet you think that now, six years later, we will magically be able to?"

"It could happen, but if you have finally found the one woman whom you won't cheat on, I apologise for asking you to facilitate my cause." She said dejectedly.

"So, just on the off chance that you might get pregnant, you want to have sex with me?"

"What other reason would there be?" She smiled provocatively. "You never needed much of a reason to hop into bed with me, or anyone else for the matter, so what's the difference now?"

"I was never unfaithful to you and you know it. I never had any reason to be. We had a pretty perfect life until your father died and we couldn't get pregnant, and your mind started to play tricks on you. I couldn't give you another child, so you threw me out accusing me of making another woman pregnant, which I didn't. You wouldn't believe me then, and I guess you don't now either even though our daughter says you have exonerated me of any wrongdoing. If I couldn't give you another baby then, why in God's name do you think I could now? What has six years of therapy done for you anyhow?" I sounded irritated and it was the last thing I wanted.

"I don't want to talk about your secretary or Beth. You haven't even given me a hug..."

"And, I am not going to. You can't come back after six years and say that you still love me and want us to try and have a baby together. That's not at all rational Em. On the off chance that all the planets were aligned and I agreed to sleep with you and you miraculously got pregnant...what then? What then Em? Do you think I would agree to you leaving again and taking another child of mine away from me? It's not going to happen. You're back living with your eccentric sisters aren't you? No wonder you've got this ridiculous idea."

"May and Noel run a very successful business even if it is a little unconventional, and what they do has nothing to do with me. I am not like them Johnny; you know that."

"A little unconventional; you call catering to black magic a little unconventional?"

"It was just a harmless little shop until all that Harry Potter business with wands and magical flying brooms became popular. Now they cater to what people want. What's the harm in that? And, if I have told you once, I have told you a hundred times that magic has no color. It doesn't work unless one is a believer anyhow, and I am not. I never once cast a spell on you even though you may have thought of me as a witch?"

I laughed a little. "You were never evil Em, but to be truthful, you did cast a spell on me."

"Should I take that as a compliment?"

"You can take it any way you like. Now, let's get back to why you are really here?" I walked over to where she was standing in the archway with a cup of coffee. She had tears in her eyes.

"Do you hate me Johnny?"

I took her hands and placed them around the coffee cup. "I could never hate you Emmy."

The door opened and Lorraine burst in with an armful of grocery bags. "You won't believe the peculiar day I had; it started..."

She saw me with my hands on my ex-wife's. Her tone changed from one of high spirits to one of apprehension. "I'm sorry; I didn't mean to barge in. I didn't know you were expecting company John."

November put her cup of coffee on the table and stepped forward to greet Lorraine before I could say anything. "Hell, I'm not company; I'm Johanna's mother, and Johnny's long-lost ex. You must be Lorraine, the new Mrs." She held out her hand and lied through her teeth. "I'm so very pleased to meet you finally."

Lorraine accepted her hand and smiled a little too nicely. "It's nice to meet you too Em."

"Actually, it's November; only Johnny calls me Em."

I believe my ex had just made a statement, and that was that only I had claim to the name Em.

"I don't think I have ever heard Johnathan refer to you as November." Lorraine said hesitantly.

"That's because he only calls me that when he is angry with me, and that is not very often is it Johnny? Actually, my given names are Autumn November. My mother named me and my three sisters after the seasons of the year; Noel for winter, she's the eldest, and May for spring, and Summer...well, you get the picture. Oh well, it's of no consequence. My ride should be here any minute and I will leave you two to do whatever."

Em walked into the living room and kept watch at the window.

Lorraine looked at me and asked under her breath if that was really "her".

I said that it most assuredly was.

"Charles is here." Em said grabbing her coat as she picked up her coffee and took a long sip.

I helped her on with her coat and said I'd walk her to the car. She smiled and told Lorraine that they'd probably be seeing a lot more of each other over the course of the next few weeks. Lorraine only nodded.

Emmy asked me if the reason I had bought this property on the banks of the ocean was because it reminded me of Seahaven. I told her that it was and that it was also pretty secluded being at the end of the road. It was also only a fifteen-minute commute to work. She said she liked the property and house very much and was happy for me. Just before we reached the car she told me that she had taken her old name back.

"So, you're a Queen again?" I asked.

"No, not that name; I liked my other one better. Actually, I never had it changed legally to DuMaurier, so I guess there are two Mrs. Jurado's now." She waited for my reaction.

I did not correct her and tell her that there was still only one Mrs. Jurado. "Okay, your choice."

"I need to get a job Johnny; do you think I could come back and work for you a few days a week again? I promise I won't be a bother."

The request appeared innocent enough, but I was pretty sure she was playing me though I wasn't sure why. Surely it had nothing to do with this baby thing.

"Do you need money Emmy?"

"No, of course not! I get my monthly intake from my share of the Queen Sisters Emporium. They asked me, my sisters that is, if I would come and work in the store, but it's not my cup of tea, so I declined the offer, and I still have some left from my inheritance."

"The proceeds from the sale of our house are still in your name in the bank, so there is another outlet for you, but if you need more just say so. You are still part owner of the business so there are dividends just waiting for you to withdraw. Are you getting a settlement from James?"

"No, I chose not to, just as I chose not to accept one from you. I have no need for the money. I don't want or need the proceeds from the sale of the house, but we can use it to pay for Johanna's wedding if you like. My shares of your company stay put in case you run into financial difficulty. I just need to find something to do. We worked pretty well together before didn't we?"

That all depended on what she was referring to. "Em, I'm sorry, but I don't have any job openings right now with the remodeling going on, and even if I did, I don't think it would be good for either of us."

"Of course, I understand."

I opened the limo door for her. I was surprized that Charles was still driving for the sisters as he must be ninety. Em stood on her tiptoes and kissed me on my cheek. She climbed in the car, smiled sweetly, and ran her fingers through her hair. That had always been her signal to tell me that she wanted me. She winked at me as I closed the door. My wife, or should I say my ex-wife, was definitely playing games, and I looked forward to playing. I watched until the limo carrying her was out of sight just as I had that taxi on that foggy night six years ago.

I called to Lorraine through the back door that I was taking Leo for a walk. The last time I had seen Em was August 31st, 2011. The date would stick with me forever as it was the day our divorce was finalized.

The divorce decree had been messaged to my office that morning. I signed for it, opened the envelope, glanced at it, and threw it in the trash basket. I tried not to think about what those papers actually meant for the rest of the day. Before I left I fished them out of the bin and stuffed them in my pocket. It was raining slightly when I got home. It hadn't felt like home since Em had taken Johanna and moved to Queensland in Ridgewood, her family home, six weeks ago. Now she was moving to England. Actually, if I was being honest, I hadn't wanted to set foot in our once loving home for almost a year before that. It had become a living hell due to Em's illness. I had hung on because I loved her, and there was Johanna to think about. But, it was all over with now. I had thrown the divorce papers on the kitchen table; poured myself a stiff drink, walked into the living room, lit a match, tossed it into the fireplace and watched the kindling come to life. It was the end of August, but it felt more like November. I laughed to myself bitterly; yeah, the end of my life with November. The doorbell rang. I wasn't expecting anyone so I thought of ignoring it, but curiosity got the best of me. I opened the door to find her standing in the rain.

She said, "Hi Johnny."

I said, "Hi Emmy; I thought you'd already gone to London."

She asked if she could come in.

"I'm sorry, of course. This is still your house too. You look cold…come sit by the fire."

She asked if she could have one of whatever it was that I was drinking. She never liked whiskey so I offered her vodka and tonic, but she said it was a whiskey kind of day. She went into the bathroom and grabbed a towel to dry her sodden hair. She sat next to the fire on her old chair and I sat on mine across from her. She had something in her hand.

"Thirteen years summarized unto a little piece of paper. It took so little to dissolve our marriage Johnny."

"It took a lot Em. I take full responsibility for what happened. I didn't, and couldn't understand your obsessions which led you down the path to depression. But, for me, it was a lot longer than thirteen years because I have loved you since I was twelve years old… you know that."

She smiled. "Puppy love, yes, how sweet and innocent it all was."

I got up, walked into the kitchen and picked up my divorce decree. "These papers may as well be empty because they mean nothing to me. You will always be my wife."

I threw them into the fire. We watched them burn. Em asked for another drink. When I returned with two full glasses she was standing in front of the fireplace tearing her decree into little pieces. I opened the screen for her and she threw them into the hot coals. She just stood there watching the flame until it diminished. I put my hands on her shoulders. She downed her drink in one long swig and threw the glass into the fire. It shattered into a thousand pieces. She turned to me with tears streaming down her face.

"Did we give up too soon Johnny…did we just take the easy way out?"

"Nothing about this was ever easy Em, and we are not done with each other. We will always be connected because of our daughter."

She came into my arms naturally, just like she had been doing for years. I kissed her lovingly and she returned the kiss with passion that had been absent for quite some time. I picked her up and carried her into what was once our bedroom and laid her on the bed that we had shared so much love in. No, we would never be over. We fell asleep in each other's arms.

I woke up a few hours later and she was gone. I heard the front door close.

I yanked on a pair of pants and ran to the door to see a taxicab waiting at the curb. I called her name. She turned. That night is still etched in my mind; her standing in the mist and the rain, smiling and running her hand through her hair. I watched until the taxi was out of sight. She had left her wedding rings on top of a note on the kitchen table.

Will you keep these for me for a while Johnny? I will never love anyone the way I do you, and no one will ever love me the way you once did.

Em

That was six years ago almost to the day. I still had the note and her rings.

CHAPTER 2

Em Comes Around

Lorraine was washing potatoes at the kitchen sink when I returned. I poured myself a cup of hot coffee and topped it off with a generous shot of Brandy. I was chilled to the bone.

Without turning around Lorraine asked me what November wanted. I told her that she had just come to say hello. She put the potatoes down and began unpacking one of the grocery bags. "She just wanted to say hello...after all these years of silence she suddenly stops by? I don't believe it for a minute!"

"Well, she did ask me if I would father a baby with her."

The carton of sour cream slipped out of her hands, hit the floor and splayed all over her. I told her to go change her clothes and I would clean up and salvage what I could. Ten minutes later she was sitting next to me by the fire.

"Her pictures don't do her justice. I felt very inadequate standing next to her in my faded blue jeans and mousy brown hair up in a ponytail. She was so immaculately dressed, and she is so petite, and young looking."

I did not comment except to say that she wasn't what I would call petite.

"What's with her calling you Johnny...you hate to be called that, and how come you are the only one who can call her Em? November, who has ever heard that for a name anyhow?"

"I think she explained how she and her sisters were named. We go back a long way Lorraine and have always called each other by those names."

"Thirteen years isn't all that long, so were you seventeen or so when you met her?"

"I've known her since I was twelve."

"What, you never told me that before...did you go to the same school, is that how you met?"

"No, I lived in Seahaven and she lived in Ridgewood, a suburb of Victoria. You know that her sisters still live there in Queensland, the family home, as Johanna stays there when she comes over. November and I met in July 1989 while we were staying with our respective relatives; me with Sarge, and Emmy with her Aunt Zuzzie whom you know as AnnieZu, Johanna's name for her since she was two."

"Yes, I know all of that. I just didn't know that you and November were childhood friends. Why haven't you told me before? I have been to your uncle's house, and you never pointed out that the stately home next door was AnnieZu's...why?"

"I think I probably did tell you that it was Johanna's great aunt's place, but maybe I didn't. No big deal though."

"Is AnnieZu November's father's sister?"

"No, she's Emmy's mother's sister."

"So, there is money on both sides of the family? Oh God, I just thought of something...the mother is going to be here for Jo's wedding isn't she?""I imagine so as Johanna is her only granddaughter. Why does that seem to unnerve you?"

"I don't know, maybe too many of your ex-wife's relatives...maybe I shouldn't go to the wedding. What do you think? I mean, if she is still unstable, and I am assuming she is or why else would she come up with the ridiculous idea to ask you to have a baby with her? Isn't the fact that you couldn't have any more children the reason you divorced? And, she's way too old to have another child, and in her state of mind it wouldn't be wise... oh, poor Johanna."

"I didn't find her confused at all. Perhaps this baby thing is a little overboard, but she's always been frivolous, so I didn't put much stock in it. Is thirty-seven too old to have a baby? Don't worry about Johanna; she loves her mother just the way she is."

"Do you still love her Johnathan?"

"I suppose I do in a way, and we will always be connected because of our daughter."

"Do you love me?"

"What do you think?"

"I think you do, but a gal likes to be told so once in a while."

She smiled, "Maybe I'll let you show me how much later then."

She went back into the kitchen leaving me alone with my thoughts. It wasn't going to happen, not tonight, and probably not tomorrow. I wasn't going to be one of those guys who held one woman in his arms while wishing it was another. Oh hell, who was I kidding? I'd been doing that for years.

It was eleven thirty Monday morning. I was sitting in my temporary office at Woodworks Manufacturing going over the cost of the facelift that was under construction below me. For the last six months I had been housed in a dusty and noisy room upstairs from the main production building after the demolition of the old facility. My secretary Nancy had a cramped office at the bottom of the stairs as it was a climb of twenty-four steps to reach the upper level, and I wouldn't subject her to the climb in her condition. Hopefully, the new administrative centre would be completed before the end of the year. I had spared no expense for the new structure which would occupy space outside of the work area. I deserved it after almost twenty years of existing in overcrowded quarters even if I did spend most of my time in the hangars supervising construction of the low-income homes.

My pit boss Alex radioed that I had a visitor. I told him to send him up. He said it wasn't a "he". I asked who it was then.

"She says she's your wife, but I've seen your wife Boss, and this sure as hell ain't her."

I grinned. "Does she have shoulder length wavy dark hair, a soft seductive voice, and a twinkle in her big hazel eyes, and a beguiling smile?"

"I can't vouch for the eyes as the light ain't too good down here, but the rest, hell yes!"

"Bring her on over."

I walked out and stood on the landing watching the two of them cross the floor. Alex had only come to work for me three years ago so did not know my ex-wife. I could tell that he was mesmerized by her by the way he looked at her. Poor sap. She had linked her arm through his and was amiably chatting with him. He was carrying a large satchel which I assumed was hers. She kept adjusting the mandatory hard hat. I smiled knowing how she must hate it messing up her hair. She saw me looking down when they were halfway across. She held on to her hat and waved. I waved back wondering why she was here, and why she had said she was my wife. She arrived a little out of breath a few minutes later. She took the bag from Alex and thanked him. He winked at me and said to call when she required an escort back.

"What do I owe this unexpected pleasure to Emmy?" I asked curiously.

"And hello to you too." She passed the bag to me.

"I brought you lunch."

"Why would you do that?"

"Because I wanted to, and I didn't think Lorraine was the kind to get up at the crack of dawn and send you off with a nutritious meal."

She was right about that, but I didn't tell her so.

"Edie sent one of those little jam tarts of hers that you used to love."

"Thank her for the lunch and the tart will you?"

"I made the lunch." She stated emphatically.

"Thank-you then. Is that the only reason you are here?"

"No, I want to know if you have changed your mind."

"About what Em?"

"About helping me with the baby thing."

I shook my head. "Nope; actually I never gave it another thought."

"I hardly doubt that, but I will let you sleep on it for another night or two."

"And, if the answer is still no, then what?"

"I guess I will just have to shop around for another donor then. Alex seems like a nice guy."

I laughed. "He already has three kids and is about to become a grandfather, so I think not. Why didn't you and James have another child?"

"I don't want to talk about James as he has nothing to do with any of this. I told you why I want you to be the father."

"You did, but it makes no more sense today than it did yesterday. Now, you are saying that if I don't agree to your nonsensical plan you'll find someone else, so I'm replaceable then?"

She donned the hard hat but not before running her fingers through her hair. "Do I have to wear this silly thing?"

"Yes, you do."

"Okay, you can call Alex." She started down the stairs.

"You are not replaceable Johnny, and you'll come to see why very soon. See you tomorrow okay."

She blew me a kiss. I told her to wait at the bottom of the stairs for Alex. I watched her from the landing again. She peered into my secretary's office, and not seeing anyone, shrugged her shoulders and went off to meet Alex. I did not tell Lorraine of November's visit. I feigned the sore back excuse and slept, as usual, in the spare bedroom.

At precisely eleven thirty the next morning, I got a call from Alex again saying that November was back. Again I told him to bring her up. I sat behind my desk waiting for her.

"Good morning Emmy; what brings you back today?"

She sat the duffel bag in front of me and proceeded to unpack it. "Lunch."

"Is this going to be an everyday occurrence?"

"Maybe, or at least until I get the answer I want."

I raised my eyebrows. "How long do you think you're willing to wait?"

"Oh, I am pretty sure I won't have to wait too long." She smiled impishly.

"I like your confidence, but the answer is still a resounding no." I said firmly.

"Okay, I'll take yesterdays' lunch things now so I have something for tomorrow."

I passed them to her. "So, you'll drop by again tomorrow?"

"Depends how I make out today. Enjoy your lunch."

"What are you up to?"

"Not much."

It was good to see her smile and not see the wildness and sadness in her eyes.

"You look content Em. Are you happy that you're home, or do you still consider London home? Are you planning on returning after JoJo's wedding?"

"England was never my home. I was just putting in time trying to banish my demons so that I could make amends." Her eyes met mine. "I am happy, but I can be happier and I intend to be very soon."

I knew there was a cryptic meaning in her words that were meant for me to ponder.

She turned and headed for the door. She was already part way down the stairs when I reached the rail at the landing.

"How did you get here Emmy?" I called down to her.

"By car of course." She answered matter of factually.

"Did you drive?"

"Yes."

"How did you get a licence so fast?"

She shrugged her shoulders.

"You don't have a licence do you, or are you driving on a British one?"

"I never drove in England."

"Em, you can't be driving without a licence. You need to see to that right away. Your old one expired years ago."

"Don't worry about me Johnny."

"I will always worry about you."

She spun around. "Why? I'm nothing to you. You let me go and never once came after me, so don't be playing the concerned ex-husband now."

"I was the reason for all your heartache, so no matter what I wanted, I had to leave you alone."

"Well, maybe I didn't want to be left alone... did you ever think of that?"

"I figured you would call me if you ever wanted to see me, but the years came and went with no word from you. Now after six years you come back... what do you want from me Em?"

"Only what you owe me."

Owe her...she didn't want money, so what the hell was she referring to?

"What is it that I owe you Em? Please tell me because I am at a loss here. You are the one who wanted a divorce with no compensation. If you want alimony now I will be only too glad to write a cheque covering whatever amount you think I owe you for the last six years."

"This is not about money Johnny, and you know it. If you think a blank check is restitution for the years that I lost then by all means, write me a cheque. I should be the one writing you one because I am the one who is and was at fault. I deprived you of years with your daughter, and it wasn't enough that I drove myself crazy, I dragged you down with me. No, this has nothing to do with money, and if you don't know what it is then I'm the fool for even thinking that...oh, here comes Alex. Maybe I won't come back tomorrow."

Her mood had changed from playful to one of despondency. We needed to talk, and five or ten minutes a day was not going to accomplish anything.

"I'm looking forward to seeing you tomorrow Em and hope you will reconsider. I'll be waiting for you."

She didn't answer except to run her fingers through her hair. She opened the door to my secretary's office and peered in. Not seeing anyone again, shut the door and went off with Alex. I had the feeling that my ex-wife, the only woman I had ever loved, this girl who had been my best friend since I was twelve, was about to turn my life topsy-turvy once more. I had been living a rather ho-hum existence for quite some time, so I was up for a challenge. I would have to tread lightly with her though. I had been assured by our daughter that her mother was perfectly rational, and harbored no animosity towards me, or anyone anymore, I wasn't all that convinced. In the back of my mind I seriously wondered if her main reason for coming home was to antagonise me. Was she just putting me on with her hither come smile and eyes? No, I genuinely believed that she had something in mind for me, pleasurable or sinister, I knew not what. There was a lot more behind this wanting me to father a child...a lot more.

Ten minutes later Alex arrived at my door while I was in the middle of finishing off Emmy's nutritious lunch. He had a large cardboard box in his hand.

"Ms. November asked me if I would give this to you." He set it down on my desk. I asked him what was in it. He said he hadn't a clue. I thanked him and told him that there was a possibility that November was going to be a regular guest so he could just bring her over without calling if he knew I was in my office. Curious as to what was in the box, I ripped the packing tape off after reading the note that had been scribbled and tucked under the tape.

For all the times I never thought of you.

It was Em's handwriting, though a little messy. I found a letter opener and slid it under the back flap of the first envelope and extracted a small note. It was written on stationary that depicted a country scene of a young boy carrying a fishing poll as he crossed over a wooden bridge. It resembled the bridge at Bramble Creek.

Dear Johnny, I arrived in London remembering our last night...I haven't been that happy for a very long time. I do have moments of sanity, and that night will comfort me when I descend into despair again. I will remember it for a very long time. I promise I will keep our daughter out of harm's way. I will think of you every night when I wish upon our star.
Be happy Johnny.
I'm sorry,
Em.

My eyes were stinging as I rifled through five or six dozen envelopes. My name was on them all. They bore our old street address and were even stamped. I randomly pulled another envelope up and opened it gently. It was a birthday card.

Dear Johnny, I hope you are celebrating your 33rd birthday in fine style. I'm sorry I ruined your last one, and maybe someday I will be able to make amends for all the hurt I caused.
Johanna says "Hi." Her card and gift are in the mail.
Em

I shuttered when I read the next note. It was on a jagged piece of paper.

I don't appreciate being dissected by strangers. I don't know why I had to be dragged into any of this. It's all your fault!

EMILY

Emily was the name she had taken to calling herself when her mental health had started to decline. She would say things like: "Emily is sick today, or Emily is having a bad day and doesn't want to talk to you, or Emily doesn't believe you." I hated that name.

I closed the box and carried it to my fireproof safe. Perhaps I would read some more another day, but not today...no, not today. I was pretty sure that she was my sweet Em now, and not the suspicious, unpredictable Emily, but I wouldn't let my guard down just yet.

I spent the rest of the day going over invoices with my foreman and checking on the progress of the new workplaces and offices. I was in no mood to listen to Lorraine's family problems, but she confronted me the minute I walked in the door asking me how she had to be the solution to everyone else's problems. I shrugged my shoulders and walked over to the coffee pot. It was empty, as usual. Em had always had a fresh brewed pot waiting for me. I poured myself a stiff drink instead, sat down and listened to her ramblings, not hearing a word she was saying. She complained for half an hour in a whiny voice getting up only once to turn the frozen fish and chips in the oven. Thank God I'd had a substantial lunch. It had been months since Lorraine and I had shared a bed. She asked me how my back was. I told her it was coming along slowly.

Em arrived on schedule Wednesday morning. Lucky that I was the boss so I didn't have to answer to anyone about how I spent my time. Alex was all smiles as Em reached into the lunch box and offered him a fruit tart.

"Fresh from the kitchen at Queensland, made fresh almost daily. They are not just any old blackberry tart; the berries are hand-picked at my auntie's farm in Seahaven." She smiled at me. "They are Johnny's favorite. I have never seen him refuse a raspberry or strawberry one either."

He thanked her, winked at me and went on his way. I told Em to sit down as we needed to talk.

"Not today Johnny as I have an appointment."

"With the Motor Vehicle Department I hope."

"No, I have an interview for a job at Pasteria." She said casually as she finished unpacking the lunch kit.

"I hope you don't mean the restaurant that the Marino's own?"

"I hardly doubt that there would be two restaurants named Pasteria in Victoria, so yes, Vik's and Deanna's place."

"I don't think that is wise Em?"

"Why...because he was once my fiancée, or is it because Deanna was the one who introduced you to the many pleasures of sex when I was whisked off to London when I was fourteen?"

I don't know if my expression to her brazen accusation registered shock, humiliation, or both.

"Thank-you for reminding me of a most unpleasant time in my life. What happened yesterday has no bearing on today. I have heard that they treat their employees like dirt, so I don't think you would be happy there. I'm just thinking of your well-being Em."

"Rumors are sometimes just rumors. There is no one more aware of that than me. Thank-you for your concern, and I am sorry that I threw your past in your face once more. I really need to get going, so see you when I see you." She said wistfully.

"It's not actually a rumor. Nancy's sister worked for them, but quit after only a few weeks as she refused to take their abuse as did many others."

"Just who is this Nancy?"

"She's my secretary."

"Oh, you mean the one who is never in her office?"

I grabbed my hard hat and handed hers to her. "She's there now, so come along and I will introduce you to her and walk you to your car."

"Really Johnny, are you going to make me wear that?"

I took hold of her arm. "Yes Ma'am, as soon as we hit the floor."

She was most cordial to Nancy even though she gave me the evil eye when she saw that Nancy was pregnant. Em asked her how far along she was and how much time was she planning on taking off work. Nancy replied that it all depended on how things went as she already had a four year old at home. She hinted that she may not be coming back.

Em smiled sardonically at me. "So, you will be in the market for a new secretary?"

"Maybe I already have one lined up." I answered flippantly.

The moment we were out of earshot Em asked me if there was anything she should know about Nancy and me.

"Oh, because she is pregnant you think it is my baby just as you thought that Beth was also carrying my child? You haven't changed at all have you Emmy? You still think of me as a cheating, no good poor excuse for a husband?"

She stopped walking and put her hand on my arm. "I'm pretty sure that you didn't have an affair with Beth, or your secretary Johnny, so please forgive me. I don't seem to have any control over what comes out of my mouth sometimes."

"Perhaps you should run it by your headfirst. You do know that Beth was my secretary, and that they are one and the same person, don't you?"

"Yes, I do now. I want to believe that she was just your secretary and nothing else."

"I'm telling you there was no affair."

"What happened to her and the baby? Do you ever see her?"

"She moved to New Mexico where she had a cousin. She married and has two more children. She sent me a photo of her and her family a couple of years ago. I don't ever expect to hear from her again. She was in an abusive relationship Em. I gave her the means to get away from the S.O.B. The one and only night I didn't come home to you and Johanna was the night I spent at her bedside in the hospital after he had beaten her. I tried phoning you, but you wouldn't answer. After several attempts I just gave up. She was almost unrecognizable; luckily, the baby was unharmed. I tried explaining that to you, but your mind was already made up that I was carrying on with her, so it inadvertently added to your distrust. What else can I say?"

"You were her hero Johnny just as you had always been mine until I lost touch with reality. You saved her from the abuse even though you were in an abusive relationship yourself. I'm sorry for how I mistrusted and insulted you."

I opened the gate and steered her through it and stopped. "I never thought of it as such. You weren't always irrational. You had days of lucidness, and I would have renewed hope that your verbal tantrums of suspicion and melancholy were behind us, but I was only fooling myself. I was in denial about your mental state, and so I stood by and waited too long to get you help. I watched you slip away from me day by day. You were ill Em, but I loved you so much that I thought my love could heal you...I'm sorry, I was wrong. God, I am so sorry. I've been waiting to say that to you for a very long time. I hope you can forgive me someday."

She had tears in her eyes. "Oh Johnny, I have put you through hell, haven't I? You were not responsible for my depression. It all began with my Father's death, but I didn't address it then, and it blossomed into something deplorable, and eventually led to our demise. I had a chemical imbalance Johnny; no one was to blame. We will talk more another time, but you need to know now that I do not blame you for anything anymore."

"Thank-you; I needed to hear that. All that matters now is that you are healthy."

"I am." She smiled and we continued walking.

"I see you are driving the Buick." I commented as we stopped at the steel grey car that her father had given to her mother. She unlocked it and I opened the door for her.

"Yes, Zena wanted me to have it as she never plans on moving back to Canada. Do you think I should trade it in for a new one?"

Emmy's mother's name was Zenaida. Em called her Zena over mom most of the time.

"What I would like is for you not to drive, period; you're not very good at it."

"Well, I refuse to be chauffeured ever again! I had enough of it when I was in London. A girl has to have some independence."

"A girl should also have a driver's licence. Promise me you will make an appointment with the DMV?"

"I won't pass the test Johnny, so why bother?" She stood on her tiptoes and kissed me softly.

I resisted the wanting in me from kissing her back. I just stood there smiling into her puppy-dog eyes. "Whatever am I going to do with you Em?"

"Well, I am not yours anymore, so you don't have to do anything."

She started to close the door, but I held it back. "As if I ever had control over you…I want to wish you luck with your interview as a waitress, but I just can't; sorry."

She laughed. "Don't be, and anyway the job is for the position of hostess. Maybe Vik still has a thing for me, and I'll be a shoe-in."

"And maybe Deanna will be the one interviewing you…have you thought about that?"

"Well then I won't get the job, so you are fussing about nothing. Did Alex deliver the box?"

"He did. I'm having difficulty reading them as…"

She interrupted me. "You should burn them then."

I was appalled that she would suggest such a thing. "I most certainly will not! You wrote them to me, and I intend to read every single one of them, even when you signed them Emily. You and I will always be connected, and not just through our daughter. I have never been able to come to terms with how much I was to blame for your depression, chemical imbalance or not, or how I was so unqualified to understand your anguish. Through your words and the little trinkets you bought and kept for me makes me believe that maybe you didn't lose all your love and respect for me. It is heartwarming that you thought about me now and then. One question though; does Emily still come around?"

"I did think about you." She put her fingers to her lips and then ran her hand through her hair. "I only hope that when all is revealed you will still have some compassion for me whether you think of me as Em or Emily."

I stepped away from the car as she revved the engine and backed up spewing a barrage of gravel behind her. Yup, that was my Em...well, was once. I watched her until she was out of sight wondering what she had to reveal. She had left me with another cryptic message to ponder. I had only slightly entertained the thought lightly that she might have multiple personalities when she became ill. She had never referred to herself as Emily before that. Silly lovelorn that I was, and still am I guess, I believed it was her way of saying things to me because she didn't want to hurt me, so she pretended she was someone else.

CHAPTER 3

Revelations

Em did not show up on Thursday or Friday, and she did not call. I assumed that she had been hired on at Pasteria. Lorraine reminded me that we were helping her sister and family move on the weekend the moment I stepped into the house Friday evening. I told her that I wasn't going to be much use with my back being the way it was. She asked me when I was going to do something about it. I told her that I had made an appointment with a massage therapist for Monday. I figured I would need one after the weekend.

Amy and her husband Ron along with their six-year-old son Kale and five year old daughter Cyndi were all moving in with Lorraine's mother Lucille who owned a seaside resort fifty kilometers away. Ron had lost his job due to downsizing and mortgage payments could no longer be met, so the sensible thing according to Lorraine and Amy was for them to move in with Lucille and help her run the business. Lorraine had asked me several times to offer her brother-in-law a job. My answer was always the same and that was that there wasn't anything available. I didn't have much use for the man, so I had no intention of ever hiring him. The move went smooth enough I guess. I spent the day going over financial business with Lucille, and playing board games with the kids.

Lorraine had informed everyone about my back problems so I wasn't expected to do any heavy lifting. I had been lying to her about my back for some time now. I hoped my mother's words, "God will get you for that" wouldn't come back to haunt me.

Monday came and went; there was still no word from Em. The massage therapist had another opening on Tuesday, so I made another appointment.

Apparently, I was very tense. She had asked me what was causing my stress. I told her my ex-wife had come back to town. She had laughed. I hadn't talked to Em for years until last week, so what was the urgency and need now? I called Johanna instead. She did not answer. I left a voice message for her to call me so we could synchronise the plans for Friday. My phone rang just as I pulled into the yard. I anticipated that it was her and shut the car off as I picked up the phone.

"Hi Daddy." Her voice was soft and full of sweetness.

"Hi Sweetheart, how are you?"

"Despite all that has happened, I think I am holding it all together rather well. I'm sorry I haven't called you, but Mom said she would look after everything, and I've been so darn busy at work...oh, that is no excuse. I guess my nerves are a little frayed. I don't know how I would have managed without Mom and AnnieZu."

Alarmed I asked her what had happened.

"Mom called you right?" She sounded confused.

"I haven't talked to your mother in almost a week."

"Oh my God...then you don't even know that the hall burnt down, and we have moved the whole wedding venue to AnnieZu's?"

I was mortified. "Burnt down...Freedom Hall burnt...when?"

"Last Wednesday; didn't you see it on the news or in the paper?"

"Never heard a thing, and if Lorraine did she would have told me. You and your mother thought Silvermist would be a good place to have your wedding? Isn't it a little far for out-of-town guests?"

"It's only sixty minutes from the ferry Dad, and it's a scenic drive. There aren't that many out of town guests anyhow, mostly just Pier's family. There are three guest houses that the wedding party can stay in, and four unoccupied bedrooms in the house for Pier's family. We didn't have any options Dad; every hall in Victoria was already booked solid. I love Silvermist, but never even considered it before because it would just be too difficult to make all the arrangements with me living on the mainland. But then Mom did her magic... if I ever had any doubts about her mental or emotional health Dad, it's all gone. She has single handily organized everything from caterers to the minister, and in true Queen fashion!"

I laughed. "That's refreshing because I have been a little worried about her."

"I just don't know why she didn't call you. Maybe this has all been too much for her after all. I know she was very apprehensive about seeing you, but she said it went all right...did it?"

I would not say anything that might worry Johanna so I told her that our visits had all been cordial. "She's not the same woman who left here six years ago Jo. I think we have our Em back. I take it that she is at Silvermist now?"

"Yes, she and Joey went up the very next day. Have you met Joey yet Dad?"

"No, I haven't. Do you know what ferry you and Piers will be catching on Friday?"

"We have a reservation for the nine o'clock sailing, so will be at AnnieZu's around twelve-thirty depending on traffic. Will you be staying at Uncle Sarge's?"

"Yes. Looking forward to seeing you Honey. Don't work too hard."

"I'm so excited to see everyone too. Again, I am sorry for not calling you. I hope Mom isn't off her meds. I love you Daddy."

I did not question her about the meds. "Love you too Sweetie."

"What was that all about?" Lorraine accosted me the minute I set foot in the house.

"What do you mean?"

"Who were you talking to on the phone? I guess you didn't want me to know, so it must have been your ex."

"No, it was not Em; it was Johanna. She called as I was driving into the yard, so I answered. Is that all right with you?" I snarled.

"Who the hell peed in your soup today?" She growled back.

"Do you think that just once you might have a pot of coffee ready for me when I get home? I know it's a hard chore, but what the hell." I picked up the carafe and filled it with water and set it heavily on the burner, pushed the prepared pack of coffee into place with a little too much force, and set it to brewing. I walked into the living room ignoring a wounded Lorraine.

She followed me. She was not the type that cried easily, but she was very close to tears as she said that I owed her an explanation for my irritability.

I suppose I did. I told her of my phone conversation with Johanna. She had also not heard of the hall burning. She sympathised, but not before she had some harsh words about Emmy's failure to inform me about the change of plans.

"I should have known she was the reason for your bad mood. It seems like every time her name comes up your become irritated and go on a rant. I will call Johanna and see what I can do to help. Should we have her and Piers here for dinner?"

"There is no time for that. Em has everything arranged, and if there is something that needs doing we will see to it. I'm going up on Thursday. I would go tomorrow but I have a large shipment arriving in late afternoon and I want to be there to supervise it's unloading." I got up saying I may as well throw a few things into a suitcase while I was thinking about it.

"You're going to stay overnight?" She asked edgily.

"Well, I'm not going to drive home every night when there is a perfectly good bed waiting for me at Sarge's, and it being the Labor Day holiday, weekend traffic will be horrendous."

She seemed relieved that I would be staying at my uncle's and not at Silvermist with Em, but not that I would be staying the whole weekend.

"When do I get to see Johanna?"

"I don't know how long Johanna's staying or what her plans are at the moment."

"I don't want to interfere with anything you and your family will be doing." She said scowling.

"Do you still consider November as family?"

I glanced back at her. "She is."

I left the house at nine thirty Thursday morning. Lorraine was still in bed. I had called to her from the bedroom door that I was leaving.

"Well, off with you then. I guess I don't even get a good-bye kiss." She said grouchily.

I supposed I owed her that much. I walked over to the bed, bent down and gave her a peck on the cheek. She asked me how I was feeling. I told her that I was good.

"You don't have to go right this minute do you? It's been a long time since we've made love... I'll be gentle I promise."

I pulled away from her before she could pull me into bed stating that I wasn't that good.

"No, of course not! I guess I may as well go to my mom's because I'm sure as hell not going to mope around here while your excuse for going away for the whole weekend is your daughter!"

"What the hell does that mean?"

"You know perfectly well what it means. Can you at least have the courtesy of calling me when you get there?"

"I'm only going eighty kilometers."

"Humour me please, and call."

I told her I would. It was a pleasing drive to Seahaven once I reached the Island Hiway which took me about ten minutes. Bramble Creek Road was at the junction of the Hiway and Seahaven's city limits. Bramble Creek was home to my uncle's place, Bramble Creek Farm which was at the end of the road. Dover's Reach Thoroughbred Horse Ranch was the first of the three properties one encountered as they drove down Two Mile Hill which was actually only a little over one mile. AnnieZu's Silvermist was the middle estate. One would not refer to my uncle's place as an estate as it was a hundred-year-old run-down farm house. It was situated on 20 hectares of prime real estate. It was also home to different habitat types that were absent from Silvermist and Dover's properties. The cultivated fields and the foothills of the Pacific Mountains were separated by the Little Spanish River and wetlands that were occupied year-round by water fowl, beavers and racoons. The river level was low at this time of year but had never completely dried up that I knew of. Bramble Creek, on the other hand, had but a trickle of water slowly flowing towards the sea. The creek bed, which in the spring and early summer was ideal for fishing was now just a mass of dried-up mud and sand. It had once been Emmy's and my favorite place to idle away the time. This whole land mass was known, for lack of a better word, an estuary. Some referred to it as The Bay of Seahaven. It was private land, and only opened to oceanographers or marine biologists. School children were given special permission to visit the wetlands in the spring. The land was not all fenced but posted that trespasser would be arrested. That had not persuaded many a youngster to stay clear. It was only a ten-minute hike down the wooded banks from Seahaven. I knew that all too well as my family home was at the top of said hill. My uncle owned most of the land, so I had special privileges.

I stopped at the top of the hill to let myself in the locked gate, which was a laugh, but at least it kept recreational vehicles out. Dover's properties were fenced. I hoped the password had not been changed since I had been here a few months ago and it wasn't. I proceeded slowly past AnnieZu's. No one was in the front yard. I stopped for a few minutes on the bridge and glanced down at the lifeless creek. My eyes wandered to the dry meadows on both sides of it. For a fleeting second I saw two young children running through the tall grasses, fishing poles in hand. I blinked, and they were gone. I continued on to the farm and parked in the lane on the north side of the house. Two bicycles were leaning up against the outside wall. I climbed the wooden ramp to the back porch. Sarge was at the far end smoking a cigarette. I could hear laughter coming from beyond the corn field that reached from the porch to the bramble patches which covered the banks above the backwaters of the ocean.

"Aah, the prodigal nephew has returned." My uncle proclaimed as usual.

"Well, at least one of the nephews shows up once in a while." I countered as usual.

"The other will be here soon enough."

I walked over and shook his hand. His grip was a lot stronger than I remembered it being. "What's with the walker, and what's all the commotion in the cornfield?"

"She's parked my wheelchair." He replied smugly.

"What, who's she?"

"Watch and marvel my son, watch and be awakened."

What the hell? I followed his gaze towards the pathway between the rows of corn. His old dog Champ made a feeble attempt to wag his tail. A woman was running up the path with a young child hot on her heels. He was yelling at her that she had cheated again. She was laughing. She slowed down when she was but a meter from me. The little fair-haired boy tackled her and they fell to the ground still laughing. She wrestled with him for a bit before saying they better stop acting like heathens as they had company. Sarge was applauding.

The youngster looked my way. "Hey," he said rising to his feet, "I know you. You're my sister's father."

He came up the steps, rubbed his hands on his overalls, and extended his hand to me. "Sorry, but we been picking berries. I'm Joey, Johanna's brother."

I took his little hand. I hoped I didn't sound too emotional because I was pretty sure I was looking into the eyes of my son. "Yes, I thought you were. I'm Johnathan, and I am very pleased to finally meet you."

Emmy got up and shook the dried grass out of her hair avoiding eye contact with me.

"Look Mom, its Johnathan, Jo-Jo's dad! How come you didn't tell me he was coming?"

"If you think about it; you'll remember that I did." She said nonchalantly. She brushed by me touching my arm lightly. "Hi Johnny; have you changed your mind yet? Come on Sarge; it's time for lunch."

All I managed to say with a nod was, "Em."

She waited for my uncle who said as he passed by me. "And, the curtain falls on act one."

"Come along Joey and bring Johnathan with you." Em instructed.

That was it; that was my introduction to my five-year-old son.

Joey held the screen door open for me. "Come on Johnathan; wanna have a piece of Betsy's blackberry pie with ice cream?"

I joined him and Sarge at the small kitchen table. Emmy poured Sarge and me a cup of coffee, ladled something from a pot on the counter into a bowl, and popped it in the microwave. He mumbled that it was a little early for lunch. She said she had things to do, so it was eat now or fix it himself later.

Joey laughed looking at me. "Hey, I just remembered something; Sarge is your uncle, right?"

"He is." I said agreeably. Hell, I needed time to process this. Her clues were beginning to make sense. Why couldn't she have just come out and told me?

"Thought so because when I asked Mom why we had to put new sheets on the bed the other day she said it was for when Johanna's dad comes. I asked her why he was coming here and she said it was because Sarge was his uncle. Funny isn't it?"

Emmy came over and ruffled his blond locks. "What's so funny about that?"

"Don't do that Mom, you know I don't like it!" He pushed her hand away. "It's funny 'cause Sarge is my uncle too."

She pretended to do it again smiling broadly. Joey put his hand up to block her. "Come on Mom, not in front of Johnathan."

"Why not?"

"Because. Can I have my pie now?"

"The question is, "May I?" and I say, no, not before you wash your hands."

They continued to razz each other for a few more minutes with Sarge butting in now and then with his two cents worth. I sat quietly taking it all in as an innocent bystander.

"Soup will be ready in a couple of minutes. Can I interest you in lunch Johnathan?"

I told her I was good. I was still in disbelief that I was looking at my son.

"Okay then, anytime you want, just help yourself. Excuse me while I go and check on your room. Get those hands washed Mister," she said addressing Joey, "or no pie!"

Soon as she was out of sight Sarge said that he didn't know what she was talking about because she had already checked the room half a dozen times.

"What's going on here?" I asked. "Emmy's making beds, cooking, cleaning..."

"Go easy on the cleaning bit, but she's one hell of a cook. Your ex is my new boss, and Joey here is her sidekick." Sarge said chuckling.

"Yeah," Joey chimed in, "she's pretty bossy, but she's a sweetheart ain't she Sarge?"

I had to laugh at that. "I'm guessing Sarge has you watching Humphry Bogart movies?"

Joey raised his glass. "Here's lookin at you kid." He took a long drink of water playing along.

I asked Sarge again what Emmy was doing here. He said she had taken over from his home care provider whose position had gone unfilled when she went on holidays. Emmy was here the day it happened, so she stepped in.

"Just like that, she was hired?"

"Who said anything about being hired?"

"So, just out of the goodness of her heart she assumed the position of caregiver slash homemaker, is that what you are telling me?"

"As I said, she's a damn fine cook. She's got me doing my exercises, and out of my wheelchair...hell, she's even got me painting again! Good therapy, she says, and she's right. Plus, I get to hang out with this little Picasso, alias Huckleberry Finn, wood-be carpenter."

I looked at Joey. "I guess he's talking about you Son."

Joey nodded. "Yeah, I like to paint. Hey, I just thought of something; you're JoJo's dad right? I don't have a dad anymore, and you were married to my Mom once, so maybe you could be my dad too, or do you already have a little boy?"

Sarge was snorting. "You know what they say, "Out of the mouths of babes..."

"You know what Joey, I do not have a little boy, but I always wanted one, so you've got yourself a deal." I put my hand out and he shook it beaming.

Em arrived just as we made a pact. She looked at us. "What's going on here?"

"Guess what Mom? Johnathan said he would be my new dad. Isn't that great?"

She nodded. "I see." She took the ice cream out of the fridge freezer and put a scoop on a small piece of pie and set it in front of Joey. "Hands?"

"Right now Mom." He got up and went to the sink.

Em took a sandwich out of the fridge, and the soup from the microwave, and placed them in front of Sarge. She wiped her hands on her blue jeans. "Take your time Joey as Johnathan and I have a few things to discuss."

She walked out the screen door not bothering to ask me if I was coming.

Joey said he hoped I wasn't in trouble because he knew that look. I said I hoped I wasn't too and followed my ex-wife out the door. Sarge mumbled, "And the curtain rises on Act Two."

I found Emmy sitting on the porch in Sarge's chair trying to light a cigarette. I watched, rather amused as the wind kept blowing the match out.

"You're not very good at that are you?" Not waiting for an answer I asked her when she had started smoking.

"Just now." She answered.

"Why?"

"Because I thought it might keep me calm while you yelled at me."

I took the cigarette out of her hand and laid it in the ashtray. "Well, it's not going to help, and you are only going to sputter and cough. When have I ever yelled at you anyhow?"

"Never, but then I have never kept anything so significant from you before."

"That's probably true, not counting when you got engaged to Vik."

"You were busy with someone else in Boston, or wherever you were, and my thing with Vik was always going to go away even before you came home and saved me as you said. But this...Joey is not going away."

"Can we just talk about today and leave our past in yesterday? Now, tell me, when were you going to tell me about Joey?"

"If you think about it you'll realise that I already told you."

"Refresh my memory because I remember no such confession."

"Last Sunday when I asked you if you would have another child with me..."

"Was I supposed to think that meant I already had one? That doesn't make sense Em."

"I also asked you if you ever thought that Joey could be yours."

"You did, and I said no. Wasn't that the perfect time to tell me that he was?"

"Maybe, but you didn't seem too keen on the idea that he might be, so I thought the best thing to do was to let you see him for yourself."

"You did a wonderful job raising him Em, you and James, but you know how much I loved raising Johanna, so why wouldn't you tell me I had a son? Five years Em, five years you kept him from knowing his own father. I have to believe that you really did hate me and blamed me for everything that went wrong with us. So why, why *now* did you decide it was time I knew?"

"I told you before that I never hated you, and that's true. If you had bothered to read that box of letters I wrote, you would know that. The hardest thing I have ever had to do was walk away from you, but I did it to save you. I had already gone under, and I was slowly taking you down with me. I was ill Johnny, but neither of us would admit how ill until it was too late. I had to go somewhere where you weren't, and luckily, my mother wanted me. I never planned on staying away for as long as I did, but it took that long for me to gain my sanity back. I certainly never planned on marrying ever again, but circumstance dictated differently."

She walked over to the railing that looked south towards her aunt's place. I joined her and we watched the wind pick up some feathery wisps from the

Four O'Clocks and scatter them in every direction like we had done so many times before. I commented that it had been a dry summer.

"The reason I didn't tell you before was that I only found out for sure a little over a year ago."

"Are you saying that for four years you thought James was Joey's father? Perhaps if you hadn't run off and jumped into bed with another man before the ink was even dry on our divorce papers you may have considered that I was his father...after all, we did have that night together."

I knew I had gone too far. We weren't even touching, but I felt her stiffen.

"I'm sorry Em; I shouldn't have said that."

"No, you are right. You have every right to be angry with me. But, in my own defense, you never begged me to stay, and you never came after me, and then you remarried, so I let you go. I let you go until the day Joey asked me for a puppy for his birthday. It was as if I had been blind because I looked at him, and I saw you. I saw you with Brandy, and I knew. But I had to be sure, and so I had a paternity test done. James was not Joey's father, and that meant that you were. I didn't know where to go from there. The next day I started a new kind of therapy."

"Oh God Em; you just broke my heart...again."

I wanted to take her in my arms and tell her that everything was going to be all right, but the slamming of the screen door put a stop to that, and the moment was lost.

"Mom, we got to get going. I have to get that roof on the fairy house, did you forget?"

Emmy wiped her eyes with her shirttail. "No, no, I didn't forget. Just let me say good-bye to Sarge and I'll be with you. Will you come over to Silvermist later Johnny? I know AnnieZu would love to see you."

"I'll be there." I waved to Joey. "See you later Sport."

He waved back. "See you Johnathan."

Well, that was going to change.

I found Sarge sitting in his recliner in the living room. I went to the window and watched Em and Joey racing their bikes across Bramble Bridge until they disappeared out of sight. I took a seat next to my uncle and asked him what Emmy had told him.

"She introduced me to Joey. I said that I was pretty sure I had already met him. She had smiled and said that she thought I would say that. I didn't ask her any questions and she didn't tell me any lies. That girl is a saint, and it's a damn rotten shame what happened to her, a damn rotten shame. Now, what are you going to do about it?"

"I don't know Sarge; I honestly don't know." I got up and said that I was going to clean up the kitchen and warm up a bowl of that good looking soup.

CHAPTER 4

November

Joey said a quick hello to Betsy and ran upstairs to finish the fairy house that he was making for his friend Amy's birthday. I sat down at the oversized kitchen table and proceeded to chop up the carrots that Betsy had cleaned. She asked me how my morning had gone. I told her that Johnathan was here.

She poured me a glass of iced tea and sat down next to me and asked me how I felt about seeing him for the first time in six years. I told her that I had already seen him three- or four-times last week, and so I had dealt with that, or so I thought. She asked me what I meant.

I sighed. "He knows that he is Joey's father."

"It was always your intention to tell him wasn't it?"

I nodded.

"So, how did he react when you told him?"

"I didn't come right out and tell him, but when he saw Joey he knew."

"Of course he did, just as we all did. When you are ready I guess you will enlighten us all as to how that is even possible."

I smiled. "Perhaps I will just let you all come up with your own suppositions as I am sure you already have, and one day we can sit down and see who has the best story." I got up and pushed my chair in. "Right now the only thing of importance is that we tell Joey. Johnathan will be over in an hour so I best make myself presentable."

Betsy laughed. "Right, because you look simply dreadful in a sweater and blue jeans! Ah, here is Miss Annie; let's see what she has to say."

I explained to AnnieZu what had transpired at Sarge's. "I was caught a little off guard as I wasn't expecting that Johnny would show up until tomorrow. He didn't yell at me or threaten to sue for custody or anything. I think that in a way he is afraid that I will have another break-down. I may just let him go on believing that so I'll get what I want."

"Autumn November Queen, don't you even think about doing that! You've put that man through hell a hundred times over, and I won't stand for you playing games with his heart anymore...do you hear me?"

Her words stung and I choked back tears. "He doesn't love me anymore, so how could I hurt him? He never came to see me, and he remarried..."

"Stop right there young lady! You've been gone for six years, and never once did you contact him. As far as he knew you never wanted to see him again, and the only news of your rehabilitation came from Johanna, who by the way, painted you as the picture of good health. I wasn't any help either as your talks with me were few and far between. And, as for your mother, well, you can't get blood out of a stone. I saw the pain in that poor man's eyes every time he asked about you. Did you not consider that he might fall in love with somebody else? After all, you did."

"I did not love James; it was a marriage of convenience. That all changed when I realized that Johnny was Joey's father; everything changed then."

"I've let you have your privacy and have not prompted you for details for fear of upsetting you, but that ends now. You are as sane as any of us, so sit back down, and start talking."

I wasn't really comfortable or happy staying at Queensland with my older sisters, but I had been reluctant to ask AnnieZu if Joey and I could stay with her. It would be soon enough for her to find out that Johnathan was Joey's father. I had planned on telling Johnny first, but the fire happened, and I had come here to help with Johanna's new wedding venue. She hadn't asked any questions, but one look and she knew just as Sarge had, and now Johnny knew. It was long past time for me to explain.

"When I left here I was rational enough to know that I loved Johnny, but day by day, and one accusation after another I was destroying him. The only way I could save him from the curse that had ravished me was to let him go. It took me almost four years to get control back of my life, and then one day I looked at Joey, and the neurosis started up again as I wasn't looking at my son, but I was looking at his father. Johnny was Joey's father, and all my therapy was for naught. I couldn't tell anyone, especially Johnny. He had remarried, and he and his new wife would surely take Joey away from me..."

I babbled my way through the last six years of my life randomly choosing events that had no significance at all. AnnieZu coaxed me through it all, and at the end I said to her and Betsy that I was probably still in love with Johnny, and that I despised his wife, and that she had better not cross my path. They both said that if Johnny and I were meant to be together again then love would win and we would be. They hugged me and sent me away saying that Joey's father was at the back door and that I had better go and make myself pretty for him.

I ran up the stairs stopping at Joey's door. "Your Fath...Johnathan's here." I corrected myself.

"Do you think he'll want to see my fairy house?" He asked.

"Of course he will. I'll be back in a jiffy."

I had cried a little relating my story to AnnieZu and Betsy, so I washed my face briskly, dabbed a light shade of lipstick on my lips and rubbed a tad on my cheeks. I pulled a bright yellow sundress on over my head and ran my fingers through my hair. I met Johnathan coming up the stairs. He smiled at me, and my heart fluttered a little.

"He's waiting for you. Don't criticize his work too much; he's just a little boy you know."

I had wounded him, but that had not been my intention. His look was one of empathy, but I took it as one of sympathy, or indifference. I followed him into Joey's room.

"Hi Johnathan, do you want to see my fairy house? It's not very good cause I didn't have much to work with. Mom has been so busy with JoJo's wedding that she hasn't had time to take me to a craft store, but that's okay. Pete found some pieces of wood for me in his workshop. It's missing something, but I don't know what."

Johnny examined the little structure from all sides. "You have done an excellent job with the materials that you had Son. It won't be a problem for you anymore as I can supply you with anything you need from now on. I build big houses for a living and one day I would like to take you to my shop and show you around...that is if it's okay with your mom. I can't find anything wrong with this fairy house except perhaps it needs a little greenery."

"Did you hear that Mom? I can go can't I?"

"Of course you can. Now let's hear what Johnathan has in mind for greenery."

"Should I paint the roof green?" Joey asked looking dotingly at his father.

"No, I don't think so, but maybe we could add a little greenery around the house and the grounds."

"How?" Joey asked inquisitively.

"Do you know if there is any moss growing around AnnieZu's gardens? If we can find some it might just spruce this little cottage up...what do you say?"

Joey beamed. "I think I might just know where to find some." He jumped up and called for Johnathan to follow him.

Johnny winked as he walked past me. "Can you hold down the fort and find a spray bottle for us please Mommy?"

Joey laughed. "You don't know it, but she doesn't like to be called Mommy. You don't know much about her do you Johnathan? How long were you married to her anyway?"

I barely heard Johnny's reply, but it sounded as if he said that he knew way more than he should about me and that it was going to land him in hot water. Of course, Joey asked why.

The moss, with a dab of glue was a success. I had an antique amber atomizer that I had no use for so I rinsed it out and asked Joey if it would do to keep the moss moist.

"Can Amy keep it, or do you want it back? It's awful pretty."

"She may keep it as it has no value to me."

"Are you sure, maybe it was a gift from one of your old beaus?" Johnny asked guardedly.

"Did you give it to me?"

"I don't think so."

"Then no, it means nothing to me."

He raised his eyebrows in a questioning manner. I only smiled. I knew in that instant that I was going to actively pursue my ex-husband. The question was, did I have the wiles to do so?

I told Joey that he should show Johnathan all his model airplanes and crafts.

"They aren't all mine because lots of these fighter jets were already here when I came. A friend of Mom's built them for her. Do you know her friend?"

Johnny looked at me. "Yeah, I just might. Did she say his name was Johnny?"

"You mean like your name? No, she never said."

"Well, I am pretty sure all these planes and copters are ones I made which means they are all very old. To tell you the truth Joey I'm a bit surprised that they are still flying."

"How come you never told me that they were Johnathan's Mom?"

"Well, we have only been here for a week and you just met Johnathan today so...Anyhow, we have something to tell you, and I'd like us all to go for a walk down to the fishing hole."

"But why Mom, there's no water in the creek so there ain't no fish."

"That doesn't matter. Do you want to hear the story of how Johnathan and I met? Do you want to know how you came to be born? I think you will be pleased by the ending."

"You're kinda confusing me Mom. Do you know what she is talking about Johnathan?"

"I do, and I am most interested in how the story ends."

"Okay," Joey said grabbing his cap, "let's go cause I got me a party to go to soon. Can Rover come with us?"

"He can barely walk Joey, so no, it would be too hard on him."

"Him and Champ are too old to play with. Will it ever be time for a young dog to live here?"

Joey ran ahead of us stopping only to pick a four o'clock here and there and blow the frilly tendrils into the air.

Johnny held me back with his hand. "I'd like to get a puppy for Joey, Em. Would it be all right with you? Do you think Johanna would hate me?"

"Johanna knows why you wouldn't let her have a dog Johnny. I never understood why you never told her how Brandy had died and how it had affected you. She's known since she was nine. I just couldn't keep it from her anymore. She promised she would never mention it to you, or ever ask for a puppy again."

"Why didn't you tell me she knew?"

"Why didn't you tell her about Brandy yourself?"

"You know why. Dogs don't live all that long, and I never wanted her to feel the pain of losing her best friend as I did, but I see now that I was wrong."

"She won't hate you Johnny, but I know how you felt because I lost my best friend three times over. Only difference is, he came back to me twice... third time is still up for grabs."

"Are you talking about me Em?" Johnny took hold of my arm and turned me to face him. "I want us to be friends again. I'm sorry for all the times I let you down. You forgave me before...can you forgive me this time?"

I smiled at him, but there was a tear in my eye. "Forgive you for what? What have you done besides get married while I was away?"

"I didn't, or wouldn't admit that you were ill, and then it was too late. I should have sought help, but I thought our love would see us through anything, but it didn't. I thought it would all just go away, but it didn't, and I lost you to something I couldn't fix. I had always been able to fix anything Em, but I couldn't fix you."

"Nothing was your fault Johnny. That demon took hold of *me*. I wasn't strong enough to fight it, so don't you try and take credit for something that was not of your doing. I can never go back to that darkness that consumed me because my muddled mind believed you had deceived me. So, it is me who needs to apologize to you. We need to put all that behind us and be parents to our son, that is, if you want to be. Sorry, I've just taken it for granted that you want to claim him as yours, but maybe I am totally wrong. I mean, he may be a complication to your new life..."

"Stop right there. Nothing could get in my way of being a father to that boy, nothing. I loved him from the moment I saw him just as I did Johanna. I'm sorry as ole hell that circumstances kept me from him for the first five years of his life, but I'll be damned if I'll go one more day without him knowing who I am...do you understand?"

"I do, and I will try not to let my jealousy get in the way of our parenting."

"What do you mean by that?"

"Figure it out for yourself Johnny." I said pulling away from him.

"What's taking you guys so long?" Joey yelled at us. "I'm going down to look for frogs."

I got to the edge of the embankment just before he reached the third stone step. "Get back up here Mister! Did you forget why we are here?"

"No, but I need to check for frogs." He said almost defiantly.

Johnny reached his hand out to him. "It's too dry for frogs. How about you listen to your mom and come and sit down with us?"

"They dig way down deep you know."

"I do, and you probably don't know this, but your mom is the best frog catcher I ever saw."

"Naw, she doesn't even like them, do you Mom?"

I sat on the old bench that overlooked the creek that was flowing sluggishly into the sea. I patted the space next to me inviting Joey to sit beside me. He sat leaving room for Johnathan.

"Many years ago when I was ten I met Johnathan down there in the creek. He was twelve and not very happy that a girl was digging in his fishing hole."

Joey laughed. "Didn't you like girls Johnathan?"

"Well, I really hadn't had any dealings with them, but I sure as heck didn't like one scaring all the fish away. She told me she would rather be fishing then looking for frogs, but she didn't have a fishing pole, and she didn't know how to fish anyhow. I told her I could teach her."

"I thought you didn't like her." Joey said a little confused.

"Yeah, well that didn't last long. She was different from the girls at school. She was kind of a tomboy if you can believe it. She didn't make a fuss about putting a worm on the hook or bonking the fish after she caught one. She didn't even bat an eyelash when I showed her how to pull the insides out of the fish." Johnny smiled at me over our son's curly blonde head.

Joey shuttered and said that he wouldn't even like to do that. "You were really brave Mom."

"I wasn't brave Honey; I just didn't know any better, and I didn't want your father to think that I was a sissy."

I put my hand over my mouth. It wasn't supposed to come out like that.

"She's funny isn't she Johnathan? I think she forgot that you weren't my father then, but now you are going to be. It's okay if you made a booboo Mom, right Johnathan?"

Well, now I had no choice, I had to cut right to the chase, but Johnny beat me to it.

"Sometimes best friends get married, and that's just what happened to your mom and me. She lived in Victoria and I lived here in Seahaven, so we didn't see much of each other during the school year. I lived just up the hill and my parents both worked so I spent most of the summers down here with Sarge and my Aunt Alice. Your mom started spending the summers down here with AnnieZu. Her older sister Summer used to come once in a while, but she was real bossy and didn't like the outdoors. Your mom had to move away with her parents when she was fourteen, so we didn't see each other for almost two years. When she got back, I had to go away to school, but we talked about getting married because we really liked each other."

Johnny had left out all the heartbreak of the years in between.

"Johanna says that Piers and her are in love; were you in love with Mom?" Joey asked.

Johnny nodded. "Very much so, and we got married, and then your sister Johanna was born. We were very happy and wanted to have a little boy just like you, but your mom got sick and had to go away to England to get better. She didn't know how long she would be gone so we thought it best to get a divorce. You know what a divorce is don't you?"

"Sure because Mom is getting one from James. How come you didn't love her anymore? How come you never went with her?"

"I have asked myself that question many, many times Joey...why didn't I go with her? I guess I thought I might be the problem because we weren't getting along like we used to. I never stopped loving her even after she married James. I have to admit I was jealous of him because you were born to him and not to me. But now we know that when your mother left here you were already in her tummy. That meant that I was your father all along, but your mother didn't know it right away. James was never your real father; I always was. Do you understand any of this?"

"Sort of."

Was this Johnathan's way of saying that he still loved me? Right now the important thing was Joey, so I'd just wait and see how things played out.

"What Johnathan is trying to say is that I only thought James was your father because I married him so soon after I left here. The truth is that Johnathan is your real father, but I didn't know it until a year ago." I sounded like I was still trying to convince myself that it was true.

"What made you know then Mom? Did you see the picture?"

"What picture Joey?"

"This one." He said.

He stood up in front of me and pulled something out from his back pocket. He untied a string that was wrapped around a piece of cardboard. Carefully he extracted something from inside a plastic wrapper. I had never known my son to be so meticulous. He handed it to me and said that I had to be very careful with it because it was really valuable. It was a photo of Johnny and his dog Brandy. I inhaled very deeply. Johnny asked if he could see it.

"Sure you can Johnathan because it's a picture of you. I thought it was me, but I don't have a dog. I can't read much, but I think it says "Dad" on it, so it's you."

"Where did you get this Joey?" I asked curiously.

"From Johanna's room at your sister's house. You can't tell her because she will be mad at me for snooping. I promise I will put it back. That's why I asked Johnathan if I could be his little boy because I already look like him. Is that okay Mom?"

I sat him down on my knee. "It is okay Joey because Johnathan *really* is your dad. I'm sorry I didn't figure it out sooner, but my head was still a little foggy when I was in London."

"I told you she was funny didn't I Johnathan?" Joey laughed. "It's always foggy in London."

I didn't know whether to laugh or cry, so I just hugged him and told him I loved him.

"I love you too Mom. Does JoJo know?"

"I'm pretty sure she has figured it out just as Johnathan did when he saw you."

He turned to his father and asked him if that was true.

"It is Son, and I hope someday you will think about calling me Dad."

"I kinda like calling you Johnathan."

"Whatever you want will be fine with me because we are just getting to know each other."

I was about to say something but stopped when I heard Betsy yelling at

Joey. The car would be here for him in fifteen minutes to take him to the party. I told him to run along and get cleaned up. He said he was already clean. I told him to wash his hands at least. Johnny asked him if he needed help getting the fairy house to the car. Joey said that Betsy would help him and that he should stay with me so that I wouldn't be lonesome anymore. He asked me to take good care of the photo. He turned halfway up the path and asked if he could tell Amy that he had a new dad. Johnny and I both said that it was okay. We watched him in silence until he disappeared inside the house.

"Have you been lonely Em?"

"Sometimes I was lonely for AnnieZu and here, but I had Joey."

"Do you think he understands Em?" Johnny asked solemnly.

"As much as a little five-year-old can. I'm sure that it will all come together in time. I think I will head back too."

"We need to talk Em."

"About what?"

"About us; you and me."

I got up and looked down at him. "There is no "us" Johnny. You and I ceased to exist the day you married Lorraine."

Why did I say there was no "us" when I really wanted there to be. What was I afraid of?

He rose and tried to corral me, but I edged past him and left his question hanging in the air.

"Why was it all right for you to marry, but not me...answer me that November!"

I waited until I was half way up the path, and just like Joey had, turned and yelled.

"You may see Joey whenever you want, but you may not take him to visit with *her* at your house. Joey will never call that woman mother! Now, hurry up...you know AnnieZu hates to be kept waiting."

He caught up to me. "I didn't know she was expecting me. Are you going to answer my question?"

"Not today."

CHAPTER 5

Johnathan

I was greeted warmly by Em's aunt and Betsy who was AnnieZu's cook and companion. She had been here for as long as I could remember. There was one person missing: Mrs. Parker. I believe that she had been hired on as a housekeeper some twenty odd years ago. That word took on a whole other meaning as she considered herself superior to Betsy, the girls who actually did all the housekeeping, the handyman, and the gardener. She took it upon herself to be supervisor to all. The only person she never tried to boss around was Harold who had many duties around the estate and had been the family chauffeur for thirty years. She either had a crush on him, which I found doubtful, or didn't want to lose favour with him because she relied on him to drive her everywhere. Harold's residence was a nice suite above the garage while Mrs. Parker lived in one of the cottages. Betsy had moved in with AnnieZu after the death of her husband three years ago. The arrangement had been a Godsend as Zu's own husband had passed away ten years earlier. The three women seemed to get along quite well together throughout the years. Betsy put up with Mrs. Parker's bossing just as long as she stayed out of her kitchen. I never heard anyone call her anything but Mrs. Parker. They were both on the premises when AnnieZu had her accident last February. Harold had driven Zu to Victoria for a celebratory luncheon with Em's sisters. It was their twenty fifth anniversary at the Emporium. The Chamber of Commerce had sponsored it. AnnieZu said the accident was all her fault as she had not waited for Harold to come around to open her door, plus she had drank two glasses of wine and may have been a tad tipsy. She had stepped out of the car and as she recalls, "One foot went one way, and the other foot another." She fractured her hip and bruised her tail bone. She was in the hospital for three weeks. Betsy had called me and told me of the accident the next day. I visited her every other day, and we became friends all over again. Our conversations centered mostly around Em.

It was no secret that Ms. Parker and I did not see eye to eye. The woman disliked me from day one, and the feeling was somewhat mutual. I was surprised that she was not somewhere hovering around today, so I asked AnnieZu where she was.

"You can relax Johnathan; she's not going to barge in on us like she usually does. She's off attending her new granddaughter's christening and won't be back until late tomorrow."

"So," Em said, "you two have taken up the gauntlet again?"

"I wouldn't say that, but I haven't been out to see this dear lady," I said holding on to AnnieZu's hand, "for a while, so I'm sure Mrs. Parker will tear into me about that."

"Why haven't you been out Johnathan? You always said that AnnieZu was like a mother to you, and you promised me you would look in on her while I was away, so what's changed? Is Lorraine keeping you hostage?"

"That was uncalled for November. You've been *"away"* as you say for quite some time, and Johnathan is a very busy man." AnnieZu came to my defense.

"No, it's all right Zu. A promise is a promise, right Em? Just so you know, Lorraine does not control what I do, say, or feel. I've been too wrapped up in the business, plus other things. Sorry Zu, that is no excuse, but I'm going to make amends starting right now. I won't be a stranger anymore. Is that all right with you November?"

I'm pretty sure Em caught the sharpness of my question as she answered that she certainly hoped so if I was going to have any sort of relationship with Joey.

Betsy entered with the tea and a cart full of sweets so that brought an end to what I thought may turn into a melee remembering Em's harsh words about Lorraine earlier. The rest of the visit went cordially. When I got up to leave I asked Em what time Joey would be back. She said sometime after dinner. I asked her if it was all right if I came over to say good night to him. She said that she was sure he would like that and would probably be ready for bed by seven.

AnnieZu reminded me that Sarge was invited to come to dinner tomorrow evening. I thanked her, kissed her on the cheek, told Em I would see her later, and showed myself out.

Sarge wanted to know everything that happened. I filled him in, not mincing words about how Em felt about Lorraine. He asked me how Lorraine felt about Em. I told him the feeling was totally mutual. He asked me if it came down to choosing, who would it be?

"Well, Em is not too fond of me, so there probably won't be any choosing."

He slapped his knee and said. "I love a good fight. I don't know where Lorraine was when they were handing out boobs, but November cleaned up on her in that category, and from what I remember, a hell of a lot more! I've never once heard you say that Lorraine has rocked your world like I know November did. Act three comin up."

"You're a dirty old man, you know that? And, quit comparing my life to some Shakespeare tragedy! Let's go warm up some of that chili for supper."

I was at Silvermist a little before seven. The screen door into the kitchen was open so I went in and found Betsy kneading dough. I asked her what she was doing still working at this time of night. She said that she wanted to make overnight buns as they were Johanna's favorite, and that Miss Annie had retired to her room to watch TV. November and Joey had already gone upstairs. I said that I hoped I wasn't too late to say good night.

"I hardly doubt that Johnathan as he was tired, but said he would wait up for you. I cannot speak for November."

I muttered to myself that no one could. Joey was indeed sitting up in bed waiting for me. I asked him where his mother was.

"She has one of her headaches."

I asked him if she got the headaches often. He said not as much as she did when they were in London. I nodded and said that I hoped she would feel better tomorrow. We read a few chapters out of the timeless novel Huckleberry Flynn until I noticed Joey was having a hard time keeping his eyes open. I tucked him in and kissed him on the forehead promising him that we would have many such adventures together. There wasn't a peep out of the room next door.

There was a streetlight outside AnnieZu's house, one at the bridge, and one half- way between the bridge and Sarge's house. I approached the bridge and was compelled to look back as I had that uncanny feeling that I was being watched. Sure enough, the curtain in Emmy's window was moving slightly. I raised my arm and saluted her with two fingers. The curtain closed. I smiled wondering what my ex had in store for me next. I didn't have long to wait.

The rattling of pans awoke me. I glanced at the clock; it was 5:15. What the hell... was Sarge up already? Surely it wasn't Em because I had told her I'd get Sarge up and fed. I yanked on a pair of joggers and stumbled into the kitchen.

"I thought I told you to take the day off Em?"

She was frying bacon. She turned and asked me if I was her boss again.

"Again...when was I ever your boss?"

"Didn't I work for you in the office and at home?"

Her voice was somewhat accusatory.

"I never considered you an employee, it was our company, and it still is. I didn't know that you considered what you did at home as work. You were always content..."

She finished my sentence laughing slightly. "Until I wasn't...you should go back to bed and let me get on with breakfast." She said as she turned the bacon.

"I'll go and see if Sarge needs help getting up."

She turned, flipper in hand. "So, you want to take that away from me too!"

She turned off the electric frying pan, undid her apron and threw it towards a chair. It fell short and she walked over to it and kicked it. She had a look in her eyes that I didn't like.

In the calmest voice I could muster I asked her what I had ever taken away from her.

"My trust, my happiness, my reason for living, but most of all my future! And now, you are probably plotting on how to get custody of my son so you can give him to her!"

She was already at the door and did not look back as I cried out in utter shock that I would never try to take Joey away from her. I was bewildered. Yesterday she had smiled at me in that old familiar way when she said she would see me later. She had raised her hand to her head impulsively but had stopped short of making the final motion of submission. Now this... accusations again that I had been unfaithful. "Oh God," I said out loud, "please tell me that Emily isn't back!"

I walked to the living room window and looked out. Em was pedaling her bike like someone possessed. I snickered a little thinking that she reminded me of "old lady what's her name" from the Wizard of Oz. Sarge called to me asking what all the commotion was. I shouted back that it was just Em being Emily. He asked me what the hell I meant by that. I said I'd explain later.

Joey phoned at nine. He said his mom had gone into town to pick up some things for Betsy. He said he wasn't allowed to ride his bike past the bridge alone so could I watch for him. I told him that I was on my way over to Silvermist as I had something I wanted to check out.

I found him sitting on the back step petting Rover. I asked if he knew where Pete was. He said he thought he was in his workshop. I told him I had to talk to AnnieZu for a minute and if he could get Pete for me then we would be all set.

"To do what?" He asked.

"Have you ever wondered why those steps in the back yard don't go anywhere?"

"There is no door to them." He answered bluntly.

"Exactly, and that is because they have another use, and hopefully you will be able to see what it is shortly."

AnnieZu was sitting in her sunroom sipping a cup of tea. I gave her a peck on the cheek.

"Good morning Beautiful."

She patted my hand and laughed. "You're flattering the wrong lady Johnathan."

"Oh, I am, am I, and just whom should I be flattering?"

"That sweet little niece of mine, of course."

"Do you mean that unpredictable ex-wife of mine?" I teased.

"I'm afraid to ask what she has done now..."AnnieZu pleaded shaking her head.

"She tore into me this morning accusing me of still taking things away from her. One day she believes that I never cheated on her, and the next she thinks I still did. I can't fight something that never happened, so I guess I'll just take it one day and one outburst at a time. Anyhow, there is something I want to discuss with you, and feel free to refuse my request at any time okay?"

"I don't think I could refuse you anything Johnathan, but first I want you to know that November still loves you. I am positive of that. She does not care for Lorraine one tiny bit.

I want you to be aware of that as I'm not sure how far she will go with this resentment."

"I'm pretty sure Lorraine feels the same way about her. Nothing will come of it Zuzz. And, just for the record, I still love Em. I always have and I always will. So yes, we still love each other, but without trust, there just isn't any conciliation."

"You must make amends anyway you know how for Joey's sake. If I was you, I would not antagonise November by talking about your wife's attributes; jealousy is a hard pill to swallow."

"You think Em is jealous of Lorraine? Believe me; she has nothing to be jealous about."

"Oh, you poor, poor foolish man. Don't you know that she would be jealous of any woman who took her place, not just Lorraine, but anyone?"

"No one has taken her place Zu... no one could."

"Then you had best be telling her that. Now, what did you really come to talk about? I have a feeling it is a lot less important than yours and November's relationship."

"I'd like to try and see if I can get the rill working again. I think it would make a delightful background for Johanna and Piers wedding. It was a special gift from your husband for your twenty-fifth wedding anniversary, and he passed away shortly after, so I'm a little hesitant because seeing it erected again may bring back unpleasant memories for you. If it would upset you, I will go no further."

"My dear Johnathan, seeing and hearing that peaceful flow of the waters cascading down the marble stairs again would not only be a beautiful adornment for the wedding, but it would be a gift to me. Eric has been gone a long time and I have many endearing memories of him. Seeing that rill working again would bring his spirit back to life. Why it quit working almost simultaneously with his passing has been an enigma for far too long. Several handy men have tried to find the problem but have been unable to get it working again. Promise me you won't be too disappointed if it proves to be a hopeless cause."

"Oh, I'm not going to fail, you can make book on that. Now I have an added incentive; it will make you happy. I guess I best get to it then.'

I planted another kiss on her cheek and told her I loved her. She told me I was telling the wrong girl again, but she loved me too, and that I must know that she regarded me as the son she had never had.

I told her I was honored and that she could quit worrying that pretty little head of hers because Em and Joey and I were going to be a family before the week was out, but I had a little work to do in that department. Then I threw in the little tidbit that I had bought my family home back.

"What?" She exclaimed.

I cautioned her with fingers to my lips. "Shh, it's yours and my little secret for the time being; are you good with that?"

"I am Johnathan, but don't be too surprised if she does not share your enthusiasm. I know you want to make a home for her and Joey, but until Lorraine is out of your life there is no chance for that happening, and then, there is the "father thing."

"Phillip has been gone for years now, and I hope that six years of therapy has finally put his death out of Em's tortured mind."

"I'm afraid there is something you don't know Johnathan. When he died, and especially under the tainted circumstances, a multitude of repressed memories were unleashed, and I believe that is what triggered November's breakdown. Personally, I don't believe that it was all due to a chemical imbalance."

"I've known her since she was ten, so I find it hard to believe that there is something I don't know about her Zuzz. I agree with you though that her father's death was a catalyst that contributed to her depression and breakdown."

"It was before your time Johnathan."

"Are you saying that she has a secret?"

Her voice was calm, yet uneasy. "We have only spoken of it twice. Once when she was ten and once again just before you and she were married. She swore me to silence and made me promise never to tell you. That time has come and gone now, and I have hope that her therapy in London may have dealt with the subject. It's much easier to bear your soul to strangers than the ones you love. Let's not broach this again until after the wedding, okay? Just be patient with her moods; she's still healing."

"I won't be satisfied until I know all the facts, but I will respect yours and her silence. If things go awry with us I am going to ask you to break your promise to her, and I won't take no for an answer. I know without a doubt that something is troubling her. I thought it was still me, but if it's something that happened before I even met her then I'm going to need to know."

"After the wedding Johnathan; after the wedding."

I hugged her again and left pondering what the secret was that Emmy had kept from me for almost thirty years.

There really wasn't much that could prevent the rill from operating. It was a pretty simple mechanism that didn't have a lot of complicated parts; a large reservoir that circulated water back and forth from it to the steps via pipes. Gauges and a water pump were all that made up the components. It was an uncomplicated device. It was activated by on/off switches which were located in the sub- basement, and on the outside wall at the top of the steps behind the large copper wall. A stream of trickling water would flow down the wall and cascade down the steps. The flow was controlled by a gauge on the pump. At the bottom of the steps, the water would disappear underground and then return and circulate continuously. The sounds and movement of the waterfalls were calming and pleasing to the senses. Johanna had been mesmerized by it when she was a child. She would sit on the bottom step and be splashed by the spray as it trickled down to nothing as it returned underground. Annie Zu's husband Eric was a bit of a romantic constructing it himself for his wife on their twenty fifth wedding anniversary. He would hold Johanna on his knee and tell her magical tales about how the fairies would come at night to bathe and frolic in the never-ending stream. She had us buying her little porcelain replicas of fairies to play in the falls with her. Those little dolls disappeared when Eric passed away, and the water mysteriously stopped flowing.

I briefly wondered if maybe I was doing the wrong thing as perhaps it would upset Jo instead of pleasing her. AnnieZu was good with it, and so if I could get it working again I would ask Em her opinion before I put it into service. She had gone into town to run some errands for Betsy so I wanted to be finished before she returned.

The door to the sub-basement was padlocked. Pete opened it saying that he had been given strict orders from Miss November to never take Joey down there, so her wrath would be on me. I told him I could handle whatever she had to throw at me and that Joey was my son too, and that he would be perfectly safe with us. Joey said he wouldn't tell her if we didn't. I laughed.

Pete and I found the problem within a few minutes; the water pump was kaput. Any decent mechanic would have discovered that immediately as we had, so there must be another problem. We ran water into the vat via a garden hose. It disappeared as fast as it came in. Where it was going was a mystery, but it definitely meant that the vat had a hole or holes in it. Well, that was that, the pump could be replaced, but the vat was pretty much a permanent fixture so it would take months to replace, and the wedding was in a week. I was disappointed but admitted defeat.

"Just a minute John," Pete said, "let's not give up so soon. I have a buddy in the city that has a machine shop and I bet he could set us up with a new pump plus aluminum or tin sheets that will fit inside the vat. There's plenty of room in here to meld them together and lower into the vat. We may require a welder and a few extra hands, but we can do it, what do you say?"

"I suppose that could work, but there just isn't enough time."

Joey had been sitting quietly on an old stool at the work bench sorting out wrenches watching us intently. I patted his head forgetting that he hated his mom doing that. "Sorry Son, I know you were looking forward to seeing how this thing worked, but it's not achievable right now; another time maybe."

"Can't you just plug the holes or glue them or something?" Joey asked disappointedly.

"Those are all good remedies Joey, and maybe they could work if we had the time. How about you help me put away these tools and clean you up before your mom gets back?"

Pete hadn't let it go yet. "Hold the fort...what about a bladder?"

I turned back and grinned. "Pete, you're a genius! Why didn't I think of that?"

"Don't know, but it could work, right?"

"Damn right it could! Only one problem; where would we find one large enough?"

"You leave that to me as you have enough on your plate. Give me half an hour to track down a retired friend of mine who used to work for the forestry."

Joey asked what a bladder was. I told him it was sort of like a big balloon only much stronger.

Pete and I shook hands. I wished him luck just as we heard Emmy calling out for Joey.

My son flinched. "Oh, oh, I'm in trouble; hide me Johnathan!"

Emmy appeared at the open doorway. Pete tipped his hat to her, "Miss November." He turned and gave me thumbs up.

Emmy acknowledged Pete stepping inside. "You can come out from hiding young man. You know this place is off limits to you, but seeing you are with your father, it is all right. What are you guys doing in here anyhow?"

"Can I tell her Dad?"

I looked down at him, beaming because he had called me dad. "Does your mother like surprises?"

"I don't know, do you Mom?"

"Is it a good surprise?"

"It's a surprise for JoJo, but it isn't finished yet, but Dad and Pete are working on it."

Emmy put her arm around him. "Sounds intriguing but think I will wait and be surprised with your sister."

"I'm not in trouble am I?"

"No, you are not in trouble. Come along, I have something for you."

"What is it?" Joey asked eagerly.

"Well, you will just have to wait and see. Wait for me at the car all right? I need to say something to your father."

"He's not in trouble is he?"

"No, now get going!" She turned to me. "Johnny, I am sorry about this morning. I reacted badly. I hope you can give me another chance."

"Another chance...for what Em?"

"For me to prove that I am a good mother, and that I am not useless."

"You've never been useless Em, and no child could ask for a kinder and more loving mother. What's this really about? Are you worried that I am planning on suing for custody of our son?"

She shook her head. "I don't think you would do that, but then you have a new wife and maybe she couldn't have children..."

I stopped her right there. "Lorraine has two grown children and believe me; she would not want to raise a five year old."

"Maybe you don't either."

"Well, you can debunk that idea right away. If I haven't already made it clear, I love that kid, and I am going to do right by him, and you too...if you will let me."

"What do you mean by that?"

I shrugged my shoulders. "Hell if I know."

Joey appeared saving me from trying to explain what I meant. "Mom, what's taking you so long?"

"I'm coming, I'm coming. I have something for you and Sarge too Johnny, so will you walk with us?"

We walked around the house to the driveway to her car in silence. She seemed to be in a very good mood, so I didn't want to say anything that may set her off. She opened the trunk of her car. Inside were two wooden crates each holding a dozen bottles of ginger beer and root beer. She selected a bottle of each and passed them to Joey telling him that the ginger was for Betsy and the root beer was for him.

"This is my present?" Joey asked disappointed.

"Don't be silly. If you look under Cassidy Cat's bed you will see a bag for you. Now run along...no, don't run because you might fall and hurt yourself if the bottles break. Ask Betsy to put some ice in your glass."

"Do I like root beer?"

"Everyone likes Big Ed's root beer. I'll be down in a minute."

She slammed the trunk shut and passed me her keys. "Take my car Johnny because they are too heavy to carry. Just bring me a couple bottles back please. Now, you better get a move on as Johanna will be here soon."

I guess I was being dismissed. I took the keys from her. "That was thoughtful of you to get Sarge some of his favorite drinks. I didn't know Big Ed's was still open."

"Only on Fridays and Saturdays; see you later."

I pulled on her arm. "Am I to assume that among all this confusion with the wedding that you have had time to renew your driver's licence?"

She was emotionless. "You can assume all you want."

"So, the answer is no. One of these days you are going to be stopped by the local constabulary and find yourself in jail."

She laughed brushing my hand off her shoulder. "That's a little extreme don't you think? Anyhow, I have already met the local constabulary, as you call him, and I am good. He has asked me out, so there!"

"Really, or are you just making it up to placate me?"

"Why would I do that...anyhow ask Ed as he was the one who introduced me to Constable Jim. Now I really have to go." She said walking away.

"I worry about you Em." I called after her.

"I'm not yours to worry about anymore. Remember... you gave that up when you remarried."

CHAPTER 6

Em

Joey and I were on the front porch waiting for Johanna and Piers to arrive. Joey would look up the hill and then down the road to Sarge's continuously. Johnny came into view first and Joey was up and running to meet him. I shook my head. One would think that he hadn't seen his father for years. Well, I guess in essence that was true. I yelled after him to slow down, but it was to no avail. Johnny picked him up and swung him around. They arrived on the porch in little fits of laughter. I smiled as Johnny sat down next to me.

"You look lovey Em."

I guess he had forgiven me for not telling him why it was all right for me to remarry, but not for him. I thanked him and said that he didn't look so bad himself. Joey asked him if he thought that I was pretty.

Johnny laughed and winked at me. "She is that Son, beautiful and enchanting, and mystifying all at once."

"What does mystifying mean?" Joey asked.

"It means she is somewhat like a puzzle, hard to figure out, confusing and challenging, but once you do, the end result is your reward. Do you agree Em?" Johnny quipped.

I wasn't sure whether I was amused or bemused as Johnny had just depicted me as an enigma.

"Here she comes Mom! What do you think she will say when I tell her? Do you think she knows?" Joey pulled on Johnny encouraging him to get up. "Come on Dad..."

Apparently, I was suddenly immaterial. I took the reunion in from the comfort of the porch swing. There was much hugging and laughing. I did not interrupt as Joey related his news to his sister whose eyes opened wide as she played along pretending that it was a surprise to her.

Johnny mounted the steps and took my hands in his. "Come on Sweetheart, this is your love-fest too."

Johnny never calls me sweetheart.

Lunch was on the table. Johnny and Joey had gone to pick Sarge up. Johanna put her arm through mine and asked if she could have a minute with me. We went into the conservatory.

"How are you Mom?" She asked.

"How do I look?"

"You have this glow to you; is Daddy the reason why?"

"Though I am happy to see him and especially so to see him with Joey, he's not the reason. You are my dear. I have missed you so very much. That three hour visit we had two weeks ago was not nearly enough."

"I know Mom." she said hugging me. "I really wanted to come over last week and help you with the altered wedding plans, but I just couldn't get away. I'm so glad you were here to take command. I'm thinking about changing jobs after the honeymoon."

"But, you love your job."

"Not as much as I love Piers. I would be away from home too much, and that's not good for a relationship is it Mom?"

I smiled. "No, it isn't Sweetie, although some would say that absence can make the heart grow fonder."

"You mean in Daddy's and your case?"

"I am very fond of your father, and I know he cares for me, but he is married, and I was, so that train must leave the station."

"It hasn't left yet then?"

"Come on; we're holding up lunch."

"One more question Mom; what did you think of Lorraine?"

"Well, I was only in her presence that once, but she seemed very nice. I thought she and Johnny were a good match."

"You hated her didn't you?" Johanna dared me to tell the truth.

"Hate is such a powerful word, and can get one into a lot of trouble as

AnnieZu so warned me. If I never see her again, it will be too soon, but she will probably show up this weekend, and at your wedding, and, on and on. I've already told Johnathan that Joey cannot go to his house in the city and that he better not expect Joey to call her mother."

"I can't imagine what daddy would do if you and Lorraine ever got into it."

"Well, he'd have to take her side wouldn't he because she's his wife, and his ex-wife is a crazy bitch? Let's go as I am very hungry."

"Oh Mommy, I love you."

Lunch was very pleasant. I sat at the far end of the table and let Joey sit between his sister and his dad; Piers was to my left. Betsy and Mrs. Parker had left to bring dessert in. Piers turned to me and asked if we could pardon him for a few minutes as he had something he would like to discuss with Johnathan. I said, "Certainly."

He asked Johnny if he would accompany him outside. Johnny rose and made Joey promise to save him a piece of pie. I asked Johanna what that was all about. She said she wasn't sure. Half an hour later, we found out. Piers joined us, and said that Johnathan would be right in.

Piers explained laughing. "Sorry for the interruption of lunch folks, but I needed to ask the father of the bride for an answer to an improbable task I have been contemplating. I thought he'd tell me that the idea was a good one, but just as I had thought, impossible to accomplish in such a short time. On the contrary, he said it could be done in one day."

Sarge was never one for small talk. "Are you going to beat around the bush all day Son, or are you going to tell us what the hell you're talking about?"

"Right you are Sarge. The gardens are beautiful, and the perfect setting for a wedding. We cannot thank you enough AnnieZu for the offering, and to you November for all the work you have done. Now, I have Johnathan to thank also. My dilemma was that there wasn't an adequate platform for the band. As you know they are all my band buddies, and one is also in the wedding party. They told me not to worry about it as they would manage. But, there also wasn't a dance floor, so I had a brainstorm; let's combine them into one floor."

"Piers," Johanna interrupted, "we discussed that, and I thought we had decided that if people wanted to dance, they could in the grass or on the patio square?"

"I know, but I wanted your Dad's opinion about how we could erect a bandstand. He said he had been a little worried about where the caterers were going to set up, so maybe the two could be combined into one large piazza, and that it could also be large enough to accommodate dancers. He paced the area off, and made some measurements in his head, and told me to leave the rest up to him."

Johanna passed him a piece of apple pie. "So, where is he?"

"He said he'd only be a few minutes. I hope I didn't put him on the spot. I told him that if this platform could really be built that it would be somewhat of a miracle. He said, and I quote: "A few days ago I received two miracles; Em came back and brought me Joey. I need to play it forward. Besides, it's for my daughter, who just happens to be the apple of mine and Em's eye." I'm too sure if I was supposed to share that."

I patted him on the hand. "Yes, you were. Johnathan is the smartest man I have ever known, so if he says something can be done, then it can be."

Johnny had returned, and I think he heard what I had said because he smiled at me affectionately. He placed his hand on Pier's shoulder. "All done ole chap. Crews will be here at eight sharp tomorrow morning with everything we need, and construction of the stage and flooring will commence. Zuzzs, are you all right with me taking the south fence down enough to allow the lumber truck through?"

"Anything you need Johnathan. How many men are you expecting?" She asked.

"Twelve."

"That's almost your whole crew Dad! It's a holiday; how did you manage that?"

"I left it in my foreman's hand. If he can't find enough volunteers, he'll hire. There are lots of able-bodied men out there who need work."

"But, that would be overtime Daddy and that'd be too costly. Piers, we should reconsider." Johanna implored.

"Do you want to tell them Em, or should I?" Johnny asked winking at me.

I had no idea what he was talking about, so said that he should.

"The money from the sale of our old house has been sitting in a savings account in Em's name for almost six years. It was her idea that we use the money to pay for the wedding, and I concurred. The interest alone will pay for the construction, so it's a go my dear."

"It's a grand gesture Daddy, but suppose if Mom or you need that money?"

"You heard your father Johanna; he's the boss." I said

Johnny shook his head as he looked at me. "If only that was so. Now, where's my blackberry pie Joey?"

"I think I ate the last piece. There's lots of apple though." Joey lamented.

Betsy laughed as she placed a whole blackberry pie in front of Johnny. "I think your son has been spending too much time with Sarge as he has inherited his quirky sense of humor."

Johnny asked who was going to join him in the indulgence of the sinfully delicious pastry.   Everyone declined as they had already had their full. I hadn't, so walked over, told Joey to scoot over, and sat down beside my ex. He smiled at me, ran his hand through his hair, cut me a generous portion, smothered it with ice cream, and passed it to me. He had just made a blatant suggestion to me. He had never done that before, so I had to wonder if he was copying my practice of an invitation to seduction, or had he only been clearing a wayward hair off his face. Thank God no one else knew the significance of the gesture. His hand brushed mine. He told me to enjoy. I replied that I had every intention of doing so.

The next day was a hub of activity. Johnny's crew arrived bright and early, and had a good start on the pavilion before some of us were even up. Johanna and I had plans to spend the day in Victoria, so I had a quick shower and tried to wash the cobwebs out of my head trying to remember last night. We had withdrawn to the living room after dinner and had spent a most enjoyable evening getting to know our soon to be son-in-law better, and listening to Sarge's recollections of Johnny's and my childhood. Apparently, I had imbibed a little too much and was helped into bed by my daughter and Betsy. And, apparently I had asked if Johnny was going to come to bed with me. Johanna informed me of my blabbering when we were on the road to Victoria. She asked me what I had meant.

"Seeing that I don't remember saying anything, I can't tell you what I may have meant."

"Is something going on between you and Daddy?"

"Didn't you ask me that yesterday?"

"Sort of I guess. I have to tell you Mom that I was fearful of you and Dad seeing each other again. I mean, you had no contact with each other for six years, and then you just show up unannounced on his doorstep…"

"What did you think was going to happen?"

"You never once spoke ill of him while I lived with you in London, but you had married James so quickly after you left here, so I always thought you didn't love Daddy anymore. I always knew that he still loved you, and that he blamed himself for your illness, but I never had a clear picture of how you felt about him. You have both told me that your reunion went smoothly, but I am a little suspect that neither of you are telling me the truth. Are you holding something in Mom…like suspicions and blame? Are you just putting on an act for all of us because of Joey and my wedding?"

I opened my window and gazed out wondering how much I was ready to reveal to my daughter. I fiddled with my locket; it was one Johnny had given me. A photo of him and Johanna and me were the precious memories it held inside.

I opened the locket. "I need to replace this picture with one of you and Joey."

"You mean one without you and Daddy?"

"I think so. I will answer your questions now because I don't want you worrying about anything. I've told you this many times over; your father was not to blame for my illness. The chemical imbalance of neurotransmitters in my brain did not let me differentiate between fact and fiction. It played games with me until it completely took over my life. I did believe your dad was unfaithful to me, and that only added to the turmoil boiling in my already unstable mind-set. You need to know that I did not love James, and we did not have a love life. Neither of us was interested in one. Unfortunately, we did have a "somewhat" physical relationship a few times. This is not easy talking about this with you."

"Mom, I am the same age you were when you married Daddy. I'm pretty sure you didn't discuss your love life with Zena, but you are not her, and I am not you, so it does not embarrass me, and I hope it won't you. Yes, Shelia has explained the clinical name for your disorder many times. I know you have tried a multitude of different drug concoctions that didn't really remedy the problem, but you seem to have found the right combination now haven't you?"

"Yes, I am on an all- natural regime and it seems to be working. You haven't asked me how Johnathan came to be Joey's father."

"Oh, you bet I have wondered. Nothing I have come up makes any sense though. I know you and Daddy were finished with each other six weeks or so before we went to England, but I guess I was wrong about that wasn't I?"

"No; not really. Your father gave me all the space he thought I needed. He respected my decision to move out of the house and take you with me. He didn't like it, but he was afraid to antagonise me anymore. He did not come and see me at the house in Ridgewood or even phone me. I went to him. It was the night before you and I boarded the airplane to London. It was also the night I received my divorce papers. Your dad received his too. He let me in saying it was still my house. We burnt our papers in the fireplace, and then we made love. I wrote him a note as he slept, left it and my rings on the table, and left. He came to the door just as I was getting into a cab. That was the night Joey was conceived. If I had never slept with James those few times, I would have been home the minute I discovered that I was pregnant. I would have come home to Johnathan and to hell with my mental turmoil...at least I think now that I would have. I have lived with that ever since I realised that he was Joey's dad. I've never stopped loving him, but it's a different kind of love now."

"Thank-you for telling me Mom. Does Daddy know how you feel?"

I laughed. "I think he does, but then sometimes he thinks I'm Emily, so..."

"Emily; I kind of remember that name from when you and Dad were arguing...who is she? Please tell me that he wasn't having an affair with her?"

"Well, he was in a way Honey because I'm Emily, so it was sort of okay."

"I don't understand...why would you suddenly want to be called Emily?"

"She kind of took over for me. She seemed to be able to handle my situation better than I could, so I let her take command again."

"Again...are you saying you have a split personality, and that Emily steps in when the situation is too much for you to handle as Em?"

"We are all a myriad of personas Honey. I am not much different from anyone else except   that I know when to hide because a stronger me will emerge and take over. Not to worry though as I am not Emily anymore though your dad's not too sure." I giggled a little.

"Mom, are you playing games with Dad?"

"No more than he is playing with me. I don't mean anything by that because the field is not fair anymore. I can never forgive him for remarrying." I suppose I sounded bitter.

"Why was it okay for you to marry someone else, but not for Daddy to? Did you not want him to be happy?"

"He has asked me the same thing several times. I have yet to give him an answer, so I guess you will know when he knows. Can we talk about the wedding now please? Just one last thing, I tried to write a little something to your father every week. I even bought him little mementos. I put the letters into envelopes, addressed them to him at our old residence, stamped them, and stored them away. Your dad has them now. He has read a few but finds them too upsetting. So you see, he was always on my mind. I was working hard to gain control of my life and get back to him. I was winning the battle, but I never told him, and he remarried, so that ended that."

"Does Daddy know all of this?"

"I think he does."

Johanna and I arrived back at Silvermist at four p.m. We dropped all the packages off at the back door and went to see how the construction project was going. Johnny spotted us and walked over and asked us what we thought.

"I see it, and yet I can't believe it!" Johanna gushed. "It's absolutely amazing Daddy! Where's Piers?"

"That's him sanding the dance floor. Hold on young lady; you know the rules, hard hat in a construction site." He popped his on her head, told her to watch her step, and asked me how my day was.

"Obviously, not as productive as yours was, but we did everything that we set out to do. You've done an incredible job Johnny. What happens to it all after the wedding?"

"It'll all come down the same way it went up. Pete and I'll see to putting the yard back the way it was. The lawn will probably require reseeding. I'm very proud of the way my crew came through for us. They are a hard-working bunch and will be handsomely rewarded although they expect nothing. I think a few days off with pay would be adequate; what do you think?"

"Sounds good; and what about you, what's your reward?"

"The look in our daughter's eyes."

I smiled. "I'm counting, and along with Piers, Pete, and you, the number is up to nineteen. Oh, is that Sarge and Joey sitting on the bandstand?"

"Sarge wasn't going to miss out on the "barn raising" as he called it. He and Joey are my supervising supervisors." Johnny laughed. "Do you think you can do me a favor Em?"

"Anything; just tell me what you need."

"I've ordered fried chicken with all the fixings for supper from Jenny's diner. It's scheduled to arrive at six and hopefully, we will be done by then. Mrs. Parker went into the village and picked up paper products, and half a dozen cases of beer, so that is all looked after. Do you think you could organise the seating and such?"

"Of course I can. I can't visualize Mrs. Parker going into the liquor store... actually, I can't even see you asking her for help."

"I didn't Honey; she volunteered. She and Betsy came over with iced tea, coffee, and sodas, and cookies at lunch when the pizzas arrived. She asked me what my plans were for dinner. I told her, and she said she'd look after the rest. Good thing because I hadn't even thought about plates and eating utensils. I'm pretty sure that Harold purchased the beer though."

I mumbled something stupid and turned to go. He put his hand on my arm and asked me what I said.

"I know the way things are Johnathan, and I'm working hard at keeping things at the status-quo, so just let me be. You should only be calling your daughter and your wife pet names."

He called my name as I walked away. I hauled all the packages in and took them into the kitchen to sort out. Betsy and Mrs. Parker were having tea. Mrs. Parker volunteered to get me a cup. Who was this woman? I put all the wedding decorations in a pile for Johanna. I had bought Joey a few things, so put them aside also, and then pulled the dress I had chosen for the rehearsal dinner out of a bag and asked them what they thought. A low whistle came from the doorway. I cradled the dress to my breast, and mockingly walked by

Johnny telling him that he wasn't supposed to see it yet. I looked back down the stairs from the top. He was still standing there with a stunned look on his face. He shrugged his shoulders and went into the kitchen. I was going to have to change my tactics as I was probably confusing him and giving him the wrong idea. A voice in my head said, "The wrong idea about what November?" I told Emily to shut up.

It was nine o'clock when the last vehicle pulled out of the south gate. Johnny told us to remind him to fix the fence tomorrow as he was too beat to do it tonight. He thanked us all; the kitchen staff I guess is who he meant for accommodating him. I let all the others do the responding. Joey wanted to go home with his dad and Sarge. I had to veto that and was met by an indignant young boy. I explained that his dad and uncle had worked hard all day and were going to have an early bedtime, and his was already past due.

"Your mom is right Joey. I promise we will have many nights in the future to spend together, and don't forget, we have our big hiking day on Monday. I'm going to need your help tomorrow with the surprise so you had better be up to it." Johnathan said trying to appease him.

Joey hit his head. "Jeeze, I almost forgot about that! Thanks for reminding me Johnathan."

"And, just what is this surprise?" I asked. Joey reminded me that I wanted to be surprised, and Johnny concurred. I said, "Whatever."

The next morning AnnieZu announced that we were going to church. She was already dressed in her Sunday best, and told Johanna and I to get cracking as she didn't want to be late. She used to drag me and Johnathan with her every other Sunday when we were young. She told me that it was high time that Joey learned some of the scriptures. I told her that there were churches in England. She asked me if I had ever set foot in one. I said, "Maybe."

"Just as I thought. Well, Joey is busy today, so his initiation will have to wait for another day." She announced.

I asked her what he was doing.

"You know perfectly well that he is helping Johnathan."

"Oh, so Johnny's exempt too is he?"

"Yes, and I imagine Piers will want to stay behind also. Betsy needs a break from the kitchen, so we'll all go out for a nice lunch afterwards at Kelly's.

Mrs. Palmer has already made reservations. No short skirts, jeans, or low cut blouses girls. Hats are in my bedroom."

It had been many years since I had worn one of her 'Sunday go-to-meeting hats.' I offered to stay behind and make lunch for the boys.

AnnieZu was not stymied. "Betsy left sandwich fixings for them. Get a move on girls."

She and I had exchanged ideas on religion many times. It was always a good argument, and I always lost. Sarge had been her accomplice in seeing that Johnny and I had a good Christian upbringing. He'd round us up Sunday mornings calling us little heathens and deliver us to her. I guess I could use a good sermon, and maybe a little blessing on the side, so I didn't put up much of a fight. A good time was held by all, inside and outside. Mrs. Parker kept us entertained at the restaurant. There was only one explanation for her new persona; she had to be in love. Now, the twenty-four-thousand-dollar question was: who was the lucky or unlucky man?

The men were nowhere to be seen when we returned at two. Betsy went straight to the kitchen fully expecting to find a mess. She checked the fridge suspecting that they hadn't even eaten.

"Well, I'll be darned. You two girls trained your men well." She said to Joanna and me.

I reminded her that I didn't have a man and went out to find Joey. I found him running circles around Johnny and Piers. He saw me and made a beeline towards me.

"Guess what we saw Mom, guess what?"

"I don't know; could it have been a frog?"

"Naw, it was a turtle, a really big turtle Mom! He was green and brown. I wanted to bring him home, but Johnathan said that he was too big and that he probably had a family so we shouldn't take him away from them. Do you think he has a family Mom?"

"I hope he does as everyone should have a family. Maybe you will see more on your hike tomorrow. I hope you haven't worn yourself out. What else have you been up to?"

"Nothin. Can I go with Johnathan to pick Sarge up?"

"I didn't know Sarge was coming over today."

"Of course he is. He wants to see the surprise too. Can I go?"

"I think you should come in the house, get cleaned up and have a little rest okay?"

"I'm not tired Mom."

"I wish someone would tell me to take a nap." Piers said as he and Johnny caught up.

Johnny asked me how church was. I replied that it was quite enlightening

"Maybe I'll join you all next time. We'll catch up later okay; right now I have to get Sarge."

"Can I go with him Mom?" Joey asked again.

"I believe I heard your mother suggest a little rest and a clean-up didn't I?"

Joey looked down-hearted and kicked the ground. "Okay, but I'm not napping!"

He followed Piers into the house. Johnny asked me if I wanted to go for a ride.

"Are you trying to start a row between Joey and me?"

He laughed. "Wouldn't think of it."

"Off with you then. Oh, by the way, Mrs. Parker wants us to call her Ada from now on."

"What's up with that?"

"I think she's in love...it's not you is it?"

"Well, she has been extra nice to me, but in all honesty, she's not my type. She's too tall, and a little too stern and she smells like peppermint." He said walking away from me.

I reminded him that Lorraine was tall. He gave me a backwards wave.

We were all ushered out of the house at three P.M. Chairs and patio heaters had been set up on either side of the stairs that led to nowhere. Unbeknownst to me, Joey had invited his friend Amy. She had arrived a few minutes before hand. She was a darling little girl. I sort of likened myself and Johnny to her and Joey. Her mother had passed away when she was three years old. Her father's business was troubleshooting for some oil company. He could not supply her with a stable home, so she had been pawned off to his parents, Cecil and Mary Dover, AnnieZu's neighbors. I hadn't seen Justin Dover for twenty years. Although he was Johnny's age, the two had never been friends. Cecil and Mary doted on Amy.

I took her little hand as we walked outside and sat her in between Johanna and myself. She asked me what the surprise was. I told her that I hadn't a clue.

"Come on Mom; you have to know what is going on! Is it what I think?" Johanna pleaded.

"Seeing I don't know what you are thinking, I will have to tell you the same thing I told Amy; I haven't a clue."

She snorted. "I hardly doubt that! Did you hear that…sounds like a vehicle just drove in?"

Piers said he'd see who it was.

I heard her before I saw her. She rounded the corner of the house on Pier's arm.

"Oh, this is just lovely! What a beautiful venue for a wedding! Hi everyone… what's happening here? There you are Johanna; how are you dear? I'm so excited for you."

Johanna was most gracious. She returned her hug.

"You must be so excited too November? How are you managing?" She cooed.

"We have everything under control, thank-you Lorraine. I wasn't aware that you were joining us today; Johnny never mentioned anything."

"That's just like him isn't it? Where is he? Is this the matriarch Miss AnnieZu"? She walked past me and practically threw herself at my aunt. I momentarily entertained the thought of tripping her.

It seemed senseless for an introduction as they both knew who the other was. AnnieZu was polite as always. She told her that it was nice that she could join us for the celebrations. I wasn't aware that we were celebrating anything.

Piers said it was time, offered Lorraine his seat next to Sarge across from us telling her that we were all in for some sort of surprise, and that her husband was behind it all. She gushed over Sarge telling him how good he looked, and how wonderful it was to see him. He told her that he had a good nurse, and then he winked at me. I winked back.

Joey came running out and stood in front of AnnieZu. "Johnathan wants you to do the honors Zuzzs. Here, I will help you up."

I was going to have a talk with him about calling her Zuzzs. Only Johnny called her that. Joey had definitely picked it up from him.

"I am honoured dear boy, but I am going to decline. I know what is coming, and I don't want to miss one second of it. The honour is all yours."

Joey whispered something to her. She laughed, and told him not to worry because Johnathan knew what he was doing and it was going to be perfect. I guess the procedure had been rehearsed, because Piers got up and gave Joey a lift so that he could reach the button behind the copper wall. He yelled, "Ready...go!"

It started out as a trickle. Amy had crawled up on my lap without me even noticing. AnnieZu and Johanna grasped my hands. Joey ran over to us as the waters started to bubble. He started clapping louder and louder as the flow settled into a relaxing, yet effervescent stream. Suddenly, the waters started to sparkle and turn blue, then orange, then red, and then lavender. It was a rainbow of wonders. It was going to be even better in the dark. Everyone had joined Joey in applauding. Tears slid down my face. My husband was a miracle worker. Did I hear Emily cautioning me because I hadn't said ex-husband?

"It's working, it's working Dad!" Joey chorused as he ran to find his father.

"Whose darling little boy is that?" The uninvited guest inquired.

Johnathan rounded the corner all smiles with Joey sitting atop his shoulders.

I stood up and looked directly at Lorraine. "He's my little boy; mine and Johnny's."

I don't know who gasped more, Lorraine or AnnieZu. I stood up and embraced Johnny and said out loud that he had worked another miracle. Then I whispered, "Your wife is here."

Without saying another word I took my leave. Johanna accosted me just as I was closing the front door unto the veranda. She asked me where I was going. I told her that I was going out to the garden to eat worms.

"Oh good, you always feel better after that." My daughter knew me too well.

Fifteen minutes later I joined Betsy and Mrs. Parker in the kitchen. I waited while they loaded one of the carts up with the casseroles. I guess I was supposed to deliver it as Betsy passed me the oven mitts reminding me that they had just come out of the oven. Tables had been set up in my absence a distance back from the spew of the waterfall. Two people were absent from the table. I took my place next to AnnieZu and Johanna. Joey and Amy sat across from us. They were giggling and whispering to each other. Johnny and Lorraine emerged from wherever they had been. Johnny took his place next to Joey, and she sat down beside Johnny looking rather smug. AnnieZu asked us if we would join her in a toast to Johnathan thanking him for the gift for her and Johanna and Piers. He thanked her and said that it was his pleasure to be able to re-erect the rill on such a momentous day for her. I didn't know what he meant. He walked over to her and kissed her on the cheek. She said that he had made her anniversary one of celebration again, and she was very thrilled that she could share the honour of his gift with Johanna and Piers.

After my uncle Eric had passed away we quit wishing AnnieZu a happy anniversary as it didn't apply anymore. I had forgotten the date, but Johnny hadn't. After we made a little fuss over her she told us to get on with the meal. The large lasagne dish was sitting in front of Johnny. It was too heavy to pass around so he ladled it out for everyone. I shook my head when he reached for my plate.

"What, the chef isn't going to eat her own creation?" He teased.

"You don't know that I made it." I stated.

He looked at Betsy. She nodded. Johanna said that I'd ate too many worms.

Johnny laughed. "Are you still doing that?"

"That's not funny is it Mom?" Joey scolded.

"It's just a joke Son; she doesn't actually eat the worms." Johnny tried to clarify.

"I don't get it either Joey." Lorraine uttered. "I suppose it's some sort of a family thing."

AnnieZu wiped her eyes because she had been laughing so much that she was crying. "Oh my, I haven't thought of that for a very long time. It really isn't just a little family thing Lorraine. The saying comes from a children's song. The child in it is unhappy and says that he is going out to the garden to eat worms. One day when these two," She looked at me and Johnny in turn, "were young, Johnathan had to go into the city with his parents. He had come to the door to tell November the bad news. You have to realise that they were joined at the hip back then, so being separated for a whole day did not sit well with them. They were both upset as they had special plans for the day, which I am sure was catching frogs or fishing. November had stormed upstairs complaining about adults and their expectations for their children. A few minutes later she came back down telling me not to call her for breakfast because she was going out to the garden to eat worms. That became her catch phrase for whenever things didn't go her way. I believe she still uses it today. Am I right Johnathan?"

"It's been a while since I've been privy to her adages, but I'm sure they are still with her. One thing though, I much prefer that she eats worms than spit nails."

That brought another questioning look from Lorraine.

"Thanks guys." I said joining in on the laughter. Silently, I said a thank-you to AnnieZu for cementing Johnny's and my eternal connection. I was pretty sure that the anecdote was meant for Lorraine to ponder.

Mr. Dover arrived to pick up Amy. He marvelled at the rill, and asked Johnathan about it. I walked with them and the kids to the car. Joey took off running back to the rill as soon as the car drove away. I asked Johnny how Lorraine had taken to the news about Joey. He said she was fine with it and was looking forward to getting to know him better. He was testing me. I could tell by the inflection in his voice.

"Over my dead body!" I exclaimed.

He had the nerve to grin. "Come on, I'm kidding, but you have to see her side of the coin."

"I do not have to see anything. I told you what would happen..."

"Please, can we not argue about this right now?"

"When do you suggest that we do then? Do you want to make an appointment?"

"I don't want to argue at all with you Em. On the other hand, our arguments usually ended up with a satisfying outcome." He said humorously.

He tried to take my hand. I pushed him away. "Leave me alone; I am not one bit amused. I'm going into the house and spit nails as you so suggested that I do. Take your wife and get the hell out of here! You have no idea how much trouble you are in."

I didn't want to go back to the patio, so I stormed off towards the back entrance. He followed me right up to when I slammed the door. I'm pretty sure I heard him say, "I love you Emmy."

I leaned against the door. I whispered, "I love you too Johnny." I dare not go back outside so I started unloading the carts of leftovers, and dirty plates.

"What are you doing November? Leave that to me and Betsy." Mrs. Parker took a scraper out of my hands. "You should be outside with everyone else and not working as a scullery maid."

I laughed. "Well, it's not your job either, and I have to do something to earn my keep. I thought Betsy's daughter was coming to help."

"She couldn't make it. If you want to do something, I could really use a cup of tea. How about you put the kettle on?"

"Did you hear that? It sounds like someone is running up the stairs." I walked out into the foyer, and there was Joey at the top of the stairs. I asked him if he was going to bed without saying goodnight. His answer was to slam his bedroom door. Something was wrong. I sighed and went up to see what had upset him. I knocked on his door and asked him if I could come in. He didn't answer.

I opened the door timidly asking if he was angry with me. He was lying face down on the bed crying. I tried coaxing him to sit up, but he wouldn't budge.

"Come on Honey; it can't be all that bad." I said as I rubbed his back. "Are you just overtired? It's been a really busy day, so it's probably a good idea if you get a good nights' sleep so you're rested for tomorrow, don't you think? Is your rucksack all packed?"

"I don't need it." He said between sobs.

I asked why not. He said because Johnathan had something else he had to do tomorrow, so there was no hike. I saw red. I told him in the calmest voice I could muster to get up, brush his teeth and that I'd be back to tuck him in.

I didn't relish confronting Johnny in front of AnnieZu and Johanna. Thank goodness I didn't have to as he was coming out of the kitchen with a cup of coffee as I reached the bottom stair. He started to say something. I stopped him before he had the chance.

"How could you, how could you break that little boy's heart? He was so looking forward to tomorrow, but no, you can't go because you have other plans! It's her isn't it...you haven't been home for two nights, so you need to make it up to her. I could so kill you right now!" I made a fist and punched him. The cup and its contents went flying across the floor.

He let me beat on him. Betsy and Ada had emerged from the kitchen and watched in stunned shock. After a few minutes he took hold of my hands, told me to calm down, and asked me what the hell I was talking about. I said he knew perfectly well because Joey had just told me everything. He said he needed to get the story, whatever it was from Joey. He asked Betsy to take care of me. I yelled at him as he ran up the stairs that I didn't need looking after.

"Let us look after you anyhow." Betsy said leading me back into the kitchen. Ada said she'd get me a cup of tea. Why did everyone think that a cup of tea could fix anything? I let Betsy rock me. "What's wrong with me Betsy? Am I going crazy again?"

"Shish Sweetie; you're not crazy, and you never were. I don't know what happened, but I'm sure Johnathan will straighten it all out."

"Of course he will because he's Johnathan, and he can never do any wrong. I'm the one who's to blame, I always have been, and I always will be."

Ada set a cup of tea in front of me. "No one said you did anything November. We don't know the story. We don't know why you attacked Johnathan so vehemently, but I'm sure you had a very good reason."

"It wasn't the first time tonight." I sobbed.

"Well, there are only a few reasons why you would attack him. One, you hate him; I find that difficult to believe. Two, you love him, and he's hurt you in some way. Would it have anything to do with the other woman?" Ada asked.

"I'm the other woman." I stammered.

"I wouldn't be so sure of that. Let's all just calm down, and talk things out okay?"

"What did you do with Mrs. Parker?"

That got the two of them chuckling. Betsy asked Ada if she was going to tell me. I said she didn't have to because I already knew.

"And, just what do you know young lady?"

"What's his name, and when are we going to meet him?"

"Who said it was a he?"

Ten minutes later the swinging doors opened. Johnny beckoned me with his finger. "Come here November."

I shook my head. Betsy gave me a nudge. He repeated the order adding please making it sound more like a request. I got up and walked slowly towards him. He closed the doors.

"Did it ever occur to you to ask me if what Joey had told you was true? No, you went right ahead and accused me of hurting him. Do you think so little of me that you believe I would welch on a promise, a promise to my son? Are you sorry that you brought him home to me? Do you want me out of your life? I can do that. I'll get out of your life, but there's no way in hell I'm giving up Joey!"

He started to leave. "I would never ask you to give him up."

"Well, we can't be together for more than ten minutes before you start in on me about something, so it's best if I make myself scarce. It won't be long before Joey tunes into our bickering, so right after our daughter's wedding I'll petition the courts for joint custody and arrange my visits when you aren't around. I'll try to stay out of your way until then."

I was crying. "You don't have to do that Johnathan."

"I think I do."

Johanna walked in. She took one look at us and knew something was up.

"Are you two fighting?" She asked nervously.

"Nothing for you to worry about Honey." Johnny said.

"Okay; Sarge and Lorraine are waiting for you. No, somethings wrong; what is it?"

"It's as I said, nothing at all is going on with us. Your mother is just being Emily again."

He asked her if he was going to see her before she left. She said she'd be up when he came to pick Joey up. He kissed her and opened the door. Lorraine was lurking in the shadows. She stepped out and asked Johnathan if he was ready to go home. She smiled maliciously in my direction.

Johanna followed me upstairs. "Are you all right Mom; he said you were Emily?"

"I'm not Emily. Everything's fine Dear; not to worry. Your dad and I just had a slight disagreement."

"He seemed to be annoyed with you."

"That's nothing new. I need to learn to bite my tongue."

"We all do Mom. If you don't need me then I'm going to go help AnnieZu."

I told her to get going as I was going to check in on Joey. He was a much calmer little boy. He was sitting up in bed playing with a compass. I asked him where it had come from. He said his dad had given it to him.

"Everything is good then; the hike is still on? Did he tell you why he had told you that he had to cancel?"

"He never told me that Mom. It was her."

I knew it. "What exactly did she say to you?"

"She said that they had a lot of things to do tomorrow so I probably wouldn't be seeing my dad for a few days, but soon as they got caught up I could come and visit them."

"Did she say what they had to do?"

"I don't remember. Maybe they had to go and see her mother or go shopping. Dad told me that she had got things wrong, and that the hike was still on. When can I go to his house?"

"We'll talk about that another day." I picked up Huckleberry Finn and turned it to the earmarked page. Joey asked me what I was doing.

I laughed. "What does it look like? I'm going to read you a chapter before you go to sleep."

He took the book out of my hands. "That's Dad's and my book. You can get another one."

I kissed him, and asked if I could take a rain check. "Sure Mom cause I'm tired anyhow."

I thought I may as well find something to read because I knew sleep was not going to come easy. Betsy always had a "who done it" mystery lying around in the kitchen, so I'd see if I could find one.. The house was quiet. It was only eight o'clock. I guess everyone had retired early. I saw Betsy's long sweater hanging on the back of a chair. I thought it would keep me warm in the night air. I put it on and headed out the back door. I thought that I had best stick to the road as there was light from the lamp posts. Sarge would most likely be in bed, so I resisted the urge to dump my problems on him.

I stopped halfway across Bramble Creek Bridge. I leaned on the railing and gazed out into nothingness. So, that was that; a near perfect weekend had been ruined by Johnny's bitch of a wife, and my uncontrollable tongue. Many nights I had lain awake in London reminiscing about my life with Johnny. Funny, I never saw him with anyone but me in my dreams. The nightmares saw him with a faceless woman. He had remarried, so I guess it must have been her. I had tried to believe that she didn't exist, but now I had met her, and she was all too real. She really wasn't his type though. What was I saying? Any woman was his type. I could hear the faint sound of the ocean waves slapping up against the seawall. It was too dark to see anything but the dim lights of a few late-night fishing boats. I heard the sound of a motor running. It sounded like it was coming from Sarge's. I wondered who it could be. The car approached the bridge, slowing down deliberately as the wheels hit the corroded planks. It came to a stop on the other side. I heard a door open and footsteps coming around the back of the vehicle. I inhaled deeply as a gust of wind blew his intoxicating scent towards me. He didn't wear cologne, but he emitted this natural musk that heightened my heart rate and breathing. The night air seemed to be saturated with his aroma, and then I heard his deep voice.

"Are you okay Em?" He sounded concerned.

"Of course I am...why wouldn't I be?" I lied trying to still my heart.

"Us," he said, "something is not right with us, and we need to fix it for Joey's sake. I'm sorry for yelling at you. I'm always stepping on your toes, so tell me what to do to remedy that."

Get rid of your wife is what I wanted to say.

"You didn't yell at me. I did all the yelling, so I'm the one who needs to apologise. What are you doing here anyhow? I thought you'd be nice and cozy in your bed back in the city by now." I did not add "with her" though I had to bite my tongue not to.

"I'd promised Sarge a few games of crib, and contrary to what you may think Em, I never go back on my promises. I will be here bright and early for Joey tomorrow just as I promised."

Had he not promised me that he'd wait for me forever?

"Then you had better get going. I'm sure Lorraine is wondering what is taking you so long."

"I can stay if you want me to."

"Don't be silly, like you said, a promise is a promise, and you promised her you'd be home."

"Did I? Did you hear me say that?"

"Not exactly, but..."

"You're postulating again. Now, do you want me to stay or not?"

"No, you should go."

"All right, but all you have to do is ask, and I'll stay."

He walked away and opened the car door. In a second he'd be gone. I turned and said softly, "I don't want you to go Johnny."

He spoke over the car door. "Well come on, get in."

He reached over and opened my door. I asked where we were going. He said, "Not far."

I opened my window, closed my eyes and pretended that I was on my very first actual date with him. I would have been sixteen and just home from living in London for two years. Johnny and I had been friends for six years. Holding hands as we ran through the fields of clover on the way to our fishing hole was the apex of our relationship when we were young. But now I was sixteen, and Johnny was eighteen. He had bought a light blue convertible with his wages from working at his dad's pharmacy after school for the past five years. We had been at odds ever since I had returned from England because he had cheated on me while I was away. We were going to be married someday he had promised when I went away, but he didn't wait for me, and I could not forgive him. Then one day he arrived at my door with a bouquet of blue daisies and asked me if I would do him the honor of going out with him as I was the only girl who meant anything to him. It was the first time he told me that he loved me in a way that was way more than just a friend. Two months later he was off to a trade school in Boston Massachusetts where he cheated on me again. Maybe he never considered it cheating because we had never been intimate...I don't know, but it did put a damper on our relationship again.

I felt the car come to a stop. We had barely gotten off Bramble Creek Road. I opened my eyes to discover that we were in the driveway of Johnny's old childhood home.

"Why did you stop here Johnny? AnnieZu said that Mrs. McFadden passed away and that the house had been sold again. It looked like it was undergoing some remodeling when I drove by last week."

He asked me why I had come by. I said, "Nostalgia, I guess."

"Let's go in and check it out." He said opening the car door.

"Are you crazy? We can't go barging in just because your family once owned it."

He came around and opened my door. "Well, we will soon find out. Where's your sense of adventure Kid?"

"This isn't adventure...it's ..."

He took my arm and led me around to the back of the car where he popped the trunk and took out a bottle of champagne.

"Why do you have a bottle of bubbly in your trunk?"

"One has to be prepared at all times."

I mumbled all the way to the front door where I stopped and said I wasn't taking another step.

He told me to suit myself and inserted a key into the lock. The door swung open. He grinned and asked me if I was coming.

I shot him a dirty look. "You go ahead. I'm not in the mood to get arrested for trespassing." Wondering why he would have a key I peered over his shoulder into the short hallway that led into the living room on one side and what was once his dad's office on the other side. Everything was bright and cheery. The only piece of furniture that was visible was a maroon-colored loveseat sitting in front of the old fireplace. I stepped timidly inside as curiosity had gotten the better of me. I called out timidly. "Hello; is anybody home?"

He shut the door behind me and said laughing. "Just the Jurado's'... just the Jurado's'; they have come home at long last to roost."

"You bought the house back Johnny?" I asked disbelievingly.

Before he could answer I headed over to the stairway, found a light switch and ran up the stairs. A few minutes later I stood on the landing and yelled down at him. "You are so lucky Johnny Jurado! If you had of removed that window seat I would never have spoken to you ever again!"

He came up the stairs with the bottle of bubbly and a big grin on his face. He said he had made a few improvements to the little nook. He had installed several wall lights that emitted a soft glow. He pulled a lever and the two windows opened unto a veranda-like enclosure on the roof.

"We can now sit on the roof and gaze at the stars and the ocean without worrying about falling off like we did when we were young."

"Is this the same "we" as in "us"? I asked.

"Yes, I want this to be "our" place."

"What is Lorraine going to say about that?"

"She has nothing to do with us. She doesn't even know I bought this house. You and I have a history here, and we always said we'd live here one day. That day is now Em. I bought back this house for you and me. I want you and Joey to come and live with me here."

It took me a minute to digest what he had just said. I needed to be sure I understood what he was asking of me. "So, you want me to come live here with you, is that right? In other words, you want me to be your mistress?"

"That sounds scandalous, so yes, and no. I want you to be my wife again. Truth of the matter is that I've never accepted the fact that we aren't still married."

"Well, we are not and haven't been for six years. What you are asking for is impossible. We can't take back all the things that have happened to us. We were best friends; we married and divorced, and then married other people. We can't make right what was wrong."

"I disagree with you. Nothing is impossible. I love you, and I know you love me, so we have to try and make things right again."

"What makes you think that I love you?"

"Because you have told me so, and I see it in your eyes and your smile."

"Oh, you mean when I am not berating you."

He popped the cork on the champagne and passed the bottle to me. "Sorry Hon; no glasses."

Reluctantly, I took a small swig. I covered my mouth as the fizziness exploded and threatened to escape. Champagne always made me feel like a human bubble machine.

Johnny laughed as he took the bottle from me. "You haven't changed at all have you?"

"Yes, I have; you just can't see it. I'm different inside. I spent six years away from you trying to heal what I had done to myself and you, and our daughter. I can't ever go back to where I was again Johnny, and that means I can't be with you. We can be friends and parents to our children, but that is all." I turned away from him so he couldn't see the agony on my face.

He moved closer to me on the window seat and asked me to look at him. I shook my head.

"Look at me November."

He only called me November when he was cross with me.

"That's bullshit, and you know it! First of all, you had no control over your illness. It was an imbalance in your brain; it had nothing to do with your soul. You didn't deliberately set out to hurt me or yourself. Yes, your illness had its way with us, but that was then, and this is now, and we deserve another chance at happiness. I can only be completely happy if I'm with you Em."

"How can you say that? Have you already forgotten how I attacked you at AnnieZu's, and all the other times I exploded for no reason? It's still here Johnny." I touched my head. "The distrust, the jealousy…it's still with me."

"Then quit listening to your head and listen to your heart. You've admitted to me over and over that you know that I didn't cheat on you, so why has this suspicion started up again?"

I couldn't control the bitterness in my answer. "You've always cheated on me Johnny. When I was fourteen and moving to England you promised me that you would wait for me didn't you? Yet when I came back you were entwined in extra-curricular sex with Deanna. You were supposed to experience your first time with me…you took that away from me. After we got back together you cheated on me again when you went off to school in Boston. But, the biggest wound of all is that you married somebody else. You didn't wait for me to conquer my demons and come home. And, you never once came to see if I was all right."

"Has this been festering in you all this time? I truly believed that you had forgiven me for my trespasses when I was a teenager. I have never loved anyone but you from day one. I can't go back and change things…if I could, I would." He sighed. "I'm sorry Em. I'm sorry that you weren't happy all those years. I thought we had it all. Again, why was it all right for you to fall in love with someone else and not me, but let's make it perfectly clear again; I have never loved anyone but you."

I knew this day was coming, I just hadn't thought it would be so soon. I wasn't sure that I was prepared. "I was not in love with James. I have never loved anyone but you; but I know you wouldn't marry without love, so that is the difference."

He started to say something, but I asked him to let me finish.

"There is a lot you are probably not aware of, and I suppose you deserve an explanation. Maybe then you will understand why there is no future for us. When I went to visit my mother in London I had no plans for staying, but she introduced me to James and Sheila Dickens and they convinced me to stay. You know all of this I'm sure, but I will refresh your memory. Sheila is the co-founder of Wellington Wellness Centre. She is a fully qualified doctor who diagnoses and treats mental disorders. She is also James's sister and was my primary therapist. Mother had filled them in on my emotional or mental breakdown, psychotic behaviour, or whatever you want to call it; craziness is the right word I guess."

"I do know all of that, and I never considered you as crazy. I don't like that word."

I laughed. "There are many definitions of "crazy" Johnny. We used to be crazy in love with each other, but I fixed that didn't I?" I took another small sip of the champagne; it tasted bitter.

"If we are talking that kind of crazy, then yes, I'm still guilty. I need to know where I went wrong Em because I feel that it was me who triggered your depression by something I said or did, or didn't do."

I swung my feet over the newly upholstered window seat and went and stood at the window looking out upon the black sky. I turned to face him. "I suppose that you were to blame in a way; no, that is wrong, it was love that was to blame, unyielding, adulating, gullible love. When the man you so worshiped falls from grace something shatters in your naïve little world and nothing is ever the same again. The descent has begun, but you are not even aware of it until it spirals into madness many years later."

Johnny was visibly disturbed. "Are you telling me that I put all of this into motion years ago when you returned from England and found that I had been unfaithful?"

"You can quit playing the martyr Johnny Dear because it was not you... it was my father, and it started before I even knew you existed. You always thought that I was my father's golden child, that he loved me more than the others didn't you? Well, you were wrong because there was another child younger and more golden than me; her name is Rachel. The night I found out is the first time I met Emily."

Johnny was on his feet. He pulled me into his arms, and then sat me down. "Oh Baby, I am so sorry. Why didn't you ever tell me?"

"It was a long time ago. I was young, and I suppose I was ashamed."

"You had nothing to be ashamed of; you know that don't you?"

"I suppose I do now, but I blamed myself for a long time. I wasn't Daddy's little girl anymore. He had a younger, much prettier one than me. I suppose that is where my distrust of men began. We came back to Canada, and I came here to stay with AnnieZu. It was the summer I met you. Then we moved back to England again. I didn't want to go because I knew he would make me see her again, and I didn't want to leave you. You were my only friend Johnny." I was trying not to cry, but the tears fell anyway.

"We've always been best friends Em. I've missed my friend more than you can imagine. I've always been here for you, and I am now, so how about you let me take some of the burden off you. Let me be your sounding board. You can even beat on me some more…"

"I might just take you up on that later. The night I found out I was supposed to be having a sleepover at my friend Josie's house which was next door. I woke up about ten not feeling well. I wanted my mother. I got up and went home still in my pyjamas. As I was going up the stairs I heard my mother and father talking loudly. Actually, Mom was yelling and crying. As best as I can remember she told my father that she had been looking the other way for years but she had enough and was taking Summer and me home, and that he could have all the mistresses he wanted. Daddy said he wouldn't allow it. She said she was going to sue for divorce, and that he, and his new harlot and bastard daughter wouldn't get one red cent. I didn't know what any of it meant. I told Summer, and she explained it to me. Mother had kicked Dad out but granted him one last visit with Summer and me. He took us to a movie and an ice cream shop afterwards. I guess he had planned it all, because his mistress, Summer had said that was what this woman was called, and her daughter were there waiting for us. Daddy's plan was for us to stay in London with him and his new family. You know that didn't happen, and somehow him and mother got back together. It was a sham of course, but money was involved. Mother was the glue that kept his company together so somehow they compromised, but it didn't solve any of their marriage problems. You know the way it ended."

"I guess I had blinders on because I thought they got along fine. You're wrong Em because he doted on you. His eyes lit up every time he saw you, and I thought you felt the same way about him. Was I wrong?"

"I don't think you were wrong. For years I was his little girl again, and then we went back to England. He didn't make me or Summer see Rachel, but as luck would have it, we ended up as opponents on soccer teams. I didn't even know until a teammate asked me if I was related to her as we both had the same last name. I quit soccer, and Summer ran away with a sailor to Australia. You had quit corresponding with me, so I knew before I even came home that you were just like my dad, and probably every other man. One girl would never be enough for you."

"Em..."

"I'm not finished yet. I know not how many affairs my father had just as I don't know how many affairs you've had, but what I do know is that my father's last one was one too many. You, Zena, May and Noel all know that he died in the arms of a shady lady. You were all trying to shield me, but I knew. What you don't know is that my father died penniless. Thankfully, Mother had some control of the bank accounts, and so she has a bit of money. I'm afraid I cut into that nest egg a bit, but it was her idea that I should go to the Wellness Clinic, and so she funded my treatments until I was able to be recognised by James's medical plan. As you know he was a French attaché to the British government so the health plan was all inclusive. That is the only reason I married him. You're wondering about my inheritance aren't you? Well, when all was said and done, my sisters and I each came out five thousand dollars richer. I tried to pay Zena back, but she refused it, so I have a few dollars left of that tainted money. If you are wondering what happened to Daddy's fortune you'd have to ask his concubines. I told you that James and I did not share a marriage bed except for those three times, but he was a nice man and a good father to Joey. That is it in a nutshell. You say you want me to live with you, but I will not be the other woman. Believing that you think you're in love with me does not give you a license to be unfaithful. I don't want your money, so don't you dare offer. I can't live at Silvermist all my life, so I will start job hunting next week. That is the end of the story. Now, I would like to go home please, and you can go home to your wife."

He took a long swig of the champagne. "Yes, I'll take you back to Silvermist for now. I am not going away, and I hope that you will give me the opportunity to say my piece. This is not the end of the story by any means. You have said many times that you were waiting for me to come and get you from London. but how was I supposed to know that Em? You never so much as even sent me a postcard or picked up the telephone to call me, did you?"

"I wrote to you practically every day."

"Too bad you hadn't the sense to mail them. Sorry, that was uncalled for. What I am trying to say is that maybe things would have turned out differently, but that train left the depot a long time ago, so we will never know what the outcome would have been. You need to know that I wanted to come and see you, but your mother advised me not to, and then I found out you were pregnant. My ego was deflated Em. Another man had given you what I couldn't."

"It was devastating to find out that I was pregnant from another man. I didn't think I would ever be able to face you again. My treatments were put on hold for almost two years while I dealt with that guilt. I refused all medications. I didn't know you were in contact with Zena as she never told me that you were. If I had of been of sound mind I might have had the sense to realise that you might be the father of my baby, but I wasn't, and so the years went by. I have been accusing you of cheating on me, but I was the bigger cheater as I cheated you out of being a father to Joey."

"I don't look at it that way Emmy. We can't change what happened, but you and Joey are here now, and I am the happiest I have been in a very long time. I came pretty close to losing it when you married James, but our daughter's constant phone calls kept me from going bonkers. Then she came to live with me, and I started to live again. Despite my personal despair I had somehow managed to keep the business that you and I had started together afloat. Even then, I wanted you to be proud of me. Then it took off in a whole new successful and economically sound direction. I don't owe a cent to any creditor; the seaside property and this house are all paid for. You say that you don't want a penny from me, but half of everything I have is yours, and you are damn well going to take it! If you still want to come and take over Nancy's position at Woodworks, the job is yours. I don't want you to worry about a thing. Are you good with that?"

"I am not, but you need to know that I have always been proud of you."

"Well then, how about giving me a little love and let me take care of you?"

"I'm going home now. If you don't want to drive me I will walk."

He laughed. "Sure you will. Come on, let's go."

Neither of us spoke until we drove into AnnieZu's driveway. Johnny started to open his door. I told him he needn't bother as I was perfectly capable of seeing myself into the house.

"A gentleman always sees his date to the door." He said taking my arm.

"This was not a date."

"I prefer to think otherwise. Can the condemned man get a little kiss?"

I pushed his hand off the door. "Go home to your wife."

"See you tomorrow November."

"You will not." I said as I closed the front door. I watched from the living room window as he drove out of the yard. To my surprise he turned left towards Sarge's. Was I wrong...had he never planned on going back to the city and Lorraine, or had his encounter with me changed his mind?

Would I have the nerve to ask him tomorrow? I'd have to sleep on it. One thing was for sure. I was going to sleep a lot sounder now that I had finally told Johnny how Emily came to be, but I also have to convince him that she no longer existed. First, I had to convince myself.

CHAPTER 7

The Week That Was

I shut the engine off when I reached the little knoll and coasted into Sarge's not wanting to wake him. Champ greeted me with an uncertain growl. I assured him that I wasn't a burglar. He wagged his tail and went back to his bed. I opened the door as quietly as I could. I walked in and was greeted by a shot gun aimed at my head. I put my hands up and surrendered.

"Jesus Christ Johnathan, are you trying to get yourself killed?" He said as he lowered the gun. "What the hell are you doing back here anyhow? I thought you'd be sound asleep back in the city with the giraffe's long legs wrapped around you. What's brought you back?"

"Emmy was waiting for me on the bridge. I picked her up and took her to the house. Sorry, I didn't mean to wake you." I smiled as I headed for the bedroom.

"Stop right there! What the hell were you doing with my girl? Last I heard, which was from you by the way, was that you two were at odds with each other."

"We still are."

"That's not an answer. What happened up at the house?"

"Why do I feel as if I am being interrogated by my father? Not too much of anything Sarge except I understand a little more about her father and her life in London."

"Like what? I never did care for Phillip Queen, so give me the scoop."

"Can we hash it over tomorrow? I really need to get some shuteye."

"Sure. There isn't a bed in that house is there?"

I shook my head. "No Sarge, there is not. It arrives on Thursday. If the real question there was did Emmy and I have sex... the answer is no, not even close."

"Good. I've made the bed fresh for your brother, so don't mess it up."

I didn't ask him when Archie was arriving because I didn't give a damn.

I was awakened by pans rattling early next morning. I jumped out of bed, threw my khakis on and headed for the kitchen. She was standing at the sink running water. She turned when she heard me.

"Well boy, don't you look yummy in the morning."

I laughed bashfully feeling that I needed to go and put a shirt on.

"What's all the commotion about? Oh, it's just you two. Don't tell me that November is taking another day off?" Sarge bellowed.

"Sorry boys, I know you were expecting her, but she asked me to sub."

"You know you're my second-best girl Betsy, and I do like your flapjack cakes. We are having them aren't we?"

"Sure as shoot in; soon as the little man gets here."

So, I'd see Em after all when she dropped Joey off.

I was standing at the window facing Bramble Creek Bridge drinking a much-needed cup of coffee when Em and Joey approached on their bikes. They stopped halfway across. She watched Joey until he reached the house. It was my turn to close the curtain. That was probably as close as I was going to get to Em all day. I didn't let it get me down and went off with my son to have a most enjoyable day. He was plum tuckered out when I dropped him off at Silvermist at three in the afternoon. Betsy ushered him off to the bath while I chatted with Ada about our day for a few minutes. I got the feeling that it was in my best interest not to ask where Em was. I spent an enjoyable evening with my uncle playing cards. We did not talk about Em; not much anyhow.

Sarge's relief worker was supposed to be on the job at eight, so I only made coffee the next morning. I slurped a wake-up cup and headed over to Silvermist. It was Joey's first day of kindergarten, and I wasn't going to miss it for anything despite what his mother might want.

I went in the back door, poured myself a cup of Betsy's coffee, sat down and waited.

"You know," she said grinning, "we should really quit these morning trysts."

"I kind of enjoy them, but hopefully I will have someone else to share them with soon."

She asked me how Joey's and my day had gone yesterday. She said he was so tired when I dropped him off that he went straight to bed. She didn't think he even had a bath. I told her that I thought we'd had a very good day

"November let him have supper in bed, but he was still too tired to eat. I haven't heard a peep out of either of them yet today. I'm not even sure they are here."

"Where would they be at seven-thirty in the morning on Joey's first day of school?"

"You tell me. Miss November has been tight lipped ever since her late-night rendezvous with you the other night."

"It wasn't a rendezvous Betsy. I took her up to the house and showed her around. We talked. There was nothing clandestine about it. You know I bought the old family home back right?"

"Yes, Miss Annie told me, and that I was not to whisper a word to November about it. Is there furniture in the house?"

"If you are asking if there is a bed... the answer is no. You're a tad more diplomatic than Sarge was. Nothing happened. I didn't even rate a kiss good night."

"You can't pursue her Johnathan until you get rid of long legs."

"Jeeze Betsy, do you and my uncle sit around dissecting Em's and my life all day?"

"Dad!" Joey shouted as he hobbled over to me.

I opened up my arms. "Hey, what's with the limp?"

"It's nothin. Remember, when that bramble bush tripped me yesterday? Leg is a little sore, but it don't hurt."

"Says my little Christopher Columbus." Em said, as she ran her fingers through his golden locks. He warned her off as usual. Eyes twinkling, she asked me what I was doing here so early. She sat down opposite me. Betsy handed her a cup of coffee and told us to play nice.

I felt like I was supposed to come up with some outlandish reason. I thought I may as well play her little game. "Oh, just thought that I'd see if my partner here was up for another adventure. What do you say Son?"

"Can I Mom, can I?" Joey begged.

"If you were trying to piss me off first thing in the morning then you've succeeded. What the hell is wrong with you Johnathan Lee Jurado?" Em stood up fuming.

"There's no reason to spit nails November Queen Jurado. How about you sit back down and listen to my plan?"

"I didn't know mom's name was the same as yours Dad. Is mine?"

Em looked uncomfortable.

"Yup, you're Joey Dean Jurado, right Mommy?" I got the evil eye again. "Your mom knows why I am here Joey. The adventure you are going on is one to a whole new world."

"Are we all going?"

"Sorry Son, but we can't go with you. We can deliver you, but you'll be on your own after that. Do you think you can handle kindergarten without us? I envy you as you are going to make so many new friends while I am slaving away at work."

"I already have a best friend."

"And, she will probably be your best friend for life, but a guy can always do with a few more."

"Just like you and Mom. You're best friends aren't you?"

"Are we Mommy?" I asked wondering why I was asking for trouble.

Joey covered his eyes. "I told you she didn't like to be called that remember?"

"Oh, he remembers all right. Your dad is just being a turd, and he's an expert at making female friends." Em answered pouring milk on his cereal.

"What's a turd Mom?"

She shot daggers at me. Betsy threw a towel at me and asked me if it was my day to die. I answered that it just might be. I was pretty sure that I was never going to win with my ex, so it didn't really matter what I said or did.

She would not ride with me to the school. Joey rode with me, and she drove the Buick; one of several in the yard that she didn't have a licence to drive. We met up and walked into the classroom with him in between us. His teacher greeted us warmly with a clip board in her hand. Amy came running up and stood by Joey.

"This must be Joey, Amy's best friend. I've heard a lot about you young man. I feel like I already know you. I am Miss Lamb, your teacher. Amy has saved you a seat beside her; do you want to check it out and see if it is to your liking while I talk to your parents?"

Amy asked Joey why he was limping. He replied that it was a long story and started talking. He called back to us. "See you Mom, see you Johnathan."

Miss Lamb introduced herself to Em and then me, shaking and holding our hands for a few seconds. Her name was Jenny. I guessed her to be in her late twenties.

"Does your son usually call you by your given name Mr. Jurado?" She asked inquisitively.

Before I could answer Em supplied her with an explanation. "This is a small close-knit village Miss Lamb, and you will hear the story probably sooner than later, so you may as well get it straight from the source. I have been living in England for the past six years and have only returned recently. Joey was born in London unbeknownst to Johnathan. He did not know that he had a son until a few days ago. I'm sure you will hear the rest of the story from your colleagues. Anyhow, they have both adjusted to each other extremely well. Joey's father has forgiven me for my imprudence, haven't you Honey?" She linked her arm through mine smiling like the Cheshire cat.

"Yup, we are one big happy family." I agreed smiling and patting her hand.

Miss Lamb, I'm sure felt like she had been put in her place but smiled. "I have Joey living at 1324 Silvermist, Bramble Creek Road. Is that right? Do you all share the same address?"

"No Ma'am, November and Joey reside at Silvermist with her aunt. I live on River Road. I am contemplating that the major repairs to my old family home will be completed shortly, and then I will be moving my family in with me."

I think Em quit breathing.

"Thank-you for your candour. If you can just dot down all the phone numbers where you can all be reached, I will let you get on with your day. I'm sure we'll be seeing each other again over the next ten months. Have a lovely day."

I shook her hand again and explained that I worked in the city so Em would be driving and picking Joey up every day for the time being. She asked me who Em was. I said, "My wife."

She was on me the minute I stepped out the door. "Well, you sure screwed that up royally didn't you genius?"

"You started it *Honey*." I sang.

"I think she likes you by the way she kept looking at you and holding your hand, so you can do the explaining when the shit hits the fan!"

"Are you jealous already?"

She stomped down the steps. God, she was beautiful when she was angry.

"Joey knows that I'm working late tonight and tomorrow, so I will try and call him after he gets out of school. He can call me on my private line anytime he wants though." I called out to her as she walked to her car. I think she gave me the finger.

God, I loved that woman!

It was late afternoon on Wednesday when Nancy beeped me on my walkie and said that November had phoned and needed to talk to me.

"I thought she had my cell number."

"She hung up before I could ask her if she had it."

Damn, I couldn't remember *her* cell number. I dialed Silvermist. Betsy answered. I asked her if she knew what November wanted.

"Joey's sick Johnathan. We're really worried. You'd better talk to November. Here, I'm walking up the stairs with the portable because she won't leave his side."

A second later I heard her panicky voice. "I'm sorry Johnny, I didn't want to call you at work, but he's asking for you, and I'm really scared. He's not eating or drinking, and AnnieZu called her doctor to come look at him. I don't know what to do Johnny…"

"First thing you have to do is slow down, okay? Listen, are you thinking that he needs to go to the hospital?"

"Is he that sick? Do you think I should call an ambulance?"

"Honey, I can't see him…"

She interrupted me. "I'll take his picture and you can see…oh, this phone doesn't take pictures."

"It's the house phone Em. How about you pass the phone to Betsy and then you can send me the photo from your phone. I pinned my cell number in for you last week, remember?"

"Betsy isn't here, but AnnieZu is."

"Good, let me speak to her. I'll be there in forty minutes. You there Zuzzs? How bad is he? Please tell me that Em is overreacting?"

"He's sick Johnathan; I mean really sick. He has a fever and..."

"How soon will the doctor be there?"

"I'm expecting him around four."

"Okay; I'm on my way. Tell Em I'll be there as fast as I can. Try and keep her calm Zuzzs."

I called my foreman Ken over and explained the situation. "You know I wanted to be here when the beams and columns arrived. You are going to have to open at least half a dozen of the crates before you accept the load. If there is even one scratch on any of them..."

"Don't worry John. I have no problem refusing the load. Now, how about you get the hell out of here before rush hour?"

I told him I'd call him later. We were almost two months behind in the last phase of the new low-income homes we were constructing thanks to defective fiberglass porch columns. Colder weather would soon be upon us, so it was imperative that we owned up to our contract. I told myself to settle down. Ken knew as much about the business as I did, so why was I fretting? Maybe it was worrying about Joey. I remembered sitting up with Johanna when she had the flu or the measles...hell, I was young then. I had no idea what child diseases were out there now. I could see Em worrying, but Betsy and AnnieZu too? I pulled out onto the hi-way and stepped on the gas. I kept checking my phone, but Em never did send me the photo of Joey.

I followed a car down Two Mile Hill. It was 3:55, so I hoped it was the doctor, and it was.

I extended my hand to him. "Well, you are not AnnieZu's regular physician, so I take it that you are subbing for him...Johnathan Jurado here."

"Nelson Black; actually Dr. Perkins is thinking of retiring soon, so he's brought me on board to see if I am interested in taking over his practice."

I walked him to the back door and asked him how it was going so far. He said it was looking pretty good and asked me if Miss Annie was my aunt.

"She's my wife's aunt." I stated.

He asked if I was Joey's father. I said I was.

We reached Joey's room in tandem. Betsy was standing in the doorway, AnnieZu was sitting in a chair in the corner. Emmy was sitting by the bed holding Joey's hand. Betsy informed her that Doc Black was here. She looked up, saw us, and ran straight over to me crying like a baby. I put my arms around her and told her everything was going to be all right. I had a quick look at my son, told him I was here, and that I loved him. I couldn't tell if he heard me or not.

"How about we all give the doctor some time alone with Joey? You stay right where you are Zuzzs; how did you get up here anyhow?"

"I walked."

"No kidding. The hip was all right with the climb?"

She said it was, and to look after November.

"She shouldn't have climbed the stairs Johnathan, but she wouldn't listen to any of us. You're the only one she listens to." Em blubbered still holding on to me.

"I'll see that she gets back down in a bit. Right now I want to hear about Joey. When did he get sick? He seemed all right except for the little limp yesterday."

"He said he wasn't feeling well when Harold and I picked him up after school. He wanted to go to bed. That was so not like him, but I thought that he was still tired from the hike. He didn't want to eat or drink. He wasn't running a fever then, but did feel hot to the touch. It wasn't until noon that his temperature started to climb. AnnieZu called the doctor and I called you."

"I didn't get the message that you had phoned until two-thirty."

"That's because I couldn't remember your phone number at the time. I called three different numbers and was just upsetting myself. I thought his fever would break, but it didn't so I told Betsy to call the main office. I'm sorry Johnathan. Please don't be angry with me. I'm so worried about Joey."

I told her to look at me. "I'm not angry with you Em. The doctor is here now, so let's just wait and see what he says."

He called us in a few minutes later. Joey saw me and called out my name. I guess the doctor had wakened him. I walked over to him. He tried to sit up. "Not necessary Sport. How about you just lie back down and take it easy while we hear what the doctor has to say?"

"It was just an accident Dad. I didn't want to spoil our day."

"Nothing would have spoiled our day. Did the brambles you tripped over hurt you more than you let on?" I was confused as how that could have made him sick.

Dr. Black pulled back the covers and lifted up Joey's left foot. The sole was covered with some ruddy looking substance. I said, "What the hell?"

"Oh my God!" Em gasped. "What is that?"

"I take it that Joey wouldn't let you take his socks off Ms. Queen; is that right? He didn't want me to either, but he said he had a sore leg, so I insisted that I check out the feet also. He admitted to me that he stepped on a nail. I'm assuming that it was a rusty one. It penetrated about twenty millimeters. It might be a good idea if we had a look at the shoes he was wearing. I'll know more after it is cleansed."

"That's so deep!" Em exclaimed.

"It's less than an inch Em." I explained because I knew she wasn't thinking rationally and may have confused millimeters with inches.

"He wouldn't let me take his socks off because he said his feet were cold. Tell me that the red gook isn't blood?"

"I think it might be iodine or mercurochrome Honey." I suggested.

The doctor concurred. "That's my guess. Mercurochrome is not widely used anymore because of its mercury content. I am not even sure if it is available for purchase at the pharmacies. However, Iodine is better and safer as it has antibacterial properties. I'm supposing that Joey did the doctoring himself?"

"I don't know where he would get it because I have never seen any around. I think you used some on me when I was young didn't you AnnieZu?" Em asked her aunt.

"I very well could have because that is what we used when I was young, but there shouldn't be any still around. We best ask Betsy or Mrs. Parker."

"How about if we just ask Joey? I know he's running a fever, but he's nowhere near delirium." I bent down and asked Joey if he could open his eyes for me. He said he was too tired.

"You stepped on a nail eh Sport? That's gotta hurt and that's why your leg is sore I'm thinking. How did you know to put iodine on the wound Son? That was really smart."

"Pete put it on his finger once. Can I go back to sleep Dad?"

"You sure can. I think that's our answer folks. I'll just have a little gander in the workshop and see what I come up with. Where are his boots Em?"

She started crying again. "I should have made him wear something heavier, but he wanted to wear his rubbers because he said there might be water."

I walked to his closet and found his rubbers. There was indeed a puncture mark in one. The boot also contained a blood-soaked sock. "It's not your fault Em. I should have paid more attention to his footwear or examined him after he tripped. As far as I know the swamp and area have been free of fallen fence posts or wooden structures that might harbor nails for years, but obviously I was wrong."

Dr. Black asked me if there was a possibility that Joey had stepped on something in the yard.

"Anything is possible. We'll know more when he can stay awake for longer than a minute. So, what's the damage here Doc? Does he require a tetanus shot?"

Em shook her head. "He had a booster shot when he was four. Is that recent enough?"

I was glad to see that Em had calmed down.

"It definitely is. I'm reasonably sure that we don't have to worry about that. He is not exhibiting any signs of tetanus, but he definitely has an infection. I would like to administer an anti-biotic but am not too sure if he will be able to swallow it or keep it down. It might have to be given intravenously which will be more effective anyhow, and he needs hydration so the sooner we get him to the clinic the better."

"What clinic is that?" I asked.

"We have recently opened up an Urgent Care Clinic in the old Hartford building in Seahaven. It is staffed 24/7 by competent staff. This area has needed one for some time I understand. We can call an ambulance which could take some time to get here, so my advice is for you to transport him yourselves. Are you okay with that Mr. Jurado, Ms. Queen?"

Before we could answer Mrs. Palmer said she'd get Harold to bring the car to the front door. I hadn't even heard the woman come in. Em asked the doctor, who insisted she call him Nelson, if he'd be there. I wondered if that meant me also; then I wondered if he was married. He assured Em that he'd be monitoring Joey for a while.

I picked Joey up, tucked his blankets around him, and carried him to the car. Em walked beside me holding his hand and reassuring him that he was going to be okay. The three of us got in the back seat. Ada Parker was apparently going with us because she jumped in the front with Harold. We followed behind Doc Black.

It was less than a ten-minute ride to the clinic. Two nurses were waiting for us at the entrance. I laid Joey on the bed and went to wait with Em while they attended to our son. Mrs. Parker said she had called her friend and that he was coming over, so she was sending Harold home. She went out to wait for him. I asked Em who Ada's friend was. She said she had no idea.

I sat down beside her on the small sofa. She asked me if I was going to stay with her.

"Of course I am! Why would you think otherwise?"

"I'm so scared Johnny."

I put my arm around her. "He's going to be all right Em; they'll have him fixed up in no time."

She leaned into me and buried her face in my chest. "I didn't supervise his bath. I should have. It's my fault. I can't lose him Johnny. I can't lose another baby." She rambled.

"Joey's not dying. What baby are you talking about?" Perhaps I had heard her wrong.

She murmured something unintelligible about a baby again. What the hell was she talking about? I tried to get an answer out of her, but she wasn't talking anymore. Her body had relaxed against mine. She had fallen asleep.

A few minutes later Mrs. Parker came back with a tall distinguished looking gentle man. She introduced him as her friend George Patterson. I waved a hello with my one free hand. Ada asked me if November was sleeping.

"She's exhausted; do you think you can get her home to bed?"

"Poor little thing. I don't think she slept a wink last night. Let's see what we can do here."

Together we roused Em. She didn't appear to know where she was at first, but when she came around she asked if it was Joey, and what was wrong. I assured he was fine and walked her into see him. He was sleeping peacefully. It took a fair bit of talking to get her to agree to go home for a few hours. I promised I would call her if anything changed.

At seven another nurse arrived to relieve the other two. Her name was Karol. Apparently, one nurse was all that was required at night unless there was an emergency. Dr. Black checked in at eight. He was pleased with Joey's progress. His temperature was down, and he was not exhibiting any adverse effects to the antibiotics, so Joey would most likely be able to go home tomorrow if all his vitals stayed steady. He then asked me if November had gone home. What did I miss? He'd only called her Ms. Queen back at the house. I blamed my reaction to fatigue. He told Karol to page him if anything came up. He left and Ada arrived with sandwiches and drinks. She said that November had fallen asleep the minute her head hit the pillow.

Karol popped in now and then to check on Joey. At ten-thirty she arrived with fresh coffee, said she was all caught up on her paperwork and had time for a break. I asked her to join me. I had been fighting sleep for the past few hours, so the coffee was a nice pick-up. Karol said there was nothing that I could do for Joey so I should go home and get some sleep. I didn't want to tell her that I didn't have a home to go to, so said I'd stay a while longer as I had promised his mother that I would.

"I understand from the day nurses that you and your wife are long- time residents here?" Karol questioned though it was more of a statement.

"Yes and no. While I was born and raised here, Em lived in Victoria, that is, when she and her family weren't living in England. She used to come and spend the summers with her aunt at Silvermist. That's how we met as my uncle lives next door to her aunt."

"I have only been in the vicinity a few months so am not too familiar with the local landscapes. Silvermist is a romantic name for a district."

"Actually, it is not a district, but the name of the estate."

"Ooh, a mansion; how intriguing!"

I laughed. "I've never considered it as such. It's always been just a house and home to me."

"Are you and your wife and Joey living there now?"

"Joey's mother and I are not together at the moment. Our daughter is getting married this weekend so it has brought us all together."

"I'm sorry; but a wedding, how exciting!"

"No need to be sorry. Em and I get along quite well most of the time."

"You don't live here anymore then?"

"I have a house in Victoria, but last April I bought my old family home back. It is just a few blocks away. I've had it remodelled and I'm looking forward to taking up residence there again. I'll be close to Joey as Silvermist is just down the hill, and it's only a thirty or forty commute into the city. Meanwhile I'm staying at my uncle's."

"You work in the city?"

I nodded and asked her a few questions about herself. She was from Dawson Creek, had graduated three years ago from a nursing academy in Nanaimo where she had been living and working until she took a position here. She was unattached. I estimated her to be about twenty-five. I thought our conversing was a good time to ask her about Dr. Black. He was a bachelor and currently residing at the Davenport Inn. Great.

Karol talked me into going home and getting a few hours' sleep as there was nothing I could do for Joey. She said he'd need me tomorrow so I best be rested up. I agreed, but that I didn't want to wake anyone to come and get me, so I'd just hang around. She said that was nonsense, gave me the keys to her car, and told me to be back by 7:15 the next morning. I thanked her and told her that I would definitely be back by then.

There was no place to sleep at my house except the little marron love seat, and I dare not wake Sarge up again, so I guessed I'd have to crash at Silvermist. One of the bungalows was bound to be unlocked, or I'd just crash on one of the sofas if the back door was still open. It was. I decided to check on Em. I tip-toed up the stairs, stopped at her bedroom door and listened to her breathing for a few seconds.

"I'm awake Johnathan."

I walked over to her bedside. "How did you know it was me?"

She sat up. "I know your scent."

I laughed. "Yeah, I suppose I reek. Nothing that a shower won't fix.

I don't want to wake Sarge up, so I thought I might camp out in one of the bungalows if one is open."

She patted the bed. "You can take a shower here, but first I want to know how Joey is."

"He was sleeping peacefully when I left. The doc checked in and was pleased with his progress. I planned on sitting with him all night but Karol talked me into going home and getting a few winks. I don't really have a home, but here I am."

"You'll always have a home here Johnny. Who is this Carol?"

"She's the night nurse; spells her name with a K; unusual isn't it? I didn't have a vehicle so she lent me hers. I have to be back by seven so I better go find a place to lay my head."

"You can stay right here Johnny. Go and have a shower."

"You want me to sleep with you?"

"Your idea of sleep might be different from mine. You'll find clean clothes in the bottom drawer of the dresser."

I was surprised that I still had clothes here. She said AnnieZu had not thrown anything out. I pulled out a T-shirt and a pair of chinos and headed for the bathroom. When I returned Em was gone. She had left me a pair of socks and a note on the bed that read, "Sweet dreams in the bed you made for me." Thank God she had signed it "Em."

The bed thing was not entirely accurate as I had not made the bedframe, just the headboard. It was my very first attempt at carpentry. It was a surprise for Em's return from England. I was pretty naïve then. I loved her but had been seeing someone else in her absence. Had I really thought that she would never find out about my transgression with Deanna? That was almost the end of Emmy and me, but love endured that fiasco. Did I learn my lesson? No, I did not, and I almost lost her again when I shacked up with a single mother in Boston. Somehow, Em forgave me again when I came home and rescued her from marrying Victor Marino. She had never given up on me and had said that if she couldn't be with me then she would remain chaste all her life. If she had of been any other woman that headboard would have been taken down and burned a hundred times over. It still stood, and so far I was still standing, but the question still remained... was this thing with Lorraine going to be the end of us for good? Why hadn't I told her yet? Tomorrow was D-Day; truth and face the consequences day.

I was aroused the next morning by the pungent smell of coffee. I opened my eyes to find Betsy standing beside the bed with cup of coffee in her hand. I said I hoped that it was for me.

"She told me to wake you at six fifteen as you had an appointment with Carol."

I sat up. "It's not an appointment Betsy. She lent me her car to get home on last night, and she's off shift at seven, so I have to return it so she can get home. Good coffee; where's Em?"

"At the clinic. You're in her bed, and you still consider this as home, so I take it that all is well between the two of you?"

"I don't know where she slept, but it wasn't with me if that is what you are wondering."

"None of my business. If you want breakfast, it'll be on the table in ten."

"None of your business eh; don't make me laugh."

I dug into the bureau drawer and found underwear. On a whim, I checked the closet, and sure enough, two white shirts, and one khaki green hung there. They looked like they'd just been laundered and pressed. I chose the green one as I had hopes of getting into work later. I joined Betsy for a second cup of coffee, a slice of toast and scrambled eggs. I thanked her, planted a juicy kiss on her cheek, and left for the clinic. I passed the car keys to Karol. She gave me a quick update on Joey. I thanked her and went in to see my son. Em was fussing with his blankets.

"Good morning." I said cheerfully. "Karol told me that Joey was awake..."

"Yes, I have met your Carol. He has been awake for almost an hour but closed his eyes a few minutes ago. He was expecting to see you, but you weren't here so..."

"First thing; she is not my Karol; she was Joey's nurse for the night. I would have been here earlier if you had of awakened me. Did you have barbwire for breakfast again?"

"You know I don't eat breakfast."

"Maybe you should start then as it might put you in a better mood. I saw the Buick in the parking lot. I thought you weren't going to drive anymore until you got a driver's licence?"

"Are you ordering me not to drive? The judge tried that, but that was in London, so it doesn't carry any jurisdiction here."

"You told me that you didn't drive in England. Did you just say that to humor me?"

She sat down beside me. "We should keep our voices down. We don't want Joey to hear us arguing again."

"I have no intention of arguing with you Em. How about humoring me and tell me about your driving spree in London. I was under the impression that you had a driver."

"Not at first. I had to call a service if I wanted to go anywhere. One day about three or four months into my pregnancy I just decided to take myself on a little outing. I ended up in the ditch thanks to a careless driver, and in traffic court the next day. I was asked how I pleaded by a man in a white wig. I did not expect that my little misdemeanour would take me to court. Anyhow, I pleaded guilty as I truly was. He gave me a lecture, something along the lines of what might be considered a minor offense in Canada wasn't so here. He fined me three hundred pounds and told me where I could pay it. I told him I had no money, and so could not pay, and he'd have to come up with another way of punishing me."

I couldn't believe what I was hearing. I waited a minute, but she didn't seem to be in any hurry in revealing what happened next. "Are you going to keep me in suspense?"

She did not look at me and spoke in a very emotionless voice. "He said he found that hard to believe as according to my file...really, I had a file? He said that I did. Anyhow, the vehicle I had ditched was registered to James DuMaurier, and my name was November Queen, so was I in his employ, or should he add theft to my lawbreaking? I informed him that I was James's wife. He asked me if Mr. DuMaurier knew that I didn't have a valid driver's licence but let me drive anyhow. I said that we had never discussed it. He asked where James was. I told him he was in France. He asked me if there was someone else who might like to pay my fine in my husband's absence. I said that my mother might if she had any money left. He shook his head and said that he assumed that my mother was also broke. I told him she was because she had been footing my medical bills. He then asked me if I was ill.

I told him that I was a little bit crazy according to Shelia Dickens, but that I was also a little bit pregnant, so one might consider me as being ill. An officer came over and whispered something to the judge. Apparently, he knew the name Sheila Dickens or was told who James was because his demeanour changed. He told me I was free to go, but to stay out of trouble. I told James when he got home. It was then he hired a chauffeur who doubled as a butler, grounds keeper, etc. etc. Needless to say, I never drove again."

"Really, you expect me to believe that? I might concede that you were let off scout free because of your connections, but I don't believe that you were as composed as you so pictured yourself, so how do you account for that?"

"Dad, you're here! Can I go home now?" Joey was awake. "Did I fall asleep again Mom?"

"You did Darling, but it's okay because you need lots of rest. The doctor should be here any minute, and then we'll go home."

I asked him how he felt. He said he didn't think he was going to be running any races for a while, but his leg didn't hurt anymore. We chatted some more about the hike, and he told me when he had stepped on the board with the nail in it. He said it was when I'd gone to pee. I didn't ask him why he didn't tell me because it could wait for later, and Dr. Black had just arrived.

Joey was given the all clear and sent home with some meds and told to stay off the foot as much as possible. I asked Em for the keys to the Buick so I could warm it up while she finished her conversation with the doctor. That was something else I was going to have to talk to her about. The two of them walked out together with Joey in a wheelchair. I got out and lifted him into the back seat. Em climbed in beside him.

"Oh, sorry Johnathan, I never did answer your question inquiring as to how I was so unruffled with the judge did I? Maybe I was the mythical Emily."

"We'll talk about that later." I replied not knowing what else to say.

"And, maybe we won't."

Joey asked her if he was going to kindergarten.

"Not today Honey; you need to stay off your foot as much as possible. Remember JoJo's wedding is in a few days, and you don't want to miss that do you?" Em reasoned with him.

"No, but Amy is going to be worried about me."

"I talked to her on the phone yesterday so she knows you are all right."

"Can I call her?"

"Yes, you certainly may."

The whole household, plus Sarge were waiting on the front veranda for Joey. Em helped him climb up on my shoulders and we went to join the crowd. Inside I was directed to sit him down in AnnieZu's big chair where a dozen or so balloons billowed from the ceiling. There was a basket of wrapped gifts in a basket on the floor. Joey asked Em if it was his birthday again.

She laughed. "No, it's not your birthday. You only get one a year, but when someone is sick it's a custom to give them gifts and cards. Do you want to open them now, or have breakfast first?"

"I don't think I want to eat."

I asked him why. He said it was because he had thrown up our picnic lunch, and that it had hurt so he didn't want to eat until he wasn't sick anymore. Em asked him why he hadn't told her that he was sick after the hike.

"You would have just worried Mom, and I didn't want Johnathan to know."

"You're right Son, we would have been a little worried, but we could have gotten you to the doctor sooner, and maybe you wouldn't have needed to go to the hospital. I want you to promise that you will tell your mother right away if you ever feel sick again. Can you do that for me?"

"Suppose if Mom isn't around, can I tell you?"

I messed with his hair a little. "You can tell me, or AnnieZu, or Pete, or anyone else. The important thing is that you tell someone."

"That goes double for me. How come you let your dad mess with your hair, and didn't give him heck like you always do me?"

Joey grinned and told his mother that I didn't know him that well yet, so I didn't know he didn't like it. That was going to change because soon I was going to know everything there was to know about him, and in doing so, I would also get to know more about Em's last six years.

Em started passing Joey his gifts. He radiated joy with everyone he opened. The women of the house and Harold had given him a treasure box filled with comic books, puzzles, a baseball, bat, and mitt, and everything else a five-year-old boy could possibly need to pass the time away. Pete had made him up a toolbox that contained half a dozen different carpenters' tools, and

Sarge had given him two small canvases, brushes and paints. Em passed me the last gift and told me to give it to our son. The card said that it was from Mom and Dad. I had no idea what the gift was. I should have known.

Joey's eyes lit up when he unwrapped it. "A fighter jet! How did you know that I was wishin for one Mom? I'm going to need help with this Dad cause it's mighty big! I hope it won't break the ceiling."

"I'm pretty sure it won't Son." I wanted to kiss his mother.

Joey thanked everyone again. Betsy and Ada scurried off to the kitchen to make breakfast. Joey had settled on cream of wheat. AnnieZu and Em said that sounded really good to them too. I told Joey I would be right back as I needed to talk to Mrs. Parker for a minute. She appeared to be delighted that I would ask her for help. A week ago I would never have dreamed of asking her for anything.

I spent the next hour with the family while we all had breakfast. Joey asked if he could go to his room for a while as he was a little tired. He seemed worried that he was sleeping so much. Em explained that it was the medication, and that it was a good thing because that was the way he'd get better faster. I piggy-packed him upstairs. We looked at the fighter jet model kit together to make sure that it contained everything we needed to build it. I told him that we would get a start on it later as I had to go into work for a few hours. He asked me if I had any balsa wood around my factory as he could use some, and did I know how to make an easel. I told him that we'd build one together and I was pretty sure I could find some balsa. Em asked if she could have a word with me. I was pretty sure that I was going to catch hell for leaving Joey and going to work. Instead she thanked me for spending the night with him, and with her. That surprised me a little as I had only spent five minutes with her. I mentioned that. She said I had been here and that was all that mattered.

"I should be the one thanking you Emmy because I had a good night's sleep in your bed, as I always have had. And the model plane, thanks for including me. I would never have thought to bring a present. When did you have time?"

She laughed. "You give me too much credit. It's been sitting in my closet for a while. I was saving it for Christmas or a special occasion. Betsy knew I had bought it, so it was all her doing."

"Good call on her part then. Can I bring you anything from the city?"

"I have everything I need now that Joey is on the mend. Will you spend the night here again?"

"Would you like me to?"

"That's your call isn't it? I hope you'll be back in time for dinner. We've all become accustomed to having you at the table you know."

"Not half as much as I enjoy being here."

She smiled and started to turn back into Joey's room. I stopped her and told her she had forgotten something. She asked me what. I said, "This." I kissed her lightly on the lips. I did not stick around for her reaction.

Six hours later I was back in Seahaven. I stopped by the house to see if Mrs. Parker had come through for me. I found a note from her stating that she didn't buy new sheets because they would have to be laundered before use, so she had brought lightly used ones from Silvermist. She said she hoped that met with my approval, and that everything else was in place. All I had asked her for was the bedding and towels. Not only were there towels in the ensuite, but everything else a bathroom could possibly need including three toothbrushes. I took that as a subtle assumption. A brand-new coffee pot, several different flavors of coffee and boxes of crackers sat on the counter. The fridge contained an assortment of cheeses and meats and a variety of Betsy's tarts. I closed up the house and drove to the florist to pick up the flowers that

I had ordered earlier. Fifteen minutes later I was back at Silvermist. I entered through the kitchen at Silvermist hoping that Em wouldn't be there, and she wasn't. I gave Ada and Betsy each a bouquet and placed another one on the dining room table. Ada actually blushed when I gave her a quick peck on the cheek. Betsy reacted as usual saying that I was kissing the wrong girl. I told her everything in due time. I picked up the orchid and went to find AnnieZu. She was in the conservatory snipping dead growth off the plants.

"Hi Gorgeous." I said and presented her with the lavender orchid. She thanked me and placed it beside the pink one I had bought her after her accident. She asked me if we needed to talk. I didn't think we did, and was going to tell her that all was good when Em and Joey arrived to escort her into dinner. The four of us made our way to the table.

Em commented on the bouquet of flowers that was sitting in front of her saying they were beautiful, and that someone had impeccable good taste. She started to move the vase into the centre of the table. Joey said that he thought they were for her because her name was on the card. He removed it saying he wondered who had sent them.

"I don't have to read the card to know who they are from Joey." Em stated.

"How come?" He asked.

"Because only one person has ever given me blue daisies."

"How do they make them blue? All the ones in the field are white, and look Mom, there's a red rose in the middle."

I explained to him that his mother was the rose and the daisies were all slaves to her beauty. He asked her if she knew what that meant. She didn't answer him but asked me what the occasion was. Before I could answer her Joey passed her the note and asked her if it was my name.

"Yes, the flowers are from your father. Again, what's the occasion Johnathan?"

I didn't think she expected an answer.

"What does the rest of the note say Mom?"

"Nothing much. Can we get on with dinner now? Where's Pete? I thought he was eating with us while his wife is out of town."

Betsy explained that he'd gone over to Sarge's and that they were fending for themselves. Just before dessert was brought out Joey asked me if I had found any balsa. I said that there was a large box of different samples of wood in the kitchen which he could inspect after dinner. Then he threw me for a loop and asked if I had asked his mother yet. Em asked him what he meant.

"Asked you for a date. He asked me if it was okay with me, and I told him I was cause you're my mom and he's my dad, so it's okay."

God, I loved that kid.

Em was not amused. "No, it is not all right Joey, and your dad knows that. He is married, but sometimes he forgets that and acts like a schoolboy again. A married man does not ask another woman out on a date."

"But Mom, it's to JoJo's supper tomorrow. Don't you want to go?"

"Of course I'm going. I'm just not going on your father's arm."

AnnieZu made a suggestion. "Well, you are not supposed to drive are you

November, and Harold will be busy with the wedding party, so I think you should save him a trip and go with Johnathan. There is no reason to consider it a date is there? The mother and father of the bride should not be feuding over a little outdated word like "date."

Em scowled at me. "Have you told everyone about my run-in with the law over my driving misadventure in London?"

"He never told me anything Dear. Your mother and I do talk now and then you know."

Em was close to tears when AnnieZu defended me. I apologized though I wasn't too sure what I was apologizing for. "I'm sorry Emmy; I just wanted to brighten your day a little, and I thought a cheery bouquet might do the trick. The date thing was in bad taste." I got up and reached for the vase of flowers. "Here, I'll get these out of your way as they seem to be upsetting you."

She hit my fingers with the back of her knife. "Don't you dare touch them!" She picked up the vase, asked to be excused, and left the table. She turned around at the door and addressed me. "I'll go with you to our daughter's rehearsal dinner, but it is NOT A DATE!"

She stormed off. Betsy and Ada made a quick retreat to the kitchen trying hard not to giggle. Joey followed them saying he wanted to see what I had brought him.

"That girl has it bad for you Johnathan. I wish I had a crystal ball. I'm a might feared of the outcome if she doesn't get what she wants." AnnieZu sighed.

"What exactly is it that you think she wants?"

"Don't be glib Johnathan; you know damn well what she wants! Any fool can see that she is still in love with you."

I laughed a little. "You think that her admonishing me every few minutes is her way of saying she loves me do you?"

"Perhaps if you stop giving her reasons to do so would help. How many times have you given her blue daisies in the past? Were they always for special occasions or just because?"

"Both I guess. Do you think I made a mistake giving them to her?"

"I honestly don't know. She's a complicated lady, and everything in her life is just as complicated. We really don't know how much damage her illness has done to her. She is not the same person who left here six years ago that's for sure. It is my belief that she would never have returned if she hadn't discovered that you were Joey's father. I am sorry that it took her so long. I want my sweet niece back Johnathan. If you care for her the way you say you do then quit playing games with her and make it happen. Only you can put the light back in her eyes."

"I'm not playing games Zuzzs. Perhaps I have tested the waters too long, and we both may be wrong about her feelings for me, but I don't think we are. I promise all will be resolved in the next few days. She'll either accept my proposal, or she'll reject it. If she rejects it, I think I will be in for the fight of my life. I've kept something from her that may very well end any chance of conciliation. One thing is for certain though; I will not be going back to Lorraine whatever the outcome. I have tried calling her, but she's not answering. I have not the time or desire to talk to her in person. I left a message for her asking her to honour our agreement and vacate the house, and not to attend Johanna's wedding."

"I have no idea what your agreement is with her, but I trust that you know what you're doing. It's not just you and November I worry about. It's like you two are still married and a divorce is looming, and Joey will be the bargaining chip."

"Never going to happen Zuzzs. It'd be hard, but I'd give him up if it was the only solution in keeping Em's happiness and sanity. Now I think I'll go see what that little boy is up to. Don't worry; I'm going to fix things."

I hugged her, went in the kitchen to thank Betsy and Ada for dinner, and went to spend time with Joey. I did not see Em, but stopped outside her door, and whispered, "Sweet dreams."

Sarge lit into me about the way I had been treating November the minute I stepped in the door. He said that while I had been sifting through stones I had overlooked the diamond. He said that I had lost her once and I would again if I didn't do something about it before it was too late.

"Believe me Sarge, I want that girl more than you'll ever know, and tomorrow is D-Day."

"Humph, I suppose you want to crash here and mess up the bed I made for Archie again."

CHAPTER 8

D-Day

I heard Johnny outside my door. If I had any brains at all I would have ran after him. It's what I wanted to do, but six years of therapy had taught me that it was patience and hard work that would win out. The time was not right because Johanna's wedding and Joey's health had to take priority over anything I was thirsting for.

It was a very busy day Friday at Silvermist. Johanna and Piers, his parents, and Uncle Sebastian plus two elderly aunts arrived at eleven a.m. The wedding party of six arrived right behind them. By the time everyone was settled into their bungalows and bedrooms, it was four o'clock. I had just sat down in a comfy chair in the living room to spend some time with Joey when the doorbell rang. I seemed to be the only one in the house, so answered it. On the other side of the door stood my mother and my brother-in-law, Archie.

I thought they weren't coming until Saturday. How they had ended up at the door together was a mystery. Archie said he had encountered my mother on the ferry and offered her a ride so she wouldn't have to get a taxi. I was a bit surprised that he had recognised her, or her, him. Zena said that she hadn't at first, and then he spoke and she saw the resemblance to Johnathan. She gave me a quick hug and wanted to know where her baby was and rushed off to find Joey. I was left alone in the foyer with Johnny's brother. He was, and had always been a little too free with his welcomes. He had always thought that he was God's gift to women. He had never married because he knew he could never be monogamous, divorce was messy, and he didn't want children. He used to tease Johnny and me all the time when we were young saying that we were in puppy love. He thought that I was a tomboy. Archie was three years the elder. The two brothers tolerated each other, but not much more. The day he hit on me was the end of any brotherly love.

I took as much as I could from his cooing and complements and ushered him in to meet Joey. I snuck out the back door to look for Johnny. He had been outside all day doing what he does best; organizing and giving instructions. I found him sitting on a bench having a beer with Piers. He asked me if I would like to join them. I told him that Zena and Archie were here. He swore under his breath. I said that I would keep Piers company.

"Oh no you don't! There's no way I'm going in there if you're not by my side!"

Piers asked if there was a problem.

"You haven't met my mother yet have you? Well, she is pretty tolerable, but she is no AnnieZu. I'll let you judge Archie for yourself."

Johnny said that we were going in united. He asked how Archie greeted me.

"The same as always."

"Did he paw you?"

"I didn't give him the chance. I don't need another Jurado pining after me."

"Another, how many are there?

"Actually Darling, only three."

My calling him darling meant that we were going to present ourselves to my mother and his brother as a loving couple. We would be playing a game, but I was tired of playing by the rules, and I was ready to let it all out. Then Johnny's words changed my mind.

"Sarge seems to think that you and I are in some play, and that the curtain is going to close on us if I don't do something. You're my leading lady Em, always have been, and always will be. Question is, do you want to play?"

I said, "Lead the way Shakespeare."

We walked in hand and hand.

Archie met us halfway across the room. "Hey, lookin good there little brother. What's this, you two hooking up again?"

"You don't look so bad yourself Bro." Johnny answered giving Archie a casual hug. "You know Em and I have been friends forever, and that will never end. I see you have met Joey. Mom told you the news I guess. Too bad she and dad couldn't make it. How is the ole boy?"

"Doc says he will make a full recovery. I think they are planning on a trip out west soon."

"Johnny, you didn't tell me that your dad was ill. What happened?" I asked.

"He had a stroke in June. He was already on the mend by the time I got out there. Sorry, guess I just forgot to tell you with everything else going on. You're coming to the rehearsal dinner tonight aren't you Arch?"

"Nah, think I'll pass and spend the night with Sarge."

"Okay, catch you tomorrow. Em, can you entertain Archie while I say hello to your mother?"

"I've already played; it's your turn." I contested.

Archie laughed. "I'm glad to see you still have that warped sense of humor November."

"It's reserved only for you. Come on; let's go see if we can find Johanna. Oh, here she is."

"Mom, you're not going to believe...oh, Uncle Archie's here!"

I let them catch up for a few minutes before I asked her what she had been so excited about.

"James just called me. He's in Vancouver, and he's coming to the wedding! Isn't that wonderful? I'm so excited to see him."

"That's just peachy Dear. Why don't you take Archie out to meet Piers while I go and rescue your father from my mother?"

"Grandma's here too? I thought she was coming tomorrow with the sisters?"

"Change of mind I guess."

I watched the two of them go off arm in arm. Johanna was Archie's weak spot.

"What kind of a household are you running here? Where's Betsy and that Mrs. Parsons? I haven't even been offered a cup of tea! Looks like you and I are on our own for dinner Joey; guess its soup and grilled cheese." My mother complained.

"It's Mrs. Parker Mom; we call her Ada now, and this is not my house to manage. Aren't you coming to Johanna's and Pier's dinner?"

"No, I am going to stay and visit with my sister and my grandson."

"Okay, Johnny do you want to show Zena to her room?"

"How about I go and make the tea and you and Joey take Gramma upstairs?"

"Zena doesn't like being called Gramma, Johnathan! Only JoJo and I can." Joey moaned smacking his head. "We should have told you."

Zena laughed faintly and asked Joey if he always called his father Johnathan. He said that he did sometimes. Johnny blew me a kiss. I was getting a headache. Archie and my mother had arrived a day early, Piers uptight parents were arguing continually, my self-proclaimed witch sisters, May and Noel would be here tomorrow, and now James was coming. All I needed to complete the dysfunctional family picture was for Johnny's wife to show up. I needed a drink, and it sure as hell wasn't that magical tea.

We took our places in front of the rill for the wedding rehearsal an hour later. I didn't really need to be present because I wasn't in the wedding party, but Johnny insisted. He informed Reverend McDonnell that we were both going to walk our daughter down the aisle. The reverend thought it was a great idea. Johanna held back a sniffle. I was very touched, but made a joke saying that I wasn't too sure the three of us could walk side by side down the path. Johnny took Johanna's and my hand and led us to the edge of the bandstand.

"So, we have to walk up here and then back again?" I was confused as I had thought we were only coming from behind the house.

Johnny smiled. "No, once is enough."

"How do we get here then?"

"Are you ladies up for a little surprise?" He teased.

Johanna said she was. I told him to lay it on me. He said I'd have to wait until tomorrow.

In the car on the way to the restaurant Johnny asked what was up with me and Zena. He thought that he had detected a hint of animosity between us.

I laughed. "Just a hint? She was against me moving back here. She has always thought that you were the root of all my problems, and that seeing you would send me back into therapy."

"Was she right?"

"Of course she wasn't. I think that you and I have a special relationship and seeing you and Joey together makes my heart purr. I think it's about time I told my mother what really sent me on the road to lunacy."

"I wish you wouldn't label yourself like that Em. I find it hard to believe that you never confided in her in the six years you were gone. All this time she has blamed me hasn't she?"

"No, not just you. She thought that the way my father lived and died was also the cause of my downhill slide, and of course she believed that you had been unfaithful, but there was one other thing she didn't know; no one knows. Oh look, the kids are just going in. I thought we were late, but we're not." I undid my seatbelt and started to get out. Johnny put his hand on my arm.

"That's the second time you have said that no one knows...knows what Em? What are you keeping from me and your mother? Does your therapist know?"

"I am not sure if it came out in my psychoanalysis or not. I've dealt with it, so it is not an issue anymore. Can we please just go in and have a lovely time?"

"I can guarantee you that we are going to have a wonderful evening, and before the night is over there will be no more secrets between us, understood?"

I only had the one secret besides the one that I wanted my husband back. I wasn't aware that Johnny had any. It wasn't like him to keep things to himself. I only hoped he wasn't going to divulge something personal at the celebration dinner, and he didn't. Piers had rented the whole upstairs of the hotel restaurant, so it was very private. At eight o'clock I said that I had best be getting back to check up on Joey. I didn't want to drag Johnny away from the party, so I was going to phone Harold to pick me up. Of course Johnny wouldn't hear of it. He said we had come together and we were going to leave together. I didn't argue with him until he turned the car in the wrong direction. I asked him where he was going. He said we weren't going far, and stopped in the driveway of his newly remodeled childhood home.

"Again Johnny...why? I thought you were taking me home." I did not open my door. He came around, opened it, and extended his hand to me.

"You know I want this to be yours and Joey's home Em, so I want to show you around."

I sighed. "I thought we had come to an agreement regarding that last Sunday?"

"I never agreed to anything. I told you I needed to have my say and I am going to. There's a reason why we can be together. I should have told you that Sunday when you first came to see me almost three weeks ago."

"So, you have a secret. I can't imagine what it could possibly be, but I'm listening."

"Not here. I want you where you can't run away."

"Are you planning on locking me up?"

"I'm hoping it won't come to that."

"Just five minutes as I need to get back to Silvermist to make sure Joey is all right."

Johnny passed me his phone. "Look, Betsy just sent this. He's sleeping peacefully, and she told us not to hurry home. If he's not safe with four grown women then I don't know what will ease your mind. Are you coming, or are you afraid to be alone with me?"

"Oh yes, I am dreadfully afraid to be alone with you." I answered sassily. "Let's go so you can tell me this big secret you've been harbouring."

He led me through the downstairs rooms. He had made a few notable changes that I hadn't noticed on Sunday. The wall between the living room and dining room had been removed and replaced by an archway. Now the view of the estuary was more prominent. The kitchen had been completely remodeled. It was also open to a picturesque window and a little breakfast nook. Johnny said he didn't have a use for his dad's old office room yet, but one would surely surface. The whole thing was just as I would have designed it, contemporary, yet antiquated thanks to the beams and crown mouldings. I especially liked the pale pink ornate living and dining room ceilings. I followed him upstairs where he showed me the room that would be Joey's. It was his old room, freshly painted and boasting a skylight. I asked Johnny when he had designed the room as he didn't even know Joey was his until a week ago.

He shrugged his shoulders. "You're right I didn't, but I had the faint hope that you were coming home to stay and if it meant with your son then it was all right with me. Archie's old room and the bathroom all needed a facelift, so it had to be done. Want to see what I've done with the master bedroom? I think it will be to your liking."

"I'd just as soon sit here in the window seat if you don't mind." I replied.

"I do mind because I have something to give you…" He pulled me along, opened the bedroom door and hit a light switch. A million golden stars danced around the sky-blue walls. "It's beautiful Johnny." I whispered wondrously.

"I always told you I'd get you the stars and moon didn't I? Sorry, I've come up short on that promise. Hopefully, the moon will make an appearance later."

He led me to the bed, sat me down and pulled up a chair opposite me. He took my hand and looked into my eyes.

"Have you thought anymore about my offer Sunday night?" He asked touchingly.

"You mean where Joey and I come to live with you, and I become your mistress?"

"Something along those lines, but I can make the mistress title go away." He smiled intimately.

I pushed his hand away, got up and walked over to the window. Silvermist was aglow in the dark night. The lights from fishing vessels shone in the distance. I loved this view. I half expected that Johnny would come up behind me and put his arms around me, but he didn't. I turned and leaned against the wall between the two windows.

"You can't change things Johnny. I told you that I can't, and I won't be the other woman, and I won't subject you to my neurosis ever again. I will tell you what I can do though. As soon as you furnish this house I will bring Joey by to visit with you as you two need some alone time. I hope you will honor my wishes and not take him to the house you share with Lorraine. You told me that she won't be staying with you here, but I don't see how you can avoid that. She showed up uninvited at Silvermist last week, so she'll surely show up at Johanna's wedding, and she'll find out about your retreat here. Maybe in time I will come to tolerate her being around Joey. I mean, he's your son too, and maybe someday there will be another man in my life, and you will have to accept that there is another man in Joey's life too. Can you give me a little more time to come to terms with this Johnny?"

"Suppose if you don't have to?"

"I don't know what you mean?"

He went to the bureau, opened a drawer and took out a little box. I was afraid of what the box held. I thought it best if I didn't find out. I said that I wanted to go home.

He approached me, undid the clasp and extracted my engagement and our wedding rings.

"I want you to wear these again Em."

"Stop it, stop it Johnny! What on earth is wrong with you? I've spent the last six pitiful years in what virtually passed as a mental institution. I worked very hard to vanquish my demons with you being my biggest one, and now you want to send me back there…why Johnny why?" I cried.

He put the case down and took me in his arms. "The last thing I want is to hurt you. I love you more than you can even imagine Em. Not being with you is driving *me* crazy, but I will gladly go there if I can go there with you. I should have come for you years ago, but I was a coward, and I was also clinging to the dream that you would come back to me, and you have. You can't deny that you still love me can you?"

I shook my head. Tears were welling up in my eyes.

"Then listen to me. I told you that I never stopped thinking of you as my wife, and that is why I could never marry anyone else. Lorraine and I aren't married Em. I never bought her a ring; I never asked her to marry me. It's all a sham. I'm sorry; I should have told you."

I pushed him away and sank to the floor holding my head in my hands. He sat down beside me and asked me to look at him.

"I don't want to. I don't like you very much right now."

"I don't like myself very much either Em. I need you to tell me that you can forgive me for not telling you sooner… can you do that?"

"No, I don't think I can, but it's not me you need to worry about. How do you think your daughter is going to react to your outrageous lie? For almost three years you have let everyone believe that you and Lorraine are married. How does she feel about living a lie? You say you don't love her, but I find that very hard to believe. You've been testing me haven't you? You had to keep me at bay because if f I didn't accept your proposals you didn't want to close the door to her bed did you?"

"You are wrong about that because I have been thinking of ending it with her for a long time, and I am regretful that I didn't. It was over for us the minute I saw you. Hell, it was over the minute JoJo announced her engagement because I knew you would be coming home for her wedding. There never was much to my relationship with her anyhow. I'm not defending myself, but I never actually told Johanna I had married Lorraine. One day she had asked me if I was going to marry her. I told her that I was already married. She asked why we were keeping it a secret. I guess I came up with some stupid reason, and next thing I know everyone thinks we are married, including you. I didn't want Jo to think that I was just shacking up, and I knew she would tell you, and maybe I wanted you to hurt like I did when you married James. It took me two and a half years before I could even look at another woman. I was still living in the fantasy world that you'd come back to me. I was working sixteen hours a day just so I didn't have to go home to an empty house. Two drunken nights with two different unsavoury women was the start of my descent into hell. Who knows how long it would have lasted, but Johanna saved me when she asked if she could come and live with me. You saved me too Em by allowing her to come. Is it too late to thank you?"

"I should never have taken her away from you, but I needed her I thought more than you did. She always looked forward to her visits with you. She was so brave getting on that big airplane all by herself. I cried every time she left, and every time she came back. Then all of a sudden she was fourteen and asking if she could go and live with you permanently. I surprised myself and let her go. I had Joey, and you had no one, so yes, you may thank me. It couldn't have been easy for a young girl to live with an irrational mother. One day I was perfectly lucid, and then the next I wasn't. I never want to go back to those days Johnny. It's been pointed out to me that you are my poison, so I should really keep my distance from you. I need to go home now."

"Do you think I am poison Em?"

"Perhaps you and my father contributed to my emotional state, but it was the chemical imbalance that was really to blame... that, and my guilt. I was up and down like a yo-yo. It wasn't just a matter of finding the right drugs to combat the imbalance, but I had to learn to deal with the other contributing factors, and forgive myself."

"What could you possibly have to forgive yourself for Em? You've never done anything wrong in all your life except love me, and here I am asking you to love me again. If it's too much for you, just say so, and I'll be gone. I'll never love anyone but you, but I'll give up everything to keep you happy and healthy."

"What do you mean by *everything*?"

"The business, this house, everything ...I'd move away."

"What about Joey?"

"I'd hope that you would let him visit." Johnny said downhearted.

"Neither of us is going anywhere. I am here to stay. I am healthy, and I intend to stay that way. I'm adjusting to a new healing protocol, so I hope you will be patient with me."

"Honey, are you saying that there's hope for us?"

I didn't give him an answer, but instead blurted out what I'd kept from him for six years. "I think the baby would have been a girl."

"Is this your introductory into what you've have been keeping from me? What happened Em...when and how did you lose a baby? It was mine wasn't it?"

"How long have you known?"

"For about one minute." He took my hand and squeezed it very hard. "You can tell me if it is going to ease this guilt that has been causing you so much grief, or if you'd rather not, that is all right too. Whatever, I'll understand."

"It was that night that you didn't come home. You said that you had called me all night long, but I never answered. The reason was because I wasn't home. I drove myself to the hospital because I knew something was wrong. I had just found out a few days before that I was pregnant. My moods were sky rocking then, so I was waiting for a better mood to tell you..."

"So, while I was saving the life of Beth's baby, you were alone and losing ours, is that right, and you have lived with this for six years? How do I react to something like that Em?" Johnny got up and looked down at me. He was hurting. "I don't deserve you Em. Come on, I'll take you back to Silvermist."

"I can't get up?"

"What do you mean? Do you just want me to go away and leave you alone?"

"You can if you want, but first help me up or I'll be here all night, and I can't breathe."

He pulled me up. I thanked him and asked him if he could find me something to wear. I was struggling to get my breath.

"You're scaring me Em; what's the matter?"

"Nothing, nothing... dress too tight."

"It isn't tight Honey. I think you're having some sort of panic attack."

"Take it off, take it off...it's the corset, hurry, turn around, turn around so I can get it off. Get me a towel or something to cover up with." I undid the lacing and let it drop to the floor and took a deep breath.

He passed me one of his white shirts. I slipped into it and collapsed on the bed. He asked me why I was wearing a corset. I told him it was because the dress was too tight and I wanted to wear it for him because he had seen it and liked it, and so I had no choice but to don a tortuous under garment from the dark ages so I could wear it.

"If all this was just a ploy to make me feel less guilty then you succeeded. Next time try not scaring the daylights out of me first okay?" He pleaded.

"I never wanted you to have any guilt about the miscarriage, so I chose not to tell you, but we were being honest, so...I have dealt with it finally, and I need you to also. I blamed myself for losing our baby because I was so off kilter. The emergency room doctor said that it wasn't anything I had done, and that it was doubtful that I would have carried the baby to term because there was a problem with the chromosomes. He said that I should look at the miscarriage as a blessing for it would have been impossible for the fetus to develop normally. I thought that was the end of my dream to have another child, but miraculously it wasn't. I fretted all through my pregnancy with Joey, but I needn't have. In fact, I had little difficulty, and it was an easy birth. I actually felt better while I was carrying him. I wrote all about those days in the letters I wrote you. Maybe someday you will read them, and then you will know how I lamented that you weren't the father. If I hadn't of been so muddled in my head I might have been able to put two and two together Johnny, but I didn't, and I am so sorry." I cried.

"Don't cry Baby, please don't cry. You can't blame yourself for what happened to you, the baby, or us. I have tried to read your letters, but then I feel your melancholy, and I have to stop because the sorrow overwhelms me. Every day I am becoming more aware of the toil the illness had on you, and I am so ashamed that I wasn't more understanding. I should have done this and I should have done that. I should have ignored your mother and went to check on you myself. I told you I was a coward. I was afraid that I would see you, and the disappointment and blame in your eyes would mean that I had lost you for good. Sorry, I've been wallowing in self-pity for too long, and it's time for me to make amends."

"I was never disappointed in you Johnny, and there are no atonements to be made. We both cried when our divorce became final because we still loved each other. I drew on the memories of our last night together over and over, and all the wonderful years we had shared. Now, I'd like to make some new memories, so I've decided to revise my proposal of earlier. Maybe instead of me just dropping Joey off for a visit or the night, I might stay for a little while also if you wish. I may even make you dinner once in a while."

"If I wish...look at me; you've just made me the happiest man in the world for even considering spending time with me. I'm hoping that you'll come with me to pick out furniture and everything else that goes into making a house a home. I'll never give up on the dream that we can be a family again."

"We're already a family Johnny. When was it exactly that you decided to buy this house?"

"April the nineteenth; the day Johanna called and said that she and Piers had set a wedding date for September 9th. That meant that you would be coming back for a little while."

"That's the day I decided that I was bringing Joey home to you."

I think the look in my eyes matched the one in his. It was one of realization that we belonged together, and the future was ours to command.

"I love you Em." Johnny picked up the ring box.

"I love you too Johnny." I offered him my hand and he gave me his. Simultaneously we slipped the rings on each other's fingers. Then he took my hand and ran it through his hair, and then through mine. He pulled me up and into his arms and kissed me tenderly. I responded with everything I had been holding in since the moment I had first seen him.

Half an hour later I was still in his arms. I was still vibrating with contentment, and he was still kissing me and whispering sweet love promises in my ear.

"I don't want this night to end, but I know I have to take you down the hill so that you'll be there when Joey wakes up. Can we just postpone it for a little while longer?"

"I don't want to leave the shelter of your arms either, but it'll only be for another day."

"That's music to my ears Em. First thing we'll have to do is to get Joey a bed."

"The first thing you have to do is tell Lorraine. I know you're not married, but common-in-law marriages are recognised as legal these days. What do you think she'll want from you?"

"Nothing; we have a cohabitation agreement. She takes what she brought into the relationship and anything else that she might have contributed to the household. It is legally binding. I have left her half a dozen messages to call me when she gets home, but she has chosen not to call. I finally left her a message asking her to vacate the house as soon as possible, and not to come to Jo's wedding. She had to know that it was over the minute she met you."

I sat up. "What do you mean?"

"After you left that day, I went for a long walk because I didn't want to go back in the house and face her. You had asked for a hug, but I didn't dare because I still loved you, but you said you could never trust me again, and I had to deal with that. You wanting to have a baby with me really threw me for a loop. She asked me if I still loved you, and I said I did. Then she asked me if I loved her. I asked her what she thought and she said she thought I did, but I never tell her so. I guessed I loved her in a way, but I definitely wasn't *in* love with her. I couldn't tell her I loved her, so she knew."

"Why did you have her move in with you if you weren't in love with her and never intended on marrying her?"

"Because I was lonely, and I wanted to...no, I needed to replace you. I wanted to be happy again and I foolishly thought by making that commitment I would be. I think you know how that turned out."

"Were you happy for a while?"

"No damn it, I wasn't! What passed for happiness was nothing compared to what I feel when I'm with you. Even when you're angry at me, I'm in good spirits because I've seen a light at the end of the long dark tunnel."

"I should have let you know that my marriage to James was a sham, and that I still loved you. I should have told you it was a marriage of convenience only. Maybe you wouldn't have made that mistake with Lorraine then."

"And, I should have come after you. Yup, should have, could have... we lost six years Em, six bloody years!"

"I was ill Johnny, so it had to be that way. Now I can see how wrong my decisions were never planned on the 'baby thing' when I went to see you. I wanted to tell you the truth about Joey, but something stopped me, so I just blurted out that I wanted you to father a child with me which was true. You really should have hugged and kissed me that day."

"Yeah, I regretted that, but I honest to God thought you were playing games with me."

"I was, and maybe I still am." I cooed and tried to get out of bed.

"Oh no, you don't! I'm not through with you yet."

I laughed. "And, I'm not through with you, but I really should go. Can I tell you something?"

"Anything, you know that."

"I'm not like one of those girls that you have picked up in some dimly lit bar. You knew what you were getting all along because we have known each other a very long time. You say that I threw you for a loop, well you threw me for one too when you admitted that you weren't married. But, here's the part you don't know. I had every intention of turning my wicked self loose on you tonight and seducing you, and to hell with respecting your marriage vows!"

"And you knew I would take the bait?"

"There never was any doubt."

"So that's why you didn't insist that I take you home as you had plans of your own for me?"

"Now you're getting the picture. I caution you not to burn the negatives."

"I need you to know that there hasn't been anything between Lorraine and me for a long time."

"How long, and how did you two meet? Did she sell you the house?"

"She was a spoke person for the land company I was supplying ready-made homes to. She did not sell me the house."

"A little more please. Who initiated the lovefest?"

"It wasn't a lovefest Em. We had a few lunches together, then dinners and movies. We seemed to have the same taste in music and theatre. One thing led to another...you know how things go."

"Actually, I don't. I have only had one man in my life, and he has been there forever. We knew each other from an early age and our love for each other grew and matured over many years, so I have no idea how one just falls into bed with someone. My fifteen minutes of unpleasant awkward sex with James does not fit into that category."

"Do we have to discuss this right now?" Johnny was somewhat uncomfortable.

"You brought it up. You want me to know exactly what?"

"Okay. I was done with women who meant nothing to me except a warm body for a few hours, so nothing happened between us for a few months. Johanna was still living with me so there were no sleepovers. It was months after she left to go and live with her friend Sara in Vancouver that I asked Lorraine to move in with me."

"So, it was all you?"

"No, we talked about it, tried it for a few weeks, and we both decided that it could work. It wasn't long before I realised that I was kidding myself into believing that anyone could ever take your place. She was away half the time helping her mother adjust to running the motel after the death of her husband who was Lorraine's stepdad. I never missed her when she was gone and had no close friends to commiserate with so I started spending more and more time at work. Johanna met Piers last autumn, so I'd hop the ferry once a month to spend the weekend with them. Next thing I know they set a wedding date and that meant that you would be coming home. I started planning on how I was going to convince you to stay. You know the rest."

"No, I really don't Johnny. I did not get the feeling that you wanted me at all the day I came to see you at your house. I felt like I was intruding."

"I was surprised as hell to see you Em. You may not have noticed, but I was quaking inside."

"You've never been unsure of yourself one day in your life so don't give me that line of bull Johnathan Jurado!"

"You really have no idea how seeing you affected me do you? When you came to my office the next day, and the next, and the next, I was hopeful that you might come to love me again even though I thought you were playing games and had an agenda. I had to take it slow because I wasn't at all sure what you wanted. I should have told you then that Lorraine and I weren't married. Like I said, you asking me to have a baby with you was something I couldn't understand. And then you abruptly stopped coming... no message no phone call, nothing. I was back at square one and broken again."

"I will apologise for that Johnny, and yes, you should have told me about your non-marriage then, and I should have told you more about mine...there we go again with the "should-offs". I really thought Johanna would have told you about Joey though. I had never actually told her that you were his father. It turned out okay though didn't it?"

"Well I can't think of a more dramatic way of being introduced to a son I never knew existed."

"Should I have informed you the minute I found out...perhaps, but it was so overwhelming that I shut down for a while. I had to come to terms with it before I could tell you. Sorry it took me so long." I said remorsefully.

He patted my hand. "I didn't know, so no harm done. I don't want you to feel that you have to keep apologising. It's only onward from here Hon. How did we get on this anyway?"

"Something about me meeting Lorraine I think."

"Yeah, nothing good was going to come from that."

"Really; did you not think that we may become friends?"

"I did not, but what I started to tell you five minutes ago is that there has been nothing between us for months."

"And I asked you for how long?"

"Five months."

I laughed. "You expect me to believe that?"

"Yes I do because it's the truth. There wasn't a hell of a lot of passion in our relationship anyhow, so I fabricated a back problem and moved into the spare bedroom."

"I do believe you because I want to, and I don't want to think that what we just shared you could ever have attained with anyone else but me. I promise I will be respectful of your sore back."

"I've been seeing a massage therapist so it's all taken care of." He said grinning.

"I bet she took care of you all right." I said playfully.

"You don't even know if it was a woman, do you?"

"Is her name Janice Jetson, or something like that?"

"How the hell would you know that?" He was stunned.

"You shouldn't be leaving women's calling cards in your coat pocket where one may fall out."

"I take it you found the appointment card that I lost?"

"You can assume anything you want."

"Are you going to be suspicious of every woman I have contact with?"

"Probably."

"I guess that means I've got my Emmy back then?"

"Careful because Emily watches over her." I joshed.

"Tell me honestly...how well do I know Emily?"

"If you're wondering if you ever slept with her you're just going to have to keep wondering." I answered as I scooted out of bed. I grabbed my dress off the floor and made a beeline for the door which I assumed led into an ensuite. I put myself back together as best I could and went out to find my shoes, dress and Johnny's shirt.. He passed me my corset and stockings. I told him to leave them for the maid.

"I don't have a maid or housekeeper Hon." He said almost apologetic.

"Well, I don't do floors or windows so you had better find one, and she better be at least sixty."

"God, how I love you November Queen."

"As I do you Johnathan Jurado."

Johnny wanted to check in on Joey so I said okay. We tiptoed up the stairs and into his room. He was sleeping peacefully. Johnny was kissing me good night at my bedroom door when Johanna emerged from her room. A light went on, and there we were in each other's arms.

"What are you two doing?" She demanded.

"What does it look like Missy? Your father is kissing your mother good night." Johnny said.

"I see that. Where have you two been? Have you been together all this time? Mom, why are you wearing Daddy's shirt? Oh my God, you've been together, oh, my God!

"That's just what your mother said to me a little while ago; actually, several times over."

I smacked Johnny and pulled the two of them into my room shushing them. "Let's not wake the rest of the household all right? Sorry we woke you Honey."

"I haven't been sleeping as I've been listening for you to come home."

"Where did you think I was?"

"Well, you left with dad so...Zena has been worried about you."

"Of course. Do you know that your father bought his childhood home back?"

"Betsy said something about it."

"That's where we were. He wanted to know what I thought of the remodeling, and we had a lot of things to talk about."

"Like what?"

"We've never stopped loving each other Jo, so we are going to be together and make a home for Joey." Johnny informed our daughter.

"Yes, I know that's your plan Daddy, but there's a complication, and her name is Lorraine. Have you already asked her for a divorce?"

Johnny asked if I wanted to tell her. "It was your boo- boo Darling, so I think that ball is in your court." I answered sweetly.

"What does she mean Dad?"

"There isn't going to be a divorce Jo because we were never married. I let you assume that I had married her I guess because I didn't want you to think I was a sleazebag. I didn't, and I never actually said that I had married her."

"You said you were married." Johanna said solemnly.

"I'm sorry that I let you assume that I was married to Lorraine. I'd never marry anyone else because I always believed that I was still married to your mom."

"So, you've known all along?"

"Known that I was still in love with your mom, yes."

"I have to sit down for this." Johanna said as she plunked herself down on my bed. "I was going to wait until after my honeymoon to tell you because I didn't think either of you was anywhere near to a romantic reunion yet. I should have known better. But, seeing you are already playing house I guess knowing this might ease your minds. It appears as though there was some inconsistency in the paperwork regarding your divorce, so guess what; you are still married to each other."

I sat down beside her. "I don't know where you would get such an idea from Jo, but your dad and I received our divorce decrees on the same day. I already told you that I visited your father at the old house and we burnt them."

"You did, and you also told me that was the night Joey was conceived. Did either of you even bother to read the papers?"

Johnny sat down on the other side of her and took her hand. "We knew what they were Jo; we didn't need to read them. I glanced at mine and saw the word 'divorce' and tossed it in the garbage. For some unknown reason I rescued it only to burn it later. Now tell us where this cockamamie idea of yours is coming from."

"From the court clerk who filed your petition."

"Oh, so you just happened to run into him? How the hell would you even know who he is...none of this makes any sense Johanna." Johnny was like me, astounded.

"First, I want to ask you why you think you were granted a divorce so quickly?"

Johnny explained that ours was a simple petition; we had agreed on everything; nothing was contested by either of us.

"Well, apparently it can take up to a year even if it is a mutual decision. If you had bothered to read the document that you both received, you would have discovered that it was a notice for you to set a date for your court hearing. Did they not explain that you would be receiving one? You are both very smart people, but obviously you didn't pay attention."

Johnny stood up and looked down at Johanna. "You are right about that. I never heard a word that was said. It was the worst day of my life and I just wanted the hell out of there."

I got up and put my arms around him. "It's actually good news Dear; we don't have to get married again because we already are."

"There's just one problem Mom. You married James, so you committed bigamy. I guess you are safe Dad if you never actually married Lorraine."

I was amused, but Johnny was furious. "It can't be bigamy if she didn't know she was committing it now, can it be? I think that's enough for this night Johanna. I have a thousand questions, but we will table the rest of this inquisition until you get back from Italy."

"Daddy, I didn't mean to upset you. Nothing is going to happen; I mean Mom isn't going to jail or anything."

"Damn right she isn't! This is all a misunderstanding, and how you came to gather this information is a little troubling to say the least. Let's get you off to bed; your big day is tomorrow and you need some sleep."

"I'm not going to be able to get any sleep until I tell you the story, so please bear with me a few more minutes. Naomi Strachan is the gal that I have trained to fill in for me. She asked me to dinner a few weeks ago, and that is where I met her dad Allan Strachan who just used to be a court clerk in Victoria; the one you two were assigned to."

"Are you saying that he remembered us?" I asked.

"He did. He commented on my last name and asked if I had a lot of relatives in Vancouver. I told him I was born and raised in Victoria. He then said that he used to work as a divorce court clerk in Victoria, and that my last name reminded him of a sweet couple whom he had taken a filing for a few years back. He said that if he had ever seen a couple who shouldn't be divorcing it was them, and he told them so. He told them that should be seeing a marriage counsellor not filing for divorce. He said he had assumed that they had taken his advice as they never filed the final papers. Out of curiosity I asked him if he remembered all the cases that were put before him. He laughed and said no, but those two were not your average couple applying for divorce. I asked him what he meant. He said they held hands all the time, and every time they looked at each other their eyes would tear up. He was pretty sure there was some outside interference that had driven them to the decision to divorce, but there wasn't anything he could do about it except recommend the councillor. I asked him if he remembered their names. He couldn't recall the gentleman's name, but hers was one he had never heard before. He said it was November."

"So I was right all along Em. I told you I never felt like I was divorced from you, and I wasn't. Is that it Johanna, tells us that's all there is to it?" Johnny probed.

"All I understand is that you never made the appointment with the courts. That letter you both received was for that purpose, but you didn't read it or act on it, so it was never filed. After a year it would have been dismissed according to Mr. Strachan because of lack of activity. It appears as though your supposed divorce is invalid and that you are technically still married. Any new marriage would also be invalid, so I don't think you have to worry Mom about your marriage to James."

"I wasn't worried at all Dear. What did you tell Mr. Strachan about us?"

"I told him that I was their daughter and that the two of you were together and still very much in love, and that you had a five-year-old son. I did not mention Lorraine and James. He was very happy and told me to give you his blessings and was glad that you had worked things out."

"He sounds like a very compassionate man Johanna. It was a very emotional day, so I can honestly day that I don't remember him or his advice. I guess it was some sort of divine intervention that you just happened to have this conversation with him. It's kind of a wedding present to us from you." Johnny laughed happily. "Come on now, you need to get to bed and I need to get up the hill."

"Why? What's there? Weren't you planning on staying the rest of the night with Mom?"

"We need to keep this just between us Jo until after the wedding, so your dad should go."

She asked me if I wanted him to leave. I said no.

"Well then, he should stay. I'm sure you'll figure something out for morning. You've been sleeping here pretty much all week haven't you Daddy?"

"Yes, because Joey was sick. Your mother and I did not share a bed."

"There really is no sense for you to leave now is there unless you don't want to stay."

He didn't answer but took our daughter's hand and walked her across the hall to her room. I heard him thank her for being the voice of reason, and for being our daughter.

He was waiting for me arms outstretched in the bed when I returned from changing into a nightie. "It was nice of our daughter to give us her permission to sleep together wasn't it?"

I told him that his idea and mine about sleeping didn't differ anymore. He said I was right.

CHAPTER 9

The Wedding Day

The day was almost perfect. I woke up at eight a.m. Johnny was gone, and so was Joey. I quickly dressed and made my way downstairs. Laughter was coming from the kitchen. Betsy and Ada were giving father and son advice on how to assemble the fighter jet. My mother was sitting at the table folding napkins.

"Good morning my dear. I trust you had a good nights' sleep." She said smiling.

Zena never gets up before ten. First Mrs. Parker, and now my mother. They must be taking happy and pleasant pills, or maybe there was some secret ingredient in the tea.

"Good morning." I cooed. "Why didn't anyone wake me?"

"We thought you needed your sleep." Betsy said with a wink.

"Yeah Mom, me and Johnathan thought so too." Joey chimed in.

Betsy brought me a cup of coffee and asked me what I wanted for breakfast.

"I don't have time. I have to get over to Sarge's and…"

Johnny interceded. "No, you don't Honey. Remember, Archie's here."

I didn't think he should be calling me honey in front of Ada and Betsy, but then he called everyone 'honey', so what did it matter? "Oh, I forgot." I mumbled.

"I'm sure you have a lot of more important things on your mind November. I guess I better see if Miss Annie needs my help." Ada said squeezing my shoulder when she walked by. Betsy was all smiles as she followed Ada saying that she had things to do outside of the kitchen.

Zena asked me if I had any idea when James would be arriving. I said that

I didn't. Johnny asked if I was apprehensive about seeing him.

"Of course I'm not. Why would I be? It was just a few weeks ago that I last saw him, and nothing has changed in our relationship."

Zena got up and poured herself another cup of coffee and started for the doorway. She turned around and addressed both Johnny and me. "No, nothing in your relationship with James has changed, but it has with Johnny." She held up her hand to stop me from speaking. "I always knew that you would end up together again, and especially after you found out that Johnathan was Joey's father. I was against it as you know, but I was wrong. I've only been around the two of you for a day, but the eyes do not lie. If it's not love shining in your eyes for each other then I don't know what love is. Johnathan, I trust that you will look after my daughter and grandson and do right by them. I think you know what I am referring to. See you all later."

"Hold on a second Zena; I'll walk with you as I need a word." Johnny said following her.

"What was she talking about Mom?" Joey asked.

"I think that she wants your dad and me to get back together."

"Doesn't she know?"

"Know what Dear?"

"That we're going to go live with Daddy up the hill in his new house?"

Oh dear, I hadn't expected that Johnny would have had time to talk to Joey yet. "Would you like it if we were to leave Silvermist and go to live with your dad?"

"Yeah, because I get to get a puppy!" Joey said jubilantly.

What time had those two got up this morning I wondered? Johnny was already making promises. I wasn't too sure how I felt about that. He returned a few minutes later smiling.

He kissed me. "Your mother gave us her blessings. I told her about my non-marriage. She didn't seem surprised at all. She told me to get on with my plans. I asked her to keep it to herself until after Johanna's wedding. She said, "Sure, because no one else suspects a thing.""

"I think the bigger problem is keeping Joey from spilling the beans. I understand that you two have been having a little powwow this morning."

"Powwow; I told you she was funny didn't I Dad? Mom, do you think me and Daddy were playing cowboys and Indians?" Joey giggled.

I hugged him. "I'm going to go and find Johanna...where is everyone anyhow?"

"Piers took the whole crew out for breakfast. Good thinking on his part as it would have been too much for Betsy. I imagine they will be back soon."

I kissed my husband. "Well, I'm out of here anyhow as I have things to do, and you need another talk with your son."

James arrived at eleven. Johnny called me from the front entrance telling me that I had visitors. James was not alone. Standing behind him was a woman hidden from view by a huge bouquet of flowers. She was his sister Sheila Dickens, my London therapist. Johanna squealed with delight and ran to greet her once stepfather. They were truly happy to see each other. I introduced the duo to Johnny. He was quite amiable to them, but immediately asked to be excused after introductions saying he had to check on the seating arrangements. Sheila stepped forward quickly saying she would love to see the gardens and could she accompany him. I pictured him mulling the idea over in his head deciding to tell her that it wasn't a good time, but instead he said that he would be delighted to show her around. He didn't even glance my way when he offered her his arm. He did it on purpose just to see how I would react to his behavior around another gorgeous woman I told myself. I trusted Johnny. I did not trust Sheila as I knew that she was always man hunting. I had shown her a picture of Johnny once. Remembering her words now made me realise that they were not professional at all.

"I would ask you if you were 'crazy' for divorcing him, but we don't use that word around here, so I won't, but what could this Adonis have possibly done to cause you such heartache? Did he not love you, was he a poor lover... oh yes, he cheated on you, right?" She had stated.

I had snatched the photo away from her. "He did not cheat on me! I cheated him out of life and love when I gave in to these demons that you are supposed to be vanquishing. He is not the reason I am here. I do not want to talk about this ever again!" I had answered adamantly.

Of course she had said that was going to be difficult as he surely had a part in my psychoses. Now she was here, and I wondered why? James would know and so I invited him into the den where we could have a heart to heart.

I offered to make him tea and toast, but he said they'd had a light breakfast on the ferry so didn't require anything. He took my hand as we sat side by side on the sofa.

"How are you November?" he asked straightaway. "I mean…really?"

I assured him that I was doing just fine. "I will be glad to see Johanna and Piers married and off on their honeymoon as it has been a whirlwind of activities around here."

"Yes, Johanna told me on the phone that you had made all the arrangements single handily."

"She gives me too much credit. The ladies of the house all did their part, and then Johnny arrived, and everything just fell into place."

"Which leads me to the next question; how are you and your ex getting along? How did he take to the revelation that Joey is his son? I'm assuming that you hadn't informed him before as you led me to believe that you weren't sure if you were ever going to."

I laughed. "I would have had to keep Joey behind closed doors then because one look at him and everyone knew that Johnathan was his father. We are all getting along fantastically, so you need not worry. Johnathan understands what I went through and does not blame me for anything. He still believes that he was a big part of my depression and that he should have been more understanding. I am working hard to dispel all of that."

"And, you and his wife get along?"

"James," I scolded, "you sound like your sister."

"Sorry, just curious. I always knew that you still loved Johnathan, so it must be hard for you to see him with another woman."

"Believe me James, she is not a problem." I hope he caught the magnitude of my statement.

"You know that you always have a home back in London don't you? You were, and are the best friend I ever had, and your hostess skills outshone everyone else's. I always felt like a king in a castle when we were entertaining because I had the queen of the social order of the day."

"Oh James, that is the nicest thing that anyone has ever said about me, but you are paying the compliment to the wrong person." I lamented.

"I don't understand what you…"

Thankfully we were interrupted by Joey running into the room and jumping on James. Johnny was standing at the doorway. He apologised for interrupting. I assured him that he hadn't as I needed to start getting ready. I left James and Joey catching up as I followed Johnny out. I asked him what he had done with Sheila. He said he had left her and Pier's uncle Sebastian wandering the grounds.

"Good that she's got her eyes on someone else."

"What do you mean by that?" He asked innocently.

"You can't offer a woman like that your arm and tell her that it would be your pleasure."

"Honey, I was just being a good host. Please tell me that you are not jealous. We talked about this, remember? My god, she's your therapist."

"She *was my therapist.* I said I'd try not to be jealous of every woman who looked at you, but then she arrived. Come along; I need to know everything that she said to you."

"We were only gone a few minutes before Joey caught up to us so we hardly had time to talk. I did not question her or ask for her opinion on your illness or recovery, nor did she volunteer anything if that is what you are wondering. Neither of us betrayed your trust."

I waited until we entered the privacy of the bedroom before I answered him. "No, that is not what I am worried about. I love Sheila; she knows almost all of my deepest darkest secrets. Not only was she my analyst, but she was my friend. I'd like to keep it that way. I will tell you a little secret about her. She likes men, especially ones who are as handsome and charming as you are. She has no male patients because she doesn't trust that she wouldn't fall for one. Off the clock, she has a handful of men. I trust you will keep this under your hat. I probably shouldn't have told you, but I trust you, and just want you to be on guard. Let Pier's uncle have her."

Johnny seemed to be dissecting what I had just told him. He focused his eyes on mine. He was not smiling when he finally spoke.

"So what you are saying is that Uncle Sebastian can handle her, but apparently I can't. Thanks for the warning. I didn't need it though as I am already involved with a woman who just happens to be the love of my life, and I would never do anything to jeopardise that ever again. There is a problem though; she says she trusts me, but she really doesn't. I guess she never has, and never will. If you see her around, tell her I love her anyhow."

I grabbed his shirt as he tried to leave. "Tell her yourself because she is right here."

"Is she? I knew she was here last night and this morning, but now I'm having my doubts."

"I do trust you; it's her I don't trust."

"Okay then. I'll do my best to avoid her and all the other women who smile at me. Anything to keep you happy Em." He smiled glumly.

He walked over to the closet and took his wedding clothes out and started for the door. I asked him where he was going. He said he was going up to the house to shower and change.

"I thought your plan was to do that here?" I questioned.

"That was the original plan, but I think you need some time to yourself, so I'll give it to you." He said sadly opening the door.

"JOHNNY!"

He turned, puckered his eyebrows, smirked and said, "Yes."

The door across the hall opened. "What's going on over here?" Johanna demanded.

"Nothing Honey; your mother is just exercising her vocal chords."

"Can you do it a little quieter Mom? You two are worse than two love-sick teenagers. I hope you have your feelings all in check before the actual wedding march."

Johnny promised that we would and shut the door. "So, you want me to stay?"

I shook my head. "Yes; I never want you to ever leave me."

"Okay, I guess I can put up with your uncertainties about me for a little while longer."

"How long do you think you can do that for?"

"Until the twelve of never, but not one day more."

Half an hour later I was sitting on the bed in my bra and slip watching Johnny get dressed. I asked him to throw me the beige briefs in my top drawer. He held them up and said they didn't look like something I would wear.

"Well, I'm not the same girl that left here six years ago, and neither is my body. It's sagging here and there, and oh yeah, I had a baby..."

"Still looks and feels pretty damn good to me."

"Says the man who hasn't gained a pound in forty years. Do you still run?"

"Nope, gave that up when my partner left."

"I never ran Johnny. You have me mixed up with someone else."

"Don't think so."

"If you call me trying to keep up to your walking pace, then I guess one could call it running. Do you like the way I wear my hair?"

He said he did. I said I guessed Johanna didn't as she had me scheduled to have my hair done by the stylist so that I would be presentable.

He laughed. "Do or don't; either way you will be beautiful. Where's your dress?"

"In Johanna's room."

"Can I see it?"

"You can...when I meet you at the bottom of the stairs."

"Okay then, I'll see you in two hours." He kissed my forehead.

"Where are you going now?"

"To check on things one last time, mingle with the guests for a bit and then I'll get Joey ready."

"Don't get too personal."

"That goes double for you."

"And just who do you think I'd be getting friendly with?"

"James, Doc Black, Policeman Jim, the next-door neighbor, the best man... shall I go on?"

I threw a pillow at him.

Johanna and I walked arm and arm down the stairs at three forty as Johnny had requested. He and Joey were waiting at the bottom for us. The photographer must have snapped two dozen photos of us as we descended. Johnny stepped forward beaming with pride.

"We are the luckiest guys in the world Joey to have these two beautiful women on our arms. Your carriage awaits ladies. May we have the honor of escorting you?" Johnny said stepping in between our daughter and me. Jo offered her other arm to her brother.

I laughed. "Carriage...I can't imagine what you have in store."

Johnny walked us to the front door, opened it, stepped aside, and bowed slightly nodding towards the horse and buggy at the end of the walkway. Joey asked if it was for us. Johnny said it most definitely was and that he should go ahead. He ran down the steps bellowing in delight as he saw Amy in the front seat waiting for him.

"Shall we girls? Don't want to be late for the wedding now do we?"

"Oh Daddy; this is just like in my fairy-tale dream!" Jo exclaimed kissing her father.

"I know Honey, and it has always been my dream that your mother and I would walk you down the aisle." He laughed a little. "We just need some help getting there and luckily for us Justin Dover happened to be home for the weekend and offered up the family conveyance. He said it had been in storage much too long, and that his old friends' daughter's wedding seemed to be the perfect reason to resurrect it."

"We were hardy acquaintances, let alone friends Johnny." I quipped.

"It's not the day to cite differences Em."

"You're right. It's a lovely gesture on his part, but I'm pretty sure you were the driving force behind the whole thing."

He practically pushed me in the back next to Johanna saying we could talk about it later. He took his seat beside me and spoke with authority to Justin. "To the wedding venue if you please my good man."

"Right you are Sir, forward please Miss Polly. Hold on to your hats ladies as it's going to get a little bumpy when we hit the field." Justin cautioned. "It's a beautiful day for a wedding isn't it? Thank-you all so much for including me and my family in it."

I looked at Johnny curiously. He smiled, winked at me, and told Justin that it was our pleasure. I would thank him later wondering why I hadn't thought of inviting Amy's grandparents. Maybe Johanna had, but I had the feeling that it had all been Johnny.

He got out and escorted Joey and Amy alongside the wedding party as soon as Justin pulled up behind the bandstand. He cued up the band to start playing the wedding march and came back for JoJo and me. Justin asked if we thought Joey would like to accompany him and Amy when they returned Polly back to the stables after the ceremony. I laughed and asked him if he was kidding as Joey would like nothing better. Johnny and Jo concurred.

Everything went according to plan. I was so very happy for Johanna, and yet every time I looked at Johnny I couldn't help wishing that it was him and I saying "I do" again. I was so very proud of him. I knew our reunion was probably evident to everyone as it had been for my mother because love radiated from our eyes every time we looked at each other.

The day sped by quickly. Johnny and I mingled with all the wedding guests, sometimes together and sometimes singularly. We had been seated at the head table which was situated on the bandstand platform with Jo and Piers, his parents, the maid of honor, the best man, and of course Joey and Amy for the dinner hour. Afterwards I visited between the two tables that seated Betsy and Ada and the rest of the household staff. Their table was right beside AnnieZu's where my mother, my sisters, Sarge and Archie, James and Shelia sat, so conversation was shared. At seven the canned tranquil music was turned off and the band started playing. The best man announced that the bride and groom were about to have the first dance, and that the parents and family should join in afterward. I excused myself and went off to find Johnny who was deep in conversation with Justin and his parents. I asked if they would excuse us as we had to participate in the customary waltz. I sent Johnny in search of Joey and Amy telling him I would meet them all on the dance floor. I was halfway to the band shell when someone called my name. I recognised the voice so chose not to answer and kept walking.

"November," she called again. I kept walking. "Em, or is it Emmy?"

Damn it; where was Johnny?

"EM-I-LY!"

Well, that got my attention. I turned to face her. How the hell did she know about Emily?

"What are you doing here Lorraine? Johnny asked you not to come, but I see you chose to come anyhow and make a spectacle of yourself. You are not welcome here, so please leave." I turned around. She grabbed me by the shoulder.

"Not until you hear what I've come to say. Believe me, it's for your own good."

"All right if it will get you out of here. Please lower your voice."

"You need to take your rose-tinted glasses off, and once and for all see Johnathan for the man he really is. He's been gaslighting you from the get-go. He's a woman chaser, wife- cheating reprobate. He can't help himself; it's a disease. He'll break you in two again, so get out before he sends you back to the looney bin that he put you in."

"Is that a threat because I don't take well to threats. If Johnny cheated on you then that was your problem, not mine. You never were his wife anyhow were you? He couldn't bring himself to marry you when he was still in love with me. Funny thing: our divorce was never final, so it appears as if we are still married. Now, you can take your revolting accusations and stuff them where the sun doesn't shine you crazy bitch!"

"You'll live to regret your choice, and you won't come out on top. You are not strong enough to weather the storm of his infidelities again. You're an idiot; you and that bastard son of yours!"

I climbed the two steps up to the bandstand, turned around and hurled myself at her. We fell hard to the ground. She screamed obscenities at me. I matched her word for word. We rolled around, scratching and pulling each other's hair. In the distance I could hear voices yelling, and then suddenly there were hands tearing me away from her while others grabbed her and someone put her in a choke hold. She reached for me one last time and ripped the chain that had hidden my engagement and wedding rings off my neck and sent it flying. I watched in horror and then amazement as my mother caught them before they hit the ground. Johanna was crying. I heard Johnny calling my name. He arrived and took me in his arms and told some man I had never seen before to shut Lorraine up and escort her off the property. I told everyone I was all right and that only my dignity had been tarnished a little. I let him help me up, bowed to the crowd who were clapping, brushed myself off, and told him that I had to put in a request to the band for our dance. I encouraged others to join Johnny and me on the dance floor. I knew I was a mess as I could feel the upsweep that the hairdresser had given me coming undone. My beautiful dress was grass stained and ripped. Johnny asked me if I wanted to change and have our waltz later. He said he was worried that she had hurt me. I told him to hush and that I was perfectly fine, and to concentrate on the song. He held me away from him, and then asked me why I had requested such a sad song. I said that it seemed fitting. I danced away from him just as the songstress sang the last words to "Dance With Me One More Time." I kicked what was left of my shoes off and scurried down the steps and ran as fast as I could for the house. Zena called out to me asking if I was all right. I panted that I had to change my clothes. I was pretty sure that Johnny would come after me. I did not want to talk to him so I hid in AnnieZu's room. Sure enough he came in the house calling out my name as he bounded up the stairs. I heard doors opening and shutting, and him yelling as he descended asking me why I was hiding from him. I had hid in AnnieZu's room behind her dressing screen just in case he dared come in. I knew I was acting like a child, but I needed more time to decide what I was going to do. Another voice caught me off guard. It was my mother's.

"Is she here Johnathan?"

"No, she's not! I'm worried Zena; she might be hurt more than she would let on."

"I don't think she is hurt, but if she is we will find out sooner or later. Right now you need to go and comfort Joey because he thinks Lorraine hurt his mother and that you have taken her to the hospital."

"Who in the hell would tell him that..."

The door shut on the rest of his words. Oh god, how had I forgotten about Joey. I needed to get cleaned up and go comfort my son and to hell with Johnny.

In my room I washed and checked myself for cuts. Finding nothing substantial except for the scratch marks and the beginning of bruises I pulled on a pair of jeans and dolled them up with a frilly white blouse. I was sitting on the bed doing my sandals up when the door opened. He took the key from off my dresser and locked the door behind him.

"Why didn't you answer me before, and what the hell is up with that song you requested? What is wrong with you November? This was supposed to be one of the happiest days of our life, but you sure put a damper on that!"

"If you mean when I got into a fight with your girlfriend... well, I am not one bit sorry about that. No one calls my son a bastard!"

"Will you please start at the beginning and tell me everything she said and did?"

"I am sure someone has it all on their camera, so you can view it yourself."

"I already have, but the conversation is not clear."

"Conversation…you think we were conversing?" I laughed rudely.

"Sorry, I know it was she who accosted you. What happened next?"

"Have I not made it clear that I don't want to talk to you?"

"Yes, hostilely so, but if you think that I'm going to let some trivial run-in with Lorraine wipe out everything that we have accomplished in this past week then you don't know me the way I thought you did. I have the key, so start talking if you want your freedom."

"Suppose if that is what I want; my freedom from you?"

"Then you shall have it. I told you that I would do anything for you, but I need to know why you have done a complete reversal on your feelings for me. We were going to meet up on the bandstand and have our first dance in almost seven years, and then you did an about turn. What did she say to you? I need to know Em. I deserve an explanation."

I told myself to stay angry so I wouldn't cry. "I heard someone calling my name. I was about ten feet from the bandstand. I recognised her voice so I did not respond. She came up behind me and said "November" again. I didn't answer. 'Emmy, or Em, whatever you go by, stop, and listen to me." I took another step. "EMILY", she shouted. I could feel everyone's eyes on us, so I faced her and asked her what she was doing here. She said she'd come to keep me from destroying myself again, and that you were still deceiving me, and had been gaslighting me from the get-go. She seemed to take great delight in informing me of all your wrongdoings. She went on and on about your thirst for women, something along these lines. "Did you not learn anything in your six years of therapy? Did you not learn that he is poison to someone as delicate as you? You came back and he insinuated his cheating self back in your life with a thousand promises, didn't he? Take off the rose-colored glasses woman, and for once in your life see him for the lying cheat that he is. He's been unfaithful to you all your life, and you know it. Just ask me; I know all too well. He seems to take delight about reminiscing in great detail about all his past discretions. He can't help himself; it's a disease. The thing is, I'm strong enough to take the deceit, but you aren't. No one woman will ever satisfy that man, so get out while you can."

"I called her a crazy bitch and told her to take her trashy self off the property. She said she truly felt sorry for me and my bastard son. I climbed the steps to the bandstand, and without batting an eyelash, I turned and pounced on her. You know the rest."

"No, I don't. By the time I got to you the melee was over. James and your mother had pulled her off you while our daughter stood by mortified. As she was being led off the property, you bowed and apologised to the crowd who were applauding you. You told me that I shouldn't look so concerned because you weren't hurt. You took my hand and said it was time for our dance as if nothing had happened. You put in a request for a song, and we started dancing. It took me a minute to tune in to the lyrics. What the hell was I to make of that?"

"It was my second choice. Connie, the vocalist, thought that "Your Cheating Heart" wasn't suitable for a wedding celebration. I thought about asking her to sing "Crazy" because we all know that I *am*, so it was fitting. Your bitch of a girlfriend reminded me of that. But, then I thought a song about us having our last dance together was more fitting."

"Well, it wasn't and it isn't. Did it ever cross your mind that she was lying? Did you ever think of defending me against her accusations?"

"There wasn't any use; she believes what she believes, and maybe she is right. Maybe I've let myself be mesmerized by you and your lies again."

"Oh, for God's sake Em, listen to yourself. I'm the one who has been spellbound by you, and it all started when I was twelve years old. Nothing has ever changed, I love you, and I have not lied to you or cheated, not once in all the years we were married, not yesterday, not today, and I won't tomorrow. I am sorry you chose to believe her. When you come to your senses and want to apologise I'll be at the house waiting."

He walked to the door, unlocked it, replaced the key, and opened the door. "I am sorry for what she did to you, and for what she called Joey. You can bet she will pay for that. Good-night Em...don't let it be good-bye. Oh, and by the way, you need to find Joey and let him know that you are not hurt."

"I was on my way to do just that." I lamented as he closed the door.

Apologise; what did I have to apologise for? It was his nauseating non-wife who needed to apologise. Did he think that we were through discussing this? Just because I said I didn't want to talk to him didn't mean I wanted him to dismiss the accusations as hogwash. What did I want? Did I want him to beg me to forgive him for past indiscretions? I'd already done that before I married him. That was almost twenty years ago. Did I believe that he had cheated on me during our marriage? No, I did not... so why was I still here?

I found my old tennis shoes in the closet and a sweater and hoodie in a drawer. I thought that I'd better grab a flashlight because once I was halfway up Two Mile Hill I'd be without light from the street lamps. I pocketed the keys to my car just in case it wasn't hemmed in by other vehicles. First I had to track down Joey, and I guess say goodnight to the guests.

I sniffled as I walked by the rainbow waters that Johnny had magically re-erected for our daughter's wedding. I found Joey sitting between Zena and AnnieZu. He cried when he saw me. I comforted him and talked him into going to bed. He did not fight me. He asked me if she hurt me, and was I mad at Johnathan. I try to assure him that I wasn't hurt. I couldn't imagine how traumatized he must have been seeing his mother rolling around in the grass with his father's ex, and hearing everyone yelling. I told him that I wasn't angry with his father, but that I best go and tell him that as it certainly wasn't his fault, but he might be thinking it was. I asked him if he would be all right with Zena for a few hours. He said he would be and that I better find Johnathan. He fell asleep while I was telling him how much I loved him.

My mother was standing in the doorway. She nodded and put the chain with my rings in my hand and told me to go find the man I loved. I kissed her and told her that I loved her too.

I scrambled down the stairs, found that my car was indeed hemmed in, put myself in second gear, and lit out for the twenty-minute hike. The revel makers were still going strong. The low purring of a guitar and voices singing "Me and Bobby McGee", and "Country Roads" accompanied me up Bramble Road.

The Jurado homestead was the fourth house down on River Road. It was a large property surrounded on three sides by Arbutus and other billowy trees. The front yard that faced the street had a low growth of hedges. The whole thing was going to have to be fenced if Johnny made good on his promise to get Joey a dog, and I knew he would. Two houses past our house was the deep ravine where Bramble Creek meandered through. Look at me, calling it *our* house.

Johnny was sitting on the top step of the covered porch. He had a glass in his hand and a bottle sat at his side.

He said, "Hi Em, did you have a nice hike?"

"Thank-you, yes. Do you think you could get the mother of your children a glass of water?"

"That I can do." He rose, went into the house and returned with a bottle of water and a glass. "I haven't had the tap water tested yet, so we'll have to drink bottled until then. I suppose I had better contact a commercial water supplier."

I didn't think that I needed to respond. He took me by surprise a few minutes later when he asked if I had ever thought about ending my life when I was ill.

I answered honestly. "I suppose I did once or twice."

"Were you with me at the time?"

"No, it was when I was without you. I had believed that I would be cured after a few months, but that didn't happen, so I became even more depressed than I had been at home. So yes, I wanted to die, but then I found out that I was pregnant, and all those ugly thoughts went away."

"How do you think you would have done it?"

Where was this going I wondered. "Well, I wouldn't have slit my wrists because I'm not that patient or brave, and it's messy. I don't like guns, so I guess poison or an overdose of barbiturates, or maybe I would have filled my pockets with pebbles and walk into the ocean."

"Oh, the old Virginia Wolf trick?"

"It wasn't a trick because it worked."

"Well, I'm sick, so am wondering if three or four bottles of booze would do the trick. What do you think?" He said mournfully.

"I hadn't realized that you were sick. What is the nature of your illness?" I was pretty sure that it was just the alcohol talking.

"I'm love-sick Emmy. I've loved this girl since I was a boy of twelve. We had a few ups and downs in the early years, thanks to my stupidity, but we were always meant to be together, so we worked everything out. She left me for a while, but she came back, but it was short lived, and she is going to leave me again. Life means nothing to me without her. I can't take another heartbreak, so I'd just as soon end it all. Have you ever been in love like that Em?"

I got up, picked up the bottle of whisky and dumped it unto the lawn. "As a matter of fact I have. It's late and I'm tired, so I am going to bed."

I made a quick sweep of the cupboards and finding no more liquor bottles proceeded upstairs. I undressed and was standing naked in front of the closet when I heard him come up the stairs. He came in, drink still in his hand, leaned against the wall, crossed his arms, and asked me if I was looking for something.

I took his last shirt out and started to put it on. "I need to borrow another shirt as I don't have a nightgown and you know I always sleep with something on. We really should think about bringing our clothes here, don't you think?"

"So, you're staying then?" He asked optimistically.

"That's the plan." I answered positively and climbed into bed. "Are you going to stand there all night holding the wall up, or are you going to come to bed?"

"I suppose I had better brush my teeth." He put his drink down and started for the bathroom.

"While you're in there you should wash your mouth out with soap."

A few minutes later he came out, sat on the bed and took his socks and shoes off. He plumped a pillow up, set it against the headboard, and seated himself on top of the bedspread without saying a word. "I take it that you think I have a dirty mouth?"

"I take it that you don't want to sleep with me. Well, I am not going to walk another five miles back to Silvermist so you are going to have to drive me." I said making a move to get out of bed.

He reached for me. "Hold on; you're not going anywhere. This is your house, so if anyone is leaving it'll be me."

"I have another home to go to, but you don't...oh, unless you're going back to Lorraine?"

"I'm not crazy about your warped sense of humor. I have a few things I want to say to you and then you can decide if you want me to stay. First, let's talk about you. I noticed some ugly red welts on your shoulders and neck... are they battle wounds? Tell me truthfully please."

"I think I will have a few colorful bruises, but I don't have any pain. Okay, I'm a little sore, but I'm contributing it to the long walk. Petty, but I hope she is suffering more."

"I don't give a damn about her, only you. Tomorrow we are going to look at the video, and I hope to laugh about it. I know it wasn't funny at the time, and I doubt if you were even aware of everyone yelling and trying to break you two apart. Thirty-five years, and I just saw a side of you that I didn't know existed."

"Are you thinking that it was Emily, or that I am her now?" I asked fearing his answer.

"No, it was all you."

"So, what do you have a problem with?"

"I don't, but you may after I tell you what I've done." He looked at me gloomily.

"Did you have sex with another woman?" I asked mockingly.

He shook his head in disdain. "You know the answer to that ridiculous question."

"That is the only reason why I would have a problem, so go on, tell me what you've done."

"It's not so much as to what I have done, but what I have been asked and my responses. I've had quite the enlightening conversations with your ex and your therapist."

I closed my eyes. I'm sure the look I gave him cautioned him that he was treading on sacred ground. What was I afraid of? I had nothing to hide. I told him that he better make it quick because I was tired and wanted to go to sleep as that five-mile hike had really done me in. I sat up and braced myself for whatever he was about to reveal.

He laughed lightly. "Five miles eh? Your therapist is first on the list."

I put my hand up. He smirked and said, "Yes..."

"Am I allowed to interject?"

"If you find it necessary to do so."

"She is not my therapist anymore."

"Point taken. Anyhow, she waylaid me when I went to look for you after the melee. She asked who Emily was, and why did you seem to be perturbed when Lorraine called you that. Did you not discuss Emily with her?"

"Obviously not."

"So, you never told her that you have dual personalities?"

"No, because I don't."

"Who do you believe Emily is then Em?"

"Do you not have a name for the "other you"? You know like when you get angry and swear and slam doors, and then you say, "Sorry, I don't know who that guy is." Well, I named my other self, Emily. If something goes wrong, or if it's something I don't want to deal with I let Emily take the blame and face the consequences. That's it Johnny; that's all there is to it."

He nodded, but I don't think he understood. I asked him what he told her.

"I asked her if she liked being called Shiel. She said she didn't. I said that you didn't like being called Emily, so I guess Lorraine perturbed you by calling you that."

I laughed. "Oh yes, she perturbed me all right. And James..."

"I hadn't really met him before the wedding, so he introduced himself after dinner. He said he hoped that I understood about yours and his relationship. I told him I did, and that it made no difference in my feelings for you. He asked outright if I was still in love with you. I said I was, and he told me that I best do something about it as he knew that you still loved me. I told him that plans were already in motion for us to make a home for Joey together. I told him about the house. He was pleased and said that you were the best friend that he had ever had, and the best damn hostess in all of London. He wished us the best and asked me if I minded if he kept in touch with you. I told him that I didn't mind in the least. I thanked him for providing a home for you and Joey and looking after you. He said that it was his pleasure, and that Joey had been a delight, but that he was right where he belonged now. I had the funny feeling that he never really believed that Joey was his to begin with. Am I right about that?"

"Maybe, but he was a good father. Is that all; can you come to bed now?"

"Don't you want to hear about my chats with Doc Black and Justin?"

"I could care less, but if you have something to confess."

"I guess that I let them know in no uncertain terms that you were already taken."

I asked him to pass me my broken chain from the nightstand. I removed my rings from the chain and put them on again. "Yes, I am taken. These rings will never leave my hand ever again unless you give me cause to throw them in the ocean, or if I am making bread, of course."

Johnny shook his head and laughed. "I will never give you cause Em, and not just because I love you, but because I like you. I must have told you a million times that I love you, but have I ever told you how much I like you?"

"I'm not sure, but I like you too. It was "like" at first sight when I was ten and first ran into you in the creek, but I am all grown up now, so love kind of took over. Now, what do you want to do about it?"

"I have a few things in mind Mrs. Jurado. And, oh yeah, your sisters put a curse on Lorraine."

I laughed. "Good for them."

CHAPTER 10

Only Em

Em woke to find me staring at her. I said, "Good morning." She returned the greeting and then asked if we were going to talk about yesterday now that I was sober.

"It was a lovely day wasn't it?" I affirmed.

"So, are we just going to pretend that Lorraine didn't show up and tried to turn me against you with all her innuendoes?"

"I thought we took care of all that last night, but I guess we didn't."

"I am sure our so-called chick- fight has already hit the internet. I just hope that the dialogue isn't audible when she threatened to choke the fifin life out of me, and I replied that it was going to be pretty hard for her to do from her fifin grave which was where she was going to be when I finished with her."

"I didn't hear it on the video that Larry took. You didn't really say that did you?"

"Maybe; who's Larry and who is the man that you sent to escort her off the grounds?"

"Larry was the drummer, and Cliff was the man I hired to look out for her. He failed in that attempt; sorry. Did any of her lies ring true to you?"

"They stung, but not nearly as much as what she called Joey. She did not have the power to turn me against you; only you can do that."

"That is never going to happen. I'm going to take out a restraining order against her so that she can't come near you again. I have no qualms about taking her stuff to the garbage dump if she hasn't vacated the house. She needs to be gone. She was the biggest mistake of my life Em. I apologise for her behavior. Can you forgive me for my foolhardiness?"

"You have no control over someone else, or what they are thinking, or going to do Johnny. I am not afraid of her, but I do hope she stays out of our lives. I think you had genuine feelings for her at one time, so you asking for forgiveness is not necessary. Poor thing: she didn't know that the connection you and I have was never going to go away. Can you answer one thing for me though...what did she mean when she said that you have been gaslighting me all along? I'm afraid the meaning of the word is not clear at the moment."

"Do you, or did you ever feel that I was manipulating you, that I was controlling your sanity by sowing seeds of doubt in your mind, or that I made you feel inadequate?"

"No, only that other person in my troubled head did that. You were always honest and supporting. You aren't, and you never were demeaning. We know what caused my illness, so that word she accused you of has nothing to do with us. Can we be done with this now?"

"Yes, we can. You are absolutely right Mrs. Jurado; our feelings for each other will never go away. By the way, I accept your apology."

She kissed me. "If you are up to it, I would like to apologise again. I mean is there another woman who would hike five miles up a dark, deserted road at midnight for you?"

I laughed. "There is not. We have to get going though Hon because Joey is waiting for us." I got out of bed and presented her with a CD player and turned it on for her. "Listen to that while I get dressed and write you a check."

"What...oh Johnny; the Platters...it's been a long time since I heard Only You." A few tears escaped from her eyes.

"There is no one like you Em, no one in the whole world."

"Lucky for us that there isn't. Now, what's this about a cheque? Are you paying me for services rendered by any chance?"

"Honey, there wouldn't be enough room on a cheque to write an amount of what you mean to me...in and out of bed. Hell, not even in my secret bank account. I never carry cash so I just want you to have some spending money in case you need it before we get to the bank."

"Why would I need money? I'm going to be with you all the time, aren't I, and what's this about a secret account? Is it one you didn't want Lorraine knowing about?"

"No, nothing like that. We did not share bank accounts anyhow. I'll tell you all about it someday. But, just in case you need to pick up a loaf of bread or a quart of milk…"

"I'm going to make my own bread remember?"

"Yup, and I will believe that the same time I see you walk five miles."

She threw a pillow at me.

Our new life had strong roots. It was as if we had never been apart for all those years. I took a week off work so that we could put the house together. By the end of the week, the cupboards were stocked, and most of the furnishings had been purchased. There was also a new addition to the family. Her name was Bella. She was two years old. Joey picked her over all the other puppies and dogs at the first shelter that we had visited. He said he could tell that she had been waiting for him. He accepted full responsibility for her care, but asked Em if she would keep an eye on her while he was in kindergarten. I'd had a fence erected so there wouldn't be a possibility of her running out into the street and getting hit by a car. She was a medium sized spayed Lab- cross, house trained, and obedient on a leash. Her owner had to relinquish her when he became ill. Joey wanted to let him know that she had gone to a good home, so we made plans to take her for a visit to the care home he resided in. Em decided that she didn't want to come to work at the factory after all as she was having too much fun decorating and just being a mother and wife, and dog sitter. She was what she called "an old-fashioned gal with old fashioned tastes." Having spent so much time at AnnieZu's, she had a definite taste for antiques, and that included vintage furniture. She had yet to find the perfect dining room furnishings and was always on the hunt. We were getting by with an old table from AnnieZu's attic.

Suddenly, September turned into October. We'd had a lovely family Thanksgiving dinner at Silvermist. Johanna and Piers came over and spent a couple of nights with us. A week later we had a surprise visit from my parents. They had moved to Alberta before Em's and my troubles had begun to help Mom's sister Ruth run the farm after her husband had died. I had only seen them once in the last six years. They blamed our divorce on me because "of my roving eye". Em set them straight on that, and we ended up having a nice visit. Mom asked if Joey could come and stay with them next summer. I was pretty sure that was never going to happen.

Friday October 21ˢᵗ

"Is it time to get up already?" Em asked me sleepily.

"Why don't you stay in bed a little longer if you're tired? I'll get Joey up and make his breakfast and take him to school."

She asked me if it was Friday. I replied that it was.

"I have to go and pick up the drapes today, and Mr. March is expecting a new shipment of antiquated pieces, so I best get on with it."

"Can't it wait until tomorrow? I'm free all day and we can make a day of it in town."

"No, I don't want to wreck your days off. If I leave by nine, I'll still have lots of time to be home before Joey gets out of school."

"Have you already made arrangements with Harold to drive you?"

"No, but I will. How long have we been together Johnny?"

"Do you mean since we first met, or since we were first married?"

"No, I know that. I mean now, you know together, together?"

"Well Jo was married on the tenth of September, so since the ninth, if you mean it that way."

"About six weeks then?"

"I guess, take a day or two. Why?"

"I just wanted to know how far along I was."

"How far along...for what?"

"How many weeks I am into my pregnancy... that's all." She beamed.

Dazed, I asked if she was pregnant.

"I think that's what I said."

I walked over to the bed and took her in my arms. "How long; why didn't you tell me, are you sure? I didn't think it could ever happen again...I mean..."

"I just told you, maybe six weeks. No, I am not sure, and no one ever said you were sterile, so there was always a possibility. Had you never thought about us getting pregnant again? I did ask you if you would father a baby with me didn't I?'

I laughed heartily. "Yeah, you did, didn't you? Would you want another child? I mean, we're not young."

"I guess it entered my mind now and then. I never even considered birth control. Maybe because I didn't care one way or the other, and we're not that old Johnny?"

Joey was calling for his mother saying he couldn't find his running shoes and that Bella needed to go out. I told her we would talk about the baby thing later, kissed her and went to help Joey.

I got Joey his breakfast and set him up in his chair and table in the "other" room in front of the television where he always watched his cartoons in the morning. We had made the small room which had been my father's office into the TV room. It was kid and dog friendly. Em joined me ten minutes later sitting down at the kitchen table next to me. I put my newspaper down and poured her a cup of green tea from the carafe.

"What on earth is this?" She asked mystified making a sour face.

"DE caff green tea; just what you always drank when you were pregnant with Jo."

"Why do we even have it in the house? Thank-you, but I'm not there for sure yet." She got up and dumped it down the sink and poured herself a cup of coffee.

"Okay. Here, have a look. Out of curiosity I went online and found that Dr. Jean Lawry is still practicing. Would you want her to see you through another pregnancy?" I passed her the laptop.

"How interesting. Yes, I think I will give her a call. I think I'll pick up a pregnancy test kit first. At least that way I'll know."

"Are those things accurate?" I asked in doubt.

"I think so, but I'm not some little teenager who just had sex for the first time and has to know immediately, so it's not that important that I find out by peeing on a stick. I am, or I'm not, whatever." She answered nonchalantly. She got up, called Joey, gave him a kiss, told him to have fun, and said she'd see him after school.

"What about me Mommy, don't I warrant a kiss?" I cajoled.

"You're so needy." She said throwing her arms around me. "Now get a move on, and try not to have too much fun without me. By the way, did you keep my pots and pans?"

"Strange question, but yeah, I did; I kept everything. It's all in the kitchen or the shed out back at the house in town. Why do you want to know?"

"Do you remember seeing my red cast iron bean pot?"

"Yeah, I used it once, but the beans wouldn't cook."

"Did you soak them overnight?"

"Can't remember. Anyhow, it's in the broiler oven. Do you want me to go and pick it up?"

"No, I have lots of time. Anything I can get for you?"

"Yeah, shirts. I have this wife who likes them better than her own nighties." I handed her the phone. "Call Harold."

She started to punch in a number and shooed us out, running her hand through her hair. "See you tonight boys." She winked.

I blew her a kiss from the door and said, "Love you Babe."

First thing on my agenda was to move Nancy into her new office. I had prioritized it as her due date was only a few weeks away, and I wanted her where I could keep an eye on her. My foreman Ron and I were surveying the new lunchroom after we had settled her in when my cell rang. It was AnnieZu.

"Tell me November is with you Johnathan!" She demanded excitedly.

"No, she should be at home." I looked at my watch. It was three forty- five. "What's wrong?"

"She didn't pick Joey up from school. She's not answering her phone."

"Is Harold back?"

"Yes, he drove Betsy to pick Joey up. She brought him here because she isn't at the house."

I knew the answer, but I asked it anyway. "Didn't Harold drive her into the city today?"

"Was he supposed to?"

"Damn it! Did Betsy notice if the Buick was gone?" I knew the answer to that also.

I didn't hear her response because Nancy told me there was a Detective Ramsey on the phone asking for me. I told Zuzz that I would get back to her in a minute. I took the portable from Sally.

"Johnathan Jurado here. It's my wife isn't it? Please tell me she hasn't been in an accident?"

"Mr. Jurado, can you verify that you own a house at 2900 Park Avenue?"

"I own the house, yes. What's the problem Detective?"

"I have a very serious and sensitive situation here. I am not at all comfortable discussing it over the phone. A patrol car has been dispatched for you Sir. I trust you will comply."

"I'm not going anywhere until you answer my question...has Em been in an accident?"

"Mr. Jurado; I do not know who Em is. The situation here is serious ..."

I passed the phone to Ron. "To hell with the police car; I'll drive myself! Lord knows what trouble that girl has got herself into. Call AnnieZu back will you Nancy and tell her I'll phone as soon as I know anything."

I met the police car turning unto Commercial Drive as I exited. What could possibly be going on at my old house that involved Em? Just a minute, the detective said that he didn't know who Em was, so it wasn't about her. I took a deep breath feeling relieved. It was short lived as it suddenly dawned on me that no one called her Em except me. Damn it! The car was in her mother's name and any identification would be under Zenaida or November Queen. Damn.

I must have hit every red light possible before I turned off The Island Hiway. I turned unto Orchard. One more block before Park...Christ, my road looked like a bloody crime scene. I didn't even bother to count the police cars...hell, was that an ambulance? I was running the second my feet hit the pavement. I weaved my way in and out of yellow tape avoiding arms that were bent on stopping me. Several officers and my neighbour Jock were standing conversing in the back yard. Jock lowered his eyes and shook his head when he saw me. I tried stepping into the doorway which was barred by two burly cops. Through their bulk I could see something on the floor under what appeared to be a tarp.

I tried to push my way through them stating very sharply that it was my bloody house. A plain- clothed chap stepped forward extending his hand.

"Mr. Jurado, I'm Detective Court Ramsey, and this is Detective Steve Stewart. I am sorry to inform you that there has been a tragic accident..."

I cut him off. "Is that a body bag? Who is it covering up...is it my wife?" I approached the bag trepidation at every step. I didn't recognise my own voice.

"Sir, she has already been identified as your wife by your neighbour Jock Reynolds, so there is no need for you to see her this way. Let's have the coroner remove her, and you can visit her later." The detective said putting a hand on my shoulder as I kneeled down next to the bag.

I brushed him off and unzipped it. I had a moment of revulsion before zipping the bag back up. I straightened, cursed, and asked the detective what had happened here.

He looked at me questioningly. I knew he was waiting for some sort of reaction from me.

"That is not my wife; that is not Em." I said simply.

"That is not your wife Lorraine Jurado?"

"Her name is Lorraine Kelly. She is not my wife, nor ever was. So, that begs the question again... where is Em, and what has taken place here? Why have you tossed the house?" I started to wander over to the table where the red bean pot was lying by it on the floor. I bent to pick it up but was met with the forceful hands of Detective Stewart.

"Evidence Sir." Ramsey said. "Let's say you and I have a little chat? How is it that your neighbour says that Lorraine Kelly was your wife, yet you say she isn't? He said he hasn't seen either of you around for a while; yet, here she is today...dead it seems from a powerful blow to the head. Do you and Ms. Kelly not reside here Mr. Jurado, and who is this Em you keep referring to as your wife? What makes you think she was here?"

"That pot is Em's. I brought it from our old house. She wanted to make beans, so came down to get it. Apparently, she drove herself instead of asking Harold to drive her. I have no idea what Lorraine was doing here." I rambled.

He shook his head. "Thanks for clearing that up. If anything I am more confused than ever. I think there is a possibility that you are in shock Sir. I think we will continue this down at headquarters and let the CSU team get on with their job."

"I'm not going anywhere until I get some answers and see my son."

"I have no answers for you at the moment, but many questions, and until you answer them sufficiently, there is no way you are going to see your son. Now, is it headquarters or what?"

"May I make a phone call?"

"To your lawyer? You haven't been charged with anything Mr. Jurado."

"No, I need to call Silvermist and find out if anyone has heard from Em yet, and then talk to my son. He is only five. Em didn't pick him up from kindergarten today, so he'll be worried as we all are. Em is not supposed to drive..."

"Make your call Mr. Jurado." He said backing away.

Five minutes later I hung up. I asked Detective Ramsey if he had got the gist of the conversation. He said he had, asked me what Silvermist was, and who were AnnieZu and Zena. He nodded at my explanations, and then asked why we were all so worried about Em, and why wasn't she supposed to drive, and who the hell was Lorraine to me.

"Em not showing up to pick Joey up is reason enough to be concerned. She is not supposed to drive and we worry because she continues to do so, and she is not very good at it."

"Back to my original question; was Ms. Kelly living here, and what was your relationship?"

"We had been co-habiting for a couple of years. I asked her to move out last September. As far as I know she had, so I have no explanation as to why she was here."

"Was there bad blood between her and your wife Mr. Jurado? Is it possible that they had scheduled a tete-a-tete, and things got out of hand...and thus..." He pointed to the body bag.

I laughed. "Yeah sure; that's it." I said mockingly. "Em hated Lorraine, and vice-versa. She would never agree to meet her, not after what happened at our daughter's wedding. And, if you are suggesting that Em had a hand in Lorraine's demise then you are sorely wrong. Em is half her size."

"You keep volunteering all this information, but you are not explaining anything to my satisfaction. Now, what transpired between your lover and your wife at your daughter's wedding...is she yours and this Em's daughter?"

"Everyone calls her November. I am the only one who calls her Em or Emmy. Lorraine was not my lover per say as Em and I were divorced at the time we were involved."

"Oh Christ," Ramsey said rubbing his head, "I've stumbled onto the set of a soap opera." He turned to his partner. "Please tell me Steve that none of this is real? Tell me that this house hasn't been trashed, that there isn't a trail of blood on the floor and on the shovel, and that there isn't a corpse of a woman under that sheet?"

Steve shook his head. "Sorry Court; looks like a real crime to me. Is it okay if Rocky takes the body away?"

Ramsey looked at me for confirmation. Seemed like a good idea to me. An officer appeared at the door saying that Court needed to take a phone call from Sargent Manly. Ramsey growled asking what the hell he wanted and took the phone from him.

"Yeah Duke, what's up? I'm up to my knees in alligators right now... November Queen?"

"That's Em!" I jumped in. "Has she been found; is she all right?"

Ramsey raised his hand to silence me. "Yeah okay, we're on our way." He asked me if I knew where Lilac Lane was. I said that it was five blocks over and was it Em.

"All I know at the moment is that she may have put her car in the ditch. Come on; we're out of here. Hold the fort down Steve."

"That sounds like Em." Was all I could say.

The Buick's hood was up having come in contact with a pine tree. The back of the car had sufficient damage to it. It appeared as though it had been rammed. Ramsey and I both swore. We made our way past a police officer whom I assumed was Sargent Manly, and a bystander. The officer said he hadn't touched anything except an ID card, and then had radioed it in. He said that there were multiple footprints leading up from the car so we should approach it from the passenger side. Ramsey pulled a blue glove out of his pocket and picked up Em's phone through the open window. He asked me if I knew her password. I laughed, and told him that she didn't have one, and that he could just turn it on. It appeared as if she had been attempting to call me as my name and partial number popped up. It also blinked 12:15 p.m. That was almost four hours ago. There was dried blood on the steering wheel and door. My heart was racing. The officer called out to us that there was a witness to the accident. We scurried back up the incline. The bystander's name was Cliff. He himself had not witnessed anything, but Mrs. Carter had. She had been traumatized, called him and he in turn called her husband

George at work. He stayed with Mrs. Carter until Mr. Carter got home and then the two of them had come over to investigate. He said they had made sure no one else was in the car and then called the police.

"So, she was taken to the hospital then?" I asked before Ramsey could.

"That I do not know, but Sandra, Mrs. Carter might, as she is the one who saw it all go down from her living room window. She is eight months pregnant and is on bed rest."

"That house over there? Is that all you have to offer Cliff?" Ramsey asked.

"As I said before, I was not a witness."

"So, did she say what happened to the woman from the car? She couldn't have disappeared into thin air?"

"No, apparently the other car's passengers picked her up and drove off. They may have taken her to the hospital I guess. You best to ask Sandra."

"Let's go speak with Mrs. Carter, shall we Johnathan?"

I guess we were on a first name basis now. I followed him mumbling about it being a baby day.

George met us at the front door. Court asked him if he thought his wife was up to answering a few questions. He said that she definitely was as she was very worried about the woman in the car, and she hoped that we could set her mind at ease that the woman wasn't injured too badly.

Sandra Carter was indeed very pregnant. In seven or eight months, Em could look like that.

"Thank-you for seeing us Mrs. Carter. I am Detective Court Ramsey, and this is Johnathan Jurado. We believe that the woman in the car may be his wife. Can you tell us what you witnessed Ma'am?"

"Oh," she lamented, "I am so sorry Mr. Jurado." Tears were forming in her eyes.

I walked over to her and took her hands in mine. "Thank-you, but there may very well be nothing to worry about. I am sorry that you had to witness such an event, and just because it is her car doesn't mean to say that she was the one driving."

"Johnathan is right, but whoever it was, we hope that she has been taken to the hospital. Can you tell us everything you witnessed? Take your time; there is no hurry." Court said softly.

"Two seconds later and I would have missed it all, as I am not very speedy. I had just returned from the kitchen with a glass of water and was going to return to George's recliner." She smiled at her husband explaining that it was the only chair that she was comfortable in. "This is a very quiet street, so when I heard the squealing of tires I looked out to see a silver car streak by. A black older large vehicle was close behind. The first car swerved at the corner, and I think tried to correct the move, was hit by the other car, and careened into the ditch coming to rest up against the tree. Two men got out of the black car, pulled a woman out of the ditched car, put her in theirs and took off."

"It's a good distance from here to there, so I don't suppose you can describe any of them, but anything you have to add will be of assistance. Sometimes if you close your eyes, the scene may become a little clearer. Can you give it a try Sandra?" Court asked encouragingly.

"I don't have to close my eyes as the scene is all still very fresh. I have perfect eyesight, but George leaves me his binoculars so that I can watch the comings and goings of the bird population, so I had the sense to pick them up after the accident. I can tell you that the first three letters on the black car's licence were DJD. I could not make out the rest as the plate was bent. One man was of average build, light colored hair. He got in the driver's seat, yet he had got out on the passenger side. The other man was taller, maybe six feet seven, very bulky. He had longish dark hair. I did not get a good look at the third man as he stayed by the car standing behind the right open door of the back seat. He helped the woman into the back with him."

Court was impressed and told her so recording it all on his phone.

"For two months I have had to stay quiet and have become very bored at times. I'm sure that I have seen every movie that was ever made. Alfred Hitchcock has given me the most enjoyment. One movie in particular comes to mind...Rear Window starring James Stewart. I'm thankful that I didn't witness a murder. The accident was enough."

Court laughed. "I know the movie well. I would not think that a young woman such as you would be impressed with a 1950's thriller."

"It puts the suspense movies of today to shame. Now, about the young woman..." She turned her attention towards me. "I wish I had better news for you. I cannot tell you even if she was conscious as the two men were practically carrying her."

"Did you get a look at her?" I asked.

"Not really as her head was down, and her hair, which was dark, was covering her face. She was wearing a knee length blue skirt and boots that came up to the hemline. Next to the two men, she seemed quite petite. I don't know if this is good news or not for you Mr. Jurado."

I thanked her and said it sounded like my Em. I told her to have a healthy baby and excused myself. She asked if I would let her know if it was my wife and hoped that she had come to no harm. I smiled and said goodbye again.

George saw me to the door. I heard Ramsey thank her and say that he'd be in touch, and that he could be reached at any time at the numbers on his card if she thought of anything else. I headed down the street. He yelled at me asking where I was going. I told him I was going home.

He pulled the car up alongside of me, rolled the window down, and asked me if I was kidding. I told him he had no reason to detain me anymore.

"You crazy son of a bitch; I know just what you're thinking!"

"Oh yeah, so you're a mind reader on your days off are you?"

"Yeah, you're gonna do just what I would do...go home and wait for the kidnappers to call."

"Is that what you would do? Being a copper and all, I would think you'd call the cavalry first."

"I don't always do things by the books, but if it was my wife I would think it over seriously, relent, and get all the help I could. If we deduce that your wife has been kidnapped, you're gonna need some assistance, and that's what I'm here for. Will you just get in the car?"

"What makes you think she's been kidnapped?"

"Something went on in that house that you're not telling me...like what were those goons looking for? It sure as hell wasn't a casserole dish."

I corrected him and told him that it was a bean pot.

"I can't force you to come with me, but I would think you'd want to know if any hospital or clinic had admitted anyone who matched her description. I can get results a lot faster than you can. How about I check right now?"

"I already know the answer but go ahead."

"Who's the clairvoyant now?" He asked as he made a call to one of his soldiers.

"You can't find ten million dollars and believe that no one is ever going to come for it. You can't stuff it into a vault and believe that the owner is dead, and that no one will ever be the wiser. You can't get back the only woman you have ever loved and believe that you'll live happily ever after, and that evil will never cross your path again. Nope, not unless you're me."

"So, I'm not only looking at a murder and a kidnapping, but a heist of some sort also...is that what you are telling me Jurado? Ten million dollars; you got to be fuckin kidding me!"

I crossed in front of the car, and got in. "Wish I was."

"So, why did you tell me? You could just pick up the loot, wait for the call, deliver it, and hopefully get your wife back. No one would be the wiser."

Laughing I asked him if he thought I was dumber than I looked.

"Oh, there is nothing dumb about you Mr. Jurado. I would not be so foolish as to underestimate you or your plan to rescue your wife."

"I have no plan, but going out on a limb on my own I know would be a mistake. I'm pretty sure you would put a tail on me and know my every move. If I was lucky enough to have the whole thing go off without a hitch, your goons would arrive and screw things up. Am I right?"

"I would have placed a tail on you that is for sure, and I still might if it is warranted. I had a good look at your profile while I was waiting for you to arrive. You are an upright citizen with not even a parking infraction, so I don't understand how you came into contact with a suitcase of stolen money and not feel obligated to turn it in?"

"I discovered the suitcase wedged behind an old dresser that had been nailed to the wall. I was doing a remodel on that bedroom as my daughter was coming to live with me. I didn't have time to deal with the authorities at the time, so I deposited it in a safety deposit box, and promptly forgot about it. Actually, that is not true because just recently I mentioned by mistake to Em that I had a secret bank account and would tell her about it someday. How did you know the money was in a suitcase?"

"Lucky guess. So, are we partnering up on finding your wife?"

"We are because I have Joey to think about, and I am not about to let kidnappers get away with murder and abusing my wife for their greedy needs. I have never had to resort to violence before, but the way my blood is boiling right now, anything is possible. I will do the bargaining and let the law deal with the linguistics."

"Let's get a couple of uniforms to drive your car home. I'll radio for a crew to set up phone surveillance on your cell phone. Do you have a land line?"

"I doubt that Em will remember our house number, but she will my cell, and also AnnieZu's numbers, so I suppose we should have Silvermist monitored also. Are you going to be the top cop on this Detective Ramsey?"

"Call me Court. Would you believe that this was supposed to be my day off? It's my collar, and I wouldn't pass on it for a million dollars...oh, you have that amount in spades, right?"

I laughed. "Yeah, I do, but for all I know it could all be counterfeit."

"I doubt that, but I'll know the minute I see it. If it came from a bank it will probably be traceable. How long ago did you find the cache?"

"I don't know the exact date, but as I said it was just before my daughter came to live with me, so about three years ago. It would have been in late spring or early summer as she was here for the start of the new school year."

"So, you and your wife weren't together at the time?"

"Nope, we were divorced. Em took Johanna with her to live in England."

"How did that sit with you?"

"Not good, but Em was ill, so I did not protest."

"Now you are all back together, and all is well, right?"

"You have a sick sense of wellness if you think kidnapping falls into that category."

"Sorry; guess that came out all wrong. I'm not some smart alecky cop who is going to grill you about your personal life, but if you are up to confiding in me you'll find that I am a good listener, and whatever you tell me will remain confidential unless it is material to the case. You say that your wife was ill; is she fully recovered?"

"Physically, she is of good health, and I can only hope and pray that she wasn't injured when the suspect car drove her off the road. I am a little worried about her emotional and mental state of mind however."

"Is there a reason for that?"

"Let's just say that November Queen is a very complicated lady. As I said before, you might want to hand over the case to someone else."

"Most cases are predictable, but once in a while, one comes along that I can sink my teeth into, and there is no doubt in my mind that this one is going to be out of the ordinary. I'm hopeful that we will get your wife back without incident, but then there is still the matter of the murder, and the mysterious money, so no Johnathan, I am not surrendering the collar to anyone. The FBI will want to be involved, but hopefully the exchange will have taken place before they arrive. I suppose we should pick up the suitcase just in case the trade happens swiftly. I am not all that comfortable with having that amount of cash in my possession, and will have to take precautions, so will put in a call to Detective Stewart to meet us at the bank. You okay with that?"

"Whatever. I did mention that it's in U.S. currency didn't I?"

He turned and looked at me dumbfounded. "You're screwing with me right?"

"I'm not in the habit of joking, but now I wish I had of let you discover it for yourself."

"Thanks; now, what bank, and are there any more surprises that you'll be springing on me?"

I glanced at the dash clock. It was 5:33. "Banks closed; I guess you could get an order to have it opened, but it'll still be there tomorrow, and I need to get home to Joey."

"Yeah, let's do that. It's imperative we get the equipment set up in hopes that the abductors call. I'll drop you off and you can open the house for the technicians and designate where you want them to set up the equipment, grab your car and head over to see your son."

"They can have the whole bloody house. Nothing matters except getting Em home."

"I'm with you Buddy."

Betsy had the front door open before the car even came to a halt. I stepped out as she yelled. "He's here; he's here, Johnathan's here!"

The first one out the door was Joey. I caught him in full flight as he swung his little body into my arms. "Hey Cowboy, that's some welcome. I missed you too Son."

"Mom didn't pick me up Dad. Everyone's worried about her. How come she's not with you?"

"She had a little accident and is resting for a few days in the hospital. How about we go into the house so I can talk to everyone at the same time?"

"Yeah, okay Dad. Is she hurting like I did when I went to the hospital?"

"Nope, not so much. She's going to be just fine and doesn't want you to worry about her."

"Okay; I'll try not to."

Everyone was talking at once asking me what I knew. I put my hands up. "In a minute people, in a minute; first things first. Have you had your supper Joey?" He said he had. "Well I haven't and my tummy's rumbling. How about you go into the kitchen and help Betsy make me a sandwich? A big glass of milk and a tart would be nice too."

"You got it Dad. Come on Betsy. Should we make one for Mom too?"

"I'm pretty sure that she has already eaten Son."

Zena couldn't contain herself any longer. "Johnathan, tell us where she is right now!"

"For God's sake Zena wait until Joey's out of earshot!" Ada flashed Em's mother a dirty look.

"You all have a right to be concerned because at this moment in time I do not know where Em is. Shortly after you called me Zuzz, I got a call from a Detective Court Ramsey. He said there was a serious incident at my house on Park Avenue. I knew right away that Em was involved, but I figured she'd had an accident with the car. In all honesty I believed she had asked Harold to drive her into the city, and to the house. She wanted to pick up her old bean pot." I cleared my throat. "What I found at the house was not pretty."

There were gasps and crying.

"Hold on; I don't want you all to jump to conclusions. As far as I know Em is okay...but Lorraine isn't."

"What was she doing there? What are you saying Johnathan...no, it can't be." Zena moaned.

I sat down between her and Zuzz and took their hands. "Listen to me; Lorraine is dead, but I'm sure that Em had nothing to do with it. She was there as the bean pot was still there on the floor, and she may have very well witnessed Lorraine's demise. Nothing is clear at this point. Now I need to make this quick, so don't interrupt me. We found the Buick. It was in a ditch a few blocks away, and there was evidence that it had been deliberately run off the road. There was a witness. She saw Em being dragged out by two men and put into their car..."

"They took her to the hospital right?"

"No Zena, they did not. Detective Ramsey has checked all the clinics and hospitals. There is no sign of her. At this point it appears as if she has been abducted."

AnnieZu was on her feet. "Get me my phonebook Ada. I'll call my banker... whatever they want, we'll get it. We have to be ready Johnathan."

"I'm pretty sure I have what they want. Without going into great detail I will tell you that a few years back I uncovered a suitcase of money in the wall that I was remodeling. I put it in the bank and forgot about it. There were men at the house searching for the suitcase today; they are responsible for Lorraine's death I'm sure. Em must have got away, but didn't make it very far. This is all on me folks. I'm the reason Em is missing. You can hate me, but do not interfere in her rescue. The house phone up the hill and my cell is being set up to monitor calls. I've suggested that your phones here should be too, so you can expect visitors later on this evening. Now, if you'll excuse me I will say good night to my son before I head back to the house."

"Not so fast Johnathan. This is a horrible thing that has happened, but no one is going to blame you. There will be things to talk about after we have November home. We all know how much you love her, so I, for one will be right by your side."

"Thanks Zuzz."

"I will reserve judgement also, but I'm already ruing the day I gave you my blessings. Love may not be the rescuer here. I dreadfully fear for her state of mind." Zena said crossly.

"I am too Zena, I am too. I have no idea if we will receive a call tonight or not, but I will keep you informed. Hey Buddy, what took you so long?"

"Sorry Dad, but Betsy is real fussy."

I told him I had to take the sandwich to go because I was expecting a phone call from his mother. He asked me if I was coming back after I talked to her. I looked around at the family.

"You bet he is Joey, and if you are sleeping I'll make sure he wakes you up." Zuzz answered.

Ada and Joey walked me to the car. Ada said I wasn't to worry and that she would look after everyone. I asked her to call Sarge.

The night dragged on. Besides Court and his partner Steve Stewart, one technician was left to monitor the phones. His name was Donny Sloan. He was a funny little guy with horned rimmed glasses, smoked like a trooper so was always taking smoke breaks on the half- finished back veranda. He kept us entertained with his many humorous tales of his legitimate and sometimes not so legitimate phone conversations that he had been privy to. It didn't keep me from pacing from one room to the other. The clock was ticking ever so slowly. At 10:10, the phone rang.

His name was Daniel, and he had my wife, and I would get her back when I gave him what he wanted. Court's hands were on my shoulders every time I lost my cool. I was allowed to talk to Em, but it wasn't my sweet loving wife who came to the phone.

"I clicked the disconnect switch. Well, that's that." I asked Donny if I could bum a cancer stick from him. I lit it and walked out the glass doors and over to the bank that overlooked Silvermist. Court followed close behind me.

"That went pretty much the way I expected it would. November didn't sound too distressed..."

"You think so eh? Well, I can quit worrying about her because Emily is back."

"Yes, I noticed that Daniel called her Emily. Does she go by that sometimes?"

"Yes and no. Did I not mention that Em has multiple personalities?"

I could see that Court was stunned, but he quickly recovered. "You did not. Is this going to prove to be a big problem for her and you?"

"On the contrary; it might be beneficial. Em has assured me that Emily is dead and gone. However, when I asked to talk to Em, it was Emily who came to the phone. She calls me Johnathan, never Johnny. She did not say she loved me so that's how I know that she's back. She hates me and blames me for everything bad that has happened to Em. She first made an appearance, or so I thought when Em was sick. Two months ago I found out that she has been a part of Em for over thirty years. She says Emily doesn't exist, but the proof is in the pudding isn't it, and this may be the last I ever see of Em."

Court had a thousand questions, but I needed to get down the hill and fill the family in, so I told him that we would talk tomorrow. I said the house was his, but not Em's and my bedroom. He said that he and Steve were going back to Victoria, but that Donny had no one to go home to so would crash on one of the chesterfields and monitor the phone…just in case.

"See you at 9:30 at the bank." I called as I scooted down the bank to Silvermist.

"Jesus Christ Jurado; you're gonna kill yourself!"

The family was all assembled in the main living room. I told them what I thought they should know about my conversation with Em. I did not mention that she had taken on the persona of Emily again. I didn't think anyone knew about her DID except Johanna anyway whom I was about to phone from the privacy of Em's old bedroom. It was a very tearful conversation even though I tried my best to assure her that her mom would be home tomorrow. She said she was catching the earliest ferry that she could. I didn't even try and talk her out of coming because if anything went wrong I was going to need her. I hung up reluctantly and aroused Joey and brought him into bed with me. The next morning he told me that I was in trouble because I had slept in my clothes and Mom didn't like that, but he wouldn't tell her.

Everyone, including Sarge was already seated around the kitchen table enjoying Betsy's blackberry pancakes. I fixed one for Joey, but didn't feel like I could keep one down at the moment. I was on my second cup of coffee when the doorbell chimed. Joey jumped up and said he'd get it as he was expecting Amy. I doubted it was her as it was only 7:45 a.m. We all heard the door open and slam shut. I asked who was at the door. He said it was only that lady who looked like Mom. What? He sat back down and I went to see who he was talking about. He had shut the door on her. I opened it.

I threw my arms around her. "God, I'm glad to see you Summer!"

She laughed hugging me. "I'm very glad to see you too Johnny, but I am not Summer."

I held her away from me and looked into her pale hazel eyes. Someone laughed maliciously behind me. I turned to see Zena.

"That woman is no daughter of mine, but she is the frogspawn that sprung from my cheating husband's loins. Send her away before she infects the whole household with her lies. It wouldn't surprise me one bit to discover that she is behind November's kidnapping!"

"Kidnapping...what is she talking about Johnny?" This stranger at the door demanded.

"My name is Johnathan. I'm assuming you are Rachel, but what I don't know is why you are here?" I said confusedly.

"November invited me."

"I'm reasonably sure that she did not invite you. How did you get here?"

"I hired a hackney."

"Too bad you sent him away because now you are just going to have to call for another one. I have no time for this nonsense, so hopefully Betsy will give you a cup of coffee while you wait." I brushed her hand off my arm.

"Where are you going? I don't want to wait here with a house full of Zena's friends, so can I please go with you?"

"NO, you cannot! I don't know you from Adam, and maybe it is as Zena says."

"She doesn't know, but November and I became friends. She really did invite me." She begged me again to take her with me.

If anyone invited her, it would have been Emily.

AnnieZu, Sarge, Ada and Betsy had emerged from the kitchen and were all sizing her up.

"I'm going to find my wife. I would advise that you not be here when I return." I said sharply.

AnnieZu invited her in and told me that she would see that her sister didn't drop a house on her head. I wanted to laugh, but I couldn't. I stepped around everyone and asked Sarge if he could entertain Joey until I got back, gave my son a hug and a promise and slipped out the back door.

I found the two detectives sitting on a bench outside of the First National. Court passed me a Tim Horton's coffee. I thanked him and asked if he had his flask on him.

"Little early for that isn't it John?" he asked.

"Not if you awoke to what was waiting for me at the front door it isn't."

I had tried to dismiss the whole event from my mind on the drive into

Victoria as I was sure Rachel couldn't have any connection to Em's abduction regardless of what Zena had suggested. I gave the boys a brief rundown of my morning.

Court seemed suspicious of her sudden arrival and said that he'd do a search on her and her whereabouts over the last few days. I told him not to waste his time.

The suitcase looked exactly as it had three years ago. Court wanted me to open it so I did. He and Steve both whistled. Court removed a stack of bills and rifled through it, passed it to Steve and removed another stack. After he had scrutinized another seven or eight stacks, he shook his head and said, "Very interesting. We have another mystery on our hands Jurado."

CHAPTER 11

Emily, November and Em

I couldn't breathe. Why couldn't I see? Was something covering my face? I tried to lift my arms but was met with resistance. The pain radiated up to my shoulders. I yelped painfully. Two different voices...where were they coming from?

"Shut her up Billy!"

"She's panicking...I'm taking the bandana off; it's too tight."

"Leave it be you little shit!"

"Try calming her Billy."

A third voice, who were these people, where was I?

"I'm taking it off."

"Like hell you are! Stop the car Dan...I'll deal with her."

"I'll stop the car all right because this is your stop, and you're out of here!"

"This is no way near my stop asshole!"

I felt a hand on my shoulder. "I'm going to untie the bandana Miss November. You'll be all right in a minute. There, take some deep breaths. So sorry."

The harsh voice again. "We should have left her in that fucking house with the other one! She'll be the ruin of us, just you wait and see. Take her up the gully and dump her!"

"How do you think we'll recover the loot if we don't have her as a bargaining chip genius?"

Oh my God; that was the voice of the man who had tackled me and that gravel voice and face belonged to the man that had attacked Lorraine. Was she dead? They were going to kill me too as I was a witness. I screamed and tried to open the door demanding that they let me go. The door wouldn't budge. The young man who had removed the scarf tried to assure me that they weren't going to hurt me and that I should stay still as I might have a concussion and that Daniel would look after me when we got to the lodge. The lodge...where were they taking me and who in hell was Daniel?

The brute who had attacked Lorraine was laughing mockingly telling them that they were making a big mistake as he slammed the car door. "Mark my words Cassidy; you're going to regret this!"

"I already regret agreeing to include you. I doubt that your brother even knows what a psychopath you are. I don't want to see you or hear from you again!" The man sitting in the driver's seat cautioned. "We wouldn't be in this mess if it wasn't for your stupidity."

"How do you figure that?"

"Breaking and entering is one thing, but thanks to you, we're facing a murder rap you idiot!"

So, she was dead, and my fate was uncertain...wait, did he say that I was a bargaining chip...a bargaining chip for what? What had they been looking for in Johnny's house, and what was Lorraine doing there?

That brute had called the young man beside me Billy, and he seemed kind. I asked him what they were going to do to me.

He patted my hand. "Don't you worry none Miss November; we aren't going to hurt you. How much further Danny? Her head is bleeding again. I think we should take her to the hospital."

"Not much further buddy, she'll be all right. It's just a surface wound."

So, the driver's name was Danny. I suppose that was a tag for Daniel.

"He's the reason I'm bleeding, and my head and neck hurt." I said mournfully trying to gain Billy's sympathy.

"He didn't mean to hurt you Miss November."

I asked him how he knew my name. He said they had got my identity from my purse which they had found in my car. I closed my eyes and sat back and tried to sort out the events that had led me to be in a car with complete strangers who were probably going to kill me.

I remember parking on the curve on Park Avenue, Johnny's old home. He was going to put the property up for sale, but just hadn't got around to it. I had shut the car off but didn't bother taking the keys out of the ignition or locking it as I would only be a minute if the bean pot was where Johnny said it was. I found it and was turning to leave when I came face to face with a strange man. We both uttered exclamations of surprise. For a brief second I wondered if it was Jock, Johnny's neighbor. That idea was immediately dismissed when the man asked me who the hell I was and I realized he was way too young to be Jock. Instinctively I attempted to hit him with the bean pot. He caught my arm in mid –flight, and the pot went flying over his head. I had tried to escape into the living room, but he threw himself at me and we both went careening to the floor with him landing on top of me. I hit my head sharply on the corner of the doorway. There was a commotion to my left. The man swore and told me to stay put as he removed himself from me. I glanced towards the back door and saw Lorraine entering. I screamed out her name as a huge man came up behind her with a shovel in his hands. She started to say something. The brute brought the shovel heavily down on her shoulders, and then again on her head. I screamed again as she crumpled to the floor. A much younger man came out of the bedroom asking what was going on. He and the man who had attacked me cursed out the brute and bent down to examine Lorraine. I crawled as quietly as I could towards the front door. I righted myself. A wave of dizziness stopped me in my tracks. I fought it off and managed to release the dead bolt, opened the door and ran as fast as I could to my car. I started the engine, locked the doors, pulled a U-turn, and stepped on the gas as I saw the three of them in hot pursuit. Silly girl that I was, I had figured I could outrun them. Blood was streaming down my face and my shoulder hurt like hell. I must have hit my head and then my shoulder when I was tackled to the floor. I had only gone a few blocks before I saw them in the rear-view mirror. A sharp corner took me by surprise. I turned the steering wheel sharply, but it was too late. The other car careened into the back of the Buick. My hand instinctively tried to shield my face as a tree came up to greet me. And now, I was their prisoner, and I knew not what was in store for me. One thing to be thankful for perhaps was that the brute had been thrown out. The young man who had been called Billy appeared to be concerned for my well-being. I guess I would have to play on his empathies. I wondered what time it was. I had arrived at the house at 1:15. Lots of time to get home to pick Joey up...oh God. My thoughts were interrupted by the driver telling Billy that it was time to blindfold me again.

"Please don't." I cried. "I'll close my eyes. I promise I won't look."

The driver laughed. "Sure you will. Put the bandana on her Billy."

"Nope; she doesn't need it. I'll make sure she doesn't open her eyes 'til you say it's okay."

"Christ Billy, can't you ever do as you're told?"

"Not when I'm right and you're wrong."

The driver snickered.

I had absolutely no idea where we were anyhow. I thought we had been on the Island Hiway but couldn't be sure. It hurt too much to turn my head, so I could only see what was right in front of me. Now the road was rough, and we had slowed down to a crawl. The car came to a halt about twenty minutes later. Billy told me I could open my eyes. I did. In front of me was a very large building in what appeared to be a heavily treed forest. I guessed this was to be my prison.

Billy came around to help me out of the car. I shook my head and said I wasn't going. He told me I had to so Danny could fix me up. I refused again.

"Leave her then Billy. She ain't going anywhere."

"You can't leave her out here all alone."

"She'll be fine; I'll crack the window."

"Then I will stay with her. I'll go get some water and clean up her wound."

"You're exhausting my patience little brother. Go and get the door open."

"What are you going to do?"

No answer came from the man standing in front of me. I estimated him to be in his early thirties and about six feet tall. He was very brawny. He bent over me. I told him to stay away from me. He undid the seatbelt. I tried scooting across the seat, but his arms were around me and he pulled me towards the door. He stood me on my feet, threw me over his shoulder and carried me into the house. Billy was smiling as we passed by him. My wailing and resisting was all in vain. I was set down on a large chesterfield in an enormous room in front of heavily draped windows that appeared to run the length of the room.

Stupidly I asked where I was.

"It's your home for the next few days which all depends on how badly your husband wants you back Mrs. Jurado."

"I don't have a husband." I said pathetically.

He laughed. "Do you think we didn't do our homework? We know who you are November Queen Jurado, and we know where you live, and oh yeah, you have a little boy don't you. He's a cute little muffin isn't he Billy?"

"I'm going to be sick." I moaned.

"Take your little friend to the ladies' room Bill. We wouldn't want her puking all over her bed now would we?"

"Come on Miss November, I'll help you into the bathroom." Billy glared at his brother. "You don't have to be so crude Danny."

"I'm not here to win any popularity contests little brother."

"She's a lady, and you of all people should know what a lady looks like."

Where was I? This was no ordinary bathroom. There were four stalls and four sinks. The countertops and the floor seemed to be marble. I couldn't avoid looking at myself as the mirrors ran from one end to the other. I washed the dry blood off only to have my forehead start to bleed all over again. There was a huge lump under my right eye. I laughed envisioning it turning black and blue matching the lingering bruises from my frolic with Lorraine. Damn it; why had she been at the house? I ran my head under the cold water hoping to quench the pounding in my head. I pulled a plush towel off the rack, threw it to the floor, lowered myself, and laid my head on it. Billy was outside the door asking if I was all right. I didn't answer him. A few minutes later he said he was coming in.

"Oh, Miss November you scared me. Are you all right?"

"I'm just peachy thank you. My head hurts, I can't raise my arm, and my shoulder hurts like hell. I'll take two aspirins and I'll be fine in the morning. Do you have any aspirins?"

"Danny does. He has everything in his doctor's bag. He'll fix you up."

"Why would he have a doctor's bag? Did he steal it too?"

"No Ma'am; he's a doctor."

This was all so melodramatic. "Sure he is, and you're his assistant, right?"

"No, I'm not that smart Miss November."

"Help me up will you Billy? And by the way, I prefer to be called Emily."

The throbbing did not lessen at all when I laid my head on the pillows. I asked Billy where his brother was. He said he was on the phone.

"I suppose he is calling Johnathan and asking for my ransom?" I queried.

"No ma'am; he's talking to our mother."

"Is she in on this too?"

"What do you mean?"

"I have no idea what you were up to at Johnathan's house. It's obvious that you were looking for something, but I have no clue as to what it could possibly be. I'm assuming that it is something incriminating, to whom I do not know. Is your mother somehow involved?"

"I guess she is because she's the reason we need the money."

"Is she in trouble?"

"She's very sick, and..."

He was cut off from volunteering anything more as Daniel entered the room and told him to be very careful of what he was revealing.

"I didn't say anything Danny, just that mom was ill."

"And, that is too much information. Now, shall we talk Miss November?"

"She likes to be called Emily."

"Okay Emily; shall we talk?"

"I have nothing to say to you." I replied in my snarkiest voice.

"She's really hurting Danny. You have to do something for her."

"What is it you think I should do?"

"Give her some aspirin and work on her neck."

I glared at Billy. "I'll take the aspirin, but he's not touching me!"

Daniel got up, left the room and returned a minute later with a bottle of water, a glass, and a black bag. He opened the bottle, poured some in the glass, and passed it to me with some tablets. He said they were Tylenol and they may help with the pain. He instructed Billy to go to the kitchen and make me a cold pack. He looked at me and asked if he could examine my head and my neck. I told him he may not.

"Okay then, your choice, but you may have a concussion."

"Thanks to you." I snapped.

"I am sorry for the tackle and anything else that is causing you pain. There wasn't supposed to be anyone at the house. I'm afraid you were just in the wrong place at the wrong time."

"I had every right to be there, but you did not, and what about Lorraine? Was it her destiny to be brutally attacked in the house she once lived in?"

"That was an unfortunate blunder on Baron's part."

I laughed vulgarly. "Unfortunate, is that what you call it?"

"I am deeply sorry for the loss of your friend."

That did it. I propelled myself forward spewing my wrath at him. "She was NO FRIEND of mine! Don't ever make that mistake again!"

He grabbed hold of me as I collapsed in his arms. He lowered me back unto the sofa and gently manoeuvred me into a sitting position. He placed his hands firmly on my shoulders and told me to relax. There was an immediate ebbing of pain. His hands then travelled up and down my neck and my head. If this was what they called "the laying on of hands", then I was a believer. He assured me that I didn't have a concussion. I did not reply. I knew not who this man was, but I knew I didn't want him to take his hands off me. He asked me if he could do some light massage to my collarbone. I nodded as tears slid down my face. I was no stranger to emotional pain, but this physical pain was something I had never encountered before, so anything else he could do to relieve the agony was welcome.

Billy came in with a large plastic bag filled with ice. He smiled at me. "I told you that he had healing hands didn't I?"

"She needs to keep still so hold up on the talking for a bit. Put the ice pack back in the freezer for now okay. Hand me the warming lotion from my bag please. Go into the maroon suitcase in room 12 and get Emily something to replace her blouse as it is soaking wet."

Billy was hesitant. "You mean something of Sarah's?"

"Yes; there should be a nightshirt and dressing gown."

Okay, there was a mother, and now someone named Sarah. Who were these people? I knew I had been taken against my will, but Billy and Daniel did not fit the description of any kidnappers that I had ever read about or seen depicted anywhere. What was it that Johnathan had that they wanted? He wasn't rich, so it couldn't be money... so, what did they want from him?

"I'll turn away while you remove your blouse. You can pull the blanket up to cover yourself." Daniel instructed.

I unbuttoned it with my left hand, but I couldn't take it off. I told him so.

"It needs to come off so I can work on you, so try again."

"No, it hurts too much. You do it. You're a doctor, so I don't have anything you haven't seen before. Take the bra off too as it is adding to my discomfort."

"I'm not a doctor." He said.

"Billy says you are."

"That's because he has a hard time pronouncing physiotherapist, which is what I am. You're sure you all right with a complete stranger removing your clothes?"

"At this point I don't give a damn as long as I have some relief from the pain."

He said he wouldn't risk aggravating the shoulder so if the blouse wasn't a favorite could he cut it up the back so it would be easier to remove. I told him to go ahead. Billy returned and handed the clothes to his brother and was told to leave the room for a few minutes while I was made decent. I wanted to laugh. As quickly as the bra was removed I was covered up with the robe. I asked who it belonged to. I did not get an answer.

At first the discomfort was very intense from the manipulation, massage, or whatever it was called, and it brought renewed tears. The warmth of the lotion and his hands was very soothing. Gradually, the pain subsided, and I was told it was enough for now. I told him that my neck still hurt. He put his hands on the sides of my head again. I yielded, arching my head into his gentle, yet strong hands. A few minutes later he said that I needed to rest and let the Tylenol and ice do its' work. Billy returned with the ice pack and three more pillows. Daniel settled me until I told him that I was somewhat comfortable. He said I could put the nightgown on later. I didn't want them to leave so said that I was ready to talk.

"Later; right now I want you to rest. I'm going out to get us all something to eat. I hope you like fast food. Billy will be right outside the door if you need him." Daniel said as the two of them walked toward the door.

"Who are you guys anyhow?" I lamented not expecting an answer, and I didn't get one.

I fought sleep as long as I could, but it wasn't long before the mistress of the dream world visited me. It was dark; so very dark. A voice told me to get up and open the drapes. I did as I was told, and before me I saw a luxuriant bed of trees all laden with a covering of ice and snow. The sun came out and I could feel water running down my body as the icicles started to melt. A voice, a young man's voice from somewhere in the distance was calling me, but he didn't know my name and kept calling me Emily. I guess he didn't know that Emily was dead.

"I'm so sorry Emily; I should have checked on you sooner. I didn't know that the ice pack would leak so soon. Danny is going to be mad at me."

I shook the cobwebs from my head. I patted Billy's hand. "There is no reason for him to be angry with you Billy as all ice bags leak. Get me a towel, and he'll be no wiser. How long did I sleep for? I can see it is dark out but have no idea of the time."

"It is 9:30. I see you opened the curtains. Not much to see in the dark is there?"

"I don't remember opening the curtains. Maybe I did so in my sleep."

He laughed, and said he'd better get busy setting the table before Danny got back with the food. He asked me if I thought I would be able to sit on a chair at the table. Where had the table and chairs come from...they weren't here before. I asked him what this place was and how long had they been living here.

"Danny says it is an old hotel or hostel. I can't remember which. He found this place after something happened with him and Sarah. He said he had a plan to get mom back to Canada."

I was lost. I hoped I could get something more out of him before his brother came back. "Who is Sarah, and where is your mother?"

"They were going to get married. I never met her because I was with Mom in Tennessee."

What? The door opened and Daniel walked in with an armful of take-out bags. He said he hoped I liked strawberry and set a milkshake in front of me. He asked me if he could help me sit up. I nodded, and then he asked if I would like a chicken burger or a hamburger."

"I'm not very hungry, so maybe just a few fries. I don't think I could wrap my mouth around anything else." What was I saying? Was I really going to break bread with my abductors?

He flattened the chicken burger with the palm of his hand and cut it into four pieces and told me to try it now. No one spoke for what seemed an eternity. I don't know who was scrutinising who more...me, them, or them, me. I pushed my plate away having eaten more than I thought I could. I was about to thank them when Daniel asked me if I thought it was too late to phone my husband. It was 10 p.m. The question took me completely by surprise. He was asking my opinion. I stammered that he'd be worried, and no, it wasn't too late.

"Will you let him know that I am all right?" I asked hesitantly.

"You can tell him yourself." He dialed the number and gave me a quick wink, and a sly grin.

I was going to be able to talk to Johnny. I had better be very careful and talk to him as if I was Emily. He'd worry way too much about me if he knew I was Em. I could hear a phone ringing...had he turned it to speaker?"

He picked it up on the second ring. "Em, is that you honey?"

Oh God! I swallowed hard and held my breath. Play the game Em, play the game.

"Am I speaking to Johnathan Jurado?"

"You are, and I want to talk to my wife!" His voice was deep as black velvet.

"You will in due time, but what say we conduct a little business first? You want your wife back and I want the suitcase; so how about a trade?"

"Who am I talking to?"

"My name is Daniel."

"Daniel who?"

"That is all you need to know. Your cop friends sitting beside you can figure the rest out."

"They are not my friends and wouldn't even be involved if you hadn't decided to add fuel to the fire by killing an innocent woman, and if you harm one hair on Em's head..."

Daniel cut him off. "Yes, that was an unfortunate mistake on my cohorts' part. Am I to understand that she was a close personal friend of yours?"

He was baiting Johnny, and Johnny took the bait.

"You rotten son of a bitch!"

"I just call them as I see them. Now, back to the exchange...you have the goods?"

"How the hell could I; the damn bank is closed!"

"Well, we will talk when you get the goods out of the damn bank then...say at noon tomorrow?"

"I'll be here. Now let me speak to my wife."

"Please goes a long way." Daniel teased.

"Please, may I talk to Em?"

"Maybe she doesn't want to talk to you."

There was silence at the other end of the line. I visualized a police officer restraining Johnny.

Daniel hung up, waited a minute or so, redialed and handed me the cell, grinning. "Here's Emily, Mr. Jurado.

Well, now he would know. I grabbed the phone. "Hello Johnathan." I said calmly.

"Oh God Baby, are you all right?"

"I've been fed and watered and stitched up, so I'm all right."

"Stitched up...are you hurt?"

"I had a little fender bender, but was rescued, so not to worry."

"I saw your car Em; it's a wreck! Are you saying that your abductors rescued you? They are the ones that rammed your car!"

"Is Joey all right?"

"He misses his mother."

"What did you tell him?"

"I told him the truth. I said you had a little accident and were being looked after in the hospital for a day or so."

"Tell him his mother loves him."

"And, I love his mother."

"I'm sure she loves you too. Good night Johnathan."

Daniel was tapping his fingers to his chin when I handed him the phone. "Do you always talk about yourself in the third person Emily?"

"I don't know what you mean."

"I think you do. Why didn't you say that you loved him? Why did you say Joey's mother did?"

I glared at him. "Did it ever enter into your little pea brain that I'm mad at him? It's his fault that I'm here in the first place!"

Saturday 8 a.m.

"Emily, are you awake; breakfast is ready." It was Billy calling from outside the door.

Oh God; it wasn't a dream; I was still here... wherever *here* was. They were feeding me again. Is this really how abductions worked? Johnny would give them what they wanted and I'd be home tonight, so best just to play their strange little game. How had I got into this room anyhow? Oh yeah, after my rant on Daniel after the phone call, he had said good night and turned to leave the "viewing room" as Billy had named it. He changed his mind and turned back.

"On second thought, you'll be much more comfortable in a real bed. Bring her along to room 12 Billy." He'd ordered.

I told Billy that I was perfectly fine, but he persuaded me to go when he said that it was a nice room with a view as Danny had picked it out for Sarah. I asked him if she was going to be coming here soon. He said he didn't think so because he thought she might be dead. Well, that rattled my chain. Had Daniel killed his fiancé? Billy wouldn't answer any more questions, so I had to let it go for the time being. He asked me if I needed anything. I told him that I hadn't packed for an overnight trip so didn't have my toothbrush. He asked me if I liked Colgate or Crest best. I said that I didn't really have a preference. He left and returned a few minutes later with a new toothbrush in a plastic wrap and a travel sized tube of both Colgate and Crest. He said if I needed anything else he could get me whatever I wanted out of the machine. I took it that he meant a vending machine. He wished me a good night and left. A few minutes later when I was struggling to get the robe off came a knock on the door. It was Daniel asking me if I was comfortable. I told him I would be as soon as everyone left me alone. He had said "Sorry, just wondered if you needed another acupressure massage."

Oh yes I did, but I wasn't going to tell him so. I think I may have groaned because he said he was coming in. He told me to close my eyes if I was naked. I had asked him what good that was going to do. He said it would keep me from seeing him ogling me. I wanted to laugh at his impudence. He came right in and told me to use my unaffected arm to help the affected arm when

I was getting dressed or undressed. I told him that I knew that. He laughed a little and said that he was going to help me get to sleep. I rolled my eyes. He placed his hands on my breastbone, and applying light pressure lowered me unto the pillows. He told me that I probably had a cracked rib or two and that he'd work on them tomorrow. He massaged my neck and shoulder for a few minutes, said that should do and left.

I guess it worked as I had slept all night long. Now, I was going to open the door and see what was awaiting me. I had no idea where I was going but followed the fried bacon smell. It led me down the hallway and through a swinging door into a commercial-like kitchen. Daniel glanced at me over the newspaper he was reading. I asked him if my kidnapping had made front page. He lowered the paper and said that it hadn't. Billy pulled a chair out for me, brought me coffee and filled the plate in front of me with scrambled eggs, hash browns, bacon and toast. I told him that I didn't have much of an appetite. Daniel uttered like I could afford to put a few pounds on.

"I've never been accused of being too slim. In a few months from now I hope to have a legitimate excuse as to why I'm gaining weight... that is, if I live that long."

"I'm sure I don't know what you mean by any of that statement."

"You've assured me that I am going home, but you can't very well do that can you? I've been abducted and witnessed a murder...no, you'll have to silence me, and the only way can you do that is to hush me permanently isn't it?"

"What does she mean Danny?" Billy questioned his brother.

"I think the lady doesn't know what she is talking about." Daniel replied folding the newspaper up. He thanked Billy for the delicious breakfast and said he would be gone for a few hours, so I was his charge.

"At least I know I will be safe for another few hours then. "I quipped.

"You'll be safe with me Miss Emily; you can be sure of that." Billy asserted.

I stood up and looked him in the eye. "And, what are you going to do when your brother or his pal Brutus are leading me at gunpoint out to the woodshed?"

He genuinely appeared shocked at my suggestion and asked what I meant.

Daniel had the audacity to laugh. "She thinks we are going to murder her."

Billy was so mortified that he couldn't get any words out. He took my hand and shook his head in his brother's direction who answered nonchalantly.

"Nothing is going to happen to her Bill. She'll be safe in the arms of her family by this evening. I wouldn't have given her a two-hundred-dollar treatment if I was planning on "doing" her in now would I?"

I was not amused with his casualness. "Did you indulge Sarah in one of your therapy sessions before you killed her too?"

For a brief second I saw something in his eyes that was almost heart rendering, but it quickly turned to sharp denial. "Sarah IS not dead! Where did you get such a nonsensical idea from?"

Billy squirmed. "I may have said something."

"I'm sorry if I lead you to believe that Bill, but we had enough on our plates with mom's illness. I didn't want to add to your burden by you worrying about me. I never meant to mislead you into thinking that she was dead, but it was easier for me if you thought that then know the truth. It doesn't matter anymore. She's out of my life because she doesn't love me anymore. She gave me my engagement ring back. It really is for the best, and I am over the whole thing. I can concentrate on keeping you safe and getting mom home. It's all good Bud; there's nothing to worry about."

The two brothers hugged. Billy said he was sorry and promised he wouldn't jump to conclusions anymore. Then he asked what was going to happen to me.

"It's like I said; I'll make arrangements with her husband for the exchange later, and she'll be home before bedtime." Daniel smiled at me over his brother's shoulder. "Okay; now I have to be out of here if this plan is going to have any chance of succeeding. Why don't you bring in some wood and we can have a fire tonight and watch one of your new movies?"

"After you get the money, and Emily is home right?"

"Let's just see how things go okay. The swap hasn't been confirmed yet."

"You said she'd be home by bedtime."

"And, that is the plan. I want her back with her family just as much as you do. None of this should have happened." Daniel said dolefully.

A tear stung my eye, but I would not let it fall. I murmured that they could lock me into the other room like before so Billy wouldn't have to worry about me trying to escape.

"The door was never locked Emily. If you're bored, perhaps you could help Billy by cleaning up the kitchen."

The two brothers, my captors, walked out the front door joshing each other. Why did I not feel threatened anymore? Had I ever really? What was wrong with me? I wanted to go home. Maybe if I kept busy I could think better. I scraped the leftover breakfast off the plates. Very nice plates they were. This must have been a classy hotel at one time...so, what happened to it? I put the dishes into hot water in the sink and poured dish soap over them. Bubbles erupted from the foam and danced around. I was mesmerized as they danced and burst as they collided with each other. Somehow they reminded me of the bubbles in the champagne the night I confessed to Johnny how I first became aware of Emily. I was awakened from my child-like stupor by a familiar noise. It was the ringing of a phone. I looked around. Daniel must have left his cell behind. Where was it? I followed the buzzing down the hall afraid that it would stop and I wouldn't find it in time. How many rings was that...four or five? Behind that door, it was ringing behind that door. I knew it was Daniel's room the moment I entered. Where was the phone? There was a book on the bed and it was vibrating. I grabbed it. My heart was pounding.

"Hello." I said hoping it wasn't the brute looking for Daniel.

Silence. I said "Hello" again. A hesitant little voice asked if I was Mrs. Cassidy.

Cassidy...Cassidy, where had I heard that name before? Silly, Cassidy is the name of AnnieZu's cat. No, it was something else. I heard the brute's voice; "Mark my words Cassidy; you're going to regret it!"

My intuition kicked in. She thought I was Billy and Daniel's mother. "Are you looking for Daniel, Sarah?"

Silence again. "Talk to me Sarah." I encouraged.

"How do you know my name?"

"Daniel has mentioned you a time or two. You were engaged to him weren't you Sarah? It's a good thing you found out in time that you didn't love him isn't it? I was once engaged to someone I didn't love also..."

"It wasn't like that."

"He said it was."

"Who are you? Are you his new girlfriend?" She asked tentatively.

I laughed. "I hardly know him. I'm more a friend of Billy's."

"I never got the chance to meet him. Danny said he's very special."

"He is. You were going to come here weren't you? What went wrong?"

"Where are you?"

I laughed again. "I have no idea. I was brought here under great protest."

"What do you mean, and who are you anyway answering Danny's phone?"

"My name is November. Daniel asked me to man the phones while he was out."

"November...I've never heard that name before. It's pretty."

Well that solved that; she hadn't heard of my abduction. How could I explain where I was anyway even if I asked her to call the police or Johnny?

"I think the battery is low Sarah. Should I tell Daniel to call you back?"

"No!"

"Then why did you call him?

"I wanted to hear his voice one last time. I thought I would get his answering machine."

"One last time...are you going somewhere?"

"Yes, somewhere where I may never come back from."

"Why?"

"Because there is no second go rounds in life."

"Are you ill Sarah?" I had the feeling that she was.

She didn't answer. "I was very ill once too."

"With what?"

"I was sick in the head. I couldn't differentiate truth from falsehoods. I made my husband divorce me because I was sure he had been unfaithful. I spent six years in and out of a wellness clinic...just a polite way of saying the "looney bin". I was finally diagnosed with a chemical imbalance and am now back with the man I love...well, almost. But, if you still care for Daniel I am sure he will stand by you no matter your malady."

"He can never know. I would never subject him to such a dilemma."

"Is there a problem?"

"I could never put him in the position of having to choose between me and his mother."

"Now I am really confused. Why would he have to choose; doesn't she like you?"

"Oh, if it was only that simple."

I heard what sounded like someone being paged. I asked Sarah where she was. The phone was beeping "low power" when she hung up. Damn it. I might have just enough power to call her back if her number registered on the display screen. I was just about to redial when it rang again.

"Sarah?" I asked hopefully.

"I'm sorry I hung up. I am sure you mean well, being a friend of Billy's and all, but the matter is out of anyone's hands. I beg of you not to tell Danny that I called."

This time I definitely heard someone being paged. It was for a Dr. Drake.

"Are you in the hospital Sarah?"

If she answered I never heard her because the phone blinked off. Now what? Was I going to tell Daniel that she had called? Why...it really wasn't any of my business. He would probably be dead or arrested this evening, so why bother? I could stop all of that from happening if I wanted to. How, and did I want to? Did I want to help him and Billy? It would help if I knew what ailment Sarah and Mrs. Cassidy were afflicted with. They couldn't both have the same problem could they? Why would it be a quandary for Daniel? He was really a decent person, and Billy...I didn't want any harm to come to either of them. How could I feel anything about them after just one day, and hadn't I been abducted? Oh God, is it possible that I have Stockholm Syndrome?

I put the phone back under the book that was titled "Simple Solutions for Recovering from a Broken Heart." I laughed out loud at the author, "There ain't no easy way Justin Stewart!"

I finished in the kitchen and went to get dressed. My blouse was useless. I borrowed one and a sweater from Sarah. I was sure she wouldn't mind. Now it was time to go out to the woodpile and get some answers from Billy about his mother, and anything else that involved this caper.

I helped him unload the cut logs from the wheelbarrow into the foyer that led into a nice cozy living room. I watched him lay the fireplace for lighting later. I told him that I needed to exercise my legs and could we go for a little walk. He said he had discovered a spot not far away where a little creek ran along side of a meadow and a mother deer and her two fawns would come to drink. It was a ten-minute walk down a path through the woods. I asked him if he was worried about me trying to escape. He said no, and that I would probably get lost because he didn't even know where we were. I asked him how long he had been here.

"Danny brought me here after I got back from Tennessee about a week ago. He said that this would be our headquarters."

"Headquarters for what Billy?"

"You know, for getting the money so that we could bring mom home."

"Why do you need so much money to bring her home?"

"Because she is sick."

"Yes, I get that, but why so much? It can't be that expensive to fly her home."

"She can't come by herself."

"So, why didn't she come back with you?"

"Because she has to come on a special plane with a nurse and all."

"Do you mean an air ambulance flight?"

"I think so."

"So, she is really ill?"

"Yup; she needs a new kidney and Danny and me are going to give her one of ours"

So, this is what it was all about, and they didn't have the money to fly her home or for the transplant. I asked Billy if his mother was still a Canadian citizen. He said she was as she lived here for six months of the year and then went south for six months. Good, then her hospital bills would be paid. I told Billy that. He said he knew that but it was her care afterwards which was going to be expensive. I asked him if Daniel had a private practice. He said he used to but wasn't working anymore. I wondered why because surely a physiotherapist's salary was substantial. I took a shot.

"How long ago did Sarah break off the engagement?"

"A while ago."

"And, Daniel hasn't worked since then?"

"I don't think so. We better head back now."

"But we haven't seen the deer yet."

"I guess it's too early."

Daniel's car was in the drive. Billy ran ahead of me and into the house. I looked around a little dumbfounded. Yeah, they were seasoned kidnappers. The keys to the car were probably in it too with a map of how to get out of here. I caught the tail end of the brothers' conversation when I opened the door; something about not having to worry about "him" ever again. Oh good, another hint at something ominous. What has Daniel done now?

Billy said "good" and asked his brother if he had got everything.

"Don't worry little brother; everything you asked for is on the counter."

Billy started to unpack the grocery bags. He seemed pleased with the purchases and said that he worked best if no one was watching. I asked him what he was planning.

"I want to make a special dinner for you tonight because I will never see you again. It's simple, but Daniel says it is the best he has ever eaten."

"Whatever it is, I'm sure it will be delicious, just like breakfast was." I don't know why I said it but I did. "Maybe Johnathan hasn't got the "money", or whatever it is that you were looking for at the house, so maybe I will be here a little while longer."

Billy smiled, but Daniel put a stop to that. "I've already talked to Mr. Jurado, and he has the suitcase, so I am pretty sure she'll be gone this evening."

"And, how is that going to work? Do you really think that he will be the only one showing up for the exchange? The FBI is probably involved. There will be sharpshooters everywhere trying to get a shot at you... and Billy. Are you going to be wearing bullet proof clothing? Will you be armed? Will you hold me hostage, and is my husband's life in danger?"

"I do not have everything figured out yet and that is why I told your husband that I would call him later in the day. Billy will not be with me, and no, I will not be holding a gun to your head, and Johnathan's life is not in danger from me. It will go down without a hitch."

"You really believe they are going to let you get away with a stolen bag of money?"

"Who said the money was stolen?"

"Well, I just assumed...why else would it be hidden away, and why did you put it in Johnny's house anyway and leave it there?"

"I think it's time that I told you about our Uncle Malcolm. We'll leave you to your creations Bill. If you get a moment I could use a cup of strong coffee." Daniel said casually.

"I'm going to need something a lot stronger than coffee? Where do you keep the good stuff?"

"Sorry Emily, but if you're asking about alcoholic spirits, you will find none on the premises unless maybe one of the ladies left some behind in her boudoir from the good ole days."

Good God, what was he saying, and did I really want to know? Damn right I did!

"You don't imbibe?"

"No Ma'am; gave it up when I met Sarah."

"She was against it, or were you a wino?"

"She was three years clean, so it was only common sense."

"This is all starting to make sense now."

Daniel led the way into the "viewing room". He pulled two chairs up to the window, and offered me my choice. It didn't matter where one sat because the view was fantastic. There were rows and rows of trees in lines of perfect symmetry. They were all dressed in their very best autumn colors. Here and there below their canopy I could make out a few red roofed houses with smoke spiralling upwards out of their chimneys. A narrow roadway led down to a shoreline. A few sailboats and fishing boats dotted the waterways. It was all very far away. I asked Daniel where we were.

He laughed. "Would you believe that I have no idea? I know how to get here from the highway, but I can't say I know exactly where we are. I'm sure that little hamlet down there has a name, but I haven't been able to match the geography up. Crazy eh, and what do you mean when you say that it is all starting to make sense now?"

"I will tell you later. You know people throw that word *"crazy"* around a lot, but if you haven't been to hell and back, then you don't know crazy. Until you spend six years in some hokey specialized clinic being probed, dissected, and drugged, and circumstances have made you leave the man you love, you don't know crazy."

"Are you referring to yourself Emily?"

"Emily is the one who drove me there. She convinced me that Johnny was cheating on me. She made me mistrust him and she talked me into divorcing him and running off to London. She was supposed to protect me, but she betrayed me, so I left her in London. She is dead to me. My name is November, and you may call me that, or Em, or Emmy. I only said I was Emily so Johnny wouldn't worry about me. He thinks she is the strong one and that Em is the weak one."

"He's wrong."

"Do you understand that there used to be another person living inside of me? There are clinical words for it, but I just believe that it was me when I was scared or unhappy." I got up and stood at the window because I didn't want to see pity in his eyes. "I have absolutely no idea why I told you all that as I never talk about it except with Johnny."

"I do. I think you needed to unload to someone, anyone who is not your therapist or husband."

"My therapists don't know."

"I don't see how that is possible. Come back and sit down and let's talk." Daniel sounded so much like Johnny that it was uncanny. That must be the reason I was not afraid of him.

"I don't want to talk anymore about me; I want to hear your story."

"And, you will, but first I want to know a little bit more about you and your six years in exile."

"That's' a very good word for it. I wasn't locked up in a mental ward. I could come and go as I pleased, and I pleased not to be there most of the time. It was a wellness clinic that was owned and run by a friend of my mother's. Her name is Dr. Shelia Dickens. She had a brother who was a big supporter of the clinic. His name is James, and I married him two weeks after my divorce from Johnny became final. I did not love James, and except for a couple of times we did not have a physical relationship. Neither of us was interested. I only married him because he had money and an excellent medical plan that could fund my therapy. I was not a good patient and was not co-operative. I refused all medications which turned out to be a good thing because I was pregnant. I did not discover this myself, but one of my routine tests did. It was December the first, and I was three months along. I was devastated as

Johnny and I had been trying to have another baby for years. Now here I was pregnant by another man who was basically a stranger. Joey was born June 2nd, 2011. James was good to us, and I in turn played hostess to his many diplomatic dinners with foreign dignitaries. It was probably Emily because that kind of socializing is not my cup of tea." I sat down and asked him if he wanted me to go on.

He laughed a little. "Oh yes, Miss November; I want to hear everything."

"Well, there's not enough time for that, so I will shorten the saga. By the time Joey was four years old, I was pretty much back to my normal self, whatever that was. One day I looked at my son and realized that I was looking at his father. I had a maternity test. James was not Joey's father, so that meant Johnny was. I started a new round of therapy the next day."

"Oh Christ; you have to be kidding?"

"Nope. I had no idea how I was going to tell Johnny, or anyone for that matter. I needn't have worried because as soon as my family here saw Joey they knew. If my mother did when we were in England she never said so. I played games with Johnny for a while, and I guess he did with me too, but everything is out in the open now and we are back together and happy."

"Why the hell did you have to be at the house yesterday? None of this should have happened. It's over now; I'm taking you home right now." Daniel was on his feet.

"Oh, so you are just going to walk me up to my door and hand me over to Johnny and a house full of cops?"

"Something like that."

"This was all supposed to happen Danny. It's my belief that everything happens for a reason. It's not quite clear what that reason is just yet, but..." Suddenly I had a jarring pain in my ribcage. Through labored breath I told him I couldn't breathe.

He got up and told me to lean forward.

"I can't; it hurts too much."

He pushed on my back with such force that I yelped. Billy came running in and asked what was going on. Daniel said he was realigning me as my ribs were cutting off my breathing. Billy said okay and were we ready for coffee. I just wanted to die.

"Breathe November, deep breaths…that's a girl." Danny said soothingly.

"I was fine this morning, and I haven't done anything, so why does it hurt so much now?"

"Well, you may have overexerted yourself helping Billy with the wood and the walk, and all this talking has distressed you, so it all took its toll."

"I'm not distressed."

"I beg to differ."

Fifteen minutes or so later some of the pain had relinquished thanks to his expertise, and I could breathe again. Daniel suggested that I lie down for a while. He walked me into the bedroom, propped me up with several pillows, called Billy to bring an ice pack, placed it on my back, and turned to leave. I asked him where he was going. He said he was going to phone Johnathan and tell him that he was bringing me home.

"Not yet. Bring me a cup of coffee and tell me a story."

"You're a little bossy you know."

"Please." I added. "Just think of me as your older, wiser sister."

"I never had a sister."

"And, I never had a brother." I said as I offered up my pinky finger. He wrapped his around mine, and the pact was made.

A few minutes later I was drinking a cup of delicious mocha coffee. Danny said that Billy must have thought it was my favorite because it sure as hell wasn't his. I laughed and told him that it would grow on him just as I had, and as they had me, and I was ready to be entertained.

"All right, I'll see if I can do that. Three weeks ago I had a thriving practice, was engaged to the love of my life, and was the happiest I had ever been. Fast forward two weeks. Billy phones me from Tennessee and tells me how sick Mom is. I tell Sarah and a day later she gives me my ring back. Her only explanation was that she had made a mistake and that it wasn't love after all, and that my mother needed all my attention. We were in a restaurant. She left to go to the ladies' room and never came back. She wouldn't answer her phone so I went looking for her. A neighbor of hers told me that she had left town, so that was that. I decided to take her advice and concentrate on bringing mom home. I found out how much it was going to cost to air vac her home. It was a hell of a lot more than I had, and apparently her insurance wouldn't cover it. I decided to go and visit Uncle Malcolm and see how flush he was."

"Where does your uncle live?" I asked.

"He has a one bedroom in a little apartment in Seattle."

"What does he do there?"

"He works in the laundry when he's not confined to his room behind bars."

"You're very funny Daniel."

"Sorry, but it's the truth. This is about the fifth government facility that has welcomed him that I know of. Anyhow, I thought that he might have some dough stashed somewhere and wouldn't mind helping out the sister who had been bailing him out of jail since he was fifteen. I struck gold because he had money in spades."

"The money at Johnny's house; where did he get it?"

"Well, not where you might think. I told him I didn't want anything to do with dirty money and that I would find another way. He told me that it wasn't dirty, and that it was hard earned money. I asked how and how much. He said and I quote: "Remember that hotel that Bailey, Racoon and I invested in? It turned out to be a very lucrative business to the tune of four hundred rocks."

"What's a rock?" I asked.

"It's slang for a million."

"So, there was four million dollars hiding in the house? How did it get there, and what was the business that your uncle was in?"

"Do you just want to go on asking questions, or would you rather I continue?"

"Sorry, I have a million questions."

"Well, I trump you as I might have millions in moolah, so hold the questions, or we will be here all night. This "hotel" here was built and designated to be a bomb shelter by some government agency, defense probably. The walls are probably built of three-foot rebar. It was during the cold war, sometime in the fifties. Many years later it was still unfinished and was abandoned. Fast forward to nineteen seventy-eight and it comes up for sale. Some entrepreneur from Los Angeles gets wind of it and buys it planning on making it a tourist mecca for Americans looking for peace and quiet. The rooms which were once offices I guess needed to be converted into bedrooms, so that is where Malcolm comes in. He and his friend Bailey answer an ad in the newspaper that is looking for carpenters. They figure they can be carpenters, and call in another buddy Raccoon, and yes before you ask, he looks like one. They are given carte blanch, and the owner goes back to LA. He pops in occasionally and is pleased with the progress and decides to put in a landing strip for small planes. Now, the boys have been thinking, and they lay their plan on Mr. X. Hotels for tourists are plentiful in this little part of paradise, but what would really pull in the bucks would be a private gambling hall for heavy rollers without the tax man breathing down their necks. A flight to beautiful Vancouver Island to an all- inclusive secluded secure hotel, pretty women, and gaming round the clock...what did he think. He liked it, and so Nevada North was born."

"I wondered what the NN stood for on the towels. What kind of gaming?"

"Every kind you can think of except slot machines. Table games like high stake poker were probably the main event followed by sports betting, craps and roulette." Daniel laughed. "That reminds me, Malcolm asked me to look for the roulette wheel. Apparently, a guest lost a bundle on it and picked it up and threw it through a window in this very room, which was incidentally, the main gambling hall. That's why the far window is boarded up. He said no one went after it as it just kept bouncing and bouncing and may have made it all the way down the hill."

"I take it that it was a very lucrative business then?"

"The boys didn't know how lucrative until Mr. X died. They had all stored away a nice little nest egg from their earnings as they stayed on as employees. They decided to cash in their chips when the old man croaked. They cleared out everything that could come back to incriminate them as they were now the sole owners as Mr. X had deeded it to them. They planned on putting it up for sale, but something they found altered that decision." Daniel paused as if he was thinking twice about telling me.

"So, what was it? It has something to do with the money in the wall doesn't it?"

"Yeah, you might say that. They discovered a safe behind one of Mr. X's personal wine vaults. It contained the three or four million that your husband has in his possession."

"So, there shouldn't be a problem then because the money isn't stolen. It belongs legitimately to Malcolm, and he gave it to you. Do you think the authorities know this?"

"Hopefully they do by now. The money itself is not an issue, but the breaking and entering is, and oh yeah, your abduction."

"Aren't you leaving out the most significant thing...Lorraine's murder?"

"Baron is responsible for that and with any luck he is in custody as we speak. You and I are each other's witnesses as to that, but taking you against your will...well, that's a life sentence, so there is no way out."

"What about Billy, and just how does Baron fit into all of this?"

"Billy's fingerprints won't be found anywhere as he wore gloves, and I will claim him as an innocent bystander. Baron is Racoon's brother, and I am sure is known to the authorities. He visited Malcolm after Racoon confessed about the money as he lay dying. He found me; you know the rest. I have never had any use for him but was convinced to include him in the affair."

"I can just imagine how. There is no charge of breaking and entering because I let you in, and you took me with you because you were afraid that Baron was going to kill me next. That's my story and I am sticking to it, but I will embellish as much as I have to."

Daniel sniggered. "I think that thump to your head has caused more damage than I thought."

"I'm perfectly lucid. I am going to do everything in my power to see that neither you nor Billy will be charged with anything."

"Okay Wonder Woman, I believe you, but the facts are the facts. I'm going to run you a hot bath. You've had enough of the cold, and I think it has frozen your brain."

"You'll come to realize that my plan is one that will work. I don't have a bathtub in this room."

"There's one in mine, so come along." He handed me the phone. "First, you are going to phone your husband and tell him that you'll be coming home in a few hours."

"I will do that right after you call Sarah."

"And, why would I do that?"

"Because she is sick and needs you."

"Yup, the cold has definitely messed with your head."

"Remember, I've been to "crazy" and back several times over, so I know what I heard."

"What do you think you heard November?"

"I heard a phone ringing this morning while you were out. I followed the ringing into your bedroom and answered it. There was a woman's voice on the other end. She asked if I was Mrs. Cassidy. I told her I wasn't and asked her if she was Sarah. I asked her why she had called and she said it was because she wanted to hear your voice one last time, and had hoped she'd get the answering machine with your voice on it. I asked if she was going away and she said yes, and that she was probably never coming back. I told her that it was a good thing that she had discovered that she didn't love you in time. She said it wasn't like that and hung up. She called right back and apologized and asked me not to tell you that she had called. Twice I heard a page for a doctor go out over the intercom, so I am pretty sure that she is in the hospital and awaiting a procedure. Oh, another thing she said was that she would never ask you to choose between your mother and her."

"What the hell does that mean?"

"I think she may also be in need of a kidney."

"And, you deducted this how...oh Christ, I see where you're going with this."

"Do you know her number?"

"Of course I do. Do you really think I should call?"

"Do you love her?" I passed him the disposable phone back. "You'll have to call her on this because your other one is dead. I'll see to my own bath because I'm a big girl. Just a minute, I changed my mind, I will phone home."

"Good; I'll give you some privacy."

"No need." I said as I dialed Sarge's number. He answered on the third ring. "I'm taking a chance that Joey is with you."

"Emmy; where are you girl?" He exclaimed.

"I'm still AWOL. I don't have much time Sarge; please, is Joey there?"

"Hang on." He called Joey to get in the house. "Are you all right Emmy?"

Sarge had never called me Emmy before. I could hear the trepidation in his voice. I tried to assure him that I was fine and that I would be home soon. I asked him if Joey thought I was in the hospital. He said that he did.

"Is that really you Mommy?" My son stuttered a little.

"It is me my darling. I am going to be coming home in a day or two. I am getting better every minute. I just needed to hear your voice and tell you I love you. Are you being a good boy for Sarge and your father?"

"I am Mommy. I am trying not to miss you too much. Bella keeps me busy."

I told him that I was glad that he had her and that I loved him again.

"I love you too Mommy."

I handed the phone back to Daniel who was looking at me with questioning eyes.

"What the hell do you mean by telling your son you'd be home in a day or two? It's happening tonight November!"

"It's going to take a little longer I fear. Now call Sarah as she is waiting." I proclaimed as I walked out of the room. He called me to come back, but I ignored him.

CHAPTER 12

The Suitcase

Another mystery...what the hell was Court talking about? Steve volunteered his thoughts. "I've never seen anything like this in all my years on the force. If memory serves me right these bills were all recalled around 1969. They are still legal tender, but it's doubtful that they came from a Wells Fargo heist. These wrappers mean nothing."

"So, you're saying that the robbery took place in the sixties?" I asked as if it mattered.

"Not necessarily as these bills could have been circulating for years, but how so many have amassed in one location is unknown at this point. Hell, they could all be from a collector's stash which would be one hell of a sideline."

"You need to get on this Steve. Take five or six stacks and see what comes up on the data base. Shelly is working today, so it's just you and her okay. Find out if there is any feedback on previous owners of John's house. Something isn't sitting well with me about this whole incident, but I'll be damned if I can put my finger on it. Times getting on; we'd better head back to Seahaven and wait for the call." Court said addressing me as he picked up the suitcase.

"You're the boss, but I think you owe me more of an explanation about why you think that there is something fishy about this money."

"Yeah, that's a good name for it because there is something stink-hole about it."

Court gave one final instruction to Steve before he settled in the passenger seat of my car. "Oh, and see what you can pull up on this Rachel person... what's her last name John?"

"Could be Queen or Mohammed for all I know." I answered uninterested.

"We can't leave any stones unturned John. You are probably right, and that it is just a coincidence that she showed up the day after November's abduction. How closely does she resemble her?"

"I can see why Joey said it was the woman who looked like his mother because at first glance she does have some of Em's features like stature, facial features, and her hair style and color are the same. I thought at first it was Em's sister Summer whom I haven't seen in twenty years. The two could have passed for twins when they were young, but everything else about them was miles apart. Anyhow, one look into this Rachel's eyes and the similarities disappear. My hope is that she is long gone by the time I get back. Now, how about you enlighten me as to the questionable money in the suitcase?"

"The bills that I examined are all in pristine condition which leads me to believe that they have been in a collector's possession for quite some time. As Steve stated these denominations have been out of circulation since the sixties, so how they were acquired is the question. Do you know who owned the house before you?"

"All I know is what my neighbour told me. He said that it had been empty for quite some time, but a caretaker came once a month to keep the yard up. Jock had only moved to Park Avenue a year or so before me so had never actually met the previous owner. My realtor knew what I was looking for, and the minute it came up for sale she called. I grabbed it and didn't ask any questions."

"Right; we'll know more by end of day I hope. If this cache doesn't register as being stolen we may have a big problem." Court pondered.

"Just a supposition, but let's assume that this Daniel is the legal owner of the suitcase...where would that leave us?"

"So, the question arises as to why didn't they take more precautions for the extraction? Only an amateur would make so many mistakes. Why did it take place in broad daylight? Why was it necessary to knock Ms. Kelly off... why not just take her hostage as they did November?"

"I'm guessing that Em walked in to find the house being ransacked and was accosted and probably tied up. For some unknown reason Lorraine arrives on the scene. Perhaps at that point the thugs realize that the loot is missing and they considered her as extra baggage because one hostage is enough. I wonder if they even knew who Em was at that point. All she is to them is a bargaining chip of sorts, but then they find her identity in her car, so things take on a whole new meaning. They had to know that I was the new owner of the house don't you think?"

"I'm assuming that they did, but here is a query, how does the bean pot come into play?"

"You're thinking that Em was already in the house when they arrived, and put up a fight tossing the pot at one of them? When will the results of the fingerprints and blood be available?"

"By the end of the day I'm hoping. There is no use in speculating John; the pieces will all fit sooner or later."

"Yeah, I'm thinking much later. Tell me more about the money in question. Why were the bills all recalled?" I needed to take my mind off worrying about Em for a few minutes."

"I'm not up to date on foreign money as it doesn't come into play often in our investigations; it's more of an FBI matter. I'm fairly confident that money laundering was one of the reasons for discontinuing the large bills as it would have been easier for criminals to "clean" then small bills. Steve believes that they were recalled in nineteen sixty-nine or thereabouts, but they were probably discontinued long before that. They remain legal tender but could be worth double the face value in today's markets."

"If it's proven that the money isn't part of any heist, but from a personal collection, does Daniel and company get to keep it?"

"Let's not put the cart before the horse John. It's all just speculation at this point. As I said before, we'll know more by the end of day."

"That may be too late as I have to give Daniel my answer by noon."

"You have the suitcase, and that's all he is interested in so we can still make a deal with him to get November back."

"There's a lot more to it than that, and you know it. What happens if the exchange is successful, what happens to Daniel then? Do you arrest him, shoot him...what Court?"

"I wish I had an answer for you John, but at this point we're just playing it by ear."

Twelve Noon Saturday

"Well, I'll give the little bugger a star for punctuality." I said as I picked up the phone. "Hello, you've got Johnathan Jurado."

"Hello Mr. Jurado. Only one question for you at the time; do you have the article in question in your possession?"

"I have the suitcase and its' contents and am ready to get my wife back, so name the time and place, and the sooner the better!"

"Aah, not quite so fast Mr. Jurado. I need confirmation that the contents have been examined by law enforcement and have been deemed to be the legal possession of one Malcolm Rogers.

After this confirmation we can talk again... say at seven this evening?"

Court threw his arms in the air. "What the hell? Does he think he's calling the shots?"

"As a matter-of-fact Detective I am. If Mr. Jurado hadn't called in the cavalry his little wife would be back in his arms as we speak, and I'd be history."

Court grabbed the phone and held it in a death grip. "Look here you smart Alec prick; not only are you facing burglary and kidnapping charges, but when it comes to murder you're stomping in my back yard, and I always get my man!"

Daniel laughed. "So, I'm speaking with an officer of the R.C.M.P. am I? Flattered sir, but you need to check with headquarters because the assassin is already in custody, or should be, so there will be no murder charge, and the kidnapping charge is also up for debate. I really thought that all the law facilities talked to each other but guess I'm wrong. I will be most interested in your findings Sir. Now please return me to Mr. Jurado."

Court hissed. I didn't want to risk him hanging up. "Let me talk to Em please."

"Sorry Johnathan, but she is not here at the moment. Talk to you at seven then?"

"What do you mean she isn't there? Where the hell is she?"

"Don't get your shirt in a knot; it's not good for the blood pressure. Not to worry though as Miss November is just fine. At this moment she is out for a walk with my little brother, who by the way is quite infatuated with her charms.”

The line went dead before I could respond. Court was conversing with someone on his phone.

“What are you saying Steve? Yeah, I heard you; the fax is coming in as we speak. Get your ass back out here as soon as you have confirmation!”

“Confirmation about the money? Who is this Malcolm Rogers, and what does Daniel mean when he says that Lorraine’s killer is in custody? What the hell is going on here Court? All I want is my Em back. He’s right; it could have been so simple. Damn, I wish I had never laid eyes on you!” I kicked my chair away and started for the door.

“Hold on John; let’s see what this fax has to say. I’m just as pissed as you are believe me. I wanted this damn thing resolved before the feds arrived, but it looks like times run out on that.”

“That damn thing you are referring to is my wife.” I said angrily.

“Sorry Buddy, I didn’t mean Em. Come on, let’s check out the fax.” Court pleaded.

“Five minutes, and then I’m out of here.” I relinquished. “There won’t be another call for five or six hours, so I have no intention of wasting time with you guys when I can be with my son.”

He agreed as he ripped a sheet of paper out of the fax machine. He laid it on the table for Donny and I to read with him. “Here’s our answer as to who this Malcolm character is. It appears that he is a guest at Cascade Minimal prison in Jefferson County for theft of rare American Indian artifacts that were on display at a Casino. No accomplices listed, but here is an interesting tidbit...last registered visitor was one Daniel Jacob Cassidy, ten days ago, and a Baron Vander Hess a day before. Now why in hell would someone whom Daniel claims to be the legal owner of the suitcase’s millions have the need to rob a casino of artifacts? Makes me think that money is hot after all, and that the origin of it is suspect. What’s your take on it boys?”

“I don’t give a damn where the money came from or to whom it belongs, but if it gets me my wife back, so be it. You’re the boys in blue here, so I’ll let you do the deducing. As long as I still have the green light to deliver the goods I’m good with anything be it legal or not, understand Detective?” I answered.

"I hear you. We've still got a few more hours to investigate, so hopefully something credible will surface. Oh, one thing more before you go Jurado… that phone call from Steve should be of some interest to you. An anonymous tip was made to VPD regarding a murder that took place at 2900 Park Avenue just as Mr. Cassidy said there had been. How would he know about it unless he was the one who made it? Convenient that an address was also included in the mysterious tip isn't it? Anyhow, Malcolm's visitor, the above Baron Vander Hess should be squirming under bright lights as we speak, denying everything I'm sure."

"I'm assuming that we are of one mind on this thinking that he could be the third man that Mrs. Carter saw drag Em from the car. Perhaps I will mention his name to Em when I talk to her later; that is, if I get to talk to her."

"Let's just see what comes up John. Enjoy your time with your son."

I didn't bother stopping at Silvermist as I was reasonably sure that Joey was still at Sarge's. I also didn't want to have another unpleasant encounter with Rachael again. Hopefully, she was already long gone back to wherever she had come from.

Joey leaped off the porch and into my arms before I reached the second step. "Hey Cowboy, you took a big chance that I would catch you, didn't you?"

He giggled. "Hi Dad; did you see Mom yet? Did she tell you that she would be home in a few days? She must be almost all better right? How come I can't go see her in the hospital?"

I put him down and looked over his little blond head at my uncle who grinned and nodded. Sceptical that Joey had talked to his mother I asked him how he knew that.

"Because she said so Dad. Didn't she tell you?" He said simply.

"When did you talk to your mom Joey?" I asked still not believing that she had called him.

"You know I can't tell time very good Dad, but Sarge knows."

"Is that right Sarge?"

"I didn't check the clock, but I think it was an hour or so ago." He answered.

"Did you talk to her?"

"She caught me by surprise. I asked her where she was and if she was all right. She said she was still in the same place and that she was fine and was Joey here. I called him to the phone and they had a brief conversation. You'll have to ask him what she said. She sounded good John."

Joey said she told him that she was getting better and that she'd be home in a day or so. He also said that he had already told me that. He added that she had said she loved him. I asked him if she had been crying. He said she wasn't, and that we should go to AnnieZu's because Johanna was probably there already. I wished I had the innocence of a five-year-old.

"Ahoy mates," I hollered as we opened the front door at Silvermist. I was just playing my part as Joey had donned his Peter Pan garb before we had left Sarge's. A welcoming voice greeted us.

"Will Tiger Lily do?" JoJo cried as she came out of the kitchen and ran into my arms.

I embraced her and let her cry for a few minutes. I didn't wait for her to ask about her mother but filled her in on what was happening. She was overjoyed that Em had called Joey. After she had gained her composure she led me into the kitchen saying we had somewhat of a situation. It didn't take me more than a few seconds to clue in when I saw Rachel sitting at the table with the family. Zena was not present.

Rachel smiled at me, said "Hi Johnny", and patted the empty chair beside her. Who was this woman giving me the come-hither eye in front of my children? Em was going to kill me if I looked so much in her half- sister's direction. I best find a way to get rid of her.

"Why are you still here Rachel? I thought I asked you to be gone by the time I returned?"

An arm slipped through mine. It was my mother-in-law's.

"I'll tell you why Johnathan. It's because my bleeding-heart sister felt sorry for the little waif." Zena smirked maliciously. "And then the others all went along with her despite my objections."

"Hi Gramma," Johanna said. "I was hoping you would join us."

Zena's whole façade changed when she embraced her granddaughter, but she still had a harsh word for everyone else. "Why didn't anyone tell me that Jo had arrived?"

"We were trying to come up with a solution that would be beneficial to everyone before we disturbed you Zena. Jo has an idea; come and sit down dear sister and see if it will meet with your approval." Zuzz suggested.

I would listen to Jo's suggestion, but I wanted Zena to know that I was backing her earlier idea of putting Rachel in a cab and sending her on her way, and so I voiced it again.

"But Daddy, that is so cold. I believe that mom did invite Rachel to visit probably thinking that she wouldn't take her seriously, but she did, and she is here. Like it or not, she is mom's, Joey's and my flesh and blood. We are not her only kin here though are we? As usual, we are forgetting Noel and May. Perhaps they would like to meet their half-sister also. I called them just a few minutes ago, and they are most curious. What do you say?" Jo asked.

Her idea seemed reasonable, but that would mean that Rachel would still be around, and I wanted her out of the country. Maybe I could put the fear of God in her. "I guess none of you know that the sisters put a curse on Lorraine, and you all know where she is now."

"Daddy!" Jo admonished me.

I shrugged my shoulders. "Just sayin...you all know how protective they are of their little sis."

"Who is Lorraine, and what happened to her?" Rachel implored.

I forced myself to look at her. "She was the woman I was living with while Em was away. She was beheaded at the house where Em was taken hostage... by whose hand, we know not. I guess I was lucky that the sisters liked me."

Rachel was repulsed. For a minute I thought she was going to be sick, but she snapped back at us. "And, you want to send me to stay with *them*? Are you all sick?"

"What are you afraid of *dearie*? You don't have eyes for my son-in-law now do you?" Zena asked mischievously. There was no warmth in her voice. "That's the only way you would be in any danger from my daughters if you know what I mean."

"Yeah, I'm on my last life with them. One more strike and I am out permanently. I am stuck with Em for the rest of my life I fear."

I hadn't expected that the whole table would break out in laughter, but they did, all but Rachel of course. Betsy was beside herself. She came over and put her hand on my shoulder and said soberly that I had better pray that the fear of being stuck with her comes true. I patted her hand and told her that it was the fear that I wouldn't be that I was worried about.

"We all know that Johnathan; we all know that." She concurred.

"We haven't solved anything here except to scare Rachel half to death, so I'm going to drive her into the city and let her make up her own mind. I'm sure my aunties will welcome her. Is that okay with you Rachel? Don't let what was said here influence you. They don't practice witchcraft as was suggested by my father." My daughter shot me a cheeky smile.

"How do you explain the pentagram in the basement then?" I mumbled under my breath. No one heard me except Zena who snorted and whispered that she thought they had erased it. I wondered how long this alliance with my mother-in-law would last.

I didn't want my daughter to go alone so offered to go with her, but she said that wasn't a good idea. Ada volunteered to go instead which suited me just fine. I whispered to Jo at the door.

"This shouldn't have fallen on you Honey. Do anything you want with her...just don't bring her back here. She can't be here when your mother comes home."

"I wouldn't dream of it Daddy. Can I come and wait with you for the call tonight?"

"We'll have dinner here, and then we will go and wait together." I promised.

I planned on spending the next few hours doing whatever Joey wanted, but first I had to kowtow to Zuzz. She had suggested quite strongly that I accompany her into her sitting room. She was not pleased with my behavior. She had never known me to be so boorish to a woman.

"I'm sorry that you do not approve of how I handled things Zuzz, but Em would never have invited Rachel to visit. She told me that if she never saw her again that would be too soon. On the other hand, Emily may have."

"Yes, let's talk about Emily shall we?"

"How much do you know?"

"I really know nothing. I thought her demeanour was a little suspect whenever you were around when she first came home, but I figured that she was still trying to understand where her place was with you. Thank goodness you both realized that you were meant to be together before Jo's wedding. Then that ugly incident with Lorraine happened. We all heard her call November, Emily. That seemed to ire her, and we all saw a side of her we didn't know existed. Is this Emily a hidden personality Johnathan? Does November have a multiple personality disorder? Is it part of what triggered her breakdown?"

"I can't answer that Zuzz. I first met Emily when Em was ill six years ago. I honestly thought that Em just made her up so that she could express how unhappy she was with me. I believed that she didn't want to hurt me, so she let Emily do it. I did not even consider that she had dual personalities. I started to have my doubts when she came home and would berate me for no reason. The night that Lorraine turned up here was the turning point. She confessed that Emily came to her the night that she found out that her father had another daughter."

"Oh no, you mean she's been around that long, and none of us knew, not even her own mother? The secret I couldn't tell you was about Rachel, but November never mentioned Emily. Shelia Dickens even asked us who Emily was. How is it that her therapist doesn't even know that her patient has a split personality?"

"I'm not sure that she does anymore Zuzz. Em says she wasn't real, and then she says that Emily took over for her when she didn't want to face certain situations, so she sort of contradicts herself. Anyhow, she assures me that Emily is dead. I truly believe that she would have remained Em's secret if her illness hadn't erected the other Em."

"Do you honestly believe that? Don't you think that Emily might surface now? Who is going to come home to us Johnny?"

I assured her it would be Em. I didn't think she needed to know that Em was indeed acting as Emily again.

"We can only pray. Now tell me about the pentagram in the sister's basement?" Zuzz probed.

"You heard that?" I laughed.

"We all did, except JoJo and Rachel I hope."

I spent the next half hour telling her about what I thought was a witch's mystic symbol that I had seen when I was fourteen years old. Em had shown it to me and we had made up our minds that May and Noel were indeed witches and maybe belonged to a coven. We were always on our best behavior around them. How they hid it from Zena and Phillip was a mystery. I was pretty sure that if they were involved in anything secret it was harmless, and yet they had put a curse on Lorraine…I laughed and asked myself if I really believed in such things.

Jo and I left to await "the call" at half past six. She filled me in on the visit with her aunts on the short trip up the hill. Apparently, the sisters had welcomed their half- sister with open arms and had given her and Rachel a full tour of the house. She informed me that there weren't any signs of a pentagram, or witches alter, no unlocked doors, and no bubbling cauldrons.

"I've stayed there many times Dad, and have never seen or heard anything out of the ordinary. They are just two old spinsters whose business just happens to be a little on the quirky side. They make a very good living catering to what people want which is a little bit of hocus-pocus; anything to take them away from their drab existence. Rachel will be perfectly safe there."

"They are only five and six years older than your mother, so I wouldn't label them as old."

"I guess because they always dress in drab dark clothes, and wear those ugly cloaks, never married or even had boyfriends is why I consider them as aged."

"All part of their mystique Honey. Your mother has told me many times that they have entertained many gentleman callers throughout the years, and probably still do today, so it doesn't appear as if they are lacking in male companionship. No one knows what really goes on behind the closed doors at Queensland, or anywhere for that matter."

"Really Daddy; I find that hard to believe."

"Well, they are your grandfather's daughters after all."

"So is Mom."

"Yes, but that is where we draw the line between them and her."

I introduced her to the detectives, put on a pot of coffee and awaited the call. Seven o'clock came and went. At eight I was beside myself and when the call finally came at eight fifteen I was ready with harsh words.

"You rotten son of a bitch Cassidy; what the hell are you pulling here? I've been sitting here for almost two bloody hours waiting for your call! If you think…"

A soft voice interrupted me. "Hi Johnny."

"Emmy, oh God Honey, I'm sorry. I didn't think you'd be on the line. Are you alone?"

"No, Daniel and Billy are right here. It's my fault that the call is overdue. Daniel wanted me to call you earlier, but I hadn't made up my mind until now, so it's my fault, not his."

"What do you mean?"

"I am still not sure, but I won't be coming home tonight Johnny, and maybe not even tomorrow. It all depends upon what is going on at your end."

"You are making this sound like you have a choice. Have they brainwashed you Em?"

"No, nothing like that. Lorraine's killer should be in custody, and you must know by now that the money was not stolen, so Daniel can't be charged with anything. When that is all made clear then I will be coming home. You have to straighten things up at your end, and we will need confirmation in the form of a legal document. Do you and your cop buddies understand?"

"No, I don't damn it! You were kidnapped Em...how the hell can that go away?"

"Nothing is as it seems Johnny. I was not kidnapped. Baron Vander Hess, whom should be in custody as we speak, was intent on killing me. Daniel brought me here to save my life. I have to go now. I love you Johnny. Don't worry; I'll talk to you tomorrow."

I cried out her name as the phone went dead. I turned to Detective Ramsey, irked to the core.

"Is she right? Is Daniel innocent of everything? Has this Baron been charged?"

"It's not that simple John. Motive, means, etc. all have to be identified. I am just as stunned as you are at November's claim that she wasn't kidnapped. That might be the only charge we will be able to put forward against Mr. Cassidy if all other things prove to be true. There will also be the allegation of breaking and entering. However, it won't surprise me one bit if your wife claims that she let them in the door."

"What the hell are you insinuating Ramsey?"

He didn't get to respond before the phone rang again. "Em?" I answered hopefully.

"Sorry Mr. Jurado, but it's me. I assure you Sir that I am just as surprised as you are by your wife's plans. It is true what she said regarding Baron's intentions and the money. I do not consider bringing her here as kidnapping, but I am sure that the authorities will have a different perspective. I had full intentions of sending her back to you this evening, but there has been a fly in the ointment, so to speak, and so I guess it is as she said. Your wife is one amazing woman Mr. Jurado. The unspeakable demise of Ms. Kelly was deplorable, and I will regret my association with Baron for as long as I live. We were both traumatized as we both witnessed the brutal act. She has been a trooper throughout this whole incident, and my brother and I are most honored to have met her though the circumstances were abnormal. I shall end our conversation now and see if I can still talk her into going home to you tonight."

"This has not been a conversation as you have done all the talking! No one has to tell me what an amazing woman she is as I know all too well. You have no idea what she has been through before you and your cronies broke into my house and endangered her life and forced her to be a witness to your crimes. You've messed with her mind as my Em would never consent to go along with your demented plans. I want her home NOW! There will be no concessions until she is released. Have I made myself clear Mr. Cassidy?" I was through with the run around.

"You have, and I will say it again; your wife is not being held against her will. You are wrong also because I do know all the reasons why you have been apart for the past six years, so I understand the agony what this ordeal is doing to you. She will be back in your arms tonight if I have anything to say about it, but you know how headstrong she is, and she is bound and determined to follow the course. Good night Mr. Jurado."

The line was dead again. I hung my head. Johanna put her arms around me. "I can't lose her again Jo; I just can't!"

"You're not going to lose her Daddy. She'll me home just as she said. Why can't you trace those calls Detective Ramsey?"

"Donny's the expert so I will pass the reigns to him." Court acknowledged.

"We can start a trace as soon as the phone is turned on, but getting an exact location of its origin is another matter." Donny explained. "Inclement weather and distance from the cell tower can delay the transmissions. The weather has been good, so something else is keeping us from zeroing in on the signal. The pings which send the signal to the phone from the towers are very weak. They bounce around spasmodically, and sometimes disappear completely. It is my opinion that Mr. Cassidy is a very smart cookie and has taken preventative steps to make his phone untraceable. It may very well be a satellite phone also which gets its signal from satellite towers which orbit the earth. Usually the longer we can keep the caller on the line gives us a better chance of triangulating the call. The times vary from under one minute to under three for the transmission of Cassidy's calls, so he doesn't stick to a timed routine, and it doesn't appear that he is worried about being tracked. Cell towers can be located every six to twelve miles apart and even closer in the city, but it appears as if we are searching for a tower over one hundred kilometers away. It is still not traceable to one. It is my opinion also that we are dealing with some sort of device that is cloaking the signal. I could go into greater detail, but anything more will probably just confuse you even more as to why we haven't been able to get an exact trace."

"Thanks Donny; that helps us a bit I think. I believe that Daniel Cassidy knows his way around the law, and that this whole thing is just a drop in the hat for him. He may be clever, but I think conniving is a better word for him. All we can do is wait until tomorrow I guess. Come on Johanna; see you tomorrow gents." I said glumly. Court patted me on the back and said that she'd be home just as soon as she could which left things in his court. He said that he was going to work all night on getting a pardon of some sort for Cassidy as it seemed that he was innocent of murder and robbery. He was still not convinced of the kidnapping denial though.

"If it is of any comfort, he has a clean record...just like you do; not even a parking violation."

"Sure that helps." I responded sarcastically.

Sunday, 10 a.m.

I had just closed the front door when I heard Zena on the phone.

"He's just getting rid of some riff-raff Honey; here he is. Can't wait to see you. I love you."

She passed me my cellular with tears in her eyes. "Be nice Johnathan."

What the hell? Why was she answering my phone. I said "Hello."

"Good morning Darling. I hope I didn't catch you at a bad time?"

"Emmy," I replied somewhat dumbfounded, "I wasn't expecting to hear from you until later."

"I can call back later if it's inconvenient."

"You just surprised me Honey. I mean...hell, I don't know what I mean. I don't understand how you are able to call me anytime, and no, this is not a bad time. Please tell me you are coming home as planned."

"First, you tell me who Zena referred to as riffraff. Are you being pursued by all the lonely ladies of Seahaven? I hope you have let them know that you're not on the market again."

I wanted to laugh, but I didn't. "It was no one Em, and you know you are the only woman who I want pursuing me. Can I say the same for you?"

"It was Karol from the clinic wasn't it?" She asked teasingly.

"What the hell did Zena tell you?"

"Well, she said that if I had a choice I'd better get my ass back home because some nurse kept calling you..."

"They are only concerned for your well- being Honey; that's all. So, have you made up your mind; are you coming home today?"

"They; who are "they" Johnny?"

"No one of any concern. Please Honey, tell me you are coming home." I pleaded.

"Tomorrow; one way or the other I'll be there. I have to go now."

"No you don't. I know these calls can't be traced so you can talk to me forever."

She laughed. "That doesn't surprise me one bit considering where we are."

"And, where is that Em?"

"Time is up on twenty questions, and you would never guess as I don't even know. If you're a very good boy I may tell you sometime where I think we are."

"You know my life was way less complicated when you were in London?"

"Really?"

"Yes, but so very boring and lonely."

"Tell the kids I love them."

"Do you love me too Em?"

"More than you can even imagine. I miss you like crazy."

"Then come home."

"I'm on my way." She promised as she ended the transmission.

I turned to see five pair of eyes smiling at me. "I take it that you all got the gist of the conversation? No matter what has happened, or what Em tells us, it is of no consequence. The only thing that is important is that she is coming home, and we will stand by her and hope that she has not been emotionally scarred. Is everyone on board?" I sad "Good" as they all agreed.

CHAPTER 13

Em's Decisions

I chose not to have a bath because I feared that I might aggravate my shoulder getting in and out of the tub. Daniel had gone into his room to call Sarah, and Billy was still busy in the kitchen, so I went into the viewing room to do some serious thinking. Daniel's conversation with his ex was probably going to factor into my decision of when I was going home.

In my mind, I had two choices. One, I could stay until he was exonerated of any criminal charges, or two, I could go and let him fend for himself. That, of course was the sensible thing to do because I was the innocent bystander who had witnessed a murder and been abducted. There was no denying that I had witnessed Lorraine's brutal slaying, but by my own words I had told Johnny that I hadn't been kidnapped. I had convinced myself that my life was not in any danger, and that the Cassidy boys had saved me from Baron. I didn't think that there was any going back from that. I didn't consider it a lie; just the altered truth in their favor.

For the first time I wondered if there was another life growing inside of me. I placed my hands on my stomach and said a little prayer. I hadn't had any cramping or bleeding so the accident hadn't forced me to miscarry if I was indeed pregnant. I hoped that I was. Oh, how I longed for Johnny's arms around me, and his breath on my face just as I had for the six years I was away from him. How had I ever endured that? Oh right, I wasn't me. I needed to go home tonight!

Half an hour later I was still undecided. Daniel found me sitting at the table bent over with my head in my hands. He asked me if I was in pain.

"It's just a headache." I replied.

"It's probably your neck again." He said as he came up behind me and placed his hands on the sides of my head.

I told him it was not that kind of headache, but a tension one. He moved is hands to my temples and massaged them. A few minutes later I put my hands over his and asked him what I was going to do without him.

"I'm going to recommend another physiotherapist for you, but I think once you are back with your family a massage therapist will be all you'll need. I'm hoping this discomfort is going to fade in time."

"Where is your practice located?"

"It was in North Saanich."

"That isn't far from Seahaven so I can visit you there. I don't want to see anyone else."

He laughed lightly. "That won't be possible will it November? Have you forgotten that I will be behind bars?"

"Not if I have anything to say about it. Now how did your talk with Sarah go?"

"I regret everything about yesterday; mostly the misery, both physically and emotionally that I have caused you, but thanks to you, there is a silver lining for me. If it wasn't for your being here and answering the phone, I wouldn't be reconnecting with Sarah. Whatever you said to her made her realise that we belong together, no matter the obstacles. I will never be able to thank you enough for giving me the opportunity to see her once more before my goose is cooked."

"Quit talking like that!"

"Look little Miss Optimist, even you can't change the facts no matter how much you want to. With any luck maybe I will get off with a light sentence, but I'm prepared for the worst."

"And, I am prepared to stay in exile until all the charges have been dropped!"

He shook his head. "No, you are not! You're two hours away from making the trip off the mountain. Bill wants you here for dinner, so I have to grant him the last visit with you, but then you and I are parting ways. There are no ifs, ands, or buts about it. My word is final."

"It is uncanny how much you sound like Johnathan, and believe me, that is a compliment. There is something you don't know though, and that is that

I always get my way, so you are just wasting your breath telling me what I can and cannot do."

His smile was most amusing. "Maybe I won't take you home because maybe I will be doing Johnathan a favor by keeping you. How long has he been putting up with your impudence?"

"Since I was ten years old, so twenty-eight years minus all the years we were apart...so about twenty I guess. I think he's probably good for another twenty." I answered positively.

"I'm betting that it is probably more like fifty, so let's not keep him waiting any longer."

"We'll see. Don't keep me in suspense any longer about your talk with Sarah. You said that you are going to see her, so when, and did she tell you why she's in the hospital?"

"You nailed it; she is in the hospital...in the cancer ward. She is not in need of a kidney as she has thyroid cancer. She is having what is called papillary surgery tomorrow. Her tumor is small and only in one node, so it may be all she requires as it doesn't appear to have spread to her lymph glands. I'm going into the city to be with her tomorrow as the surgery is scheduled for eleven a.m., so that is another reason why you have to go home tonight."

"I am very sorry to hear that. How serious is it? I know nothing about that or any other cancer. What are her symptoms? Did you notice any of them? I mean you were together just two weeks ago, so there must have been something?" I questioned.

"She complained of a sore throat and said that she was having trouble swallowing, but we both just thought it was a cold. Unfortunately, thyroid cancers are one of those diseases that can be devoid of any symptoms. She is young so the prognosis is good and there is nearly a ninety per cent chance of recovery. That's all I know at this time November."

"So, she is still in love with you, and just didn't want to burden you with her problems when you had your mom to think about. Is that why she broke the engagement?"

"Something like that." He passed his cell phone to me. "It's fully charged. Do you want to call Johnathan now or after dinner?"

"Are you batty? This is your cell, so it can probably be tracked. I'll wait for the other to charge thank-you very much."

"Suit yourself, but it's probably safe."

"Why do you say that?"

"Did I not mention that this building was designed for no outside interference which includes phones being traced?"

"You did not, but why take the chance?"

Billy came to the door and told us that dinner was on the table. Daniel took my arm and led me into the dining room. I told him we were not through discussing him and Sarah. He said that we were out of time. I told him we had all night because I was spending another night here. He objected strenuously. I smiled and told him that he could drop me off somewhere tomorrow on his way into Victoria.

The dining room was large enough to accommodate fifty or more people. It was tastefully decorated for the eighties. Billy's whole dinner was delicious. His lasagna, home- made biscuits, and chocolate mousse were the best I had ever had. I asked him where he had learned to cook. He said from his mother. Daniel added that his little brother had been cooking since he was eleven. I asked if he had ever worked in a restaurant. His answer was one I had suspected.

"No, I'm not smart enough to do that."

"You are smarter than you give yourself credit for. Your skill in the kitchen speaks for itself. I know a restaurant in Seahaven that would hire you for your lasagna alone. How would you like to come and work there?"

"Oh, I couldn't. I'm not good around people. That's why I can only work in the back."

"In the back of what?"

"In the supermarket."

"Well, you are good around me, and I am no different from anyone else. You need to do something that makes you happy, and it's cooking isn't it? Cooks don't have much to do with their customers unless it is a very fancy restaurant, so do you want to give it a try?"

It was plain to see that Daniel was not pleased with me. He asked if he could talk to me for a minute privately.

"Whatever you are going to say you can say in front of Billy."

"All right then; you should stop putting ideas in Bill's head that can never be."

"Do you think that his cooking isn't good enough, or do you think he couldn't handle it?"

"He is and he could, but what you are proposing is unrealistic and you know it."

"I do not. You are going to be tied up with the authorities for God knows how long, and then there is Sarah and your mother. Where does that leave Billy? I'm suggesting that he come live with me and my family, and we look into getting him hired on as a sous chef in Seahaven. What do you think about that Billy?"

"You want me to come and live with you? What would Johnathan say? Daniel, what is she saying?" Billy asked confusedly.

"The lady doesn't know what she is saying. I'm serious November, we need to talk."

I got up and thanked Billy for the delicious meal. "I hope I haven't upset you. Your brother thinks I have blundered, and maybe I have, so I will let him reprimand me. I hope you will think about what I said, and we can talk about it tomorrow."

"You won't be here tomorrow." He lamented.

Daniel gave me the look so I thought it best not to say anything more at the moment. I followed him out of the room and back into the viewing room. I sat quietly and listened to him for five minutes about how impractical my suggestions were, and that I was unaware of Billy's difficulties with society. He said I was idealistic believing that I could fix anything. I asked him if he thought his brother was broken. That set him off on another tirade.

When at long last he stopped lecturing and chastising me, I apologised and said that I should have discussed it with him first, and then I asked if he really thought it was a bad idea. He surprised me and said that it was what he wanted for Billy, but it was the wrong time right now as they already had too much on their plates, and the future was very dismal.

"Of course it is, and that is because you took the wrong way out of a money predicament! But, as I said before our paths crossed for some purpose, and I am here to help."

"There isn't anything else you can do November."

"Yes there is. I can bring your mother home and get her into a hospital for the treatment she needs. It is up to you to see that she gets a new kidney.

I'm sure they will let you donate even if you are in prison .You or Billy may not be a match you know, so there might be a problem there, but let's cross that bridge when we come to it. I can give Billy a place to call home until this mess is all sorted out."

"How do you expect to do all that? It's a costly endeavor you know, and chances are that I'll never see one red cent of Uncle Malcolm's money." Daniel stated.

"I know, and that is why I am going to give you the money to get your mother home."

"You're going to fork over thousands of dollars to the stranger who abducted you? I do have some scruples you know, but the answer is no to your generous offer. I will not take anything else from you."

"Strangers are just friends who have yet to meet, and didn't we decide that we were siblings from another father?" I reminded him.

"I don't remember any such thing."

"Well, it is quite possible because my father was a philanderer. Do you know for sure that your mother never stepped outside of the marriage?"

"You are really grasping at straws aren't you?"

"Maybe, but I was left penniless once, by my own choosing, but was convinced to take help from strangers. I was too proud to ask Johnny for help, or I guess I may as well be honest and say that I let Emily make the decision for me. It cost me six years Daniel, so please let me do this for you and Billy." I pleaded.

"The circumstances are very different November. I am very moved by your kind and generous offer, and have to omit that I am tempted, but the answer is still no. When you thought that I wanted ransom money from your husband you said he didn't have that kind of money, but now suddenly he's worth more than you let on to, why is that?"

"You are a lot more chauvinistic that I thought. Just because I'm a woman doesn't mean that I don't have my own money." I quipped.

"You just finished saying that you were penniless. I would never demean you or any other woman that way, Sorry if I came off that way."

"You aren't far from wrong in my case though. I fully intended on getting a job when I returned from London as I wasn't going to ask Johnny for anything. I knew that Joey and I could live with my aunt forever, but I needed to make a life for myself. I asked Johnny for a job, but he didn't have anything for me and said it wasn't a good idea anyhow. That was all before he knew that Joey was his son. Then he wanted to look after us, but I refused. There was money from the sale of our house and dividends from the business we had started together all waiting for me, but I also chose to pass on it. I can tell that you are wondering why. It was because I was still in love with him, and I was pretty sure he still loved me, but there were too many obstacles in our way. Thankfully, we were able to vanquish them all. You and I have no such hurdles in our way. I still have the money as I have had no reason to spend it. Johnny has a very lucrative business, and so, I let him take care of me, as apparently, I was and am in great need of being taken care of."

He smiled. "Then let's get you home to the man that can do that."

I told him to pass me the phone. I called Johnny and told him that I would be home on Monday. Daniel tried his best to get me to reverse my decision and let him take me home immediately. I did not budge.

We spent the rest of the evening watching the movie Billy had chosen. He said that I would like it because he was sure that I believed in fairy tales. I think it was some futuristic story about the Brothers Grimm. Daniel slept through most of it. I forced myself to stay awake, but had a hard time focusing as all the problems that would surely arise with the decisions I had made were racing through my mind. One minute I was confident that Johnny would support my plan, and then the next I would see us at an impasse. I couldn't jeopardise my marriage again, so there had to be a solution that we could all live with... wasn't there?

Sunday morning dawned clear and bright. It was plain to see that Daniel had had a sleepless night. Mine had been interlaced with seeds of doubt that I was doing the right thing. Maybe it wasn't, but it was what I could live with. I was putting all my faith in Johnny's love for me. If my decisions were more than even he could understand I would have to live with the consequences, but I had to believe that it would all fall into place.

Billy and I saw Daniel to the door at seven-thirty. He told me it was still not too late for him to make a detour and drop me off somewhere close to home. I blew him a kiss and told him to give Sarah a hug from me, and we'd see him tonight. He sighed and told us to have a good day.

I asked Billy if there were any hot dogs in the house. He said there was, and did I want one for supper. It looked like a beautiful autumn day so I suggested we pack up and wander down to the pond and have a weeny roast. I had seen a rock fire pit there so thought it would be safe. I asked him if he had a fishing pole because maybe there were fish in the water and maybe we could catch one for supper. He was overjoyed at the suggestions and went directly to the refrigerator and pulled a package of wieners and buns out of the freezer. He said there were marshmallows too, but he hadn't seen any fishing poles, but it didn't matter because he didn't know how to fish anyhow. I found that hard to believe. If Daniel was any kind of a big brother he should have taken Billy fishing. I asked him why he had never learned to fish. He said it was because he was afraid to go on a boat as he had fallen out of one when he was six and had almost drowned, so he didn't like to get close to water. I assured him that we wouldn't be going on a boat and he wasn't in any danger of drowning with me around. I left him arranging the picnic basket and went searching for anything I could construct a fishing pole out of. Johnny and I used to have competitions on who could make the best pole with things we found. Wood was easy to come by and I was handy with a knife as he had taught me how to whittle. More than once I had used safety pins or something similar for hooks. There was always some sort of discarded material around that could be used for the line.

I didn't actually believe that there would be fish in the pond, but it would still be fun. There was a ramshackle shed on the grounds so I ventured into it. To my delight it was filled with all sorts of sports equipment. Golf clubs were sticking out of bags that lined the shelves. There were tennis racquets, baseball bats, lawn bowlers, and other paraphernalia. I guess the guests had needed a break from the gaming tables once in a while. Everything was covered in twenty years of dust and grime. Huge holes in the roof had let the rain in and rusted much of the equipment. In a far corner I spotted half a dozen derelict fishing rods. Only a couple would be of any use to me. I took them and made my way back out into the sunshine feeling like I needed a bath.

I searched the drawers for anything I could use for fishing line. Most of them were empty and there wasn't anything in any of the bedrooms. I decided to venture downstairs. I was curious as to what was down there anyhow. Billy would not come with me and told me that I shouldn't go. I took a flashlight with me just in case the power went out. I got to wondering why there was even electricity if the hotel hadn't been occupied for years. Surely it hadn't stayed connected, so Daniel must have had it reconnected. There wasn't much to see except empty rooms. I supposed they had been used as offices and additional bedrooms. Lord knows how many bodies had lodged here at any given time. I found a large steel door at the end of the hall. I daren't go in it as I had seen too many movies of people getting locked inside of freezers, and I expected that was what was on the other side. I was suddenly aware of a throbbing noise. It seemed to be coming from another level. Dare I explore further? I did and was amazed at what I found. I had definitely come upon which was once the control center. The door to it was hanging from its hinges.

I stepped inside a massive room which still had the remains of the bones of a command station. Instead of removing the equipment it had all been put out of commission by some sort of wrecking ball which still hung from the ceiling. Even the signs designating their tasks were destroyed. I was pretty sure that I was looking at the remains of fifty-year-old computers and listening devices. I supposed that this electronic room was home to everything needed for the bunkers operation. I looked inside a dilapidated cupboard and discovered spools and spools of wire and cable. One spool was a thin thread of sorts. Its use was unspecified, but I thought it would make a makeshift line for the fishing polls.

I still had not found the source of the steady droning which I now believed was a generator as that would explain the power source. I wished that Daniel was here to enlighten me because if it was so then he would be responsible for its operation. I would ask him when he got back.

There was yet another floor. A wobbly sign above its door read: STORES, KITCHEN, DINING. I decided that I'd had enough exploring for the day, and Billy would probably be worried. He was and he scolded me for being so bold.

Two hours later with roughly assembled fishing rods, a picnic basket, blanket and wood for the fire we set out for the pond. Billy lit a fire while I watched. I asked him where he had learned to stack the wood and kindling like that. He said he had been a Boy Scout before the accident. It was then that I found out about the accident that had injured his brain. He was racing his go- cart when a car came out of nowhere and he collided with it. We talked about that for a while until he clamed up and said that we should try fishing. He wanted me to tell him about my childhood and how I had met Johnathan.

I excluded all the heartaches of my childhood as I reminisced about the first ten years of my life. I told him that I had a loving family and was happy most of the time, but that something was missing, and that was a best friend. That was all taken care of when I met Johnny the summer of 1989. I highlighted all of our adventures at Bramble Creek. I told him about our wedding and the birth of Johanna and our life right up to when I had become ill. He knew that I had spent years in a clinic in England so I couldn't skirt around that, but I kept it light.

Billy volunteered a little more about his family. It was just as I thought; a lot more tranquil than mine had been. His father had died of a massive heart attack seven years ago. That was when his mother had started to winter in the south, and eventually called Franklin Tennessee her winter home as it was only twenty miles from Nashville. He then expressed his fear that he and Daniel might go to prison and he was scared that he would never see me again. I crossed my fingers and assured him that none of that was going to happen.

We had our wiener roast and went back to the hotel to wait for Daniel. We both fell asleep in front of the television as he didn't get back until almost midnight. He had a quick bite to eat while he told us about Sarah. There were no complications with her surgery and could be discharged as soon as Wednesday.

Daniel and I left at eight thirty the next morning. We must have reviewed the story we were going to tell the interested parties at least a dozen times in the forty minutes it took for him to drop me off at the restaurant that he had designated as Johnny's and my rendezvous point. It was imperative that our account of Friday match almost word for word. I was pretty sure that we had it down pat. He wanted to drop me off in front of the restaurant, but I insisted he let me out about a quarter of a mile before it. "See you on Tuesday." I said as I hugged him and took my leave. I'm sure he kept his eye on me until I opened the restaurant's door.

CHAPTER 14

Johnny

"Em, is that you honey?" I nervously asked answering on the first ring.

"I'm here waiting for you at Hannah's Roadside Diner Johnny. Do you know where it is?"

Her voice was music to my ears. "I do; I'm on my way. Don't move Sweetie; don't move."

"I won't. Hurry Johnny, hurry."

I ran out of the house ignoring Donny's appeals to wait for Court. I pulled out of the drive to encounter the detective about to park his car. He asked where I was going so early in the morning. I told him to get my wife. He told me to park as I was going with him. I didn't argue because I knew he'd get me to her faster clearing traffic with the siren, and frankly I didn't trust myself to drive safely.

Court said he hadn't expected her to call so early. He said it was lucky that he'd had a sleepless night and had been up since five or else he would have missed me and Daniel would have gotten away. I laughed and asked him if he really believed that Daniel would be waiting with Em. He said he could hope couldn't he. He radioed headquarters to send three cruisers to the address I had given him. He wasn't expecting any trouble, but it was policy. I told him that I had no problem with them doing whatever but warned him about interrogating Em. He then told me that an agent from the FBI had called yesterday and was supposed to arrive sometime today to confiscate the phone records and all the other evidence that had been amassed. He asked what had taken them so long to respond but didn't wait for a response and told them they were too late as everything had been resolved. There was no kidnapping, and that the woman in question was safe and sound. No charges of any kind were being laid except perhaps a mischief allegation.

"So you lied to the FBI?" I asked somewhat astounded.

"I had full confidence that November was coming home today, and so I was off by a few hours. No one needs to know any difference do they?"

"A few hours; you call a whole day a few hours? Christ Court, you could be in big trouble!"

"This isn't the first time they've pissed me off, so they can come at me guns blaring. I've got integrity and morals on my side John, so I'm good with it all. Sometimes a man just has to do what his conscience is telling him to."

"So you may have thrown away thirty years of your career and life to the wolves because of someone you have never even met?"

"I've met her through your eyes Johnny Boy. There is something about her and this whole incident that has me stumped. We are missing something, and hopefully without me having to question her she will enlighten us all on her own...what do you think?"

"I think you're expecting too much. I'm fully prepared for her to keep the whole truth from us because for whatever the reason, she has taken the Cassidy brothers under her wing, and she won't betray them. I'm good with whatever her fabrications might be, and somehow I believe it was all her idea."

"You don't believe she was coerced anymore?"

"No Court, I don't. She's not a very good liar though, so I may be in for a rude awakening."

"Yeah brother, you may be. Ten more minutes and you'll know."

CHAPTER 15

Em

I accepted the coffee the waitress offered me and took it to a bench outside. She tried talking me to stay inside where it was warm, but I was dressed warmly in Sarah's winter coat so was quite toasty. I did not think she had any inkling as to who I was. I wrapped my hands around the hot mug and fixed my eyes on the Hiway to the south. Daniel had said that Seahaven was thirty minutes away. Time ticked by slowly. I was sure that Johnny would be coming in a marked police car so paid no mind to any of the vehicles that stopped.

I heard the whoop, whoop of the siren minutes before the car came into view. It was unmarked. Two men were in the front seat. It stopped twenty feet in front of me. The passenger was out before it even came to a full stop. He just stood there and looked at me. I told myself to be cool. He took two steps and held out his arms to me.

"Come to me Baby, come to me."

I seemed to be glued to the bench, hands clutching the coffee cup. I said his name and the water works were on as he reached me. He took the cup, placed it on the bench, and took me in his arms.

"You're safe now Em; you're safe." He said as he removed my hood and kissed me all over my face. "Don't cry Baby; please don't cry."

I stuttered that I had promised myself that I would be brave when I saw him and not blubber.

"You are brave Honey; so very brave." He crooned.

"I'm so sorry Johnny; I'm so very sorry." I said through the tears.

He held me away from him. "You have no reason to be sorry. None of this was your fault."

"You asked me not to drive and I did and I wrecked Zena's car. I lied to you when I said I would call Harold when I had no intention of doing so. I led you to believe that I was Emily, but I wasn't Johnny. I just needed you to believe that I was all right, and you would if you thought I was her. I stayed in London for six years and I shouldn't have. I had to do it; I had to do everything Johnny, and if you aren't able to forgive me this time I'll understand." Tears were running down my face like rain.

"Nothing matters except that you are back in my arms where you belong. I should have come for you in London, so I am just as culpable as you. We've already sorted all of that out Em, so it's all good. Let me look at you...is this bruise on your face the sum of your injuries?"

"I have some discomfort in my neck and shoulders. It's probably whiplash, but Daniel is a physiotherapist so he was able to control my pain. I wrecked the car Johnny. Does Zena know?"

I felt him stiffen a little. I guess it was because I had mentioned Daniel. "It was your car Em. Remember your mother gave it to you. We'll get you to a real doctor tomorrow and see what he recommends. Now, I have someone I want you to meet."

"Yes, I suppose you do."

"Say hello to Detective Court Ramsey."

The detective took my hands. "Mrs. Jurado; may I say how very happy I am to see you. Your husband has told me so much about you that I feel as if I already know you."

"And, I already know your voice as I have heard it on the phone trying to calm Johnny, and talking with Daniel."

"I'm embarrassed to admit that I lost my cool with Mr. Cassidy."

"There is no need to be as you were just doing your job I am sure. I can tell that you and Johnny have become friends and I hope that will continue even though I know he is going to object to you questioning me. I know it has to be done. I am hoping that it can way until tomorrow though as I want to spend today with my family."

"The only question I have for you today Mrs. Jurado is in regards to Daniel Cassidy's whereabouts. I don't suppose he is anywhere in the vicinity is he?"

"You may call me November, Detective Ramsey, and you would suppose right."

"It's as I thought. I am Court when not at the station, November. Take your bride to the car John and keep her warm while I fill Steve in on the situation. I am sure that he will want to do a search and question the restaurant staff." The detective said throwing his car keys to Johnny.

Another unmarked car followed by two police cruisers pulled in. I was surprised to see Officer Jim behind the wheel of one of them. I asked Johnny what he was doing here and how did the other cars get here so fast. He said that Steve Stewart was Court's partner and had probably been on his way to the house when Steve radioed that I had called him to pick me up. Jim was a popular visitor at the house, and would check in twice a day to see if there was anything new and would have heard the call for assistance.

I waved to Jim as Johnny escorted me into the car. "It appears as if your detective friend was expecting an ambush or something. Daniel is only one man and is not a ferocious criminal."

"He needed to be prepared for anything Em."

"They can put their guns away as there is no need." I said huffily.

"I'm pretty sure they know that now. Let's get you warmed up."

"I'm not cold Johnny."

"I see you bought yourself a new coat. It looks warm and comfortable."

"It's not mine."

"No, whose is it then?"

"It belongs to Sarah."

"And, just who is Sarah?"

"She's Daniel's girlfriend."

"So you had female companionship?"

"No, Sarah was not at the house."

"Okay, I will quit while I am only relatively confused." Johnny said somewhat annoyed.

"I'm waiting for Detective Court so I can give you both a synopsis of the last three days. I really don't want to repeat myself, but I need you and him to know that I was not abused in anyway, and what you considered as kidnapping was only a ruse to save my life."

"He said he wasn't going to interrogate you Em, so you don't have to tell us anything."

I snuggled up to him. "I missed you Johnny."

"I missed you too Baby. I just want to take you home and have you all to myself, but I'm not that selfish, so I guess I am going to have to share you with the rest of the family for a little while. I phoned Silvermist while on my way up here to prepare them for your homecoming. Joey still believes that you were in the hospital, so I think it best we keep it that way."

"Well, we can try, but I fear that his school buddies are well aware of my disappearance and will have many questions for him. Adults talk, and children hear and misconstrue the facts. He can see that I am perfectly fine, and so we will deal with any backlash if and when we have to."

"You are right about one thing Em; you're perfectly perfect." He crooned kissing me.

"I never was before, and I didn't go under any mystical transformation, so I'm nowhere near the image you have of me. I only hope you can still love me, warts and all."

"Well let's not get creepy and put you in a league with your sisters." Johnny quipped.

"Did they take credit for Lorraine's demise?" I asked sheepishly.

"Oh Emmy no, they were sympathetic. No one even brought up the curse. You don't believe in such things do you?"

"Why was she there Johnny? Why was she there?"

"I don't know Honey. Both her mother and sister had no idea that she had plans to go there."

"Were you the one who informed them? Do they know how she died?"

"No, it was not my job. I only called Lorraine's mother and family to offer my condolences."

"It must have been traumatic for you Johnny. How did you find out?"

"Here's Court. Let's not talk about this anymore right now Hon."

Johnny seemed reluctant to answer my questions, so I would let it go for now.

"How are you two kids doing back there?" Court asked us peering over the front seat.

Johnny told him we were just fine. I asked him if my husband was in trouble for not reporting the money in the suitcase. They both were taken aback by my question.

Court said that it had been proven that the money wasn't stolen, so Johnny was not culpable.

"Good, and now Detective Ramsey if you will please turn on your recording device I will tell you what all transpired over the last few days."

He was still scrutinizing me. "I told you I would not be questioning you today so nothing has changed there. Your family is expecting you so we best get going." He said starting the car.

"I will be through talking by then, but you best have a record of my account while it is all still fresh in my head, and who knows, maybe I'll forget, or change my story tomorrow."

"She's joking Court. Tell him you're joking Em." Johnny implored.

"Yes, I'm sure she is. You did warn me about her personality quirks didn't you John?"

"Oh yes, me and Emily have him going around in circles sometimes." I mocked.

"This is not the time to be flippant November." Johnny warned.

"And there it is; you've unmasked yourself my love. You see Detective, my husband only calls me November when he is angry or displeased with me, and he is definitely that. But, not your worries; we'll hash it out at home. Now, is your recorder on?"

Johnny's eyes told me that I had wounded him. "I'm not angry with you Em. I just want you to be aware of what you are stating because I am afraid you might incriminate yourself."

"How could I do that? Remember, none of this was my fault, and you know I don't lie." I couldn't let it go and I threw in a quip. "I can't speak for Emily though. Do you know who Emily is Detective Ramsey?"

At first I thought Johnny was going to erupt, but instead he threw up his hands and laughed half-heartedly. "I give up. She's all yours Court."

"Thank-you Darling." I sat back but spoke loud and clear. "You may drive now Detective. I arrived at 2900 Park Avenue around one thirty Friday October 20th. I left my keys and purse in the car as I was only going to be a few minutes if the bean pot was where Johnny said it would be. I unlocked the back door and for some foolish reason I wanted to see the bedroom that my husband had shared with his lover for three years."

Johnny winced. I said I was sorry. "So I was in there when I heard the knocking. It was Daniel and Billy at the back door. Of course I didn't know their names at the time, but they introduced themselves to me immediately. Daniel asked me if I was Mrs. Jurado. I said I was and was then asked if Mr. Jurado was home. I explained that no one lived here anymore. I was told the story about their uncle having been the previous owner and mistakenly had left something behind. It was apparently hidden in the wall in the smaller bedroom. I was asked if Mr. Jurado had found it. I said I had no idea but they were welcome to see if the article was still there. I told them I was just there to pick up a pot and asked them to lock up when they left. Billy had already left for the bedroom. I found the pot and turned to see that Daniel was still in the kitchen. The back door opened and there stood Lorraine. I was stunned to say the least. Just as she started to say something this brute of a man came up behind her and hit her on the shoulder with a shovel. She screamed, I screamed, Daniel cursed, and the brute brought the shovel down on her head. She collapsed and Daniel told me to get the hell out of there. I ran for the front door and fought with the deadbolt all the time hearing the three men yelling and cursing. Just as I got the door open I heard the brute screaming at Daniel and Billy to stop me. I got to the car and turned around seeing the three of them in hot pursuit. I could have gotten away, but I'm not a very good driver as Johnny has probably already told you. I took a corner too fast and overcorrected at the same time as their car hit me from behind. I saw a tree come up to greet me. The next thing I was aware of was that my head and shoulders hurt. I couldn't see anything because there was something over my eyes. I tried to remove it, but I couldn't because the pain in my right arm stopped me, and then I heard the brute's voice. He was telling Billy to shut me up."

Johnny pulled me into his arms. "Oh Emmy, I am so sorry. I am so very sorry that you had to see that and that your life was threatened, and all over that stupid suitcase. It's my fault and I will spend the rest of my life making it up to you if you can forgive me. Can you Em?"

"There is nothing to forgive. It was all predestined Johnny, and it's not like I had any great feelings for your ex. I had wished her dead on more than one occasion, and then there was my sister's curse. Ha, maybe I have some of their magic."

"Don't talk like that please Honey."

"It all turned out didn't it? I survived, Mrs. Cassidy is going to get her new kidney, and I made two forever new friends. I am sorry for Lorraine's family, and you too Johnny as you loved her, and she was your family once."

"I never considered her my family Em, and I've told you that I was never in love with her. It is a tragedy, but I am not mourning, so you can put that out of your mind."

Court asked if I was all right. I said I was and that the worst telling was almost done with. He said I needn't continue and Johnny agreed with him. I ignored their suggestion.

"I realised that Billy was sitting next to me in a moving car. He was holding my hand and told Daniel that I needed to go the hospital. The brute erupted and told Daniel to stop the car as he would deal with me because they didn't have the guts to do so themselves. I think I may have screamed. Daniel did stop the car and as soon as the brute got out, locked the doors, rolled his window down just enough to talk to the raving lunatic. He called him Baron and told him to find his own way back to the boarding house and not to contact him. They had a heated argument for a few minutes each blaming the other for the turn of events. Baron wanted me dead, and suggested they take me up to the gully and dispose of me. Daniel said they needed me in order to get the money, accused him of complicating matters as they now had a murder charge on their hands. He drove off leaving Baron on the side of the road. A few minutes later he stopped the car and checked on me. He removed the bandana and assured his brother that my wound was superficial and that he would take care of me back at the house. I was relieved that he'd kicked Baron out, but I still feared for my life. Billy kept reassuring me that they weren't going to hurt me. I was supposed to be blindfolded again but begged not to be, and Billy promised he'd see that I kept my eyes shut until we reached the house. I was thankful of that. Daniel disagreed with Billy, but I also promised that I'd keep my eyes closed, and I did. Maybe thirty minutes later the car stopped and I was taken into the house and sat down on a sofa in a large room. Billy kept calling me Miss November. I asked to go to the washroom, checked out my battle wounds, tried to clean the dried blood and sat down on the cold floor. Billy came in to check on me and persuaded me to come with him back to the sofa. I told him that I was in a lot of pain. He said Danny was a doctor and would fix me up. I told him that he could call me Emily. I was given Tylenol. Daniel and I had words. He said he was sorry about my friend. I took exception to that and attacked him yelling that she was no friend of mine, and to never make that mistake again. I aggravated my already acute injury so badly that I came close to passing out. He took hold of me and gently placed me back onto the sofa. He said that he wanted to check me for a concussion and whiplash and asked my permission to do so. I relented. He started administrating pain relieving manipulation to my neck and shoulders. I had instant relief. It was then that I learned he was a physiotherapist. I never feared for my safety after that, or had a moment of apprehension." I smiled at Johnny. "I was trying to relay all of that on the phone to you, but I had already deceived you and let you think I was Emily, so I failed didn't I?"

I had only seen Johnny cry two times. Once when he told me about his dog dying, and when Johanna was born. He had come close to tears when I had accused him of cheating on me and when I had asked for a divorce. I couldn't tell for sure if he was in that state now but he was very close. I felt sick knowing I was the cause of his anguish.

"You didn't fail me Em. Hearing your voice was music to my ears. I didn't care who the hell you thought you were. You were alive and that was all that mattered. Court had checked all the clinics and hospitals after we found your car. You hadn't been admitted to any of them, but a witness from the crash had seen two men carry you into their car and drive off. I didn't know if you were alive or dead Em."

"You were there? You saw my car in the ditch...how?"

"I had been summoned to my house by Court, and soon after I got there he got the call about your car, so of course I went with him."

"Just a minute...you were at the house? Did you see Lorraine's body?"

"Yes; and how do you think I felt when I arrived and saw a body bag on the floor, and nobody knew who or where you were? They thought the body on the floor was my wife..."

I was horrified. "Why, why would they have thought that?"

"Jock Reynolds identified her as being my wife."

"Did you uncover her body?"

"I had to...I had to see if it was you." Johnny lamented.

I threw my arms around him. "I'm sorry; I'm so very sorry. If I had waited for you to take me to get the pot like you had asked, if I hadn't driven, if I..."

"Honey, we can't keep postulating. It happened, and you have to quit blaming yourself. Some good did come of it all didn't it? You have always said that things happen for a reason don't you? I don't understand all what went on, or how Mrs. Cassidy and her new kidney fit into this complicated picture, but I am sure the story will all unravel over the next few days."

"It might take longer than that, but I'm through for now. Are you all right with that Detective? I'm sorry that you had to listen to Johnny and me airing our complex laundry."

"First I will tell you that I shut my phone recorder off when I felt that your conversation was a little too personal, so no one will hear anything from the last few minutes. I thank you for your factual recollections which I believe were difficult for you to reiterate at times. We could never get a fix on where the phone calls were coming from. Do you know why?"

"I think what you are actually asking me is if I know the location I was taken to isn't it? It was down the road, or maybe up the road from where you found me." I said wittily.

"Touché, Mrs. Jurado. I look forward to more chats." Detective Court Ramsey conceded as he pulled into Silvermist. He gave two quick beeps on the siren, said he'd talk to us tomorrow, and told us to have a pleasant day with the family and not to worry about anything.

I had the last word telling him that he'd be seeing Daniel within the week if all went smoothly, and that he could return the suitcase to the uncle because Daniel didn't want any of it.

Johnny shook his hand through the open window, and said he had no idea what I meant. He turned just in time to stop Joey from hurdling himself at me. He had a huge bouquet of blue daisies in one hand. "Whoa there Cowboy; you don't want to send your Mom back to the hospital do you? Be gentle okay?"

"I won't hurt you Mommy. I just want to hug you." Joey promised.

I pulled him into my arms. "I so missed you little man." I hugged him as hard as I could ignoring the pain in my shoulder. "I'm almost all better, but will probably need some help with things around the house for a little while.

Do you think you can be my big strong boy?"

"I can Mom because I been helping Betsy and Sarge. Can you walk?"

"Yes, I certainly can." I said taking his hand. "I suppose I should go and say hello to all those people standing on the porch, what do you say?"

"They aren't people Mommy. It's Grandma, and AnnieZu, and Betsy and Ada. Look Mom, Sarge and Johanna are here too!"

I laughed as my daughter held out her arms to me. I walked hand and hand with them to greet the rest of my family. Many tears and terms of endearment, and sighs of relief later I realised that someone was missing. I asked where Johnny had got to. Joey said he'd go find him. A few minutes later he came back, and said that Johnathan was sitting on the bench at the creek. I asked how he knew to look there for his dad. His answer brought a wave of sadness.

"Because he goes there every night Mom. He says he goes there to talk to you."

"Oh, I best go to him then."

AnnieZu took my arm. "No, you shouldn't Dear. I'm sure he is talking to a higher power right now thanking Him for bringing you home. He'll be back just as soon as he makes amends."

"Amends for what?"

"He was our rock November. He never let us see his despair, but we all knew what your disappearance was doing to him. He blamed himself, he was scared, and I wouldn't be one bit surprised to find out that he make a deal with some unknown force, so he has to make amends."

"It was my impetuous nature that was the catalyst in this web of misadventures. Before this day is over you will all know everything that transpired over the last few days, and I am going to need all your understanding regarding the steps that I have to take. Right now I have to go and find my husband because I am the only one who can quell his guilty delusions, and I need him."

"And, I need you my love. How about we give them a rundown together after breakfast because frankly I am starving, and I could smell Betsy's flapjacks a mile away." Johnny replied as he came up behind me wrapping his arms around me.

"Me too." Joey chimed in following everyone into the kitchen.

I held Johnny back. "Are you trying to get even with me by disappearing on me?"

"Wouldn't think of it. Honestly I didn't even think you would notice I was gone with all the attention everyone was giving you."

"Well, I did, so don't do it again. I so want to go home and just be with you and Joey."

"We have to give them a few hours Hon as they all love you, and missed you."

"I was only gone three days."

"It felt like six years Em."

CHAPTER 16

What Goes Around

We headed for "the house up the hill" as Joey called it, at three in the afternoon. Johanna was spending the night at Silvermist before returning to the mainland the next morning, but came home with us for a longer visit and because Em wanted her to assist her in washing her hair. She was still having pain in her shoulders and neck when she raised her arms. I was concerned, but she assured me it wasn't all that bad. Joey told his mother that Bella knew a bunch of new tricks, took her hand, and pulled her into the back yard. She turned around and mouthed, "Help me."

I laughed. "It's your turn my love. We've been playing for three days, and it's not as if you are playing with my brother."

She scoffed, but enthusiastically followed Joey saying she was sure she'd be amazed.

Johanna asked if I thought that Joey could continue playing the other game.

"I think it has completely slipped his mind." I answered.

"How long are you planning on keeping it from her?"

"Tonight; I'll have to tell her tonight because she'll definitely want to call her sisters in the morning. I think she bought the story, but it seemed far-fetched to me."

Jo laughed. "What, you don't think they would visit sick children?"

"Maybe if they needed fresh recruits for their craft."

"Oh Daddy, you are so funny."

Around six we dined on Betsy's picnic basket full of Em's favorites including fried chicken and coconut cream pie. She asked us if she had told us that Billy was a very good cook. We said she had, and didn't mention that she had told us half a dozen times already. She remarked again that any decent restaurant would be fortunate to have him in their kitchen.

I got Joey ready for bed while Jo washed Em's hair over the kitchen sink. She then helped her mother into the shower. I sat with my daughter on the window seat overlooking the valley below while waiting for Em. I had left the bedroom and bathroom doors open just in case she required help. We heard the water shut off. I went in to see if she needed me while Jo checked on Joey.

I found her sitting on the edge of the bathtub. She said, "Hi."

"Hi, what are you doing there Babe? Do you need help?"

"I'm just thinking."

"Well, we can't have that. Let's get you dried and dressed so you can say go say good night to the kids."

"Is Johanna still here?"

"She's reading a bedtime story to Joey. What nightie do you want to wear?"

"Do I have to go to bed?"

"No Sugar Plum, you don't have to go to bed." I answered amused that she was asking me.

"I'd like to wear something soft and alluring. You've never called me that before."

"Are you sure? Will this black silk do, and by the way, everything you wear or don't wear is appealing to me."

"Of course you would say that. Did you like that orangey dress I was wearing before?"

"I don't think it was yours."

"You are right; it's Sarah's."

I helped her on with a housecoat and we went to see our daughter off. It was more emotional than usual. I left Em saying prayers with Joey while I drove Jo to AnnieZu's. I came back to find Em sitting in front of the mirrored dresser. She passed me a vial of something that smelled like camphor and peppermint. She asked me to rub it into her shoulders and neck. I removed her housecoat and kissed her neck before I started.

She kept her eyes focused in the mirror as she spoke. I was pretty sure she wanted to see my reaction to what she was going to say.

"Daniel and Billy were in the house when I got there. I thought the door had opened way too easily. I made a mental note to tell you that the lock probably needed replacing. I thought I heard a funny noise but shunned it off. I found the bean pot. It was exactly where you said it should be. I turned and came face to face with Daniel. I'm going to use their names even though I didn't know them at the time as it will be easier that way. I screamed and threw the pot at him. He ducked and asked me who the hell I was. I asked him the same thing. Billy came out of the small bedroom and asked what was going on. Daniel told him he could handle it and to get back to work. I tried to get around Daniel, but he grabbed me awkwardly and we fell to the floor. That's where I hurt my shoulder as it got jammed into the door pillar. He was holding me down telling me to calm down as he wasn't going to hurt me when the back door opened. I don't know who was more surprised, Lorraine to see me there on the floor with a man on top of me, or me seeing her gawking at me. She started to say something, but the words went flying off into the air as Baron snuck up behind her and brought the shovel down across her back. She staggered. I screamed. He hit her again; this time on the head and she collapsed. Daniel cursed and pulled me up and told me to get the hell out of there. I ignored the pain and the dizziness and ran as fast as I could for the car. You know the rest. I'm sorry for what I said in the car about going into your old bedroom. It was callous, and I have no idea why I said it."

"You didn't say it to hurt me Em, but maybe because you were hurting. Water under the bridge Hon. I understand why you didn't tell Court any of that. You didn't want them to face a breaking and entering charge did you? Is that because you think all the other alleged charges are going to be dismissed?"

"I guess. It's all so complicated Johnny. I've only relayed the tip of the iceberg to you and Detective Ramsey. Do you feel like talking?"

"I don't have anything to say at the moment, but I am definitely up to listening. Let's get you comfortable in bed. I'll put a pot of coffee on and we'll pull an all-nighter if we have to."

Her eyes were closed when I returned. I thought she may have fallen asleep so I retreated as quietly as I could.

"Where do you think you're going?" She asked bluntly. "I'm not through with you yet."

"You're a little bossy you know." I answered humorously.

"Daniel said the same thing. I told him to think of me as his older sister."

"Well Sweetheart, I don't fit into that category, thank God. How old are these boys anyhow?"

"Billy is twenty-three and he thought that Daniel was thirty-three. Billy openly admits that he isn't very smart and forgets things. He'd been in an accident when he was eleven and the doctors told him that he would never advance mentally or emotionally past that age because it had affected the learning part of his brain. I will tell you that is B.S. because the compassion and integrity that young man possesses is more than I have seen in most supposedly well-educated people. I've told him that I am going to find him a job as a cook, and he can come and live with us until Daniel gets his life sorted out." She stated not blinking an eyelash.

"You did WHAT?" I asked disbelieving what I had heard.

"You heard me because I spoke very clearly. I told you it was complicated. Now you can leave if you want, but please give me a cup of coffee first."

I placed her cup on the night table. It's mocha and I'm not going anywhere, but I am going to need a little more information please.

"Thank-you. Billy made me flavored coffees. Daniel is like you and doesn't care for them, so why did you make it?"

"We drank all the ordinary stuff while you were gone, and this is all that is left. I'll have to get Ada to do some shopping for us tomorrow."

"You will not! That's my job, and I am not relinquishing it!"

"We are going to be very busy tomorrow, so I thought you might like some help."

"Do you think that Detective Ramsey is going to question me all day?"

"No, I think he will be as brief as possible seeing he already has your rough outline of the events on tape."

"Is a phone conversation admissible? Are you coming with me as I have other things to do."

"You are not being charged with anything Em, so you shouldn't worry. Now, are you planning on visiting the bank, and meeting up with the Cassidy boys somewhere?"

"I've made up my mind Johnny, so please don't hinder me. You always said that the money from the sale of our old house is mine to do whatever I wish with, and what I want is to help Billy and Daniel bring their mother home and have the surgery."

"And, that's praiseworthy Em. I'm not saying that you will be monitored, but just in case you are, suddenly making a large withdrawal from your bank account might be a tad suspicious."

"You think I would be followed, and thus I'd be leading the boys to their slaughter?"

I found her choice of words amusing. "I know nothing of the sort, but erring on the side of caution is sometimes better than going off half-cocked. I have an alternate proposition, and you will be doing me a favor if you will accept my offer."

"I don't understand..."

"Good, now you know how I feel. But, one thing is for sure and that is that I know the way your mind works, and I haven't been wrong so far. You figured that the chance of the Cassidy boys ever getting the money from their uncle's suitcase was not going to materialise in time to save their mother's life, but you could solve that problem because you had money that you don't need. Well, you see I have a quarter mill just lying around gathering dust in my old safe that no one knows about, so will never be suspect. I would like to contribute it to your cause." I offered her a wafer.

"Johnny Jurado, did you pilfer from the suitcase before you stashed it? And no, I don't want a wafer; they're lemon and you know I don't like lemon!"

"Sorry, the coppers and I ate everything else. No Darling, I did not keep some of the dough from the suitcase. I just hope you won't lose any respect for me when I tell you where the money came from."

"And, I thought I was the one telling stories tonight. Explain away my love as I am most intrigued. I doubt that I would ever lose my respect for you."

I had been sitting beside the bed holding her hand. I pushed the chair away and walked over to the bureau where I had left the coffee pot. I said it was still hot and did she want another cup. She said no. I told her that I had taken a bribe, and that it was what was left of the dirty money.

"I'm sure it was more like a commission, but you interpreted it as a payoff."

"Yeah, that's just what my therapist said. I need something a little stronger than coffee, so think I will go make myself a drink. Can I get you one?"

"You're seeing a therapist?"

"Was; not anymore." I gave her a half smile and said I'd be back in a few minutes.

She found me standing at the French doors in the dining room peering out into the shadows. I thought I had put all those feelings of degradation behind me, so why had I dredged them up? I could have just told Em that it was money left over from a project that I had over budgeted. I felt them all dissipating as she encircled me in her arms and rested her head on my taut body.

"You don't need that drink Johnny; all you need is me."

The tension faded as I turned to face her. I set my glass on the table. "Thank-you Darling, you are right because you are all I need. I never planned on telling you any of that. Funny, how I just blurted it out."

"It happens. Let's go sit by the fireplace and you can tell me all the reasons why."

I threw a match into the logs and waited until they caught fire before I joined her on the maroon settee. "Are you sure you want to hear this?"

"I want to know everything."

"You have to promise me that you won't blame yourself."

"There's been enough blame going on to last us the rest of our lives. I will try not to take too much to heart though I fear my illness was the spark that ignited your so-called fall from grace."

"And, that is why I never wanted to tell you because I knew you would say just that. I told you that I buried myself in my work after you left, and that is correct because I did. I seemed to cope for about six months with help from a bottle of whiskey every night. Then I went on some sort of rampage buying up every piece of property that I could get my hands on. I maxed out six credit cards, had loans at three different institutions, and put our house up for sale because I needed more funds. One Sunday morning about two years or so into this lunacy as I was nursing a very large hangover, I looked around the house. It was a mess; clothes, papers, and take-out containers everywhere. I was thinking that there was no way out of the jam that I had gotten myself into. I had laughed to myself and said that I may as well just burn the bloody house down and all the memories that went with it, and then I'd declare bankruptcy and go live on the street."

Emmy stiffened beside me. "Oh Johnny..." she moaned.

"Relax Hon; you know this story has a happy ending. Johanna called that very day and told me she wanted to come and live with me as soon as her school year was up. I couldn't believe my ears. I told her that you would never allow it. She said you had already given her permission and blessing. I wanted so much to call you and thank you, but my pride wouldn't let me. I had less than three months to make a home for our daughter. It had to be somewhere else because I was done with the memories that were haunting me there. I realised I needed help, and that's when I decided to see a therapist. I picked one out of the phone book. Her name is Sophie. She is the mother of six children and grandmother to twenty-two. She helped bring me out of my doldrums, and self-loathing. I had to find a way to let you go and find a way to make a new life for myself and Johanna, and I was the only one who could do that. You know that didn't turn out as planned, but at least I had somewhere to start. I was seeing Sophie twice a week. I had no idea how I was going to pay her, but she wasn't worried. She had more faith in me than I had in myself. I was contemplating selling the factory to pay off some of my debts. There just didn't seem to be any other way out. Ken and a few others knew my plight, and offered to work without pay and to even take out loans to keep the company afloat until the new ventures took hold. I couldn't let them do that even though the future looked promising. Someone else needed to take the helm. Then Mike Reardon arrived at the door. I had refused his calls because I knew he had a reputation as being associated with the mob who were buying up large parcels of land for God knows what for. What mob I had no idea, but I had enough problems without inheriting anymore, and I still had enough self- respect to keep myself from making a deal with the devil, or so I thought. That was me calling the kettle black. He had a proposal for me. I listened. He offered me three million dollars for a property I had purchased for one and a half million. I say purchased, but that bill was still outstanding. He did not say why he wanted the property so badly. I discussed the offer with Ken. He told me to ask for five million as we both knew that the land was worth three times as much even if it was all quagmires. It would take a bundle for us to develop it. Against my better judgement I put forth my proposition to Reardon. We settled on four mill. I handed him the list of my creditors and told him I wanted them paid off. It was accepted hands down. I received one and half million in cash. I hired back the men I had laid off, gave everyone a raise, offered Ken a bigger role in the company with added benefits, and got started on rebuilding. I am not proud that I caved. I'd had high hopes for that parcel of land to be a scenic retirement home for low-income seniors. It overlooks the ocean, but is now home to million-dollar condominiums, and all its rich inhabitants."

I got up and stoked the fire. "This kind of reminds me of the night we burnt our divorce papers. I knew I was losing you to something I had no control over, but this I did on my own volition because of the mess I had made. I will understand if you are so disappointed with me that you feel you can no longer live with me. But of course I'm hoping you will be able to forgive me one last time."

"Come back here Johnathan." She said holding her arms out for me. "It is not me who needs to forgive you because you did what any red-blooded man would have done. There is no shame. You did not commit a crime. It is way past time for you to forgive yourself for what you deemed as being immoral for it wasn't. It did not cost anyone any hardship or loss of life. You need to be proud of yourself for the lives you have enriched because of the jobs and homes you have already created. Now, let's put this to bed for the night as I need to call my sisters and ask for their help before it's too late."

"I should never have doubted your reaction Em. Thanks for always seeing the flip side, but I fear there is another fly in the ointment. It concerns your sisters; every single one of them."

"I fail to see how Summer could be involved in anything that Noel and May have concocted."

"It's not Summer; it's your other sister."

"I don't have another sister. What are you trying so hard not to tell me?"

"It's Rachel, and she is here. She's staying at Queensland."

"What the hell were you drinking? And just for the record, she's barely half a sister."

I laughed as much as I dared and told her the story.

"You have to be fricking kidding me! She said I invited her...well, that's a blatant lie?"

"Could Emily have invited her?"

"How the hell would I know? There were days I couldn't account for, days I had no clue as to what I had done, or where I had been, but no one missed me, so I guess I was there in one form or the other."

"I didn't mean to ruffle your feathers."

"You didn't. I'm sorry I yelled at you. Whose idea was it to send her to Queensland?"

"It was Zena's, but we all went along with it. Apparently, things are going swimmingly."

"Well, not for long because November is home, and November always has the last say, and she will see that Rachel's ass is on the proverbial slow boat to China. I've had enough insanity for a lifetime. Please take your woman upstairs and love all the negativity away." She said running her hand through her hair. I told her it was already penned in on the eternal calendar.

LAST CHAPTER

Em

I awoke to find Johnny staring at me. I asked him how long he'd been watching me sleep.

"I'm trying to make up for the six years that I didn't awake to find you in my bed. I don't seem to be able to get enough of you. Am I freaking you out?"

"No my darling, you're not, but I think you could be doing something a little more constructive."

"Like what?"

"You could make me something to eat and drink, coffee, very strong coffee. I think I'm going to need it. Can you give me your phone please?"

"It's only six thirty, so maybe you should wait another hour before you call your sisters. I'm not sure if the monitoring has been taken off the phones here yet, so I know yours is safe as it was just returned to me on Sunday."

"Where is the car? I had a lot of stuff in the trunk and back seat."

"I have everything including the shirts you bought for me. Thank-you; they are much needed and appreciated. The car is a write-off Em; sorry."

"Doesn't matter because I am never going to drive again anyhow."

"You will Hon. We'll get you proper driving lessons when you are ready. One thing I didn't find in the car was the pregnancy test. Guess you didn't get around to buying one. How have you been feeling...I mean with the fall and everything else you've been through?"

"There isn't a baby Johnny. I shouldn't have jumped to conclusions so quickly, I'm sorry."

"I thought we were through with the "sorry" word. How about we put the baby talk on hold for the time being? Let's just concentrate on today, okay. Put your head back down and I'll see if there is anything left to make breakfast out of."

Joey wandered into our room rubbing his eyes. "I'm hungry Mom, and Bella has to go out."

Johnny told Joey to climb into bed with me and he'd take Bella out and make breakfast. An hour later we were still waiting for breakfast. I climbed out of bed and yelled at Johnny from the top of the stairs. He was standing at the front door saying goodbye to someone. It looked like Betsy. He smiled up at me and said that the table was set and awaiting me and Joey. I wondered if there was a chance that I could steal Betsy away from AnnieZu.

May answered on the first ring. "May, listen to me. Don't say anything; don't let on that you are talking to me. It's imperative that only you know what I am going to say, understand?"

"You want me to get May then?"

"Oh, I'm sorry Noel. You sound so much alike. No, I don't want you to get May. I just don't want Rachel to know it's me. I don't want to talk to her at all, but I need a favor from you. Are you going into the store today?"

"Yes, because we had to shut the doors for the weekend because the press wouldn't leave us alone, and I have to get the place decorated for Halloween."

"I suppose that was because of me; sorry. Please tell me that Rachel isn't going into the store with you. I understand that you are all getting along, is that right?"

"Firstly, she is not going with me, and neither is May because they are both in bed with colds, so I am all alone to do the decorating and making treats. Secondly, two days with your sister is long enough. She has outstayed her welcome."

"Firstly Noel, she is just as much your sister as she is mine. Secondly, the minute I take care of today I'll see her out of Queensland. Now, if you will help me out with my mission, I will help you with the decorating, and the baking. I think I can convince Johnathan and a couple of friends to help out also. Were your phones tapped Noel?"

"Not that I know of. What is it you require of me November? And may I say how happy I am that you are home and unscathed? We prayed every night for your safe return."

Really, they could put curses on people and then turn the other cheek and pray?

"It's best I tell you when I see you. I have to give a statement or something down at police headquarters first, so will see you as soon as I am done there."

"Can you bring Joey? I'd like to have a child's input."

"He's only five Noel, so I'll have to think about that. Are you doing gory?"

She laughed like the friendly pretend witch she was. "No Dearie; it's all fun this year."

Johnathan and I were ushered into Detective Ramsey's office. Apparently, I wasn't going to be interviewed in a tiny airless cubicle, and my husband was allowed to accompany me. The meeting took all of fifteen minutes. My phone statement from yesterday had been typed up. I read it over and was asked if I wanted to add anything to it. I didn't. I signed it and was told that there was nothing more that was needed from me at the time. I asked the detective if I was being monitored. He asked me why I would think that.

"I think you believe that I will have contact with Daniel Cassidy because I am going to help him bring his mother home, and that you think that I am naïve enough to lead you right to him. To be clear, those plans are already in motion, and I have taken full responsibility for Mrs. Cassidy's welfare." I replied a little too defensively.

"There is nothing naïve about you Mrs. Jurado, and I commend you on your compassion. I'm taking your word that Mr. Cassidy will do the right thing and turn himself in. However, that doesn't mean we aren't keeping an eye out for him. If I suspect that you are harboring a fugitive, or have helped him flee the country, I might have to take further action and request that you come in for further questioning. Is that clear?"

"He is not a fugitive as he has done nothing wrong. Now, if that is all I will take my leave as I am going to my sister's store and help decorate for Halloween. Would you like the address?"

"That won't be necessary. Thank-you for coming in Mrs. Jurado. Be talking to you soon John."

Johnny shook his hand and followed me to the door. I turned around.

"Are you planning on remaining palsy-walsy with my husband? If you are then I suggest you refrain from harassing me! Good day Sir."

Johnny had a hold of my arm. "That was uncalled for Em."

"Don't you dare apologise for me." I warned brushing his hand off my arm. "I'll be in the car."

He didn't even look at me when he started the car. "You sure put him in his place didn't you? Did you forget that he is a cop and just doing his job? I've answered my own question; you are definitely bi."

"Bi what?" I demanded.

"Bi- Em, bi-Emily."

"You might just be right. I heard what I said, and it wasn't me, and yet it was. Am I not allowed to raise my voice or get angry? Every time I do you are going to think that I am Emily no matter how many times I tell you that she's gone aren't you? Are you ever going to just let me be me, temperament and all?"

He squeezed my hand. "I suppose that I should just learn to accept you as you are and quit pointing out characteristics that I think are strange. It's just that before you became ill I never saw the cross side of you. You were always this calm sweet girl."

"Obviously you have forgotten how livid I was when I came back from England and found you in the arms of Deanna?"

"I've tried to erase that ugly part of my life from my memory banks, but you haven't erased it from yours, so here we go again blaming each other. It's never going to end is it?"

"It ends now with me sending the fictitious or whatever she is Emily back to London with the same ill wind that Rachel rode in on. Anything to please you Johnathan."

"It doesn't take all that much to please me Em as long as you are the one doing the pleasing. I am eternally grateful that you have accepted me with all my defects, and I promise that I won't mention *her* name again. Though I must admit I was a little turned on that two women might be sharing my bed." He said sheepishly.

"Sorry to burst your bubble, but it's me or no one at all…if you get my drift."

"I do, and I've just learnt to keep my fantasies of two of you to myself." He kissed me and said that it was time that I introduced him to the other men who had captured my heart.

We knew we were taking a big risk meeting up with the Cassidy boys, and very well might get caught. I couldn't change Johnny's mind about going with me even though I tried using Joey as a bargaining chip citing that we could both end up in jail and our son would be parentless. He dropped me off at the Emporium while he went to retrieve the "funds" from his office. I wasn't expecting Daniel and Billy for another hour so took my time explaining my situation to Noel. She was intrigued and said that I could count on her discreet support. She flipped the sign on the door to "CLOSED" and led me into the back room where all the holiday boxes were stored. I was astonished to see that a full kitchen had been installed. I asked her when that had come about. She said that it had been there for seven years. I wanted to cry realising that life had gone on while I was sick. I could never get those years back. She sat me down at the table and we talked while the coffee perked. She chuckled when I said I was thankful that it wasn't the tasteless tea that they served at Silvermist. She filled me in on everything that had taken place while I was away as we unpacked boxes and drank coffee. I jumped up when I heard the rapping on the back door. I had directed Daniel and Billy to come in that way as it was down a dark back alley that was only used for garbage pick-up and my sister's vehicles. The guys were a little bit late and I had started to worry.

I was astonished when I opened the door to find three figures standing there.

Johnny winked at me. "I found these two gentlemen lurking around outside so thought I'd better invite them in and see what their intentions were."

Apparently, Johnny had gone around back to make sure that no one we weren't expecting was hanging around. He recognised Daniel right away and introduced himself. He had saved me from what I had expected was going to be an unpleasant few moments. It was not possible that I could love him anymore than I did right then. I hoped my eyes relayed that.

I ushered them all in quickly and barred the door. I hugged them all and made the introductions to Noel. Billy didn't want to let me go, nor I him. Noel invited them to sit and share her table. She apologised that there weren't any sweet treats as yet. I told her about Billy's expertise in the kitchen and suggested that he could take over the making of the Halloween treats while we do the decorating. His eyes lit up. Johnny and I left them pondering over the cookbooks while we took Daniel aside and informed him of the plans already in place to bring his mother home.

He said that he and Billy had an appointment to be tested to see if their blood types were compatible with their mother's. He was going to visit Sarah and then find a place for her to live as she was being discharged from the hospital tomorrow. She had suggested that Billy could live with her. He didn't think that was a very good idea because Billy wouldn't like being cooped up in a city apartment. It wasn't practical that he go back to the hotel as he would be all alone and didn't like driving, but it just might be the only answer. His next step was to turn himself in because nothing could be resolved until he knew what kind of a jail sentence awaited him.

The whole thing upset me. I had told Johnny that I wanted Billy to come and live with us. He had voiced his disapproval so we hadn't really discussed it any further. I felt like I had no choice so I made a suggestion that Billy could go back to the hotel and I would be responsible for seeing that all his needs were met. I was shot down by both Johnny and Daniel.

"I can't allow you to do that November. You have already done enough, and by your own words you are a horrible driver, so I won't have you driving up and down that Hiway. We are not your responsibility. Malcolm is up for early parole; it is looking positive so I'll come up with something until then."

"You do know my wife don't you?" Johnny grinned. "I think she will do exactly as she wants despite our objections. The solution to that is to have Billy come and live with us. We have the room and there is plenty to do between our place and my uncles'. Maybe we can find him a part time job in one of the local restaurants also. What do you say Daniel? If things don't work out we can revert back to Em's plan, but I'll be at the helm right beside her, so not to worry."

I was dumbfounded. I tried to keep my emotions in check and struggled to find my voice.

"I could just hug you to pieces Johnny Jurado." I managed tearfully.

"Well, I'm not adverse to that." He said welcoming my arms.

Daniel eyes were a little moist as he looked at us in awe. He turned to Johnny and said, "You remember that I was the one who took your wife hostage don't you, and now you want to reward me with looking after my brother. It's enough that you borrowing me the money to bring my mom home and set Sarah up, but this is way above and beyond my wildest expectations."

"If kidnapping is now a synonym for saving Em from being killed then I am the one who owes you for she is my life. And just to be clear, this loot is not a loan. The deal is you take it and never ever think about repaying it, or no deal...got it?" Johnny stipulated.

"My deal with November was to accept the money as a loan..."

Johnny stopped Daniel from saying anymore. "You're dealing with me now, and the deal is as I said. Believe me you are doing me a big favor."

"I don't understand how that could possibly be. Who in their right mind would give strangers a staggering amount of money and not expect reimbursement?"

"Who says anything about me being in my right mind?" Johnny laughed. "Anyhow, those are the terms, and maybe someday I will let you in on the secret of the dough that's been sitting in a safe gathering dust for over three years. Don't worry; it's not *hot or embezzled*."

"Again, I was the one who intended to steal the suitcase from you so my scruples are not in trouble of being blackened here. I'll have time to mull all of this over while I'm doing my penance in the local lock-up while my fate is being decided by the courts. Time is running out so I best say my heartfelt thanks and get Billy and make our way to the hospital before I turn myself in. What was the name of that detective again?"

"You're not doing that today?" I asked petrified that he was.

"Yeah, like I said, I feel as though I am risking Billy's freedom and it's just a matter of time before we both get caught, and now both of you are involved, so it's now or never. I may just chicken out tomorrow if left unchecked."

Johnny nodded. "That might just be the right plan. Let me pave the way for you. Where's your phone Em?"

I swallowed hard. "Whatever you are thinking of doing, please don't. It's too early Johnny. He needs more time."

Daniel took my hand. "You have to trust that I know what I'm doing November. I'm ready to face the music only because I have you two on my side."

I shook my head. "No, I'm sorry, but no. You can take Sarah and hide out at the hotel for a few more days. No one will find you there, and your mother needs you remember?"

"It's bad enough that you and Johnathan are co-conspirators, but now you want to include Sarah in that league also. I know you are used to getting your way, but not this time November. It's my decision and I want Johnathan to make the call. Please give him the phone." His eyes pleaded with me.

Reluctantly I relinquished.

"Thanks Babe." Johnny said pulling a card out of his pocket. "We're not going to throw him to the wolves you know." He punched in a number and turned the conference button on, and put his free arm around me.

I knew who he was calling, and yet I shivered when I heard his voice again.

"Detective Ramsey here."

"Miss me yet?"

"Yeah, it's not the same without you giving me flack. What's your grievance now Jurado?"

"Just wondering if you're going to be around, say in three hours or so?"

"Could be depending on what the occasion is."

"It's business. Wondering how you'd feel about me escorting a new friend to the hospital for some blood tests and taking care of a little business before he surrenders to you?"

"Christ, are you telling me that Cassidy has been in contact with your wife? Where the hell is he? This isn't looking good for either of them John."

"Then it's not looking good for me either. This really isn't negotiable Court. You accept the proposal or he goes back into hiding. Trying to do what's right here. You told me that you wouldn't give this case up for anything or anyone, so how about showing a little compassion for the man who saved my wife's life? You want to see it through don't you? All those questions you have about the "suitcase" and everything else can be answered as soon as you give us the green light. I promise that even you will be amazed at the answers. What'd you say Detective?"

"I'll have to run it by my superiors. I'm not promising anything. I'll call you back."

"You're the head honcho around there so don't give me the gears. If you're homing in on the phones location thinking that Daniel is here with us then I will save you the trouble, and tell you that he is."

"I rue the day I met you Jurado! You and this fiasco might just cost me my bloody job."

"You already did that when you lied to the FBI didn't you?"

"That's not for public knowledge you ass."

Johnny surprised me and passed the phone to Daniel. "It's your turn."

Daniel smiled from ear to ear. "Your secret's save with me Detective Ramsey."

Court cursed. "Who the hell are you anyhow Cassidy? You've wooed Mrs. Jurado and now you've got her husband kowtowing to you too. It's going to take a hell of a lot to convince me that your intentions have all been honorable. I hope you realise that you have put them in one hell of a quandary."

"I do, and as hard as I tried I could not convince November to abandon me. Actually, it is because of the attachment she developed with my brother Billy that she became so involved. Johnathan is entangled in this mess I made because of his great love for her. I need for you to guarantee me that Billy will not be charged with anything before I agree to surrender."

"I can guarantee nothing Cassidy, and let's be perfectly clear here; you do not make the rules. I do understand that there might be mitigating circumstances which may exclude your brother from being charged with any crime, but that is not for you to decide. It can only benefit you if you make good on your promise to turn yourself in. I will need to hear Billy's side of the story. Please return the phone to Mr. Jurado, and I expect to see you before four this afternoon."

Johnny thanked Court and said he'd see him in a few hours.

"You're not his lawyer Jurado, so you may deliver him but then you'll make yourself scarce. Are we clear on that?"

"I've designated myself as Daniel's McKenzie friend, so I'll be there sitting beside him."

"How in hell do you know about that Jurado?"

"I'm not just a pretty face you know."

Court laughed. "This isn't a court of law you know?"

"Close enough; see you soon."

Johnny hung up before Court could reply. Daniel and I were stymied as to what a McKenzie friend was. He explained that it was a friend who sits alongside of someone who doesn't have a lawyer. His role is to provide practical and emotional support to the litigant. I asked him if we were going to be allowed to sit in on the questioning then. I didn't like his answer.

"Not we Sweetheart; just me. You are going to stay here with Noel, or else I'll put you in a car and send you home...your choice." He said dead serious.

Did he not know who he was giving an order to? I walked over to him and ran my hands through his greying locks. "I'm the cause of all of this salt- and pepper- aren't I? You are the man every woman can only dream about, and I am the lucky gal who has his heart. I will yield to your wisdom, and finish up with Noel, and then I'll see myself home. I love you."

"And, I love you. I won't lie to you, Daniel may very well be behind bars before the day is through, but I'm hoping Billy will be free to come home with me. I'll do my best to keep you posted. Just in case things don't work out, you should say your good-byes."

"I can't believe you are doing this for me and them Johnny. I don't have the words..."

"That'll be a first then won't it? You should know by now that I would do anything for you. If you're happy then I'm happy, and you know what, I kinda like your new friends."

I did not say good-bye, but told Billy that I would see him later. After the hugging I saw them to the door. Johnny kissed me and told me to keep my fingers crossed. I said that I couldn't believe he was going to meet Sarah before I did, and to give her a hug from me

I told Noel that I would come back the next day to help her as I needed to get home to Joey. She offered to drive me home and wouldn't take no for an answer. I suggested that I could just borrow her car and drive myself. That brought a hoot of laughter from her.

"Why are you laughing?" I asked innocently twisting my hair around my fingers coyly.

"Do you really think I'd still fall for your childish ploys November Queen? Shame on you."

It was my turn to laugh. "It was worth a try. By the way I'm a Jurado again."

"Exactly, and that's why I'd rather have you annoyed with me then to risk the wrath of your husband. Haven't you already had enough accidents for a lifetime anyhow?"

"Have you been talking to Zena?"

"Only when I have to."

"She's mellowed Noel. I think she is here to stay, so we are all going to have to try to include her in our lives."

"I think you are right. We had a lovely visit with her at Johanna's wedding. If she decides to stay it will be because of Joey. It's obvious that he is the apple of her eye."

"Yes, he will be the main reason she stays. Let's go by Queensland as I need to find out what brought Rachel here. She says I invited her, but I did not."

"You have enough to contend with so May and I will deal with her. She's a very lonely girl. It's not clear how close you two were in London; care to enlighten me?"

"I would if I could, but it appears as if I have blocked her out of my memory banks."

"That's the strangest retort I have ever heard."

"It's the only answer I have, so let's just leave it at that. The last thing I recollect is that her marriage was falling apart. Maybe it did collapse and she needed a different point of view to reassess her life. She has two teenage children, so how she could leave them is beyond me."

"Perhaps I have been too quick in wanting to oust her. Our father, bless his soul, may be the cause for her bitterness as he is to our mother's. Rachel is not your problem, so quit worrying. Let's get you home to your son. I'm looking forward to a visit with the little tyke myself."

I made the mistake of telling Joey that his dad might be bringing a guest home to stay with us for a few days. Now he just sat at the window waiting for their arrival. Every few minutes he'd ask me why they weren't here yet. Johnny had called at five thirty saying that things were going well and he'd be home soon. He hadn't said 'they", but I set the table for four just in case. I hoped Billy would like my Sheppard's pie. I'd borrowed all the ingredients and salad fixings from Silvermist as I still hadn't shopped. Betsy threw in a loaf of freshly baked bread and a dozen tarts.

It was almost seven when Joey screamed in delight. "They're here Mom, they're here." I wiped my hands on my apron and went out to join him in the welcome. I did a double take as a second car drove in behind Johnny's. It was Daniel's. To keep from crying I scolded my husband for absconding with the fugitives.

"What have you done Johnny Jurado? Weren't you already in enough trouble with the law?"

He embraced me grinning roguishly. "We've all been pardoned Hon; even you."

"What, how, why..." I couldn't stop the tears anymore.

"It's all good Em. Let's go inside and we'll explain what went down. We've got room for one more haven't we?"

Did he have to ask? I was overjoyed but was feared that my joy was going to be short lived.

Johnny ushered our guests to the kitchen table. He poured coffee from the newly brewed pot I had made. "I told you guys that she'd have a fresh pot waiting didn't I?"

"That you did." Daniel said holding a chair out for me. "You know the saying, "There but for the grace of God go I"? Well, it is because of your grace that Billy and I are here. Though, the circumstances of our meeting were berserk; to say the least, it was the beginning of a friendship that I will cherish for the rest of my life. You corrected the deceitful mistake I had made out of desperation. You are a beautiful woman, November Jurado. You have the heart and soul of an angel. I hope it's not asking too much for you and Johnathan to keep us in your circle of friends." He embraced me and kissed me on the forehead.

"Thanks for making my wife cry again Cassidy." Johnny teased.

"They are tears of joy." I mumbled.

"I know Hon. I don't know how much longer I can ignore those tantalising aromas coming from the oven as I am starving and I am sure our guests are also, so is it dinner or details first?"

"Can you not see that I am sitting on the edge of my seat anticipating what the judgement is? It has to be fairly good or they wouldn't be here right? Maybe they are out on bail? Tell me now please Johnathan before I burst a blood vessel."

"I told you it was all good, so you can rest easy. I don't think Billy wants to sit through this again, so how about you show him to his room Joey? We'll call you when dinners on the table."

"Thanks John; I think Billy's had about as much as he can take for one day. Let's not keep this beautiful lady in suspense anymore." Daniel said squeezing my hand.

"I'll be as brief as I can Em without holding anything pertinent back. I had visions of the questioning being conducted in a bleak, small airless room, but that wasn't the setting at all. We were escorted into a room not unlike Court's, only larger. It was the Chief of Police's office. We were seated and offered coffee or water. We all chose water. A few minutes later Court came in shook my hand and introduced himself to Billy and Daniel. He said we would be joined by Detective Stewart and Arnold Webster, the Chief of Police shortly. He would be the one conducting the interview, but the Chief may have additional questions. He cautioned them just to state the facts of the days in question, and not to ad personal feelings, or anything not relevant to the case. The interview started as soon as the Chief and Steve joined us with Daniel's version of the days in question. It did not differ from your account except for the notable remorse in his voice. Billy was asked if he concurred or had anything he wanted to ad. He said it all happened just the way his brother said."

I asked why they weren't questioned separately as I thought that was how it was done.

"I think the verdict had already been made before we even stepped foot in the police station because of your account Em. If there had of been any doubt that you were withholding key evidence I'm sure there would have been more investigating. You three were the only ones involved, except Baron Vander Hess of course, so there were no other witnesses to object to what went down at the house. By your admission, you let them into the house, so there was no breaking and entering charge. You and Daniel witnessed Lorraine's slaying, so you are each other's defence. I'm sorry, but you will probably be called to testify in Vander Hess's trial."

"It will be my pleasure. So, what happened with the kidnapping charge?" I asked tentatively.

"What kidnapping? By your own admission you weren't kidnapped but whisked away to prevent Baron from killing you. I have to admit I was a little worried because of your previous history that Court or the Chief might want you to undergo some form of questioning on your mental fitness, but thank God, it was never brought into question. I think we owe Court a debt of gratitude for that exclusion."

"I originally objected to you telling Detective Ramsey of my days of insanity..."

Johnny reached for me across the table. "Oh Sweetheart, please don't think I did that. You were never insane, and I never implied that you were." He got up and pulled me into his arms.

"Suppose if he had of done that, then how much trouble could I have caused."

"It never happened, and it never will. Let's just put the whole thing to rest okay? Let Daniel tell you his penance while I get an extra place setting and get dinner on the table?"

Daniel took over. "A few things have come about since last I saw you. First, I will relieve your anxiety. I have been exonerated on any charges that we feared would be awaiting me. The Chief said he would like to lay a charge of mischief on me because I shouldn't get off scout-free, but because of the reasons for my actions, that being my mother's dire health problem and saving your life he was going to let it go. I was to keep my nose clean and have no contact with any known felon. But, because my uncle was donating a kidney to my mother, I could have a limited relationship with him. Yes, Malcolm is a 90% match to his sister. Billy and I did not come close. He was granted early parole and we'll all meet at the hospital tomorrow. He wants mom to live with him, so I will go apartment hunting with him tomorrow. He also has an appointment regarding the legality of the monies in the suitcase with the authorities. Once they hear the story about the casino, everything should be cleared up. We can only hope."

"I am overjoyed that this all has a happy ending, but Johnny said you had a penance?"

"It's an odd one. Right after the surgery on Thursday, Detectives Ramsey and Stewart and someone named Donny have requested a tour of the hotel. Johnathan says that Donny was the expert trying to get a fix on my phone.

I'm sure they will be amazed at what they'll find."

"I want to go; please can I go too?" I pleaded.

Johnny set the salad in front of me. "Yes Dear, we are all going. I wouldn't miss the unveiling for the world. You two get started while I call the boys."

"What about Sarah? Is she being released tomorrow? I told Johnny that I would find her lodgings, but now you're free so what's your plan? Oh, you're going to take her to the hotel aren't you?"

"Do you think she will like it? Suppose if something goes wrong? It's so far away from any medical facility, and I can't leave her alone while I am visiting Mom, so maybe we should just stay in the city for a while."

"Why don't you just wait and see how she is feeling tomorrow? There is no question about her liking the place. It's roomy, quiet, and one can sit all day and just admire the views. You can always leave her here with me while you visit your mom. It's not that far away Daniel, but you need to be comfortable with your decision."

He reached into his pocket and pulled something out. "Sarah said she can't wait to meet you. Here, she wanted me to give this to you."

I took a trinket from his outstretched hand. It was an angel pin. I asked him where it had come from because she had been hospitalized for several days.

"You'll have to take that up with her. She just asked me to give it to you. She said you were the angel who had brought her back to me. You know you're my angel too don't you?"

"Damn it Cassidy! Can't I leave you alone with my wife for two minutes before you start her crying again? That's supposed to be my job." Johnny quipped.

"Sorry about that Jurado. She's an easy mark."

"Quit complaining; you'll get your turn later tonight." I promised my husband.

After dinner Billy asked me if he could have a word with me. "I'm not very good with words you know November, but I want to thank you for taking me under your wings and Johnathan too. I think you are both lucky to have each other. You're the best people I ever knew. Whenever I am here I will help you with whatever needs doing. Sometimes I might have to help Mom, or Danny. You are like a second mother to me, and I hope you will feel free to scold me if I misbehave. I'll be on my best behavior because Danny says I can be a handful sometimes. Joey asked me if I would like to be his big brother. Is it okay if I told him that I would like to be because I have a brother and everyone should have one. I told him I could teach him how to fish."

Every muscle in me wanted to laugh, but I refrained and told him that we were going to be one big happy family even though we wouldn't all be under the same roof all the time, and he was welcome to stay as long as he wanted to. I could hardly wait to introduce him to Sarge and everyone at Silvermist.

I left the guys doing the clean-up while I tucked Joey into bed. He was too tired for a story. It had been a long day. The rest of us retired to the comfort of the living room. Everyone was fatigued. Billy was the first to crash, then Daniel. Johnny saw him to the tv room where he had made up the chesterfield for him. I dragged myself up the stairs.

Johnny found me sitting up in bed. "You waiting for me Babe?"

"I'm wondering if you are too tired for a story?"

"If you're the one doing the telling then I am not."

"Then come and lay your head on my bosom and I will tell you a tale of a young fair- headed lad and raven-haired lass who fell in love many years ago."

"Oh, I think I know this story. It has a happy ending doesn't it? Tell me more my love."

I ran my fingers through his locks as he rested his head on my breast. "The story has no end as it goes on and on. It all started in 1989 in a magical land called Bramble Creek..."